A Jenetta Carver® Adventure

A GALAXY UNKNOWN®

RETURN TO DAKISTEE

Book 8

BY

THOMAS DEPRIMA

Vinnia Publishing - U.S.A.

AGU:®

Return to Dakistee

A Galaxy Unknown® series – Book 8
Copyright ©2011 by Thomas J. DePrima
15.c.1

ISBN-13 (print): **978-1-61931-016-2**

ISBN-10 (print): **1-61931-016-3**

ISBN-13 (eBook): **978-1-61931-015-5**

ISBN-10 (eBook): **1-61931-015-5**

Cover art by: Martin J. Cannon

Appendices containing political and technical data highly pertinent to this series are included at the back of this book.

To contact the author, or see information about his other novels, visit:

http://www.deprima.com

Dedication

Creating a series like this would be impossible without support from many people. I normally dedicate the book to the people who have provided help and assistance during the writing or editing processes, but this book is being dedicated to the fans who made this series a phenomenal success, and who kept asking for more. I'm delighted to add a new book to this series after a hiatus of five years.

Series and novels by the author:

A Galaxy Unknown®...

> A Galaxy Unknown®
> Valor at Vauzlee
> The Clones of Mawcett
> Trader Vyx
> Milor!
> Castle Vroman
> Against All Odds
> Return to Dakistee
> Retreat And Adapt
> Azula Carver

AGU:® Border Patrol...

> Citizen X
> Clidepp Requital
> Clidepp Déjà Vu

AGU:® SC Intelligence...

> The Star Brotherhood

Colton James novels...

> A World Without Secrets
> Vengeance Is Personal

When The Spirit...

> When The Spirit Moves You
> When The Spirit Calls

Table of Contents

CHAPTER ONE
~ March 10th, 2285 ~

"Open up, damn you!" Doctor Vlashsku screamed with all the force of his being, but his verbal attack proved as ineffective as the physical assaults preceding it. He had been talking, yelling, and then screaming at the enormous door for several hours in a bid to gain entry, but all efforts had been for naught. Lasers and plasma cutters hadn't even marred the surface, much less cut into it, and the harsh light from portable Chembrite Light panels reflecting off the surface seemed to be the only energy the door didn't soak up like a sponge.

"It's no use, Edward," the Nordakian scientist finally admitted as he hung his head and leaned gently forward until his forehead made contact with the door. To a casual observer he might appear to be in prayer, entreating God for divine intervention, or at least inspiration, but this posture was only the result of weariness from prolonged physical effort. Control over his chromatophoric cellular distensions began to return as his mood calmed, and his skin, until now fluctuating between a bright orange and a deep red, began to assume its normal, medium-aqua coloration.

Doctor Edward Peterson, leader of the expedition at Loudescott, sighed quietly and approached Vlashsku from behind. Although the tallest of the Terrans in the camp, Peterson was still a foot shorter than the Nordakian, owing to the natural height of the species. As he reached up and placed a gnarled hand on Vlashsku's shoulder, he said, "You've tried your best, Dakshiku. Tomorrow's another day. You'll feel better after a meal and a good night's sleep."

"I've already tried *everything*," the Nordakian said in despair. "Amer, Dakis— even ancient Dakis. It's hopeless,

- 1 -

Edward. There's nothing left to try— not tomorrow— nor any other day."

Doctors Anthony Ramilo, Barbara Huften, Bruce Priestley, and Glawth Djetch had slowly moved closer from their observation positions as the two men talked.

"If only we knew what you said all those years ago to get the door open at the other facility," Peterson said somberly. "It's a pity the recorders weren't running when you screamed at the door out of weariness and frustration, but who could have guessed the door would open to a vocal command."

"This door must be of the same manufacture as that other," Vlashsku said. "It's certainly proven to be just as impervious to our cutting tools."

"Yes. And, like that door, it must operate by vocal command since there's no external opening mechanism."

"Perhaps it's time to call Space Command, Edward," Dr. Huften offered.

Peterson took a deep breath and then released it slowly before saying, "Not yet, Barbara. It would end our chances of acquiring any useful knowledge. We would no doubt be barred from *this* facility just as we were from the other."

"That was only because the lab contained cloning equipment. The laws of the Galactic Alliance required Space Command to confiscate the equipment so it couldn't be used. We're lucky they didn't confiscate the clones we made."

"The cloning process was initiated accidentally," Doctor Djetch said, "and Space Command realized we never intended to manufacture clones in violation of Galactic Alliance law. I am gratified they finally recognized our brethren as citizens and accorded them the full rights of all sentient beings without reservation."

"That's how it started," Peterson said. "But once they learned of the impregnability of the material used in the lab's construction, the restriction included the whole facility as well. The cloning equipment is long gone, and yet we're still not allowed near that facility. If we can get inside this one, we can download the contents of its main computer before they learn of the discovery. Who knows what wonderful information we might discover about the ancient people of Dakistee if it isn't first filtered by Space Command censors?"

"But as with the other facility, we're locked outside without a key," Doctor Anthony Ramilo said. "We've already spent a week trying to open it."

"I have confidence that after a good night's rest Dakshiku will manage to open it."

"Then you're far more confident than I," Doctor Vlashsku said.

"If that Carver woman could solve the riddles of the other facility, we can solve this one."

"Azula Carver is *brilliant*," Vlashsku said. "I would not presume to compare my meager abilities with hers. If she were here, I have no doubt we would already be inside."

"Brilliant? It took her *weeks* just to figure out how to shut down the cloning equipment," Peterson countered.

"She proceeded slowly and methodically, just as any good scientist should. Of prime concern was that she not cause the death of any embryos or fetuses during the deactivation. In order to be assured of that, she had to fully understand the entire process first."

"Since we've already exhausted every means at our disposal, how do you suggest we proceed, Edward?" Ramilo asked.

"We should start over with the vocal sessions. Beginning tomorrow morning, we'll each spend two hours talking to the door."

The other scientists groaned aloud.

"Well, we can't just give up," Peterson said.

"Why not?" Huften asked. "I admit I have nothing more to say to this door. What I have said has already been repeated several times, and we've gotten nowhere. If I have to keep screaming at it, I refuse to be held responsible for what I say.

And if there's no cloning equipment inside this facility, Space Command wouldn't dare lock us out again."

"Don't be so sure. I've learned never to underestimate the arbitrary nature of military types."

"If we contact Space Command, it will probably take weeks for them to get a ship here. That will give us lots of time to go hoarse from shouting at the door."

Peterson fumed for a few minutes and then said, "Oh, alright. I'll make a call— but not to Space Command. I'll call Commander Carver."

"She's an admiral now, Edward."

"An admiral? Already?"

"Edward, it's been sixteen years since she was last here. You still don't listen to the news do you?"

"Why should I? It's always depressing and rarely reported accurately. Either the newsies are so eager to file their stories that they don't take time to get the facts straight, or the editors and publishers alter the reports to favor management's points of view because they're only interested in promoting their own agendas. The only thing I trust, somewhat, is the obituaries page. There are few ways you can distort the report of a death."

Huften rolled her eyes before saying, "Okay, Edward, believe what you will— but make the call."

◆　◆　◆

"Our contact on Dakistee has filed an urgent report," Councilman Ahil Fazid announced as he rose to stand in front of his chair at the Raider Lower Council table. The powerful group was in regular session and all members were present in the meeting chamber. "You'll remember that just a few days ago I spoke of our attack on Mawcett, now known as Dakistee, following the discovery of the cloning equipment there. Well, our head man on the planet reports that the same group of scientists that discovered the almost impregnable facility at that time has found a similar facility in the same region. According to the report, the new facility appears to be clad with Dakinium, so the archeologists have thus far been unable to gain entry. Most importantly for us—," Fazid paused a second for effect and looked at each of the other council members around the orotund table, "they have not yet reported their find to either Space Command *or* their own headquarters."

"You want to launch another attack on the planet, Ahil?" Councilman Bentley Blosworth asked.

"No, Bentley; at least not yet. It would certainly be pointless to attack the site before they manage to open the facility. What I'm suggesting to the Council is that we position a force of sufficient size that can charge in and confiscate whatever the facility contains once the scientists manage to open it. Our attack would be nothing so crude as the last one where we were forced to rely on Tsgardi mercenaries."

"How many people do we presently have on Dakistee?" Councilwoman Erika Overgaard asked.

"We have at least one individual at every one of the large excavation sites. At major sites, we have two or more. We've closely monitored all dig activities for some time to ensure we are immediately aware of momentous discoveries. The technology of the former inhabitants was far superior to what we, and everyone else, originally believed existed at the time, and we don't want to risk losing out again. The last treasure trove of technology and information elevated Space Command to a position of undisputed power in this part of space. Another such significant find can push them even further ahead, with us falling further behind. I don't think we can ignore this new discovery."

"So what are you asking of the Council, Ahil?" Chairman Arthur Strauss asked.

"I'm seeking agreement on a plan of action where we move as many people as possible into place. They will be ready to rush in and grab whatever is found in the new facility before Space Command can get their hands on it."

"How many people and what other support are you proposing we dedicate to this operation?"

"When the cloning equipment was found, there were only a few dozen small dig sites on the planet. That number has grown to more than a thousand. And with the influx of archeologists and laborers, towns have sprung up to support the expanding population. We already have a presence in each town for the purpose of offering— leisure time activities and for the distribution of narcotics, but few if any of those people are trained for open warfare, nor are they capable of executing a takeover. We also have a problem with weapons availability and personnel transportation. For the most part, our hidden weapons caches are limited to hand-held lattice pistols. We do have some of our people in ground transportation positions, with a select few possessing small shuttles, or at least having access to them. But we need larger weapons, explosives, and a means of quickly moving hundreds of people to the dig site at Loudescott when they're needed, and then evacuating them just as quickly."

"Shoulder-mounted weapons and explosives shouldn't be a problem," Chairman Strauss said, "but the transportation will. Perhaps you should start repositioning people as soon as possible using the available surface transportation."

"Yes, Arthur, my staff has already developed plans for using the planetary transit systems, but availability is woefully limited."

"I have no problem with the plan, in general, but we'll have to look into the transportation issue."

"In a related issue," Councilman Neil Soroman said, "assuming you are successful in acquiring the technology, how will you get it off the planet and safely away?"

"Obviously, we'll need a ship."

"Yes, but how big a ship?"

"Many of our people will, hopefully, be able to resume their former roles, but the leaders, once they drop their cover, will have to be taken off the planet with whatever it is we acquire."

"So, at the very least you'll need a small transport at your disposal."

"Yes, preferably one that can land on a planet or moon somewhere and hide until the pressure's off. A small warship would be best, because it can participate in the attack and would have the speed to escape afterwards."

"Let's have a show of support," Chairman Strauss said. "Everyone who feels we should commit the assets and put this operation into effect, raise your hand."

◆　◆　◆

"Lt. Commander Christa Carver reporting to the Admiral as ordered," Christa said after being admitted to Jenetta's magnificent office on Quesann and coming to attention. Jenetta's cats raised their heads and looked at Christa, but didn't rise from their prone positions against the walls on either side of the room.

"At ease, sis," Jenetta said, smiling. "Have a seat, unless you'd rather make yourself a mug of coffee first."

"I could use a cup," Christa said, moving towards the beverage dispenser. "I got your message as soon as I woke up and figured it must be important or you would've waited until we have dinner tomorrow night, so I came down before I even grabbed any chow."

"By tomorrow night, you'll be light-years away from here."

Christa's mind began to race as she ordered a mug of Colombian, but she didn't say anything to Jenetta until she had taken a sip and was walking towards the desk. "The *Hephaestus* is going out? I thought we were supposed to remain in port for another three weeks."

"Not the *Hephaestus*— just you."

"Me?" Christa said in surprise as she settled into an 'oh gee' chair that faced Jenetta's desk. "Where am I going without my ship?"

"I received an importunate message from Dr. Edward Peterson this morning."

"The archeologist?"

"The very same. He's still on Dakistee at the Loudescott dig site."

"Why did he contact you?"

"His message was very terse. He only said my presence is urgently required. But since we know how he feels about Space Command, there can only be one reason why he would entreat me to come."

"They've found something they can't handle and need you to pull their chestnuts from the fire?"

"That's what I assume. If it's another cloning lab, I do hope they didn't engage the equipment this time. That issue has finally dropped off the activist radar screens."

"What else *could* it be?"

"I don't know. And I won't know until you get there and send me an encrypted report. If they've found something of critical importance— something so significant that they acknowledge it should wait for me to travel back to Region One, then I don't want to treat it lightly by sending a routine request through Space Command for any ship in the deca-sector to investigate."

"But why me? I'm just getting comfortable in my role as third watch commander aboard my battleship."

"Obviously, Dr. Peterson feels we're uniquely qualified to handle this problem, whatever it is. I can't be gone for six months and Eliza won't be back from patrol for ten months. That leaves only you for this special assignment, *Commander*."

Christa understood from the use of her rank that it wasn't a request. And, sister or not, one doesn't argue with an Admiral when given an assignment. "Okay, sis. When do I leave?"

"The Quartermaster vessel *Roberts* is scheduled to depart in a few hours. They're expecting you to be aboard. I've ordered their route altered so they'll pass Dakistee. They'll drop you off near the planet so you won't have to make other connections. As it is, you'll be underway at Light-9790 for almost fifty days."

"Aye, Admiral. Uh, I trust I won't lose my position aboard the *Hephaestus* while I'm on this *temporary* duty?"

"I understand your concern. Each time I was assigned temporary duty off the *Prometheus,* I feared I would never return to the job I really wanted. I promise you that if you complete this assignment within six months, your post will be waiting. You remain part of my command while you're away, so if something unexpected happens to delay your return, I'll find you another good ship as soon as you're available for a posting. I've notified Admiral Holt that you'll be on special assignment in his sectors and asked him to supply whatever assistance is within his ability to provide."

"Then I guess I'd better get going," Christa said as she took a large gulp from the mug and returned it to the beverage center for automatic cleansing. "I don't want to cause a delay in the *Roberts'* departure."

Jenetta rose and came around the desk to walk Christa to the door. "Christa, be careful. If this is another cloning lab, I'm sure the Raiders know about it already. The war out here has displaced many of the ships that were on patrol in Region One, so help may not be as close as you'd like when you need it. Report to me as soon as you know what the situation is and I'll do everything I can to provide the support you need."

Christa smiled. "Okay, sis. Ya know, I'm already warming to the idea of returning to Dakistee. It's been a long time since we were there. I bet things have changed a lot."

"I'm sure you're right. When our books were published, Dakistee became *the* place to be for every archeologist in the GA. I understand the Expedition Headquarters staff on Anthius was inundated with applications for a while. They were said to be approving requests and assigning at least two new dig locations every single day. I wonder what the original planetary occupants would say if they could see how the scientists fawn over stuff they probably considered garbage, just because it's old."

"Well, that's nothing new. When we went to museums back on Earth when we were small, I remember seeing ancient pottery shards, broken arrowheads, and shattered bone knives. But I think the low point on Dakistee came when a publication ran a picture of a twenty-thousand-year-old disposable diaper, complete with fossilized fecal matter."

Jenetta chuckled. "Yes, I remember that. But who are we to say it doesn't have some archeological value?"

"At least it was long past the odorous stage."

"Yes. Too bad. That could have made for an interesting adjunct to the museum display. Imagine the display's audio introduction just before they activated the scent generator." After the two women shared a chuckle, Jenetta continued with, "But I'm sure they never seriously contemplated putting the find on display. Its usefulness is probably limited to providing dietary information from the period."

"Perhaps, but I always get a laugh out of imagining the excitement of the archeologists who made the discovery."

"Just think, in two months you'll be able to observe them up close," Jenetta said, giving her a slight push towards the door.

"Okay, I'm going," Christa said with a grin, then turned and hugged her sister for a couple of seconds.

"See you when you return, sis," Jenetta said.

◆　◆　◆

There was a transport waiting outside and a special shuttle waiting at the palace landing pad. Upon reaching the *Hephaestus*, Christa hastily packed her spacechest and then reported to the Captain. He was in his ready room on the bridge and the door opened as she approached.

"Come in, Christa," Captain Powers said as she entered. "The Admiral has notified me that you've received a special assignment and that you'll be leaving immediately. She said you won't be back for at least four months, but offered nothing else. Can you talk about it?"

"I don't know very much yet, sir. An archeologist on Dakistee sent an urgent request beseeching the Admiral to come as quickly as possible. She's asked me to go in her place since she can't get away."

"Dakistee, huh? Probably another cloning lab. Still, that's a long way to go when you don't know why you're going. You were born there, weren't you?"

"Yes, sir. I'm one of only seventy-nine citizens of the planet. I'm looking forward to seeing it again, but I hope to make the trip and return quickly so I can resume my duties here."

"Now that the war has ended, things are calming down. If your return should be delayed, I'll do everything in my power to keep your post open for you. You're a valuable member of this crew and I'd hate to lose you."

"Thank you, sir. I would much rather be here than going to Dakistee."

Captain Powers smiled. "You're just like your sister. You want to be aboard a ship more than any place in the galaxy, but you go where sent without complaint and do your best. You're an excellent officer, Commander, and I'll miss your services until you return."

"Thank you, sir. I'll be back just as soon as possible."

◆　◆　◆

Upon reporting aboard the *Roberts*, Christa was escorted to guest quarters in officer country. As she settled in, the enormous Quartermaster ship left orbit at Quesann. It's next planned stop was Dakistee. A special shuttle, delivered to the *Roberts* for Christa's use while she was on Dakistee, was stowed in one of the *Roberts*' flight bays.

◆　◆　◆

"Welcome to my humble retreat, Excellency," Sebaqd Gxidescu said to Nordakian high priest Kledoujk Vejrezzol as he opened the front door of his vacation lodge to the visitor.

"It is my honor to be welcomed here," Vejrezzol replied in customary Nordakian fashion as he stepped quickly inside and pushed the door closed. While approaching the building he had ascertained that, as ordered, all windows were shuttered, so he felt comfortable pulling back the hood that shielded his identity from anyone who might be watching from the woods or via satellite. He knew his home was being watched and delighted in knowing he was always able to easily evade the people who tried to follow him.

"The others are already here, Excellency," Gxidescu said.

"Good," Vejrezzol said as he removed the heavy cloak and draped it over his arm. "Show me the way."

Gxidescu turned and walked towards the rear of the house with Vejrezzol close behind. Although Gxidescu called it a vacation lodge, the house was massive and seldom used, if the sheets covering the furniture were any indication. It was just one of the innumerous perks typically afforded to those who, although not members of the nobility, were important business leaders with close ties to the church. The land was part of the estate belonging to the family Ukaloctqul, but had long ago been 'assigned in perpetuity' to the church for their use.

Their route took them almost to the kitchen at the rear of the house and then down a flight of stairs to the basement. Gxidescu shoved open a huge door and then pushed it closed after he and Vejrezzol had entered the large room. Ten men seated around a table in the center of the room had jumped to their feet as Vejrezzol entered.

"It's safe to talk openly in here, Excellency," Gxidescu said. "The room has been swept for bugs and no sound can pass through the door or walls."

Vejrezzol nodded and took time to scan the faces of the men at the table as if searching for signs of nervousness or doubt. Finding none, he said, "Be seated, gentlemen."

The high priest took his place at the head of the table, while Gxidescu took a seat at the opposite end. From their vantage points, both leaders could establish eye contact with any of the others, who constituted the inner circle of Vejrezzol's dissident sect. "Report," was all Vejrezzol said as he looked at the first man on his left.

"The freighter is in orbit and ready to begin loading. The captain has been well paid and is prepared to take on twenty of our followers as crew."

Vejrezzol nodded and looked at the next man, who immediately began his report.

"The containers that will hold our five-year food supply have been delivered and loaded. This includes the emergency rations. As planned, the fresh food will be loaded in refrigerated containers just before we're ready to leave."

Vejrezzol nodded again and shifted his gaze to the next man.

"The medical equipment and supplies have been loaded into containers and are ready for transport. The supplies with expiration dates will be delivered just before we're ready to leave to ensure they're as fresh as possible. All suppliers have been compensated for the supplies we've ordered and are only awaiting notification of our ship date. All will be ready."

"The 'farm equipment' and 'seed packs' have been procured and loaded into the special containers," the next man said in turn. "We're ready to send the loads up."

The last man on that side of the table spoke up as Vejrezzol looked towards him.

"The home furnishings and personal possessions of our followers are ready for transshipment, except for what they will bring as carry-on luggage."

Vejrezzol shifted his eyes to the other side of the table and the reports continued.

"The complete knowledge base of our people has been downloaded from the Royal Library and is securely stored in several containers."

"I assume it doesn't contain any copies of the new Almuth?" Vejrezzol asked.

"Of course not, Excellency."

"Very good."

Vejrezzol continued around the table, receiving reports on building materials, power generation and water purification equipment, livestock, communications equipment, clothing, and necessities such as paper and pens, cookware, sewing supplies, etc. The last man to report said, "The people who have traveled off planet in anticipation of this day have been collected from their locations and are all aboard. To the best of our knowledge, no one outside this group knows just how large the flock is."

"Excellent," Vejrezzol said when all reports were complete. "The day we have planned for and worked towards for so many annuals is almost upon us. When Azula Carver delivered the blasphemous document she alleges to be the original Almuth, we all knew that our ancestors would never have followed such a vile lifestyle as is espoused in that text. Why the nobility supported it and the leaders of our church accepted it as genuine we shall probably never know. But we do know that once we are out from under the thumb of the royal family and their puppets in the church, we will be able to live the lives God intended for us. I shall notify you all very soon of the departure date."

"Has the government given any indication that they intend to stop us or *attempt* to stop us?" Gxidescu asked.

"None, nor should they. We are free citizens of Nordakia and the Galactic Alliance, exercising our right to travel outside our home solar system. Slabeca has no planetary government and is not protected by the Galactic Alliance Bureau of Alien Affairs, so they cannot require us to secure advance entry permits. My friends, I promise you this— when we reach our destination, the entire galaxy will know of the sacrilege that forced us to abandon our homes on Nordakia and travel to a distant solar system. They will understand the reasons for the acts we have perpetrated and support our cause as just, no matter how many die in our struggle. Anything is acceptable when it's done by the hand of the righteous in the name of God."

CHAPTER TWO

~ April 24th, 2285 ~

"That's him leaving now," one of the analysts said to the group of senior officers watching the monitors in the command center.

Images from satellites and 'oh-gee' floating surveillance cameras filled an entire wall of the enormous operations room. Special housings, employing the battle armor technology used by Space Marines that rendered the wearer almost invisible, left little chance the cameras would be spotted. Images of the panorama behind the unit were projected onto the housing front, but a slight rippling effect might be detected if the camera was being repositioned. At night, the surveillance equipment was virtually undetectable. With the right sensors, it could be located by heat signature, but, due to the cooling feature built into the armor, chances of identifying the presence of the equipment were infinitesimal. The floating cameras had become the favorite tool of people performing surveillance work, although satellites still had a place.

"How can you possibly tell who's beneath that cloak?" one of the officers asked. "It could be almost anybody."

"The equipment uses a number of measurements when attempting to identify a suspect," the analyst said. "It has estimated his height and weight using the dimensions of objects in the environment and the impression he's left in loose soil surrounding the lodge, plus it can compare the gait of the subject with those of previously recorded instances where identification was positive. Every person walks in a different manner, and you can't fool the system for long, even if you're trying. The computer lists the probability of accuracy in this surveillance to be 99.99%. It's him, sir."

As the oh-gee vehicle departed the site, the computer announced that a routing plan entered into the vehicle's GPS device would take it to the home of Nordakian high priest Kledoujk Vejrezzol, albeit by an indirect route.

"That would seem to leave little doubt it was him," one of the senior officers said. "Shall we continue our conversation in the secure conference room?"

◆ ◆ ◆

As the door to the conference room slid silently shut, Admiral Cjolaku spoke first. "From what we know of their plans, the dissidents are ready to depart the planet. The Prime Minister has expressed his firm belief that they'll attempt to initiate a great catastrophe on our home world timed to occur after they've gone. He said he has excellent reason for his speculation, although he can't name the source. Our job is to ensure it doesn't happen."

"Sir, did the Prime Minister mention what *type* of catastrophic event they might be planning?" Commander Rlerqsop asked.

"He suggested it might be a mass poisoning or a pandemic. We'll have to be extra watchful of people who work in any field dealing with mass distribution of products, especially pharmaceuticals and food. All water reservoir security forces must be placed on heightened alert."

"Every agent on the planet, including a cell composed of retired agents reactivated just for this operation, are watching all known members of this group," Rlerqsop said. "I'll update their orders immediately to include this latest information. If the dissidents attempt anything, we'll know."

"Hopefully in time to stop them," the admiral said.

"Yes, sir."

"If they do perpetrate a great disaster, they won't escape justice," Commander Bloljuxa said. "A Space Command vessel will be monitoring their progress for at least their first month after leaving Nordakia to ensure they really are headed for Slabeca."

"Whatever made them choose Slabeca as their destination?" Rlerqsop asked. "It's a hot, dirty little planet with limited mineral resources."

"They say they intend to follow the plan of our ancestors who colonized this world millennia ago," Bloljuxa said. "On Slabeca, the dissidents will be free to establish a colony where they can follow the dictates of their false Almuth. There's no government, and the existing colonies are small and widely scattered. They say the lack of mineral resources makes the planet unattractive to mining operations with their *corrupting* influences."

"Yes, but Slabeca? Most of it's an arid wasteland because it orbits too close to its star."

"They believe the planet is ideal for their intended agrarian society because it's of so little value for anything else. It's certain that it will never be a tourist destination. The dissidents have purchased massive irrigation system supplies, in addition to their farm equipment, seeds and agricultural supplies. They believe they'll turn it into a lush paradise."

"Lotsa luck with that one. I think they'll be on their way back to Nordakia within two years."

"Vejrezzol has made everyone sign papers renouncing their Nordakian citizenship and the documents will be filed officially after they depart. They can't come back."

"They're all Nordakian born," Rlerqsop said. "If they petition to come back, I'm sure the government will restore their citizenship, unless they've perpetrated crimes during their absence, such as attempts of mass poisonings of Nordakian citizens."

"The only thing I don't understand," Bloljuxa said, "is why the women among the dissidents wish to go. The false Almuth stripped women of all privileges and made them virtual slaves in the household. The Royal family had worked at reforms long before Azula Carver returned the One True Word to our people. If the dissidents follow the dictates of the false Almuth we've reviewed, the situation on Slabeca will be ten times worse than at any time here during the past century."

"I can't answer that one," Rlerqsop said, "other than to say that I don't think they fully understand what they're getting themselves into. I think they might have romanticized this back-to-basics philosophy. It's one of the reasons I believe they'll be begging to come back within two years. Life on Slabeca won't be easy for anyone, but I pity the women most."

◆　◆　◆

Prime Minister Kulhwolpk hurried to the door and pulled it open. "Come in, Most Holy," he said to the distinguished-looking Nordakian who had just arrived in his outer office as he stepped back to allow entry.

"Thank you, Prime Minister," the priest said as he stepped through the doorway. As a Jtagual, Chlakqu Rtjweefkla occupied one of the five highest positions in the Nordakian priesthood.

"Shall we sit in my informal area, Most Holy?" Kulhwolpk asked, gesturing toward the oh-gee seating in a side alcove. "These seats are far more comfortable than the office chairs."

"That would be most satisfactory," Rtjweefkla said and turned in that direction.

Once the two men had settled into comfortable chairs, the prime Minister said, "Thank you for coming. I wish to discuss the matter of the dissidents again. They will be leaving shortly and we're on high alert for treachery and sabotage, but so far we've uncovered no plots. Have you heard anything?"

"Vejrezzol has broken off almost all contact with the church. He doesn't respond to communications and doesn't see visitors from outside the sect he's established."

Kulhwolpk shook his head slowly. "I was hoping you could tell me something we could use."

"I can tell you Vejrezzol was never granted access to the documents that proved church leaders were behind the genocide of our people on Dakistee. We've known for decades that Vejrezzol only craves power, so we've seen to it that he never rose to a position of real authority and responsibility in the church. Had he achieved such a position before we learned of the treachery, he would surely have been included in the discussions and would then have understood why the church allowed the document from Dakistee to replace the Almuth we were following. But I know he can't be trusted to keep the secret, so when I learned he was serious about leaving Nordakia, I felt you should be reminded of what happened once before. I can't guarantee Vejrezzol is unaware of it. He might have learned from a clergy member in the know."

"Then you feel confident he's capable of carrying out such an act?"

"Capable? Without a doubt. He's extremely bitter. When the church hierarchy was satisfied that the Almuth presented to the King and Queen by Azula Carver was genuine, we made a commitment to embrace it. It was difficult letting go of so much we had come to accept, but most of us were successful. Vejrezzol and his followers continued to denounce the original Almuth as heresy and pledged to prove it was a lie perpetuated by Azula Carver. He was unable to do so, of course, but he managed to gather enough believers that he was able to form his own sect. Unfortunately for them, the government never recognized their church because it tried to impose old values on a populace who had come to embrace the changes."

"And how do you feel about the changes now?"

"The church has fully accepted the changes. Our people are more faithful to the covenants of the Almuth and more content with their lives than at any point in my lifetime. I doubt any of our priests, outside of Vejrezzol's sect, would welcome a return to the Almuth we followed in the days before the changes. The recovered text of the One True Word has answered so many questions that our scholars have wondered about and argued about for millennia. A new sort of peace has developed within the priesthood. Our ancestors on Dakistee were wise indeed, and the leaders who brought our people here must have been mad. I wish we could tell both groups how we feel about them."

"If so much of the church recognizes that the changes have been beneficial, how is it that Vejrezzol has managed to find so many supporters for his dream of reinstituting the false Almuth?"

"People have trouble letting go of lifelong behaviors, even when shown the practices were wrong to begin with. We in the priesthood have accepted that what we were taught was a lie and that our teachers had themselves been deceived. This was a difficult pill to swallow, but we were unable to argue with the truth that the people who brought us here had committed a vile act. We knew it was time for us to do what we could to rectify it. Vejrezzol never reached that conclusion. He could only see that what he had been taught was being stripped away from him after a lifetime of dedication. He simply refuses to accept the truth."

"Some might say that's a sign of madness," Kulhwolpk said.

"Yes, some might. But in all other respects he seems completely rational. I hope he doesn't give me cause to regret my defense of him by attempting a heinous act like that of our distant progenitors."

◆ ◆ ◆

"Ahil, please give us your report on Dakistee," Chairman Strauss of the Raider Lower Council said at the regularly scheduled meeting.

Councilman Ahil Fazid stood in front of his chair at the enormous table and cleared his throat before beginning. "We've moved as many elements as possible into the Loudescott site and someone watches the entrance to the tunnel around the clock. We've learned that, to date, the archeologists have made no progress in their attempts to open the facility. They work down there every day but our people report they haven't been able to open the entrance door by even a nanometer. Word is they've asked Admiral Carver to come help since it was she who had so much success with the ancient technology in the past."

"Admiral Carver?" Councilwoman Erika Overgaard said in surprise. "Do they really expect the Commander of the Second Fleet and Military Governor of Regions Two and Three to come to Dakistee to handle a minor issue?"

"It's not so minor. Who knows what wealth of secrets and technology awaits behind that sealed door? They've been trying desperately for weeks to open the facility— without success. Anyway, the word is they're doing their best to open the door before Carver, or whoever she sends, arrives so they can get the first look at whatever lies within the facility and because they fear they might be excluded again."

"Are we ready to take advantage of any opportunity that presents itself?" Strauss asked.

"Not quite yet, but we'll be ready in time to move in quickly when the facility is opened. Our main problem is one of keeping the assets in place without detection. We've located as many people as possible at the dig site as laborers, food preparers, and whatnot, and established a base some two hundred kilometers away in a mountainous, densely wooded area for the rest. The terrain is so difficult to traverse on foot that the area is rarely visited. Within minutes of being summoned, our shuttles can be airborne and arrive at Loudescott quickly. The problem is one of keeping our people bottled up inside the small ships until they're needed. We don't allow them outside because, although there are no surveillance satellites around the planet, they would be visible to passing aircraft. The shuttles themselves are camouflaged to blend in with the surrounding vegetation, and the hulls can mask heat signatures."

"Do they have all the weapons and supplies they need?"

"They've been fully outfitted and the shuttle captains have been briefed. They understand their roles. They'll deliver the people to the dig site when called and then ferry them off, along with whatever prizes our people are able to retrieve."

"So what remains to be done?"

"We're completing preparations for diversionary actions that will pull every Space Marine on the planet to the opposite side of the globe. These will seem like popular uprisings for better wages. Once the Marines begin to arrive at the distant locations, we'll block all communications from Loudescott so they can't signal for help. With luck, we'll have days before the Marines begin returning to their posts around the planet."

"Excellent. How large is the Marine contingent at Loudescott?"

"Quite small, really. It's less than a squad. We estimate their total planetary strength to be only about four hundred."

"That's a significant number."

"Not for an entire planet with hundreds of dig sites to watch over. They're actually spread out pretty thin. The Marines posted at Loudescott are responsible for all security at the dig, which encompasses some fifty square kilometers."

"It would seem they'll not be able to offer much of an obstacle if half their present number have traveled to the other side of the planet when we're ready to move in. Excellent planning, Ahil."

◆ ◆ ◆

Following a smooth and uneventful trip, the *Roberts* arrived at Dakistee right on schedule. Christa had spent part of the time brushing up on her Nordakian by requiring the computer interface in her quarters to speak to her only in that language. To refresh her memory on the history of the planet, she had also reread the books that she, Eliza, and Jenetta had coauthored a decade and a half earlier. She had also spent an incredible amount of time plowing through the myriad documents and vids they had found in the underground facility's computer. All top-secret documents had long ago been removed from her computer's database, and Space Command had released most of the other documents to the archeological officials at the expeditionary headquarters on Anthius, who had no doubt disseminated them to the archeologists on Dakistee. She felt prepared for whatever awaited her on the planet.

◆ ◆ ◆

Christa lightly touched her shuttle down on a designated landing pad near the most ground activity at the Loudescott dig. The huge smile on her face conveyed how she felt. It was always a thrill to pilot a small craft after being in a command position for a time and away from the controls of a ship. Giving orders to a helmsman that would alter the course of a battleship just wasn't as satisfying as piloting the ship oneself. While aboard ship, Christa always made time for simulator practice, but it just wasn't the same.

As she shut down the engines and turned off the ship's flight systems, she saw a greeting party approaching from across the landing field. Marine Assault Transport traffic was fairly common in the area, but Space Command ship sightings were rare. The exterior markings clearly identified the shuttle as SC, and the people at the dig site had rightly guessed that it might be the representative they were expecting.

Christa emerged from the shuttle and stood on the top step for a few seconds to absorb the beautiful springtime vista before stepping down from the shuttle to greet the approaching group. They were the same group of scientists she had known when she was last here. Although Jenetta's first encounter with the group had occurred before Christa's birth, she recalled every detail of the event as though it had been she greeting the site personnel.

She smiled at the approaching party and, as they neared, said, "Hello, Doctors Peterson, Ramilo, Huften, Vlashsku, Priestley, and Djetch. Hello Mr. Hill, Ms. Steen, Ms. Tomallo, and Ms. Cheney. It's wonderful to see all of you again. It's been a long time between visits. Congratulations on earning your doctorates, Doctor Priestley and Doctor Djetch. I don't see Mr. Deeds among your party. I hope he's well."

In the lead, owing to their longer legs, Vlashsku and Djetch stopped two meters from Christa. In customary fashion, they dropped to one knee, their heads bowed, with their right hands held against their chests as required when greeting a member of the Nordakian nobility. The others stopped walking while the ritual was performed, but didn't question it since they had observed it before. When Jenetta had first landed on the planet sixteen years earlier, both Nordakians had greeted her in the same fashion.

"Gentlemen, please stand and raise your heads," Christa said. As they rose, she said, "You honor me with your greeting, and I thank you. Since we'll be working closely for the near term, perhaps we can dispense with kneeling for the remainder of my visit. Is that okay?"

"As you wish, My Lady," the two Nordakian men said in unison.

Doctor Peterson stepped forth and extended his hand, saying, as Christa accepted it, "Commander, I'm delighted you were able to come after all. When I received the message that you were sending a representative, I feared we would be saddled with someone who didn't have a clue about the technology of the ancients."

"Edward," Dr. Huften said, "don't you remember? I told you Jenetta Carver is an admiral now. This is obviously Christa or Eliza."

"Quite right, Dr. Huften, I'm Christa."

Dr. Huften smiled and said, "Welcome to Dakistee, Christa. To answer your question, Harold Deeds is well. He's not among us because he accepted a position at Expedition Headquarters here on Dakistee. He's a senior curator at the collection warehouse."

"Wonderful," Christa said with a smile. "I regret, Dr. Peterson, that Admiral Carver was unable to get away, as much as she would have loved to come, but I was fortunate to be available for a return to my homeland. I hope you consider me a suitable replacement. Just what is the urgent matter you need to discuss?"

"Since you and your sisters share a common heritage, I'm delighted you're here, Commander. We've encountered a problem not unlike the last time we requested assistance from Space Command."

"Another cloning lab?"

"We don't know. We've uncovered an impregnable facility similar to the other, but we've been unable to gain entry."

"Perhaps that's just as well. There's no telling what dangers might be inside. Would you show me the way to the new tunnel?"

"Of course. Follow me."

With Dr. Peterson in the lead, Christa and her entourage wound their way through a maze of small open pits. Most had at least one person at the bottom who was exercising great care while removing clumps of soil or painstakingly cleaning dirt from partially buried objects. Christa was glad to see that Dr. Peterson had finally made the transition to laser poles. The new poles, positioned along two axes of an area, continually drew and redrew a grid work of lines. When Christa had last been on the planet, Dr. Peterson had still been insisting on the ancient system of stakes and string to delineate the grid, and people frequently became fouled in the lines and tripped.

The surface entrance to the facility was identical to that of the cloning facility. All exterior surfaces of the two-meter-wide tunnel were faced with a highly polished, metamorphic rock resembling marble that bore tendril-like streaks of white and gave the appearance of fractures in the lustrous black surface. As they descended into the tunnel, their nostrils were continuously assaulted by the pungent odors of damp soil and mold spores that lingered in the passageway. As with the other entrance, the downward ramp turned back on itself twice and widened to four meters as it leveled out. The entire way was brightly illuminated by Chembrite Light panels.

As the black wall and door came into view, Christa experienced a flashback to the first time Jenetta had seen the other wall and door. The door and tunnel area were still as pristine here as the other had originally been. Following the attack by Tsgardi mercenaries at the other location, the entry antechamber had evidenced the severe consequences of innumerous explosions from attempts to breach the facility's impregnable construction.

"Here it is, Commander. As you can see, our attempts at entry have been fruitless. We didn't resort to explosives. They certainly didn't help the Tsgardi gain entry at the other facility."

"Yes, brute force isn't an effective tool with Dakinium. And the use of power sufficient to break in might result in the entire facility being destroyed."

"Do you think you can open it?" Doctor Huften asked anxiously.

"I'll certainly do my best. But first I have to report in. My orders are to send a detailed message to my HQ as soon as I've sized up the situation."

"But you can't announce this," Peterson said. "We've kept it a closely guarded secret to ensure the Raiders don't learn of it."

"I'm not going to announce it, Doctor. I'm going to send an encrypted message to Admiral Carver to see how she wishes to proceed."

"Humph, I know what *that* means," Peterson said.

"Please enlighten me," Christa said.

"It means you're sending for reinforcements to bar us from getting inside."

"I expect Marine personnel will arrive to protect the facility once it's opened. And I can state with some certainty that you won't be among the first to enter the facility. We must ensure there's no danger to site personnel and that there will be no situations like the cloning accident at the other facility."

"Which means we won't have an opportunity to examine whatever it is you find inside."

"As I understand it, all artifacts from the other facility, with the exception of the cloning equipment, were eventually turned over to Expedition Headquarters."

"Yes, but not for many months."

"Even so, you did eventually get everything except the illegal equipment or access to certain confidential information that Space Command deemed should remain secret."

"And how do we know that?"

"It's the truth, Doctor. If you don't believe it, I have no way of convincing you."

"Humph."

"Well," Christa said to the assembled scientists, "if you'll all excuse me, I have a report to compose and send."

The group parted so she could leave and waited until they were confident she was out of earshot before talking among themselves.

◆

"I told you," Dr. Peterson said. "We're going to be cut out of the loop just like before."

"We never expected to be included in the Military's inner circle of confidants, Edward," Dr. Huften said. "We only knew we needed their help to get into the facility. We've had months and we're no closer to learning the secrets of our find than we were before we found it. Perhaps we'll have to wait a few months to learn what's inside, but we've already wasted that much in effort. I'm happy to turn the problem over to Space Command. I know they'll share whatever information they can as soon as they can."

"We have only their word for that."

"Azula Carver and her sisters are honorable," Dr. Vlashsku said. "I believe everything they say."

"As do I," Dr. Djetch said.

"Admiral Carver and her sisters did save all our lives at great risk to their own when the Tsgardi attacked." Dr. Ramilo said. "I'm also disposed to believe what she says is the truth."

"I never said she was lying," Dr. Peterson said defensively. "I trust *her*. I just don't trust the military as a whole."

Christa climbed aboard the shuttle and relocked the hatch behind her. The shuttle Jenetta had provided was outfitted to serve as both home and base of operations. The seats in the cabin area had been removed and replaced with furnishings usually found in a deluxe shelter. The larder was stocked with enough food for six months, and she even had a gel-comfort bed. At least she would be comfortable while she waited for instructions from Jenetta.

The message to Quesann would take seventeen days to arrive and then seventeen more for the response to reach Dakistee, so, after sending her report to Jenetta, Christa sent a message to Admiral Holt at Higgins Space Command Base. As nice as it was to come home for a visit, she feared losing her dream posting on the *Hephaestus* if she remained here too long. She knew Jenetta and Captain Powers would do everything they could to hold the position open, but they couldn't hold it forever. Besides, she'd rather be aboard the *Hephaestus* than on Dakistee. The DS battleship was scheduled to leave on patrol in three days and Christa was disappointed that someone else would be handling her watch.

In preparation for an extended stay on Dakistee, Christa moved the shuttle to a small, open area nearer the new facility. The area, located just fifty meters from the tunnel entrance, would from then on serve as the shuttleport for the new outpost.

CHAPTER THREE

~ May 5th, 2285 ~

Higgins SCB was only thirty light years away, so a reply from Admiral Holt arrived the next day. Christa was having breakfast when the computer informed her of its arrival. She immediately set her meal aside and moved to the computer console.

As Christa activated the viewscreen, a head-and-shoulders image of Admiral Holt filled the image area. Jenetta had long ago learned to judge his mood from his expression and, as their interaction with him had increased, so had Christa and Eliza. They could tell when he was masking his mood and what mood he was masking. On this occasion his face was affable, and Christa could tell it was genuine even before he spoke a word.

"Hello, Christa," the Admiral said, "it's a pleasure to welcome you back to Region One. I'll naturally do everything I can to support your mission on Dakistee. After receiving Jenetta's initial message, I assigned Lt. Grace Carmoody of the GSC research ship *Heisenberg* to your operation. All reports indicate that she's an excellent officer and scientist. Her ship should arrive in orbit within two days and she'll transfer to your command there for temporary duty. I've also issued orders to the Commanding officer of the Marine battalion stationed on Dakistee to send you as many Marines as he can free up. I'm afraid the troop strength on Dakistee is woefully limited, so don't expect more than a company, and don't be surprised if you only receive a squad. But even a squad should be enough to guard the tunnel entrance from a bunch of unarmed scientists. Keep me apprised of the situation there and don't hesitate to ask if you need anything.

Our Marine resources are low in this deca-sector, but I'll give you everything else I can.

"Brian Holt, Rear Admiral, Upper Half, Higgins Space Command Base, message complete."

Christa knew she couldn't attempt to open the facility's door until she had some support. She didn't expect to need help opening the door, but she'd need a few Marines to ensure the anxious scientists stayed far enough away so they remained unaware of the procedure. Jenetta wanted to make sure that as few people as possible learned the secret to the process so Space Command would always have to be called if any additional facilities were discovered.

Christa spent the remainder of the morning reviewing files downloaded from the first facility's computer core. Just after noon, local time, the computer informed her that an Armored Personnel Carrier was approaching. Christa watched the computer-provided image on her monitor for a few seconds, then gave the computer an instruction to open the hatch. A few minutes later she heard the sounds made by someone climbing the ramp, and a Marine appeared in the hatchway.

"Sergeant Flegetti reporting, Commander," he said as he braced to attention.

"At ease, Flegetti. What are your orders?"

"To report to the Commander for temporary duty in support of the operation, Ma'am. That was all I was told."

"How many Marines do you have with you?"

"Two fire teams of four, Ma'am."

"Very well. That will be adequate for now. Where are you normally posted?"

"About two klicks from here, Ma'am. We're part of the Fort Carver squad."

Christa smiled and said, "I wasn't aware it was still being called that. I never saw the sign that was put up, but my sister told me about it."

"Technically it's the Loudescott Outpost, but everyone prefers the informal designation as a tribute to the people who fought the battle that took place here in 2270."

"A number of good people were injured or lost their lives here."

"Yes, ma'am. The Corps put up an official plaque at the entrance to the bunker and the original handmade sign was mounted on the wall in the mess hall. "

"Are you the senior noncom for your squad?"

"No ma'am. That would be Staff Sergeant Burton."

"I would have expected him or her to arrive with the teams."

"Um, I'm sorry, ma'am. I was so excited about meeting you that I forgot I was supposed to say Lt. Uronson sends his regrets and will come to see you as soon as he returns from Pendleton. Staff Sergeant Burton went with him."

"Pendleton? Camp Pendleton, California?"

"No ma'am. There's a dig site here named Fallbrook halfway around the planet. Battalion headquarters is located there on a Marine camp that's been named North Pendleton."

"I see. There's no need to be in awe of me, Sergeant. The Admiral is the one who's done all the fantastic deeds."

"Um, yes ma'am, but you're a clo…" The last word seemed to stick in his throat.

"It's okay to say it, Sergeant. Everyone in the GA knows that my sister Eliza and I are clones of the Admiral. Our birth wasn't intentional, but we're glad it happened all the same."

"Uh, yes ma'am." A bit red-faced he added, "So is everyone else."

Christa smiled, then said, "Sergeant, your assignment here is simple. The archeologists have discovered another bunker like Fort Carver. They haven't been able to gain access and it's up to us to see that they don't until it's been checked for hazards and cleared of equipment designated as contraband by the GA. You and your people will empty the tunnel of any non-military personnel and post guards at the entrance to see that no one except Space Command and Marine personnel are permitted entry unless I amend this order. Clear?"

"Yes, ma'am."

"Good. The tunnel entrance is about fifty meters off this ship's starboard bow. Your two fire teams will take responsibility for the tunnel immediately and guard it around the clock. Dismissed."

"Aye, ma'am."

Sergeant Flegetti braced to attention , then turned on his heel and left the small ship. A couple of minutes later, Christa saw the APC depart in the direction of the tunnel entrance.

◆ ◆

After completing the research she had been engaged in when the Marines arrived, Christa left the shuttle and walked to the tunnel entrance. The two Marines on duty there braced to attention until she had passed them.

The tunnel was as quiet as a tomb. Christa thought briefly about all the Mummy movies she had seen while growing up, then shook herself mentally to clear her head and think about the job at hand.

The blacker-than-black door and wall looked forbidding and ominous as they came into view on the lowest level. Impregnability was a given since they had firsthand experience with the construction material used, but there shouldn't be anything ominous about the facility. It was just a workplace that happened to be underground. Innumerous military facilities were located underground, mainly for protection from attack, and that factor had been of immense value when the Tsgardi tried to take the cloning equipment. Having the entrance underground meant they couldn't bring large equipment to bear that might have given them a better chance of breaking in. Perhaps the sensation she was experiencing now was simply the result of knowing how old the facility was, as well as the pale-yellow light given off by the Chembrite panels.

Christa walked to within a meter of the door, took another look around to make sure she was alone, and said, "Dwuthathsei." She had expected the door to open as soon as she uttered the Dakis word for open, but nothing happened. So she said it again, more clearly. Still nothing happened. Because it had worked at the other facility, she and Jenetta had expected it to work here as well. Finally, she began saying the word in slightly different ways. Ancient Dakis was marginally different than modern Dakis, although the computer at the other facility had been able to understand and bridge the subtleties. It appeared this computer was a little more dense. Or perhaps the computer was malfunctioning. If that was the case, getting inside was going to be a real chore.

After trying every phonetic variation of 'dwuthathsei' she could think of, Christa gave up. She had to find a new approach to the problem. Moving right up to the door, she placed her hand against it to see if she could feel any vibration that might indicate something was happening inside or that the door was trying to open. She felt no vibration, but she did feel something unexpected. There were scratches on a door that should have none. The tools used against the door shouldn't have been able to mar the surface at all.

Christa retrieved a Chembrite panel from against the rear wall and brought it over to the door. When it was placed off to the side, shadows created by the scratches allowed them to become barely visible, but it turned out the scratches weren't really scratches at all. They were carefully etched patterns and markings in the door. Although almost invisible, it was obvious they weren't accidental.

Christa used the camera in her viewpad to photograph the marks from several different angles and with the Chembrite panel casting light from several different directions. When she felt she had a good representation of images, she had the computer assemble a single image and increase the contrast so the marks were easy to identify. What she saw was six circles, each approximately twelve centimeters in diameter, arranged horizontally across the center of the door. Perpendicular to the circumference line of each circle were small lines, sort of like the points on a compass. Christa counted thirty-eight of the equidistant marks around each circle. A single, large symbol or icon appeared just above the row of circles.

Christa felt sure the markings were important and might hold the key to opening the door, but she didn't have a clue as to what they indicated.

◆ ◆ ◆

When the *Heisenberg* entered orbit two days later, Christa still hadn't a clue as to the meaning of the circles or the large symbol on the door, but it wasn't because she hadn't thought about them. She had thought of little else for the better part of two days. If she was going to follow this lead, she needed a starting point.

◆ ◆ ◆

Lt. Grace Carmoody arrived dirt-side early afternoon local time. By Galactic System Time it was early in the first watch when the shuttle touched down. The pad next to Christa's shuttle was vacant, so the *Heisenberg* shuttle landed there and then took off as soon as Carmoody had disembarked with her gear.

◆

"Lieutenant Grace Carmoody reporting as ordered, Commander," Carmoody said as she braced to attention.

"At ease, Lieutenant. Welcome to Dakistee. Coffee?"

"Thank you, Ma'am. A cup of coffee would be great. I was so excited about this assignment that I skipped break-fast."

"Help yourself," Christa said, gesturing towards the small galley unit installed against a forward bulkhead where two seats would normally be located, "then come sit down."

When Carmoody had fixed her coffee and was seated at the dining/work table, Christa said, "Do you know why you're here?"

"I was only told to report to you to assist on a science project. Nothing else."

"Sixteen years ago, archeologists working on this planet discovered an ancient underground lab where a cloning process had been perfected."

"Yes, I know about that. At least as much as has been released to the public."

"Then you're probably also aware that I was a product of that process, as was my sister Eliza and seven duplicates each of the eleven scientists who discovered the lab."

"Yes, I believe you're called the 'Dakistee Seventy-Nine.'"

"That's correct. Space Command confiscated the illegal equipment and that ended the cloning activity here. We still maintain control of the underground lab because the entire facility is sheathed in Dakinium and it's imperative that it not fall into enemy hands."

"I understand."

"Okay, that ends the history discussion and brings us to the current situation. Those same archeologists have discovered another facility. Like the first, it's sheathed in Dakinium. But, unlike the first, they haven't been able to gain entry. That's probably a good thing. We're here to find a way in and ensure there's no illegal equipment on the premises. We'll also probably have to take permanent command of the facility to prevent anyone from getting samples of Dakinium. The scientists won't be happy, but we have our orders."

"Yes, Ma'am."

"Since we're going to be working closely, why don't you simply use my first name when we're alone. I'm Christa."

Carmoody smiled. "I'd like that. I'm Gracie to my friends."

"Okay, Gracie, here's what I've found so far." Christa handed her a holo-magazine cylinder that contained the enhanced image of the door. "Just activate the cylinder."

As Carmoody powered on the device, a high-resolution color image of the door rose up from the device.

"What is this, Christa?" Carmoody asked after she had examined it for a couple of minutes.

They're markings I discovered on the facility's entry door. They're so faint that they're almost imperceptible, even when you're looking for them. As you've probably heard, Dakinium is almost indestructible, so the marks are there by design, not by accident."

"Does the original facility entry door have these marks?"

"I don't know. No mention of markings has ever been included in the files. Perhaps no one ever looked, or perhaps the door was so badly damaged during the Tsgardi assault that markings would have been considered mere scratches without a close examination. In any event, the door was removed by the *Prometheus'* engineers and taken away. I have no idea where it might be now, or even if it's still intact. It might have been destroyed by SC Research during the experiments to reproduce Dakinium."

"Then we have very little to go on."

"Yes. The force required to open the door might very well destroy the entire facility, so we have to find a non-violent way in. It will, therefore, be necessary to solve this puzzle. Let me add that everything we discuss regarding this issue is to be considered Most Secret. You're not to mention any of our findings to anyone."

"Do the archeologists know of the circles or the symbol?"

"Not as far as I know. I didn't tell them, and they never mentioned them to me. I suppose they spent all their time trying to open the door in a manner consistent with access to the other facility."

"And what is that?"

"A simple vocal command in Ancient Dakis, which is amazingly close to the current language equivalent in spoken Nordakian Dakis."

Carmoody simply nodded to convey understanding and returned her attention to the image on the cylinder. Christa took another holo-magazine cylinder from the table and also stared at the image, perhaps hoping for an epiphany of sorts.

After a time, Carmoody said, "These small lines around the circumference of the circles are interesting. I count thirty-eight. Could they be compass headings?"

"I suppose they could, but I doubt it. We use three hundred sixty degrees, but according to the computer files, the ancients here used a segmentation of five hundred degrees for direction. I ran the number thirty-eight as a search argument, but nothing that seemed relative was returned."

"Too bad. May I see the tunnel and door?"

"Of course. It's just across the way. I'll show you."

◆

The Marines had erected a small canopy to shade them from the hot sun when they stood guard. The two on duty at the tunnel entrance braced to attention as the two officers approached and held it until Christa and Carmoody had passed. The tunnel was cooler than the outside temperature and continued to drop slightly as the ramp led downward.

"Wow," was Carmoody's reaction when she first laid eyes on the wall and door.

Christa smiled and said, "It does create awe in people when they first see it.

"It almost looks evil," Carmoody said.

"It's just a wall and door, but I understand what you mean. Of course, there may be some great evil inside. But we won't know until we get the door open."

"I don't see the marks," Carmoody said when they were just a meter away.

"You practically have to press your face against the door. I didn't know they were there until I inadvertently felt them. Here, this will help," Christa said as she retrieved the Chembrite panel she had used to highlight the marks from the side.

"Yes, I can see them now, barely," Carmoody said when her nose was just a couple of centimeters from the door. "I can understand why most people might miss them. It's entirely possible the archeologists have no idea they're there."

As she ran her hand over the surface she said, "It's amazing you even felt them. I know they're there and can barely sense them."

"Information isn't of much use if you can't relate it to the problem at hand, and so far I haven't a clue about their importance. I could have a table moved down if you think it would be beneficial to work here instead of on the surface."

"No," Carmoody said. "Now that I've seen the door and have a better appreciation of the problem, I can work just as well on the surface."

CHAPTER FOUR
~ May 8th, 2285 ~

Several days later they were no closer to a solution.

"This is frustrating," Christa said. "It's like what we went through when we were charged with dismantling the cloning equipment in the other lab but didn't want to simply pull the plug and possibly harm developing embryos."

"What if we ask the archeologists if they know anything?"

"I don't want them to know what we've found. The Admiral wants to keep all civilians in the dark concerning the opening of facilities like this in case more are uncovered. We need to be the first ones in."

"I don't mean we should share our findings. I mean maybe we should show them the unidentified symbol and ask if it looks familiar."

"Hmm," Christa muttered as she thought, "you know, when Jenetta was working on her problem at the other lab, one of the archeologists gave her some information about symbols that were etched into the floor."

"Did it ultimately help her solve the problem?"

"No, but it gave her hope that she was making progress. I think we could use a little encouragement like that. Okay, I'll ask Dr. Vlashsku. He's always been anxious to help without expecting reciprocal favors."

◆ ◆ ◆

"My Lady, you honor me by your presence," Doctor Vlashsku said when greeting Christa at the door to his shelter. "Please come in."

Christa replied with the customary Nordakian reply, "It is my honor to be welcomed here."

"How may I be of service, My Lady. You have only to ask and I will do it."

"You were helpful when I— I mean when my sister was trying to solve the riddle of the symbols engraved into the floor of the cloning facility. I'm hoping you might recognize a new symbol. I haven't been able to find any reference to it in any of my Dakistee files, including those sent to me from Expedition Headquarters on Anthius."

"Of course, My Lady. Do you have an image with you?"

"Yes," Christa said, producing a holo-tube. "Here it is." She had reversed the large symbol to show as black on a plain white background in an attempt to disassociate it from the door. The lower resolution of the holo-tube was perfectly adequate for displaying it.

Doctor Vlashsku activated the holo-tube and looked closely at the symbol for several minutes before asking, "Is this symbol connected with the problem of accessing the new chamber?"

"It might be. I'm trying to determine its origin to see if it might have a connection."

"Seeing this on a holo-tube has reminded me of something. We had our annual conference at the Brighton dig site last year. This symbol bears a strong resemblance to one I saw there."

"Brighton?"

"Yes, the site director had a cylinder, very much like a holo-tube cylinder, and this symbol was engraved on one end. It wasn't a holo-tube of course, but the jet-black cylinder was about the same size. The director had it mounted on a desktop display stand in her office. That's all I can think of right now. I'm most sorry I can't be of more help."

"On the contrary, Doctor. I think you've been of immense help."

◆　◆　◆

"Please come in, Commander," the director of the dig site at Brighton said as she stepped aside to allow Christa and Carmoody into her office."

"Thank you, Dr. Manson. This is Lt. Grace Carmoody."

"Welcome, both of you. Would you care for a beverage?"

"Thank you," Christa said. "I'd like coffee if you have it."

"The same for me," Carmoody said.

"Marie," Ms. Manson said out the door to the office, "three coffees, please."

"Ladies, please have a seat and tell me how I may help you."

"Our visit here today stems from a conversation I had with Doctor Dakshiku Vlashsku at the Loudescott site," Christa said and then stopped as Dr. Manson's assistant brought in the coffees and placed them on the director's desk. When they had prepared their coffees, she continued. "I sought his help in identifying a unique symbol and he said he recognized it as being identical to one he observed on an artifact you have on your desk. From his description, it might be that one," Christa said, pointing to a display stand supporting a black cylinder about the size of a holo-tube cylinder.

"And what is your interest in the symbol?"

"I'm trying to determine if it has relevance to a problem reported by the archeological team at Loudescott."

"You're referring to the underground facility they recently discovered?"

The statement caught Christa off guard. She hesitated for just a moment before saying, "You're unexpectedly well informed, Doctor."

"Word of a major new discovery travels quickly. I know the team at Loudescott hasn't been able to open the facility and they contacted Space Command for help. Are you two all they sent?"

"So far. I can request additional help if we need it."

"And have you been able to gain access to the facility?"

"May I look at the cylinder while we talk?"

"Of course. Help yourself."

Christa leaned over and lifted the tube from the display stand. It appeared to be a solid, single-piece design. The symbol she was looking for was engraved on one end. The other end bore a letter from the ancient alphabet. There were no other markings. "It's remarkably pristine for something nineteen thousand, four hundred years old."

"It was sealed in a vacuum container. The container's exterior showed the effects of age, but the contents were as perfect as the day they were sealed inside."

"What else was in the container?"

"A timepiece, some letters addressed to the Regional Cultural Headquarters here, and a lengthy list of very prominent individuals."

"How do you know they were prominent?"

"There were titles associated with most, such as Minister, Doctor, Professor, etc."

"I see."

From the look and weight of the cylinder, Christa guessed was made of Dakinium.

"Yes, this is what I'm looking for. The symbol is identical to the one I'm trying to identify. Have you seen it anywhere else, Doctor?"

"No, I haven't. We've been able to identify most of the symbols we've encountered using one or the other of the reference books you and your *sisters* wrote."

Christa didn't miss the way Manson emphasized the word 'sisters' and wondered if she had a problem with clones.

"I wonder if I might borrow this for a short time?" Christa asked.

"Why?"

"I don't know, but I feel very strongly that it might help my research."

"I'm afraid I can't let you take it. It's the property of the Dakistee Archeological Expedition and can't be loaned out without approval from the headquarters on Anthius."

"Then could you show me exactly where it was found on the dig site?"

"Why?"

"Call it— curiosity."

The look Manson gave Christa indicated she was suspicious of Christa's motives for wanting the information, but she turned on a wall monitor and used a laser pointer to identify the general area where the cylinder had been found.

"You're sure it wasn't more to the left— by say a kilometer?"

Manson eyes narrowed and she said, "I may be mistaken."

"Of course. It's impossible to remember where every object has been located."

"If you have no further questions," Dr. Manson said, standing up behind her desk, "I have another meeting."

"Thank you for taking the time from your busy schedule to see us today."

"You're welcome. Goodbye."

As Carmoody and Christa exited the building and walked towards the shuttle pad, Carmoody said, "You already knew where the cylinder was found?"

"No, but she said the vacuum canister contained letters written to the Regional Cultural Headquarters. I remembered where the RCH was located from looking at a map of the city that once stood here."

"Where did you get a map of the city?"

"The files we got from the computer in the other facility provided excellent maps of the entire planet. Once the Expedition Headquarters had that information, new dig sites were assigned at all the former locations of major cities and many sites were closed down if the area they were excavating had only been a forest or some other rural area. It was just pure chance that Dr. Peterson happened to select a site where the planet's capital city was located, but the maps have since helped him make decisions regarding where his people work within the city's limits."

"So what now?" Carmoody asked.

"Now we get the cylinder Dr. Manson has."

"But she said no. You're not going to steal it, are you?"

"Of course not. But before we even lift off, I'm going to send a request to the Expedition Headquarters on Anthius that the cylinder be delivered to me at Loudescott because I require it for a research project."

"You think they'll give it to you?"

"The Expedition Headquarters owes Space Command, and especially the Carver sisters, big time. They'll loan it to me."

◆　◆　◆

"Lt. Uronson reporting to the base commander," the butter-bar Marine officer said after being invited into the shuttle and coming to attention.

"Stand easy, Lieutenant," Christa said.

"Yes, ma'am," he said as he relaxed. "I apologize for not being here to welcome you, ma'am, but I was ordered to report to battalion headquarters for a series of meetings regarding new security procedures being implemented on the planet."

"It's quite all right, Lieutenant. Sergeant Flegetti has done a splendid job in your absence. There are always two sentries on duty at the entrance to the new facility, which has been perfectly adequate. Now that you've returned, I want you to establish a proper camp like the one at Fort Carver. A perimeter trench with protective berm should be dug one hundred meters from the tunnel entrance. I realize you don't have the manpower for proper patrols, but I hope we'll soon have reinforcements. I expect this new underground facility will be every bit as important as the other."

"Yes, ma'am."

"Any questions, Lieutenant?"

"No ma'am. But I have to say that expectations of reinforcements may not be realistic. The Corps is spread really thin on this planet and everyone is requesting additional personnel."

"I'm afraid you might be right. We'll just have to see what kind of priority Space Command places on this outpost."

"Yes, ma'am."

"That's all, Lieutenant. Dismissed."

◆ ◆ ◆

Three days later, Christa received a visitor at her shuttle. "Welcome, Dr. Manson. Won't you come in?"

Manson entered the shuttle and walked to the table Christa was using for a desk. As she placed a small case on the table, she said, "The Expedition Headquarters has ordered me to deliver the cylinder to you. It's on loan for as long as you need it. I need your thumbprint on the receipt."

Christa applied her thumb to the viewpad and said, "Would you care for a cup of coffee, Doctor?"

"No thank you. I'm on a tight schedule. Good day." With that, she left the shuttle and walked to where her own was waiting.

"Wow," Carmoody said. "Did they make her bring it to you personally?"

"In my note I may have mentioned that Dr. Manson had proved to be a little less than cooperative. Perhaps that was the reason she was here today. I wouldn't have said anything if she hadn't deliberately tried to mislead us regarding where the cylinder was found. I still haven't worked that one out. There was no reason that I can see."

"Perhaps she just wanted to place an obstacle in our path and thought misleading us about where the cylinder was found might accomplish that."

"Perhaps. With luck we'll have no more contact with her. Her personality is no better than the coffee she serves to her visitors."

Christa opened the small case and removed the cylinder. She looked at the symbol on the end of the tube and smiled. "Well, we have it. Now what do we do with it?"

"It's yours for as long as you want it. You could mount it on a display stand and send a picture to Dr. Manson."

"No, I'm not looking to rub her face in it. I don't know why, but I really feel we need this object to open the door.

◆　◆　◆

After breakfast the next morning, Christa and Carmoody returned to the tunnel. They stood staring at the door and the cylinder as they thought, but there seemed to be no real connection other than the symbol on the end of the tube. There were no openings in the door where the cylinder might be inserted, as would be done with a key, and no supports where it could be hung. The breakthrough came when Christa extended her hand to compare the length of the cylinder with the diameter of one of the circles. As her open hand neared the door, the cylinder suddenly leapt up and stuck to the door. She was so startled that she just stared it for some thirty seconds as she tried to reason why it should behave like that. Recovering from her absorption, she reached out and plucked the cylinder from the door, then again held it close to the door, but a meter to the right of the first spot. She watched, fascinated, as it again leapt from her hand and clung to the door.

"This doesn't make any sense," Christa said. "Dakinium doesn't have magnetic properties, yet it's acting like it does." She plucked the cylinder from the door and carried it over to a Chembrite light where she held it against the steel support stand. There was no magnetic attraction. "Well, the magnetic properties aren't in the cylinder. It must be something in the composition of the door."

"Did you notice," Carmoody asked, "that it only stuck on circles both times?"

"Did it? Let's check that out."

After ten minutes of experimentation, the results seemed conclusive. The cylinder would only stick to the areas inside the six circles, but it stuck equally well inside any of them.

"So, either there're magnetic properties in the door and the cylinder has a steel core, or the Dakistee ancients discovered some property of Dakinium that we don't yet know," Christa said. "Did you notice the rod always aligned with one of the thirty-eight marks on the circumference?"

"Yes, I did," Carmoody said.

"It would seem we have part of our answer," Christa said.

"We do?" Carmoody said with surprise. "What is it?"

"The circles *must* represent a locking mechanism. There could be no other reason for having such an elaborate arrangement on the door. It has to be a combination lock."

"Okay, but how does it operate?"

"I can think of several possibilities. You could place the cylinder on a circle, beginning in a certain position, then twist it to a new position. We've already established that it will align in any of thirty-eight directions. But that could be problematic if there isn't a way to reset the lock since there's no visible indication of where an internal cam is presently pointed, so it's more likely that simply placing a cylinder against the door enables a mechanism. However, that theory relies on there being five more cylinders. So— to open the door, you must have the proper cylinder on the proper circle, aimed in the proper direction. It's incredibly simple and yet incredibly complex at the same time."

"I'm not following you. It doesn't sound that difficult if you have the cylinders."

"That's why it seems incredibly simple, but if I'm correct, we must not only have all six cylinders, but we must know the exact position required for each. Each of the required cylinders might have been entrusted to an important individual on the planet and only that individual knew the proper alignment of their cylinder. That makes it both a key lock and a combination lock in one. You must have all the pieces *and* the knowledge of the combination to open the door. Having only one part won't do it."

"If that's true," Carmoody said, "there's another possibility. What if one of the circles was meant to be left without a cylinder, although six cylinders were made. It would be like having six deadbolts on a door where you had no information if the bolt was currently open or closed."

"Yes. If just one of the deadbolts isn't retracted, the door remains locked."

"I wonder how many permutations are possible? Assuming that all six cylinders are required, what's thirty-eight raised to the sixth?"

"Roughly three billion, eleven million combinations," Christa said. "However, there's another consideration. I'm assuming that each cylinder has a different 'magnetic' strength value, so you must have the correct cylinder on the proper circle. This raises the possible combinations to *eighteen* billion." She released a soft sigh and added, "It might take a few days longer to open the door than I had anticipated before my arrival."

CHAPTER FIVE

~ May 16th, 2285 ~

As the two Space Command officers later relaxed in the shuttle with cups of fresh Colombian, Carmoody asked, "What now? How do we locate the other five cylinders, and where do we even begin to work out the proper combination required to open the door?"

"I'm not even going to worry about the combination unless and until we acquire the other five cylinders. If the one cylinder we do have is made of Dakinium, it stands to reason that the others are as well. We can't let them fall into the wrong hands."

"How can we determine if it's Dakinium?"

"The easiest way is to x-ray it. We know it's not made of lead— it's too light. If it's aluminum, titanium, tritanium, or some composite, it won't block all x-rays. The archeologists have x-ray equipment here."

◆ ◆ ◆

All six doctors and their chief assistants were on hand to watch the test. Christa couldn't refuse them admittance to the work shelter since it was their shelter and she needed the use of their equipment.

When the x-ray test was complete, the results were negative. No X-rays had passed through the cylinder.

"And what significance does this cylinder have with gaining access to the facility?" Dr. Peterson asked when the test was over.

"I believe the unknown symbol on the end of the cylinder plays a role in opening the door. I hope to learn what the symbol represents and how the name was pronounced."

"And what was the purpose of this test?"

"I'm looking at everything that might provide clues to opening the door."

"So it's not just the symbol you're interested in but the cylinder as well?"

"Yes."

"And what role does it play in opening the door?"

"That's remains to be seen, but it's all part of the puzzle. This door doesn't have the same simple locking mechanism the other has, which is why you were unable to open it."

"And this is all you know, or suspect, after ten days of effort?" Dr. Peterson asked acerbically.

"Since you spent months shouting at the door without success, I saw no benefit in repeating your efforts. I'm taking a different approach. I have no guarantee it will be any more successful than your months of effort, but it's my best line of reasoning right now. If you have a better idea, Doctor, I'd love to hear it."

"Humph," Peterson said before he turned and left the shelter.

"Don't mind him," Dr. Huften said. "He's just frustrated after being so excited about the discovery and then being unable to open the door."

"I understand," Christa said, smiling. "Although we've been acquainted for many years, I certainly don't know him well enough to interpret his moods, but I think that once we manage to open the door he'll cheer up."

"Only if we get to look around inside. Edward is still bitter about being shut out of the other facility."

"That's only a habitat for the Marines posted here. All of the equipment was taken away years ago, and anything that didn't violate Galactic Alliance law was turned over to the Expedition headquarters. You've had access to almost everything the facility contained."

"I know. It's more a matter of pride than anything else. He feels slighted that we were restricted from being able to examine everything before it was moved out."

◆ ◆ ◆

Christa hesitated to use a plasma torch to test the cylinder, but once back at her shuttle, she used a laser pistol to fire at the cylinder with bursts of increasing power and duration after verifying that the previous burst had no effect. The tests were performed under the shuttle's belly, using the ground as a 'bullet block', and out of sight of the dig site laborers. When a sixty-second, narrow beam burst at full power had no effect, she was satisfied the cylinder was made of Dakinium.

"So now we know it's Dakinium," Carmoody said. "How are we any closer than before?"

"That's a good question. All I can say is that each piece of a puzzle helps us towards the solution, even when we don't know the importance of the piece at the time. However, in this case we know two things. One, since the rods are Dakinium, they are definitely associated with the ancients of Dakistee, so I doubt their inherent capability for attraction to the circles is mere coincidence, and two, there is no known sensor which can detect the presence of Dakinium, so the search for the other cylinders may be long and arduous."

"If sensors can't detect Dakinium, how do we find the cylinders?"

"First, I'm going to contact Anthius and request they look through their files. Perhaps there's a cylinder sitting on another site director's desk somewhere."

◆ ◆ ◆

Christa's shuttle only had one bed so Carmoody had been billeted at Fort Carver since arriving dirt-side, but she always joined Christa for breakfast. When she arrived in the morning several days after verification of the cylinder, Christa greeted her excitedly.

"I just heard from the Expedition Headquarters on this planet. They've verified that in recent years, two more cylinders have been found. Using the coordinates they provided, I was able to determine that each excavation was over a Regional Cultural Headquarters. One cylinder has been confirmed to be on Anthius, and they'll send it at the earliest opportunity. The other cylinder was in a warehouse here on Dakistee, but it's apparently been misplaced. It's missing from the artifact box where it was stored, but they're trying to track it down and will send it when they find it. I've sent a note to Admiral Holt on Higgins requesting that he divert the next Quartermaster ship scheduled to pass within twenty light-years of Anthius to pick up the cylinder and bring it here. That shouldn't be long since Anthius is only fifteen light-years off the direct route between Earth and Higgins."

"He'll do that? He'll divert an entire Quartermaster ship just to pick up an artifact?"

"This project has the highest priority. If so many ships hadn't been sent towards the Region Two border when the war was raging, we'd probably be overrun with help."

"I can't imagine what we'd do with them. We've mostly been spending our days reviewing old records, searching for any clue that might point to locations of the cylinders. More people would only get in the way."

"You're probably right, but I'd feel a lot better if we had a warship or two in orbit overhead. Sooner or later the Raiders are going to learn of our efforts here. If Dr. Manson has heard the news all the way over in Brighton, the entire planetary archeological community probably knows by now as well."

"I wouldn't doubt that for a second. They seem to spend all their free time openly comparing notes with their fellows regarding what they've found recently." Carmoody paused for a breath, then said, "So— okay, we've tracked down three of the cylinders. We're halfway there. How do we get the rest?"

"We've deduced that the three found to date were located in the ruins of RCH buildings, and we know where the other buildings were. We simply have to get someone to set up a dig at each location."

"Simply?"

"I've asked Admiral Holt to inform the Expedition Headquarters of our pressing need for the remaining three artifacts. He'll explain that under GA law, Space Command is authorized to assume control of the area where we believe the artifacts are located. He'll explain that our earth-moving equipment is on the way to the planet and that we'll be digging up the RCH locations and sifting through the excavated soil for the cylinders, or perhaps a vacuum canister containing the cylinder."

"They'll go absolutely ballistic! Earth-moving equipment would destroy the dig sites."

"Most probably, although it won't damage the cylinders. Their reaction is what I'm counting on. Admiral Holt will be prepared to offer a compromise when they respond. If the Expedition Headquarters begins active, full-scale excavations in search of the artifacts we need, he'll hold off and let them do it their way. If we find they're not making a maximum effort, we can always move in with our earth-moving equipment, all of which will be positioned nearby to keep the consequences of moving too slowly uppermost in their minds. I think they'll be well motivated. I really hate using such tactics, but I see no other alternative. We must have those cylinders and we can't sit around for five, ten, or even twenty years until they decide to excavate the areas where we believe the cylinders are located."

Carmoody breathed deeply and let it out slowly. "I can't see any alternative either, but I can already hear the expletives that will be ringing through the halls at Anthius."

◆   ◆   ◆

Chairman Strauss looked around the ostentatious table in the Raider Lower Council chamber and fixed his eyes on Councilman Ahil Fazid. "Ahil, we haven't heard anything about our special Dakistee operation of late. Can you provide an update?"

"Of course, Arthur," Ahil said, as he stood up in front of his chair. After clearing his throat, he said, "Our assets are all in place and just waiting for the signal to move in. However, there's been a serious delay in the effort to open the newly discovered facility. Admiral Carver was unable to come to Dakistee, but she sent Lt. Commander Christa Carver, so the effort is in good hands. But we've learned the facility's entrance door will not open in the same manner as the other facility. Commander Carver has announced that she requires six cylinders created by the Dakistee ancients and has begun a planet-wide effort to recover them. They've located three so far and believe they know where the others are buried, but it will take time to locate them."

"How much time?" Strauss asked.

"Unknown. The cylinders are allegedly buried in the ruins of Regional Cultural Center buildings."

"How can these cylinders possibly be of any use after twenty thousand years of being buried in the soil of a temperate climate planet with a decent average rainfall?" Councilwoman Overgaard asked.

"The three recovered so far were all sealed in vacuum containers, which is an indication of their obvious significance. They are in perfect condition, so it's assumed the others will be as well."

"Why does she need these cylinders?" Strauss asked. "What's in them?"

"According to reports, they're a single piece of composite metal about the size of a holo-tube cylinder. Each has a special symbol engraved on it. Carver has stated that the symbols represent the key to opening the door. Perhaps she must read each aloud like a combination."

"How much time do you estimate will be required to find the remaining three cylinders?" Councilman Bentley Bosworth asked.

"Unknown. Perhaps a few months, perhaps much longer."

"Unacceptable," Strauss said.

"We have no choice, Arthur."

"Yes, we do. I want you to pass the word to our people on the planet. They're to facilitate the search operation in any way they can. Do whatever is necessary to ensure Carver gets her cylinders as quickly as possible. *Whatever* is necessary, Ahil. I don't care if you have to replace every laborer on the planet."

"The laborers are not part of our workforce, Arthur."

"It's not necessary that they be our people. A few broken arms, legs, or necks should get the message across that they'd better find those artifacts tout de suite."

"Yes, Arthur. I'll see that they get the word immediately."

◆ ◆ ◆

"How long are we supposed to shadow this old freighter, Captain?" Commander Conte, XO of the GSC destroyer *Portland* asked his Captain at their morning meeting. The *Portland* had been tailing the *Gastropod* for two days, staying back at maximum DeTect range in the hope that they wouldn't be noticed.

"The Nordakians requested a ninety-day tail. Space Command promised thirty with additional time if no emergencies required our attention."

"Are they expecting them to be attacked by Raiders?"

"According to SCI, the Nordakians suspect the freighter's stated destination is false. They think the flight plan, which will take them to Slabeca, might be a red herring. You see, the ship is carrying Nordakian dissidents who reject the Almuth that Azula Carver brought back from Dakistee. They want to follow the strict Almuth of previous generations and they can't do that on Nordakia because there can only be one 'True Word of God,' so they've gone off in search of religious freedom. Slabeca is a miserable little planet that barely supports organic life, *but* Obotymot is recovering well from the meteor strike that filled its atmosphere with dust. All reports indicate the efforts to scrub the atmosphere have been hugely successful and the planet is on track to a full recovery. In not too many years, it should again be a lush, agrarian paradise.

"Obotymot? But that's a Nordakian world. They must be observing the true Almuth there."

"They do, but Obotymot is still relatively unpopulated. Since the disaster, the population has gathered in large central locations, which could make them an easy target. The Nordakian Military Intelligence Agency suspects that if it is their true destination, the dissidents might intend to seize part of the planet so they can establish their own, isolated theocracy. The difficulty is that every square centimeter of the planet has already been apportioned to the nobility, so the dissidents would be commandeering private property. The Nordakians further believe that *if* the dissidents seize anyone's lands, it would be the estate of Azula Carver. Her estate on Obotymot spans an entire peninsula. I understand it's about the size of Texas. It's well known that they hate her with a passion because they blame her for all their problems, so it makes sense they would target her lands."

"Azula Carver? But that's *Admiral* Carver. Are they nuts?"

"I would have to give that an unqualified, 'Yes.' Anyone who has a desire to return to the ways of the old Almuth, other than the priesthood, certainly can't be firing on all thrusters."

"Yeah, the priesthood would have it easy. The people in charge *always* have it easy in a society where they have supreme power."

"Yes. They do the directing and the others do the work."

◆　◆　◆

"Enter," Nordakian high priest Kledoujk Vejrezzol said in response to the door chime.

Sebaqd Gxidescu, his top Minister, entered and walked to where Vejrezzol was reclining on an oh-gee sofa, but said nothing until given permission to speak.

"Report," Vejrezzol said finally.

"The ghost is still there. The captain insists we're being followed, but the ship is remaining at maximum Detect range. The electronics on this old scow aren't the best and we only get a glimpse every few hours. When we do, the signal only lasts for a second or two."

"But he's absolutely sure there's a ship there?"

"He says he's certain."

"It can't be just a ghost image, reflection, or some other anomaly?"

"He says no."

"Then it must either be a Nordakian military vessel or Space Command."

"Or perhaps a Raider vessel."

"The Raiders don't operate in this part of space anymore," Vejrezzol said. "We don't need to fear *them*."

"They don't openly attack ships anymore, but everyone knows they're still around. A few ships go missing every year and some people think Raiders are responsible. They believe the Raiders are being very selective by only targeting old vessels no one will miss, rather than high profile passenger liners and cargo ships with valuable loads."

"Bah! Those missing ships are all old tramps. The owners probably just scuttled them for the insurance money."

"I don't know. Most insurers won't pay off these days without some proof of what happened in case the owners are doing exactly what you say, or in case they've simply sold the vessel to someone operating in another area of space. But if the Raiders are targeting tramps, we'd be a likely candidate. This old wreck can barely make Light-75."

I'm well aware of that. You should have found us something faster."

"This was the only ship I could find where the Captain would allow us to provide most of the crew," Gxidescu said. "Having our people on the bridge will make the takeover easy when it's time to change course."

"If that ship is military, and we have to assume it is, and they continue to follow us, we might have to go all the way to Slabeca. I thought we'd be able to alter course a few days after departure from Nordakia."

"That could delay our plans by up to two years."

"Yes, yet we have no choice. If we alter course while we're being watched, the military will be on us in a minute and we'll never reach our real destination."

"Perhaps we could lose our tail..."

"I'm listening," Vejrezzol said.

"If we could arrange for someone to send a distress signal, the ship following us might have to break off to go to their assistance."

"But my entire flock is aboard this ship."

"While making arrangements with the *Gastropod's* captain, I made other contacts who might be willing to perform this favor for us, for a price."

"How much of a price?"

"Perhaps ten thousand credits. Perhaps more."

"Do it. I'll authorize up to twenty-five thousand credits if they can get the ghost off our backs."

"Very good, Excellency. I'll begin working on it immediately. It may take a month or more."

"A month or more?"

"It will take time because a ship must get into proper position so the ship following us is the logical one to come to their aid."

"I see. Very well, proceed."

◆ ◆ ◆

"Have you seen what that witch has done now?" Dr. Manson asked her assistant.

"Which witch, Doctor?"

"That Carver woman. Not only did she convince the Expedition Headquarters on Anthius to give her *my* cylinder and make me deliver it personally, now she's gotten them to throw all our schedules out the window to concentrate on uncovering the three Regional Cultural Headquarters that hadn't been excavated yet."

"Whatever for?"

"She thinks they'll find an additional cylinder in each. She claims there are six, and she needs them all to open the facility the people at Loudescott uncovered."

"Perhaps she does."

"She's a fool if she thinks I'm going to accept that at face value. Her sister didn't need the cylinders to open the other facility and she doesn't need these. She has some other purpose in mind."

"Perhaps she really does need the cylinders."

"We tested the cylinder I had with every device we own and all we proved was that it was a solid piece of composite metal fashioned to be ornamental. It doesn't have any magical powers. No, there's something else going on here. I just haven't figured out what it is. But I will. And I promise I'll get even with her for embarrassing me. I'll make her the laughing stock of the archeological community if it's the last thing I ever do."

CHAPTER SIX

~ June 3rd, 2285 ~

Admiral Jenetta Carver returned from a lengthy meeting in the Admiralty Hall at Space Command's Region Two Headquarters on Quesann and plopped tiredly into the chair behind her desk. As Military Governor of fully four-fifths of Galactic Alliance Space, meetings consumed most of her days. Supreme Space Command Headquarters on Earth still hadn't named anyone to govern Region Three. This meant that responsibility for those sectors had rested on her shoulders since she defeated the Uthlaro and forced them to cede their territory to prevent them from waging a new war when they felt sufficiently recovered from their previous devastating losses.

The monitor that covered one wall in her office was projecting a top-down, 2D map of the sectors for which she was responsible. As was the case with many galaxies, when viewed from the side at a distance, the Milky Way Galaxy looked like a child's spinning top. At the center, it was some two thousand light years from top to bottom, but the thickness fell off quickly when moving outward, so galactic maps were usually shown as a top-down, two-dimensional representation marked off in square sectors unless being projected by a holographic device.

SC officers who commanded bases had immediate responsibility for the sectors where their base was located. Because of the GA's distance from the center of the galaxy, that responsibility extended to include all territory above and below the accepted median line drawn through the horizontal center of the galaxy. Technically, their space was composed of cubic sectors and astronomers and astrogators rankled whenever Space Command personnel referred to the space in terms of square light-years, but that was the way they preferred to think of it. To denote a certain location within that space, the accepted method was to add an ante-median or post-median notation to the 2D sector address. Whenever holo-tables were used, the 3D effect gave a better feel for the complex equations used for navigation.

After enjoying a few quiet minutes with a mug of freshly brewed Colombian coffee, Jenetta raised her com screen to address the mountain of work that always greeted her arrival in the morning, or her return to the office after meetings concluded. She halted her scan of waiting messages when she spotted one from Admiral Holt at Higgins SC Base, then tapped the play button and leaned in to provide retinal scan identification. Her ID confirmed, she leaned back to listen as she sipped her coffee.

"Hello Jen, I hope this finds you well and your regions quiet. My sectors are presently quiet, but things seem to be heating up along our borders back this way. The two wars you fought were responsible for much of the Region One forces being sent to reinforce the old frontier zone border, and it will take years to get our interdiction forces back into place and working normally. Higgins has been operating at just forty-two percent of approved strength, while the Border Patrol forces along the Aguspod, Clidepp, and Gondusan borders have been pared down to bare bones. The Admiralty Board decided that decades of stability allowed all but the oldest and slowest ships to be reassigned. The 762 light-years along the Clidepp border is the most active right now. Things are heating up dramatically out there and some people in SCI are predicting a civil war will erupt in that territory within the next decade. I can't say I disagree with that prediction. We'll have to be careful lest we get sucked in.

"But I digress. The real reason I'm calling is to inform you that I've asked the Quartermaster transport *McHenry* to pick up Christa on Dakistee and bring her to Higgins so we can better discuss the situation on Dakistee. The Archeological Expedition Headquarters on Anthius has acceded to all her requests, but I'm hearing some disturbing reports that there's increasing hostility among the scientists that Space Command is responsible for disturbing all their dig site schedules and interrupting more important activities by placing unfair demands on their organization. It's important that we develop a strategy to quell the growing resentment and make them understand we have no desire to dictate the direction of their work, while stressing the importance of the current activity. Since Christa is the closest thing we have to an ambassador on Dakistee, I'd like her to take the lead in this effort.

"Brian Holt, Rear Admiral, Upper Half, Base Commander, Higgins Space Command Base, message complete."

Jenetta leaned back in her chair and thought about the situation for a few minutes before responding. It was Christa's mission and Jenetta naturally trusted her implicitly, so she wanted to avoid any hint of second-guessing her sister.

"To Brian Holt, Rear Admiral, Upper Half, Base Commander, Higgins Space Command Base, from Admiral Jenetta Carver.

"Hello Brian. It's always a pleasure to hear from you. I appreciate the assistance you're giving Christa on her mission. I know you understand the significance of this find and that we must do everything we can to gain access to the new facility, but I would be saddened if we created an atmosphere of anger or mistrust among the scientists and archeological personnel on Dakistee. I know Christa understands and agrees with this, so I'm sure she hasn't done anything contrary to our interests there if the action could have been avoided. There must be more to this than we're aware of. If you can learn who might be instigating the ill will, we might be able put a halt to it.

"Jenetta Carver, Admiral, Commander of the Second Fleet and Military Governor of Regions Two and Three, at Quesann SCB Regional Headquarters, message complete."

◆ ◆ ◆

As the SC Quartermaster transport *McHenry* established a stable position in orbit around Higgins Space Station, one of its flight bays opened and a shuttle emerged using its deuterium thrusters until far enough from the ship to engage its main engines. Christa had already received permission to enter an open bay in the giant docking collar that surrounded the station. As the shuttle lightly touched down just inside the bay using thruster power only, Christa engaged the magnetic skids and waited until the outer bay door had been closed and atmo in the air lock was reestablished. As the walls of the temporary airlock folded up and away from the shuttle, Christa used the shuttle's oh-gee engine to gently glide the shuttle across the hanger deck to an assigned docking space.

It was well into the second watch aboard the station, so Christa and Lt. Carmoody first walked to the housing office and secured quarters so they wouldn't have to sleep in the shuttle, then walked to the officers' mess to grab a bit of dinner.

They had been dining together for weeks, and Carmoody was always amused by the size of the food portions Christa consumed. When Jenetta's body was changing, she required great quantities of food to fuel the work her body was performing. By the time Christa and Eliza were cloned most of the changes had taken place and her appetite had slackened considerably, but it never fell into line with what other full-grown adult Terrans consumed. As clones, Christa and Eliza had inherited the need for increased food consumption and all three women ate like ravenous teenagers without ever putting on an extra ounce, much to the envy of fellow officers.

"I wish *I* could eat like that," Carmoody voiced yet again, as she looked at Christa's overflowing tray while they walked to a table.

"I used to get two trays like this and then a half dozen pieces of fruit to munch on later. Now this amount sustains me until breakfast unless I work out in the gym afterwards."

"It was nice having use of the gym aboard the *McHenry*. I had grown tired of simply jogging around the perimeter of the facility at the dig site and, unlike the Marines stationed there, I've never been into weightlifting."

"Yes, and it was wonderful to have some sparring partners for kickboxing. I'd gotten rusty since leaving the *Hephaestus*."

"I enjoy exercising, but I don't think I'll ever develop a taste for kicking people in the head."

"In our line of work, it can come in handy. I wouldn't be here now if Jenetta hadn't practiced religiously before I was born."

"I don't know if I could talk about my birth the way you do if I was cloned."

"Some people are uncomfortable with it, but most people accept it without a problem. It's not like Space Command is turning out clones every day; it was simply a fluke. But it was a fluke that we must ensure doesn't happen again, which is why getting into the newly discovered facility is so important. If there's cloning equipment there, we can't allow it to be activated."

"What if it's something else?"

"Such as?"

"I don't know. Perhaps a weapons research facility."

"Then we'll quietly remove all illegal materials before we allow the scientists to enter. They won't be happy about that, but we have no choice. Hey, what say we do a little shopping before we turn in? The concourse stores are open for another two hours."

"I'd love it. I haven't been shopping in over a year. The *Heisenberg* has been operating so far off the normal space lanes that we've never gotten closer than twenty light-years to a base since leaving Earth."

"Great, I need a few things."

◆　◆　◆

Christa arrived for her appointment with Admiral Holt a few minutes before 0900 the following morning and was surprised when the admiral's aide told her to go right in. She walked down the short corridor to the Admiral's inner office and stopped a few paces short of the doors to straighten her

tunic. When she was sure her uniform was perfect, she stepped into the sensor area that would activate the two doors.
Walking directly to where Admiral Holt was working, she
stopped one meter short of his desk and braced to attention.

"Lt. Commander Christa Carver, reporting to the Admiral
as ordered," she announced.

Admiral Holt looked up from his com screen, smiled, and
said, "At ease, Commander and welcome to Higgins. You're
looking well. It's been awhile since you were last here."

"Yes, sir. The last time I was here you administered the
oath of citizenship to Eliza and myself, and commissioned us
as Space Command ensigns."

"I remember it well. And now you're a senior officer commanding a mission on Dakistee. How time flies."

"Well, it has been fifteen years, sir."

Admiral Holt stood up and walked out from behind his
desk. "Let's sit in my informal area to talk. Would you like a
mug of Colombian?"

"Yes sir. That would be wonderful."

Admiral Holt smiled and gestured towards his beverage
dispenser. "Help yourself, Commander."

Christa moved to the dispenser, placed a mug under the
spout and ordered her coffee. Before moving away she turned
to where Admiral Holt had taken a seat in a large overstuffed
chair and asked, "Anything for you, sir?"

"I'm fine, Commander."

Christa selected the oh-gee chair opposite the Admiral
and sank into its comfort, careful not spill her coffee. She
took a sip and then placed it on the table on her right as she
waited for the Admiral to begin.

"I've been in communication with Jenetta," he said at last.
"I informed her of several persistent rumors on Dakistee that
we're being too heavy handed. Have you had to pressure
anyone there?"

"No, sir. But I did have to appeal to Anthius when a local
administrator refused to lend me a cylinder she was display-

ing on her desk. I explained that I needed it for my research and she informed me I would have to get permission from the Expeditionary HQ on Anthius. So I did. They might have been a little upset with her refusal to cooperate, so they apparently had her bring it to me personally. I suspect she was quite displeased for having to do that. Since then, I've only submitted my requests through your office."

"Please explain as completely as possible what it is you hope to achieve with these cylinders. I accept your statement that they're vital to your research, but I should know the complete story in case I need to defend our actions with the Admiralty Board or the GA Council."

"Of course, sir." Christa spent the next hour explaining about finding the circles on the door, the symbols, the magnetic attraction of the cylinder made of Dakinium, and her speculations about what would be required to unlock the mechanism that was keeping the door from opening. Admiral Holt asked pertinent questions, which showed he clearly understood the line of thought Christa and Carmoody were following.

"I see," Admiral Holt said when they had thoroughly discussed every aspect of the issue. "The fact that the cylinders are made of Dakinium means we won't be able to return them to Expedition Headquarters unless and until it becomes legal for people to own the material. Since its discovery, it's been listed as a controlled distribution substance. Have you told anyone else of your speculation about the composition of the cylinders?"

"My assistant, Lt. Carmoody, is the only one I've informed directly. The scientists at the site were in the lab when I tested the cylinder with the X-ray equipment, but I couldn't exclude them since it was their lab and their equipment I was using. They might *suspect* the piece is Dakinium, but I never discussed it with them. I've allowed other people to assume the cylinders are merely a solid piece of composite material and that their excellent condition is owed to being stored in vacuum containers for the past nineteen thousand, four hundred years. I've let them believe that my only interest is in the symbols engraved into the material. The fact that the symbols are engraved should make people assume the material isn't Dakinium since everyone believes it's impossible to mar its surface."

"I have to say your hypothesis outlining the procedure for opening the door certainly sounds reasonable. But if it proves to be a false trail, where will you look next?"

"At this time, I have no other avenues of investigation, Admiral. I'm pinning everything on this course of action. The evidence all points to the cylinders being key to accessing the facility. If I can't make it work, I don't know what I'll do next. But I believe more strongly every day that we're proceeding down the right path."

"Okay, Christa, keep at it. I have every confidence in your ability. I'll run whatever inference is necessary at this end. Just get that door opened as quickly as possible. Once that happens, the importance of the find will hopefully make everything else fade into the background."

"Yes, sir. Uh, Admiral, I only have a half squad of Marines, composed of two fire teams and a sergeant to guard the tunnel entrance 24/7. Right now it's adequate because the facility is inaccessible. But if I manage to open the facility, every scientist on the planet is going to want in. Half a squad may not be adequate to hold them back without using force and some of the curious could be seriously injured if it comes to that."

Admiral Holt sighed. "I know. Manpower shortages are making it increasingly difficult to keep a lid on things in this sector. I'll see if I can free up another couple of fire teams from somewhere else on the planet, but that's all I can promise. Besides, it can't be that difficult to hold back a group of scientists who spend their days brushing dirt off antiquities. It's not like they're trained as fighters. They'll probably faint or soil their underwear the first time a Marine yells at them to halt where they are."

"I have no doubt that would be the case with some, but others might surprise you. Choice of occupation is not always a good indicator of intestinal fortitude. I was once just an astrophysicist."

Admiral Holt smiled. "I recall Jenetta saying she was just a mere Ensign. I told her she was an Ensign, but never 'mere.' I doubt there's anyone on Dakistee who can measure up to you or your sisters, but I'll keep what you say about the others in mind as we move forward on this project."

◆ ◆ ◆

Before boarding the Quartermaster transport *Ferdinand* for the thirty-hour trip back to Dakistee, Christa and Carmoody spent two more days on Higgins, shopping and enjoying the other available amenities such as the fine restaurants in the civilian areas of the station. Their one visit to Gregory's was disappointing. With Gregory now operating the finest restaurant on Stewart SCB, the one on Higgins was suffering badly in the hands of his brother-in-law. The service was poor and the food bland. There was no difficulty getting a table at dinnertime as there were no waiting patrons. The other restaurants on the concourse were crowded at that hour, so the quality had obviously been slipping for a while.

The two women would have liked to stay on the station for a few more days since there was no rush to return to Dakistee, but there wouldn't be another Light-9790-capable transport headed in the general direction of Dakistee for many weeks. Without the advanced speed capability provided by Dakinium sheathing, the trip would require a full month aboard a warship.

CHAPTER SEVEN

~ August 24th, 2285 ~

"I've found it!" wafted across the dig area. Most work stopped immediately as laborers near enough to hear the muffled words stood up and scanned the dig site in an effort to determine who had shouted.

When the same voice shrieked, "It's down here!" people were able to identify the direction of the words.

Within seconds, a dozen dig site laborers were scrambling toward the hole from which the excited shouts seemed to have emanated. The first laborer to arrive peered cautiously over the berm of dirt, then almost immediately disappeared from view as he moved forward and slid head first into the cavity. Upon reaching the excavation, other laborers belly flopped onto the raised dirt berm to observe the activity. Excitement had begun to wash through the camp like a tsunami and everyone dropped whatever they were doing to race towards the excavation.

The site director pushed his way through the growing throng and peered down into the five-meter by five-meter hole where two laborers were struggling to free a tarnished cylindrical object. If it *was* the canister they were seeking, only the very top was showing, but the built-in handle allowed the laborers to tug on the cylinder with all their strength.

"Druzkil," Dr. Edolis said, "did you find it or not?"

The pair stopped what they were doing and looked up. The one who had unearthed the object said, "I think so, Doctor Edolis. It certainly looks like the top of the vacuum canister we've been told to hunt for. But it seems to be hung up on something."

"Remember, the buildings here collapsed from age. It could be almost anything. Clear the area around the canister instead of trying to muscle it out."

"Yes, Doctor."

As the two laborers resumed their activity, Edolis sighed silently. He would have preferred to have skilled people doing the excavations, but he was under extreme pressure to find the canister as quickly as possible so he was forced to use all available resources. Even now, when trained people were available to take over the excavation, he had to let the laborers continue at their task. The trained workers would resist a quick removal and would probably take several days to carefully extricate the canister lest they damage other relics in the immediate area. The laborers only had their eyes on the bonuses promised for a speedy recovery.

Despite an intensive effort that ignored possible damage to other relics, it still took another hour to raise the prize. Two large sections of rock, presumably decorative wall sections from the collapsed building, had pinned it solidly in place until an oh-gee crane was brought in to remove the wall rubble.

"At last," Dr. Edolis said as he held the canister in his hands. Turning to address the gathering he said loudly, "Clean your digging tools and store them properly, then take the rest of the day off. The next two days will be paid leave for everyone except food service and other support person-nel."

A cheer erupted and everyone raced back to where they had been working so they could wrap up for the day.

"Is that it, doctor?" Edolis' assistant asked, pointing to the canister.

"I believe so, William. I don't want to open it out here to check the contents. Let's take it back to my shelter where we can clean the cylinder first and then examine the contents away from prying eyes."

The canister wasn't really that heavy, but at one hundred twenty-six years, Dr. Edolis no longer had the strength required to carry it all the way back to his shelter. His assistant, just eighty-three years young on his last birthday, was able to handle the sixty-pound container alone and insisted upon doing just that to prevent Edolis from straining himself.

Once in the shelter, Edolis and his assistant washed the canister carefully, then spent the better part of an hour trying to open it. In the end, they had to admit the container had been slightly bent out of round by the weight of the wall sections between which it had been wedged. It wasn't grossly damaged— just enough so that the lid wouldn't unscrew, but that prevented it from being opened. Dr. Edolis finally sent for the labor supervisor, who happened to be one of the last people in the camp, everyone else having washed up and left for town as soon as they could.

◆ ◆

"You see the problem, Josef?" Dr. Edolis asked. "The top won't unscrew."

"Yes, Doctor. I see the problem. It's out of round and will never open easily. We'll have to force it. I'll have to get a torch and a few tools. I'll be right back."

Twenty minutes later, Josef returned with the tools he would need to open the canister. He ignited the torch and began applying a low heat evenly around the top, hoping heat expansion would be enough to overcome the slight deformity.

It wasn't. When the processes entailing gentle persuasion didn't work, Josef moved to the more serious tools. He clamped an enormous pipe wrench around the middle of the canister and fastened a long steel bar to the handle on the top. Again he applied heat evenly around the top for several minutes, then turned off the torch and laid the canister on its side on the floor. Placing his foot on the pipe wrench to hold the canister down, he applied as much of his body weight as possible to the steel bar. The top still refused to budge.

"That's the best I can do without damaging the canister," Josef said as he straightened up from the last effort and set the canister back on the table. "We can take it down to Los Aliosis and put it into the hydraulic twisting clamp assembly they have there. It can torque up to five thousand foot-pounds. I'm sure it would have that open in a few seconds."

"We need it open now," Dr. Edolis said. "Cut it, Josef."

"But that will permanently damage the container, Doctor."

"I realize that. Cut it open, Joseph, but only at the end so you don't damage the contents any more than necessary."

"You're the boss, Doctor Edolis," Josef said as he grabbed the laser torch and set the cutting depth.

Josef shook the canister to settle the contents towards the bottom, then began to cut as high around the top as possible. An inrush of air made a hissing noise as the canister was first punctured. It was a good sign; the vacuum had been intact. Josef continued cutting around the top of the container while Dr. Edolis' assistant sprayed the area just cut with a coolant.

When the top was being held on by a mere spec of metal, Josef stopped cutting and waited until the coolant spray and been applied. Slipping on a pair of thick work gloves, he grabbed the top and bent it backwards.

Dr. Edolis immediately rushed forward and pushed Josef away from the canister. "Thank you, Josef. That will be all. You probably want to head to town like the others."

"Someone has to stay and watch the camp so we don't have scavengers ransacking the shelters," Josef said as he picked up the tools. "I don't mind. I sort of like the peace and quiet. Besides, I've lost enough money to those chiseling SOBs in the casinos."

"Then I hope you have a peaceful evening."

"Thanks, Doc. You too. Goodnight, Mr. Portnoy."

"Goodnight, Josef," Portnoy said as he closed the door.

"It's here," Edolis said as he reached into the wrecked container and withdrew a black cylinder about the size of holo-tube cylinder.

"What's so important about that object?" William asked. "It looks rather useless to me. Does it open?"

"As I understand it, it's a piece to a puzzle that will allow Space Command to open the facility the Loudescott people uncovered. I have no idea how it will do that, but perhaps these symbols etched into the ends provide the necessary clues. In any event, we can return to our previous schedule now and this will get that damn loan-shark off my back."

"How do you figure Cozarro fits into this?"

"No idea, but he said that if we didn't make a maximum effort to find this, he was going to start having his thugs break legs and heads, starting with mine. I've never heard of Space Command employing such tactics before, but I never doubted Cozarro was serious. I wonder how much they paid him to force us into finding this as quickly as possible."

As William returned to his shelter, Edolis relaxed with a double bourbon on the rocks. The liquor warmed his insides and made him feel better than he had in days. Although he'd never tell anyone, the threat from Cozarro had nothing to do with Space Command but arose from Edolis' failure to pay up on his gambling debts. But the gambler *had* promised to wipe the slate clean if Edolis found the cylinder quickly.

◆ ◆ ◆

"The sixth cylinder has finally been found and has been sent to Commander Carver at Loudescott," Councilman Ahil Fazid announced as he gave his weekly status report in the Raider Lower Council meeting.

"It's about time," Chairman Strauss said. "It's costing us a small fortune to keep our people hidden in readiness for their attack on Loudescott. What of the cylinder the warehouse misplaced? That's all Carver needs to complete her work, is it not?"

"We've been unable to ascertain exactly how the cylinders fit into the picture," Ahil said. "Carver has told no one at

Loudescott, except possibly her assistant, Lt. Carmoody. Since Carmoody is Space Command, there's little chance she'll pass on the information to any of the archeological people.

"But we *have* been able to locate the cylinder that was missing from the warehouse. By pressuring our people who work there, we discovered that one of them had stolen it to sell on the black market. We tracked it down, but the buyer was unwilling to part with it. We were forced to use extreme prejudice with him. Following the recovery, it was returned to the warehouse where it was placed in a box of artifacts scheduled to be examined the next day. When it was identified as having been misfiled, it was sent to the proper section. The people there immediately recognized it and forwarded it to Carver.

"And the employee who stole it for personal profit?" Councilman Bosworth asked.

"He was disciplined, most severely. I doubt he will ever again steal anything from the warehouse without orders or permission."

"While the cylinder was in our possession, did we examine it?" Strauss asked.

"Yes, I've been assured that it's just a solid cylinder of lightweight composite metal with two symbols etched into the end surfaces. Other than its value as an artifact, it's nothing special."

"So Carver has all the pieces now?" Councilwoman Overgaard asked.

"If she doesn't have the sixth cylinder yet, she should have it within hours."

"Very good," Strauss said. "Make sure our people are put on alert. We may need to send them at any time."

◆　◆　◆

"Our ghost is gone," Gxidescu reported. "We've not seen a single sign of him in eleven days."

"Does the captain agree?" Vejrezzol asked.

"He does. He says that if they were still there, we would have caught sight of their sensor reflection at least once during those days."

"Excellent. It's time to take over the ship. You know what to do."

"Yes. I'll see to it immediately."

◆ ◆ ◆

"So, now that we have all six cylinders," Carmoody said, "what do we do with them? There are still eighteen *billion* possible combinations."

"I think we might narrow that down a bit using the letters engraved in the cylinders."

The characters from the ancient alphabet?"

"Yes. I've run them through an un-scrambler and come up with two possibilities in the ancient tongue. One, translated to Amer, means 'rodent hole.'"

"How delightful," Carmoody said facetiously.

"Yes," Christa said with a smile, "but the other means 'heritage.'"

"Heritage? Now we're talking. I'd go with that one."

"The question is: Go where? I agree 'heritage' sounds a lot more appropriate as a key than 'rodent hole,' but how do we apply it? Is it supposed to be stated aloud? Is it part of a popular phrase or saying from that period used to remind everyone which phrase must be read aloud, or is it simply a one-word utterance?"

"Good questions all," Carmoody said. "Here's another suggestion. Since there are six letters in their word for heritage, perhaps that's the order the cylinders should be applied to the circles, left to right."

"That sounds reasonable. Good thinking. If true, it means we've just cut the possible unknown combinations from eighteen billion to just three billion."

Carmoody smiled and said, "Wonderful. The door is practically open."

◆ ◆ ◆

Weeks later, the two women seemed no closer to opening the facility than when they first arrived on the planet.

"This is getting us nowhere," Christa said as they sat in the tunnel staring at the door. "There's something we've overlooked in all this, or possibly misinterpreted."

"Let's review what we've tried," Carmoody said. "We've placed the cylinders on the circles in the order required for 'heritage.' We're assuming the thirty-eight positions on the circles represent the twenty-eight letters of the ancient alphabet plus the first ten digits in a base-10 number system and that the numbers follow the letters. Counting from twelve o'clock, we've aligned each cylinder with the position represented by the symbol on that cylinder, then moved the cylinder within each circle, one mark at a time for all circles, until we had tried all thirty-eight marks as the starting position. Then we did the same thing over again assuming that the numbers preceded the letters in the layout. When that didn't work, we tried a progression system where only one circle at a time was altered, and we did that with the numbers and letters in both arrangements. When that failed to produce results, we did it in reverse order. Are you sure of the order they used for their alphabet?"

"Yes. It was used the same way in every reference document found in the files we recovered."

"If the people who possessed the cylinders were the highest ranking people in the Regional Cultural Centers, then it stands to reason they were older officials. How did they see the marks on the door? We're both young and yet we can barely see the etched lines when our noses are practically pressed against the surface."

"That's a good point, Gracie," Christa said. "We're only able to see them when the light is coming from the side and the etched lines create a slight shadow."

"Perhaps there are marks we can't see with the light from the Chembrite panels. Who knows what kind of light source they would have used in this tunnel?"

"That's true. What we need is a hyperspectral projector capable of projecting the entire range from ultraviolet through infrared. I'd bet they don't have one on the planet and, even if they did, I wouldn't ask to borrow it. We've already told them too much about the leads we're following."

"We had several portable units aboard the *Heisenberg*, but they're a very long way from here."

"I'll contact Admiral Holt and request that one be sent to us as quickly as possible. In the meantime, let's continue to work on finding the right combination just in case the hyperspectral projector is a bust. Why don't we try reversing the order of the cylinders in the circles?"

"Might as well," Carmoody said. "It might be a month before we get the projector."

◆　◆　◆

Almost two weeks later, a ship arrived in orbit over the Loudescott location just before sunset and a shuttle immediately began the descent to the surface. The Diplomatic Corps emblem on the Space Command shuttle drew Christa's eyes as she watched the small ship park next to her shuttle. It was another five minutes before the hatch opened and a Space Command Lieutenant emerged. He strode purposefully to where Christa was standing and came to attention. He had been told to report to Lt. Commander Carver, and years of media coverage allowed him to recognize her immediately.

"Lt. Lindall, ma'am," was all he said.

"Stand easy, Lieutenant. Are you delivering a VIP?"

"No, ma'am. We have a delivery for you from Admiral Holt. We were on our way to Nordakia to deliver a diplomatic pouch and he requested that we divert slightly to bring you important equipment."

"Thank you, Lieutenant. We've been expecting a delivery, but I thought it might be coming via Quartermaster ship."

"We're taking some of the load off the Quartermaster Corps in this deca-sector now that we have one of the new DS ships. We're ferrying small shipments and groups of person-nel."

"Your ship is DS?"

"Yes, ma'am. Fresh out of the yard three months ago."

"Is it a new design?"

"Sail to keel. And is she ever fast. The trip to Higgins from Earth takes just four days, and we made it here in one."

"Any armament?"

"Well, we *are* supposed to be a diplomatic yacht, so we don't want to look like a scout destroyer, but we have four disguised laser arrays and hidden missile tubes fore and aft. Our missiles have limited punch, unlike the serious torpedoes you line officers have, but if someone attacks us, we can mount a defense of sorts while we prepare to go to Light-9790."

As they talked, ratings had carried two large cases over to Christa's shuttle.

"There's your delivery, Commander. Is there anything else you'll be needing from us?"

"No. Thank you, Lt. Lindall. Extend my appreciation to your captain."

"Yes, ma'am."

◆　◆　◆

It took thirty minutes to set up one of the projectors the next morning. Instead of directing the beam from the side as they had been doing with the Chembrite panels, Christa and Carmoody set the projector directly in front of the door with the lens opened wide enough to cover the entire door. After they had both donned special eye protection goggles, Christa started at ten nanometers, the low end of the ultraviolet part of the spectrum, and gradually increased the wavelength. At three hundred nm, something began to appear on the door. Christa fine-tuned the wavelength and the image sharpened.

"I'll be damned," Carmoody said. "Look at that."

Christa's attention was already focused on the door and the now clearly visible markings. There was a tiny alphabetic or numeric symbol at each of the thirty-eight marks on each circle and, while the order was the same on all six circles, the starting position was different. No one would ever have chanced upon the combination. Most importantly, each circle had a large alphabetic symbol in the center.

"Damn," Christa said. "It says rodent hole. We were even using the wrong order for the cylinders."

"We would have been here a thousand years if we hadn't gotten this projector."

"Let's not gloat too quickly. There may be additional parts to this puzzle we haven't discovered yet. Let's put our new information to the test."

Five minutes later they had placed the cylinders on the right circles and aligned them with the proper symbols. Christa stood back and uttered the Ancient command for 'unlock.'

Nothing happened.

"Okay," Christa said, "it's time for Plan B." She reset the cylinders to the starting positions in each circle, then, one at time, without moving the cylinder away from the door, she twisted each until it pointed at the symbol identical to the one engraved on the cylinder. As she moved the last one into position, a rumbling sound could be heard from within the door as cams that hadn't moved in almost two hundred centuries tried to turn to new positions and bolts retracted into the door so it could move.

When no noises were heard for several seconds, Christa reached out and removed the cylinders from the door. She then said, "dwuthathsei," which was the Dakis word for 'open.' It hadn't changed very much in the nineteen thousand, four hundred years since the Ancients had occupied the planet.

The door began to rumble again, then complained loudly as it slid into the door pocket.

As the door completed its travel, Carmoody looked at Christa and said, "Now what?"

"First I have to go report our breakthrough, and then we get to find out what was so valuable that the Ancients employed these incredibly complex machinations to protect it from prying eyes."

CHAPTER EIGHT
~ October 8th, 2285 ~

As the two Space Command officers approached the surface, Christa halted to speak with Carmoody.

"We've been pretty depressed the past few weeks because we didn't seem to be making any progress. It's important that we continue to exhibit a look of depression. Right now you look much too happy, so you'll have to ratchet it down a few notches."

"Why?" Carmoody asked. "We opened the door. That's cause for celebration."

"If there's one thing I've learned when I'm not aboard ship, it's that someone is always watching. There can be any number of reasons, and most often it's innocent curiosity, but I would be willing to bet a year's salary that there's at least one Raider spy watching us whenever we're in the open."

"A Raider spy? How can you be so sure?"

"I have a deep appreciation for their intelligence-gathering and they have to have learned about this find since everyone on the planet seems to know about it. They've had plenty of time to place a dozen spies in the archeology camp so at least one can always be watching for any sign that we've been successful."

"But you've closed and locked the door again."

"It doesn't matter. I don't want them to know we've opened it. We have limited protection here and I don't want to let them think they can gain access somehow."

"But surely the Marines can stop them."

"Maybe, and maybe not. Either way, it's easier just to keep them from learning even the smallest bit of information.

Now put on your most dejected look. The one you were wearing all day yesterday would be *perfect*."

"I'm not going to be able to look depressed if you keep making jokes," Carmoody said with a grin.

"Okay. Sorry." Christa said with a smile. "Now give me a depressed look." After a couple of seconds, Christa said, "That's good. Hold that one." Masking her own face with a look of boredom and fatigue, she turned and led the way out of the tunnel into the bright afternoon sun.

◆

Once inside the shuttle, Christa said, "Okay, you can drop the act. No one can see us in here."

"What act?" Carmoody said. "I'm genuinely depressed about spies possibly watching our every move. You're not sure though, right?"

"I have no proof, but I know it as sure as I know that I need a cup of coffee. Join me?"

"Thanks. I'll get them while you send the message. Colombian, two sugars, black, right?"

"Right."

◆

When Christa returned from the cockpit, Carmoody was relaxing with her coffee. Christa's full mug was on the table and had cooled enough that she could take a big sip.

"Okay, the message is sent," Christa said as she took a seat. "But if we go back into the tunnel now, it will look suspicious. Let's wait until tomorrow. In fact, perhaps we should wait until we have some additional forces here. As soon as we start exhibiting signs of increased activity, we're going to have archeologists climbing all over us, trying to gain information about the find."

"Fine with me. I'm not in any hurry to die."

"Die?"

"Haven't you ever seen any of those old mummy movies? People walk in and disturb a tomb, and, the next thing you know, mummies are popping up everywhere, trying to kill the entire cast."

"Gracie, that only happens in the movies," Christa said with a giggle.

"Really? Look what happened the last time you opened a facility like this one. Didn't you tell me you had to live in a sewer for weeks after you escaped from the facility?"

"But we were escaping from Raiders, not mummies."

"And isn't the code word to open the door 'rodent hole?' That speaks volumes."

"It may not be a literal translation. As you said, it's a code word. Code words that mislead are often assigned to operations and projects."

"And didn't you just tell me we're being watched by Raiders?"

"There's a big difference between being watched and being attacked. We just have to make sure we don't let them know we've opened the facility until after the Marine reinforcements arrive."

"What Marine reinforcements? From what I've seen on this planet, the Corps doesn't have enough people to control a wild wedding party, much less a Raider attack."

"That was the purpose of my message. I told Admiral Holt we need every Marine he can get for us."

"I hope he comes through."

◆　◆　◆

"Ahil," Chairman Strauss said, "Costs for the operation on Dakistee are mounting. Our people have been sitting on their brains for months now just waiting to attack. What the devil is taking Carver so long to open that damned door?"

"I just received word that two cases were delivered by the diplomatic service, contents unknown. At the time of the delivery, it was believed she hadn't yet been able to open the facility."

"The Diplomatic Corps? What could the Diplomatic Corps possibly have that was required to open the door?"

"We don't know. Carver was observed carrying one of the cases into the tunnel yesterday morning where she remained until lunchtime, then returned to her shuttle. She and her assistant both appeared to be dejected, as if their latest attempt had failed. This is supported by the fact that she hasn't increased the Marine protection. She still has just two sentries at the entrance."

"Is there anything further we can do to assist her efforts— without her knowing who's behind the assistance?"

"She's been very closemouthed about her progress. No one on the planet knows what the status is or what her plans are."

"She appears to be just like her sister Jenetta," Council-woman Overgaard said. "I understand Admiral Carver has always been very closemouthed until it's necessary to let others know of her plans. But perhaps we could make it necessary."

"What do you mean?" Fazid asked.

"Suppose we were to arrange a visit by a high-ranking official from the GA Council, or better yet, from Space Command. She would have to detail her progress if they asked, wouldn't she?"

"Possibly," Strauss said thoughtfully, "depending on their position and security clearance. If we send someone, they must be high-ranking, or in a position to request secure information regarding her progress. See to it Ahil."

"But Arthur, I don't believe we have anyone in such a position," Fazid said.

"Then speak to our Intelligence Section. We have numerous sources kept in deep cover where no more than one or two members of our organization know of their existence. It's for their protection and allows us to preserve our most valuable resources for the day when we need them."

"Very well. I'll consult with the Intelligence Director today."

◆ ◆ ◆

"Before we begin," Admiral Moore announced to his fellow officers seated around the large, horseshoe-shaped table, as well as everyone else in the large hall always used for meetings of the Admiralty Board, "no word of the next topic is to leave this room." He looked around before continuing. The gallery was empty, but the usual assortment of aides and clerks were sitting behind their admirals.

"Lt. Commander Christa Carver has succeeded in opening the second Dakinium-sheathed facility found on Dakistee."

"About time," Admiral Hubera said.

"Donald," Admiral Moore said in a tone that dripped with reproach.

"Well, she's been there for more than five months working on this one problem, Richard. All she had to do was open one little door."

"As you know, Donald, we only just acquired the last of the six cylinders needed to open the door," Admiral Hillaire said. "Considering that she managed to open the facility in relatively short order once she had the proper apparatus, I'd say she's done outstanding work. And don't forget that it was *she* who uncovered the role the cylinders played in this effort."

"How could I," Hubera snapped back, "with you reminding us constantly?"

"What has she discovered inside, Richard?" Admiral Platt asked of Admiral Moore. "Is it another cloning facility?"

"The report forwarded by Admiral Holt states that at the time of the report, she had managed to open the facility but hadn't yet entered it. She's requested more Marine forces for her protection detail."

"More forces! More forces! Humph! It's always the same story with the Carvers. She's as bad as her sister."

"Donald, I remind you that with Admiral Jenetta Carver you're speaking of a senior officer," Admiral Moore said. "Be careful with your rhetoric."

Admiral Hubera clamped his mouth shut and leaned back in his chair, obviously upset by the warning. Jenetta Carver had been a mere cadet when he was a senior instructor at the Academy, and rancor towards her had increased with every promotion she received as she climbed through the ranks. Now she was senior to him, with four stars to his two, and resentment ate at his insides every time he heard her name or thought about her. He had already suffered one major heart attack when his temper got the best of him because of her military successes in Regions Two and Three.

"This facility is deep underground like the other, is it not?" Admiral Bradlee asked. "With only one entrance to guard, Commander Carver shouldn't be so concerned about being overrun by a bunch of scientists that it delays her further investigation."

"We've all seen mob violence," Admiral Moore said. "If we only have a few Marines on duty, the likelihood of violence increases. I would hate to see a shooting incident occur there. A crowd is far less likely to charge a well-staffed sentry post."

"Stun rifles should be adequate for simple crowd control," Admiral Plimley said.

"Anytime you use force, you must be prepared for the most dire of consequences," Admiral Bradlee said. "If you stun someone, they're potentially down for hours. During that time they can be trampled or suffocate from the weight of other bodies who fall on top of them. They might even be used as shields by others."

"Our Marine resources are stretched extremely thin. Is Admiral Holt requesting additional troops?" Admiral Platt asked.

"No," Admiral Moore said. "He just seems to be reporting the progress of Commander Carver and repeating her request of him. He's well aware of the staffing issues and knows we've already sent him all the personnel resources we can."

"Then I suggest we let him handle the issue. It's part of his deca-sector after all," Admiral Platt said.

"Does anyone else have a dissenting opinion?" Admiral Moore asked as he glanced around the table. When no one spoke up he said, he said, "Very well, we won't interfere with his handling of the issue."

◆ ◆ ◆

Christa waited until a barely adequate Marine presence was available at Fort Carver before she opened the facility again. Admiral Holt had done everything he could to provide as large a contingent as possible.

At 0800, Marine Lieutenant Uronson, Staff Sergeant Burton, and Sergeant Flegetti arrived with three fire teams of Marines in battle armor. Fire teams in the Space Marine Corps typically contain four members, so when combined with the fire team already providing security on site, the new fire teams gave Christa a full squad of sixteen Marines, plus two noncoms and a CO.

From that point forward, Christa believed there would never be fewer than four Marines patrolling the camp, in addition to the two posted at the entrance tunnel. Although a defensible perimeter in the form of a meter-and-half-deep trench had long ago been dug one hundred meters from the tunnel entrance, they would need at least a full company to properly defend against a concerted effort to penetrate the camp.

As Christa and Carmoody entered the tunnel, the remaining ten squad members, two noncoms, and Lt. Uronson accompanied them. They carried with them a dozen Chembrite panels and stands, as well as a small communications package that should allow her CT, and that of Carmoody, to operate inside the facility.

This would be the first time anyone outside a very small group would have any indication that she had succeeded in opening the door. Anyone watching the camp would know something big was up and she had no idea what to expect. She would have preferred that the Marines be armed with stun weapons, but she'd opted instead for laser rifles. She hoped the lethality of the weapons would further deter the curious from advancing too close to the tunnel entrance.

◆ ◆ ◆

"You look extremely nervous," Christa said to Carmoody as they walked down the tunnel ramp.

"I've always had this thing about ghosts, goblins, mummies, zombies, vampires, trolls, witches, werewolves…"

"I get the picture," Christa said, smiling. "You read too many cheap novels when you were young and developed a phobia about garden-variety monsters. This isn't a haunted house, Gracie. It's just an ancient work center."

"All haunted houses were just normal houses at one time. Then they get old and decrepit, and the monsters take up residence."

"You'll probably be amazed at how clean it is, if it's anything like the other facility. And we found no ghosts, goblins, or mummies in that one. It was only filled with spotlessly clean equipment."

"We'll see."

"I'm excited by the prospect of seeing something no one else has seen in two hundred centuries. Who knows what we'll find?"

"That's what frightens me." Carmoody said. "I have this unshakable feeling of dread— as if we're opening up a Pandora's box that will unleash unspeakable evil upon this world."

◆ ◆ ◆

When they reached the door, Carmoody set up the projector while Christa prepared to place the cylinders that would allow her to unlock the door once the markings were visible.

The process went smoothly and the door was unlocked within minutes. As the verbal command caused the door to retract into its storage pocket, Lt. Uronson announced, "Something is going on topside, Commander."

Christa turned to face him and said, "What sort of something."

"I've been told there's a large group of civilians entering the compound."

"Armed?"

"They don't appear to be."

Christa turned towards the door and said the Dakis command for 'close.' The door slid out of the pocket and resealed but didn't lock. "Let's go up," Christa said to Uronson. "When we arrive topside, I want you and your people to remain inside the tunnel and out of view unless I need you." To Carmoody, she said, "Gracie, you remain here. You know the commands for open and close, but don't enter alone."

"You needn't worry about that," Carmoody said with a nervous grin.

◆　◆　◆

As she emerged from the tunnel, Christa found the entire cadre of Loudescott scientists, the head labor supervisor, and his assistant standing a dozen paces from the tunnel entrance. They were blocked from proceeding further by the four Marines left topside to patrol the camp. The two Marines posted at the entrance were prepared to repel an attack, but their weapons were still pointed skyward with their fingers on the trigger guards. As yet, the civilians were offering no resistance to the Marines. The two Marines in the center parted to allow her through when she reached their position.

"Doctor Peterson," Christa said cheerfully to the lead scientist standing prominently in the center forefront, "I don't believe we scheduled a meeting for this morning."

"Since you've obviously been successful in your efforts to open the facility, and have so far chosen to conceal that information from us," Peterson stated angrily, "we've come to *request* that we be allowed to enter it for viewing."

"Doctor, we've been through this before. You'll be allowed to enter when we know it's safe for you to do so and not before. That time has not yet arrived."

"Then you *have* been able to enter the facility?" Peterson said as both an inquiry and statement of fact.

"No, not as yet," Christa said truthfully.

"Come now, Commander, dig site personnel have seen you entering the tunnel in the company of Marines. That wouldn't be necessary if you hadn't finally managed to open the door."

"I tell you truthfully that I have not yet been able to enter the facility," Christa said, "but I believe I'm very close to accomplishing that. The Marines will be on hand from now on, ready to assist when they're needed with whatever task is placed before them, whether that task is investigation of the unknown or repelling people who would impede our investigation."

"Are you referring to us?"

"I'm referring to anyone who would attempt to intrude uninvited. As you well know, I'm a scientist. I share your curiosity of the unknown and understand how anxious you are to tour the facility. I promise to grant you access just as soon as possible. But that time has not yet arrived. Until I open the door, no one can enter. And Doctor, I don't intend to continue having this same discussion. There's nothing more to be said, so I bid you good day. You'll be notified when the facility will be available for your inspection. Good day, Doctor. Good Day, everyone."

With that, Christa turned on her left heel and walked towards the tunnel entrance. The group behind her remained silent, but she knew she was receiving looks with the sharpness of daggers. She paused at the entrance to address the lance corporal and the PFC stationed there.

"No one is to be allowed entrance into the tunnel— no one— unless I personally authorize it. You're to use whatever force is necessary to carry out that order. Do you understand?"

When both Marines acknowledged affirmatively, she said, "Carry on," and reentered the tunnel.

"And they believed you when you said you hadn't yet opened the door?" Carmoody asked after Christa related the conversation.

"I never said I hadn't opened the door. I said I hadn't yet entered the facility, which is true, and at one point I said the door is closed, which is also true. I never said it hadn't been unlocked. If I told them that we had managed to open the door, we'd be besieged daily by requests for tours. And once the word spreads, we'll have pressure from every quarter to make the facility accessible. We still have much to do before that time arrives, so it's better that they assume we haven't managed to open the door yet.

"Now, what say we open this place and see just what it contains, and perhaps get an idea of when we can allow civilians in. For myself, I'm anxious to get back to my ship, although I might have lost my post by now. I never dreamed I'd be here for half a year. I thought it was going to be a two-month trip, a week on the surface, and then another two-month trip back to Region Two."

"I envy you. I wish I was going out there as well instead of simply cruising around this deca-sector, researching anomalous readings reported by passing vessels."

"You'll probably wind up out there eventually, Gracie. That's where we need scientists. We have an entire Region of new worlds and spacial phenomena to research."

Turning to face the door, Christa said, "Dwuthathsei."

◆ ◆ ◆

"We have a report from Dakistee," Councilman Ahil Fazid announced from his chair in the Lower Council Meeting Room. "It would appear Carver might have opened the facility at last."

"About damn time," Chairman Strauss said. "That operation has cost us plenty and the Upper Council is beginning to make noises about it. They want to see some results. Let's activate our plan."

"Have we confirmed that the door is opened?" Councilman Blosworth asked. "We don't want to move in and find the facility is still locked."

"No," Fazid said. "Our eyes on the ground only report that it *appears* Carver *might* have opened it. There's been no positioning of troops other that the original fire team."

"No positioning of troops?" Strauss echoed.

"She only has a single fire team of Marines to perform round-the-clock sentry duty at the entrance to the tunnel, although they recently established a camp perimeter by digging a trench. We've planned for sufficient strength to overcome a full company, so there's no problem."

"If the door *hasn't* been opened," Councilwoman Overgaard said, "and we attack, our entire effort to date might be wasted. We can't afford to spend a month there in the open, trying to produce a result that Carver hasn't been able to accomplish. At most, we'll only have a month before Space Command shows up in force and the operation will be a failure."

"Damn!" Strauss shouted. "Ahil, what kind of idiots have you placed in the Loudescott camp?"

"I'm sorry Arnold. I'm doing my best to work with what was available. Carver just doesn't share information, and we have no way of determining what has actually taken place below ground. The door may or may not be open."

"As Erika has said," Councilman Blosworth reminded everyone, "if we move in too soon, it might be a total loss. I don't see that we have any choice but to hold off until we have definitive information about the status of the door."

"Our people will continue to observe and report," Fazid said. "I've told them to report everything, no matter how small or insignificant they judge the event."

CHAPTER NINE

~ October 22nd, 2285 ~

Christa stepped over the sharp edge of darkness at the threshold and attempted to peer through the gloom, but the black was pervasive. The Chembrite panels had been aimed upward to properly illuminate the antechamber, so their light failed to penetrate the facility more than a meter or two. Perhaps Carmoody's words were responsible, but Christa was likewise experiencing unusual trepidation.

Taking a deep breath, Christa uttered, "Sumattah." The spoken command, which translates from Dakis as 'lights on,' had the desired result. Almost instantly, the interior of the facility was brilliantly illuminated. Since the door had responded to a spoken command, Christa knew the facility had at least some power available, and, to prevent a knee-jerk reaction to the sudden environment change, she had alerted the Marines to expect the lights. With the bright illumination, her initial sense of dread evaporated.

Before moving forward, Christa took a good look into a cavernous space that was nothing like the other facility— almost. The builders, as with Fort Carver, had used a meta-morphic stone for the floor and walls, and it's marble-like sur-faces, polished to a high gloss, gleamed brightly when the lights came on. And, like the other facility, it was as clean as a nanotech laboratory. But where the entrance to Fort Carver opened to reveal a short corridor, this one opened into a large rotunda like that found in many large commercial and government buildings.

Positioned along each side of the entranceway were narrow rooms that looked like security stations. Christa assumed that the rooms, about five meters long and two meters deep, were intended for screening people as they entered or left the facility. Security people, protected behind some sort of thick transparent material, would probably sit at the counter that faced the entranceway. Each room contained five chairs, but no other visible equipment. Remembering the work console in Fort Carver that looked like an ordinary table until activated, she turned to Lt. Uronson.

"Lieutenant," Christa said to the Marine officer standing just off her right side, "alert your people to the possible dangers in here. Tell them to touch nothing except the floor. No one is to enter either of these two rooms until they've been examined. Then have them spread out around the foyer and look for anything out of the ordinary. We're looking for sensors, switches, or booby traps, so tell them to be careful where they walk."

Uronson said, "Aye, Commander," then immediately repeated the orders to Sgt. Burton, who assigned his Marines to specific areas of the rotunda. Christa watched as they spread out and carefully examined the floor and walls. When all reports came back negative, Christa moved to the rear wall where a single set of doors interrupted the circular shape of the room.

"Only one way in?" Carmoody asked.

"Looks that way. The two rooms up front and single doorway back here indicate that this might have been a security area where people waited until their credentials were checked before being allowed inside. Well, here goes." Christa took a deep breath and said, "Dwuthathsei." Unlike her first attempts to open the entrance door, these doors groaned a little, then opened a little, then groaned some more, and finally opened wide, revealing a small room roughly five meters square.

"Is this all there is?" Carmoody said as lights flickered on in the room.

"No, look, there's another set of doors at the back of the room. This must be some sort of decontamination chamber."

"Why would they need that?"

"Perhaps they wanted to suck up any loose dirt and dust particles before entering a clean area."

"A clean area? This front area is so clean you can eat pancakes with maple syrup directly off the floor."

"I told you it would be clean."

"Yeah, but I thought you were exaggerating just a tiny bit."

"Lieutenant," Christa said, "post two men at the doors to this room. *Nobody* follows us in without orders to the contrary. Then have the rest of your people join us."

Christa and Carmoody entered the room and waited until the Marines were inside. There was more than adequate space to accommodate all of the Marines, even in their battle armor, but she wanted to ensure someone was left behind to report what happened if they became stuck inside the small room.

As the last of the Marines entered, Christa said, "Hudaksei," the Dakis word for 'close.' The double doors closed so fast she hardly saw the movement and barely had time to say, "Wow!" before the floor fell out from beneath them.

◆ ◆ ◆

"Geosynchronous orbit has been established over Loudescott, Captain," the helmsman said as he completed the orbiting track maneuver and set the ship controls to maintain the position.

"Very good, Lieutenant," Captain Kalastarus said. "Tactical, scan the site and plot LZs."

"Aye, Captain," the tactical officer said as she studied the monitors. She had already begun her work as the ship entered orbit, as any good tac officer would have done, and she had a tentative landing plot. She just wanted to verify the situation on the ground before sending coordinates to each of the waiting shuttles.

◆ ◆ ◆

As the occupants of the small room began to recover from the unexpected free fall, their legs received the full effect of rapid braking. It was a relief when the room came to a stop.

"I've heard of high-speed elevators in old buildings not having inertial compensation," Carmoody said to Christa, "but I never experienced anything like that."

"It was only bad because we weren't prepared for it. There's nothing in here to indicate this is an elevator. But— it was exhilarating for a few seconds."

Her last comment was met by a few phony coughs and sighs.

"What?" Christa said, looking around. "Is anyone in here going to tell me it didn't get their heart pumping?"

"I can definitely say it got *my* heart pumping, ma'am," Lt. Uronson said, "after it started beating again. I was truly expecting the stop to be quite a bit more sudden. I'm glad I was wrong."

Christa smiled. "I think we all expected the worst, Lieutenant." Turning serious, she said, "But it's time to get back to work. It appears we've stopped moving."

Christa took a deep breath and said, "Dwuthathsei." The doors at what had been the back of the room opened to reveal total blackness. As with the Chembrite panels and the rotunda, the light inside the elevator penetrated perhaps a few meters. It showed there was a floor there, but absolutely nothing else was visible. The Marines were ready to turn on their helmet lights when Christa said, "Sumattah." Lights immediately illuminated the area outside the elevator.

Stepping from the elevator, Christa saw she was in a corridor that stretched into darkness for roughly ten meters in both directions, but even this was enough to show that this facility was larger than Fort Carver. Like the rotunda above them, the corridor was spotlessly clean.

"It appears that the vocal command only activates the lights within an established range," Christa said, as she was joined in the corridor by Carmoody and Uronson. "We'll probably have to use it repeatedly as we proceed."

"Proceed where?" Carmoody asked. "We don't even know where we are."

"How far would you estimate we descended?"

"Based on the time and apparent speed of descent, I would guess we're somewhere between two hundred and four hundred meters below the rotunda."

"That agrees with my estimate," Christa said, "so let's say three hundred meters until we have more accurate information. There were no controls in the elevator, so this may be the only other level."

"Unless this level is simply the default stop if no level is specified."

"True. But if it is a default stop, we should investigate this floor and learn what we can before going elsewhere."

"In the rotunda you spoke of possible booby traps," Lt. Uronson said. "Do you believe that to be the case down here as well, Commander?"

"I didn't really expect to find any in the rotunda, given the effort required to enter the facility, but I wanted everyone to be extra alert. And I don't expect to find intentional booby traps down here either, but we could fall victim to alien technology if we're not especially careful. We should split up into two groups, each taking a different direction in the corridor. Make sure your people know the vocal commands that turn lights on and off, and open and close doors. Activate the tracking transponders in your battle armor and visually mark your trail with the returned coordinates as you proceed because we don't know what kind of labyrinth we're facing down here. Follow SOP and mark each door as a room is cleared. We'll use this location as Point Zero. I can use the data collected from the transponders to create a floor plan of this level as each group proceeds, unless someone moves into a shielded area. If that happens, we'll lose voice communications as well.

"Should you notice that voice communications are lost, move back to the last point where we had a confirmed connection and remain there until you reestablish contact."

"Aye, Commander," Uronson said.

The next few minutes were spent teaching the Marines the simple Dakis commands they would need and giving them instructions. Uronson then divided his people into groups and they moved out. Christa accompanied one and Carmoody another.

◆ ◆ ◆

"What do you mean we can't enter?" Captain Kalastarus said angrily to the Marine corporal. His face was becoming a mottled red color and his nose was just centimeters from that of the corporal. "Do you know who I am?"

"I'm sorry, sir," the corporal said calmly. "I don't know who you are, but I can see from your uniform that you're a Space Command captain. I mean no disrespect, sir, but I have my orders."

"And what are those orders, *exactly*?"

"Commander Carver said absolutely no one shall be permitted to enter the tunnel without her personal authorization."

"Do you think she intended that to include senior Space Command officers?" Kalastarus shouted.

"Perhaps not, sir, but my orders were quite explicit. I can't let you pass."

"And suppose I just push past you?"

"I really hope you won't try that, sir. Commander Carver said to use whatever force was necessary to see that no one entered the tunnel."

"Are you saying you would use force to stop me?"

"Most regretfully, sir. And we've only been issued laser weapons rather than stun rifles, so if I'm required to discharge my weapon there could be serious injury."

Kalastarus blanched slightly and was suddenly pushed aside by a hand from behind him. A more senior officer immediately replaced him in the corporal's face. "Do you know who I am, corporal?"

"No, sir."

"I'm Rear Admiral Hubera. I'm a member of the Admiralty Board."

"Yes, sir," the corporal said. "I've heard of you, sir."

"You will now allow me and the other officers to enter."

"No, sir, I will not."

"I'm countermanding the orders you received from Commander Carver. You will allow all Space Command officers to enter the tunnel."

"No, sir, I will not until Commander Carver authorizes your passage or amends my orders."

"I'm an Admiral, corporal. The last I heard, that outranks a Lt. Commander by a wide margin."

"Yes, sir, you do. And as such you must be familiar with regulations. An order cannot be countermanded by a senior unless the senior is in the same chain of command, or the person who gave the order is missing and assumed captured or lost."

"I'm her superior officer," Hubera screamed, his own face now becoming mottled with rage.

"Yes, sir, you have superior rank, but you're not in the same chain of command."

"I'm a member of the Admiralty Board. My authority supersedes *every* chain of command."

"No, sir, not this time. Commander Carver is currently acting under direct orders from Admiral Carver. Admiral Carver is senior to you, sir, and operating in a separate command chain."

Hubera sputtered something unintelligible and turned to face Captain Kalastarus. "Are you just going to stand for this?"

"What do you propose, sir? If you order us to attack this position and overcome the guards, I'll have our Marine complement come down from the ship, but I'll need a specific order from you to attack and overpower Marine sentries that are only following the lawful orders of their base commander. And, much as I hate to say it, there's no guarantee our Marines would obey an order to attack Marine sentries who aren't acting illegally and overtly."

"She's not the base commander," Hubera sputtered. "And this isn't a base. At best it might be considered an outpost." He knew there was no way he could order an attack on Marines doing their duty as spelled out in the regulations simply because he was being inconvenienced. Turning back to the corporal, he said, "Contact Commander Carver and tell her I'm here."

"When the shuttles began landing, I tried to contact the commander to inform her, but she's out of communication."

"What? Out of communication? What does that mean?"

"The Commander must be in a part of the new facility that is shielded. Dakinium blocks all radio signals. Whenever we conduct a drill at Fort Carver, we lose all communication to the outside when the main door is closed."

"Fort Carver?" Hubera said. It was doubtful his eyes could have opened wider.

"The other facility has been informally known by that name for about fifteen years, sir, ever since the time of the Raider attack and the battle that took place there."

Hubera groaned slightly. He hadn't known of the unofficial name. As far as the records indicated, it was only referred to as the Loudescott Outpost. "Corporal, just as soon as you regain contact with Commander Carver, you tell her to report to me aboard the *Murray*. Understand?"

"Yes, sir, Admiral."

"And regardless of the chain of command, she had better not keep me waiting long."

Hubera turned and stomped off towards oh-gee vehicles with the other Space Command officers following.

"Oh, Lordy!" the Marine corporal muttered to himself. "Methinks the Commander is in for a reaming."

♦ ♦ ♦

When Christa had used the term 'labyrinth,' she couldn't have known how accurate it would prove to be. As her team began its investigation, they were astounded by the maze of corridors, large dormitory-style rooms, and mess halls they discovered. Each dorm room was like the single dorm at Fort Carver, and there were dozens. And, like the dorm at Fort Carver, there were several small, private rooms associated with each of the large rooms.

"Have you found anything other than dorms and mess halls?" Christa asked Carmoody after two hours of searching.

"Nothing yet," Christa heard in her CT, "if you don't count the kitchens and supply rooms associated with each mess hall."

"Same here," Christa said, looking at the holo-magazine image that showed the floor plan created so far for the areas searched. As she watched, another area appeared as part of the expanding image. "Okay, let's keep at it until we reach the outside perimeter."

♦

An hour and a half later, Christa heard the soft, chime-like noise that indicated she was receiving a message on her CT.

"We've reached what appears to be the outer perimeter, Commander," Carmoody said. "We're splitting into two groups and spreading out in an effort to identify the size of the facility as we work our way back. Uronson will remain with one small group and I'll stay with the other."

"Understood," Christa said. "I'll also divide my group when we reach the outer perimeter. If we assume the elevator was in the center of the facility, we should be encountering that point ourselves pretty soon. We'll meet you back at Point Zero."

"Affirmative," Grace said. "Carmoody out."

It was another four hours before Christa and half her original team arrived back at Point Zero. Carmoody wasn't there yet, but Lt. Uronson and his half-team had returned.

"Just dormitory rooms and mess halls, Commander. At first we performed a thorough check of each room, but after about a dozen, we just visually verified that each room appeared empty and moved on. There didn't seem any point in checking closer since they were all identical."

"We did the same, Lieutenant. The only thing that changed was the location information in each section. We have what looks like a fairly complete floor plan." Looking at the diagram on her holo-magazine cylinder, she said, "It appears that the other two small groups are almost done. There are only a few areas that show no indication of having been searched yet. They should join us within ten minutes."

"So there's apparently no cloning equipment here," Uronson said. "Do we let the scientists in?"

"No, not yet. This place doesn't make sense given what I know of ancient history. I have to figure out why they built it."

"Perhaps it was intended as a shelter in the event of war."

"The other facility is quite similar in design and construction, which would seem to indicate they were built around the same time period. We know the Dakistians were aware that they were a dying race when they built that facility, so why build something like this? Who is going to start a war when you know the entire race will be extinct in a matter of decades?"

"People do strange things at times."

"My impression of the Ancient Dakistians is that they were a highly intelligent society. They knew they were looking at the end of their lineage on this world, and efforts to locate the dissidents who left were unsuccessful. I doubt anyone would be thinking of war and, if they were, it should have been difficult to garner any support. Lieutenant, have you checked in with your people top-side?"

"I've tried several times, but I haven't received any acknowledgment."

"No acknowledgment? Why didn't you report that to me?"

"I assumed communications are being blocked by the Dakinium construction of this facility. We experience such problems at Fort Carver when we run drills."

"Possibly. But if I'd known, I would have dispatched someone to go up to the surface to verify that all was well. If we can't contact them, then they can't contact us. We have no idea what's happening up there. I guess we'll need a more powerful communications system in here."

"My people are well trained and well armed, ma'am. They can certainly handle a few scientists, or even the entire Loudescott archeological complement."

"There could be situations other than an attack by scientists, Lieutenant, that require immediate attention." Christa breathed deeply and then released it. "Very well, we'll head up as soon as the rest of our people get back."

CHAPTER TEN

~ October 22nd, 2285 ~

"Gracie, this may take longer than I expected," Christa said to Carmoody via her CT. "Admiral Hubera's kept me waiting for an hour already. I have no idea how long I'll be up here."

"I understand he was pretty upset about being refused entrance to the tunnel."

"Yeah, well, he should have called ahea…"

"Attention!" Captain Robledo, Admiral Hubera's Flag Secretary, said loudly as he preceded Admiral Hubera into the room.

Christa braced to attention and held it while Hubera took a seat at the table. He didn't invite Christa to sit down.

"Lt. Commander Christa Carver reporting to the admiral as ordered, sir," Christa said as she stood in front of Hubera.

Hubera just sat and scowled at her, as he had always done when students at the Academy reported to him. He had tried it with Jenetta Carver when she had appeared at the Admiralty Board, but it hadn't unsettled her in the slightest, and it didn't seem to be working with this Carver either.

Christa's peripheral vision made her fully aware that Hubera was scowling at her as she stared straight ahead. He might be angry about being inconvenienced down on the surface of the planet, but he had no grounds for making any charges, so she wasn't nervous, and she was content to stand at attention until he spoke or returned her salute.

Hubera finally stopped scowling and decided to bully her instead. In a voice dripping with acrimony, he said, "Just what made you think you could authorize the use of deadly force against Space Command personnel, Commander?"

"I never gave such an order, sir."

"The sentry at the tunnel said you did. He said he was prepared, on your orders, to use deadly force if I tried to enter the tunnel. Is that not correct, Captain Robledo?"

Robledo, who had been standing quietly on Hubera's left, spoke up to support the Admiral's statement.

"I think you misunderstood, sir," Christa directed at Hubera. "The order to use 'whatever force deemed necessary' to stop unauthorized persons from entering the tunnel was not directed at Space Command personnel. At the time I gave the order in question, Lieutenant Carmoody and I were the only Space Command personnel on the planet, to the best of my knowledge. Had I been notified of your imminent arrival, I would surely have modified the order to exclude all Space Command personnel."

"You have an excuse for everything, don't you, Commander?"

"I'm just stating the facts as I know them, sir."

Hubera scowled again and finally returned her salute, allowing her to drop her arm.

"What have you found in the facility?"

"Today was our first day of inspection, so we moved slow…"

"I didn't ask how you moved," Hubera shouted. "I asked what you found."

Without missing a beat, Christa said, "Empty dormitories and mess halls, sir."

"That's all?"

"That all, sir."

"No cloning lab?"

"No, sir."

"No other useful technology?"

"No, sir."

"How much of the facility is still unchecked?"

"We checked every room we reached, sir."

"How big is it?"

"Unknown, sir."

"How can you not know? You were in there all day."

"The facility is enormous, sir. We haven't had time for a detailed analysis yet. Upon learning of your arrival and that you wished to see me aboard the *Murray,* I dropped everything else and came up. If the Admiral would allow me to give a detailed report instead of simply replying to pointed questions, I think he will receive a better picture of the situation."

Hubera drew in a large breath and exhaled it quickly, clearly demonstrating his exasperation at not being able to rattle Christa and not getting the answers he wanted. She hadn't once been insubordinate, and he didn't expect that she would become so. She was as bad as her sister.

"Very well, Commander. Give me your detailed report."

Over the next ten minutes Christa related everything that had happened since they first stepped into the new facility until they came topside and she learned of the *Murray's* arrival at Dakistee. Hubera had just stared at her somewhat impassively during the presentation, a remarkable achievement for someone of his temperament.

"As I said earlier, sir," Christa said in conclusion, "if I had been notified of your pending arrival I would have amended my orders to allow for Space Command officer access to the facility. I do apologize for the inconvenience you experienced."

"Carver, since the incident with Admiral Vroman, the travel plans of Admirals are held in strictest confidence."

"Yes, sir. I meant that the imminent arrival of the *Murray* should have been made known. It would not have required mention of your presence on board."

Hubera sputtered a couple of times. He knew she was right. Regulations required that a base commander, even an outpost commander, be notified before a ship arrived at his or her command. But Hubera had wanted to just drop in, hoping he could catch her doing something he could spin into a dereliction of duty accusation, even if it wasn't enough to justify a formal charge, so he had specifically ordered the *Murray's* captain not to announce their arrival.

"This is considered an inspection visit, and, as such, is excluded from the normal regulations and protocols regarding arriving ships."

"Yes, sir. Impromptu arrivals often hold surprises for both parties."

Hubera snorted slightly and then said, "So I'm supposed to return to the Admiralty Board and report that after half a year of work here, as well as considerable involvement by Space Command Headquarters to locate those damned cylinders, all you have to show for it is an empty underground bunker?"

"That's all we've found so far, sir."

"You said you searched the entire floor."

"Yes, sir. There are one hundred dormitories, each capable of housing over one hundred people, and each has its own mess hall, but there are no community areas, no libraries or work spaces, and no exercise areas. At Fort Carver…"

Hubera interrupted her with a very vocal, "That other facility is called the Loudescott Outpost, and that is the name you will use for it."

"Yes, sir. The *Loudescott Outpost* was intended merely to serve as a work location where new clones and off-duty personnel could bivouac temporarily, but the scope of this facility indicates that it was much more. I don't yet know what the purpose was, but additional investigation should tell us. There must be more to this story than a facility created simply to function as an underground bunker, and I expect it will be uncovered with analysis."

"Story? Uncovered? You're supposed to be a Space Command line officer, not a newsie. We have people enough to uncover stories. We ordered you here to open the facility, nothing more. You've accomplished your mission, and you will now return to Region Two at the earliest opportunity. Do I make myself clear?"

"Yes, sir, your order that I leave the planet as soon as possible is very clear. I shall notify Higgins immediately that I require transportation out of Region One at the earliest opportunity. Since it could take days or even weeks for transportation to be made available, may I continue my work here until then?"

Hubera snorted again. He couldn't think of a good reason to refuse her request since she would be on the planet anyway. "Very well, but don't let it delay your departure. I expect you to notify Higgins today of your transportation requirements."

"Yes, sir. I shall notify Higgins as soon as I return to my shuttle that I'm under orders from you to abandon this post and leave on the first transport out. Uh, while I *am* still here, may I borrow some of the *Murray's* people to assist my investigations? I only have one assistant and neither of us is trained as an engineer."

"Certainly not. This is a scout-destroyer, not a battleship. The *Murray* doesn't have any personnel available for loan-out; the crew complement is too small."

"I meant only while the ship is here, sir."

"Now that I know this investigation has been pure folly, we'll be departing."

"Yes, sir. I wasn't aware you were leaving immediately."

"You're dismissed, Commander."

"Yes, sir," Christa said, coming to attention.

When Hubera had returned her salute, she turned on her heel and left the compartment. After the doors had closed behind her, she snorted in imitation of Hubera's snort, then smiled and headed for the shuttle bay.

◆　◆　◆

"He ordered you to leave— before we complete the work here?" Carmoody asked in surprise.

"He said we have plenty of people who can uncover the story now that the door is open," Christa replied.

Carmoody made an exaggerated visual sweep around the shuttle with her head and eyes before grimacing and saying, "Yes, of course. I can see that now. We're definitely over-staffed. What are you going to do?"

"On the trip back down to the planet, I sent a message to Admiral Carver, with a copy to Admiral Holt at Higgins, requesting transportation to Region Two in order to comply with Admiral Hubera's direct order that I terminate my work here and immediately quit the region as a passenger on the first available transport."

"Did you explain to Hubera that we've only just begun our research here?"

"I tried, but he had already made up his mind and refused to hear anything else. But, until transportation is arranged, we'll continue our investigation. It's getting late— I'm going to grab some chow and get some rack time. We can plan the day's effort over breakfast in the morning."

◆ ◆ ◆

The following morning, Christa and Carmoody entered the facility without an escort. Since they had searched the entire lower level, they didn't presently require any additional help from available personnel. Marines patrolling the camp above would alert Christa to any change in the status quo. Christa's standing order regarding access had been amended. No Space Command or Marine personnel would be denied entrance to the tunnel, although the *Murray* had departed and there were again only two Space Command officers on the planet.

Christa had warned Carmoody about touching what look-ed like an ordinary table in the security room, so Grace was careful not to touch the console as they took seats in the room on the right side of the entrance. Despite the advance notice, Carmoody still reacted with an involuntary twitch as Christa gently touched the console near the leading edge and it illuminated. All at once, it came alive with lighted pressure points and monitor readouts.

"Where is all the power coming from?" Carmoody asked. "I mean, this place is twenty thousand years old. The electrical grid had to have crumbled to dust eons ago."

"I'd be willing to bet it uses the same system as the other facility. Our investigation there showed that it had a private generating system using thermal energy."

"They drilled a thermal shaft just for one facility?"

"They might share a common shaft, with each facility drawing what heated water it needs to power its generating equipment."

"I'm impressed."

Christa smiled and continued with her explanation of the control board. "These symbols are Dakistian. We believe the priests who led the religious dissidents from the planet millennia ago changed the shape of the characters used in the language so that previous versions of the Almuth would eventually be undecipherable, but they had to retain the phonetic sounds or risk severe communication problems. The language changed slightly down through the centuries as colloquialisms crept in and scientific and technological advances were made, but the Dakis language has remained remarkably close to Ancient Dakis. My sisters and I have credited the Almuth for the phonetic purity. Every Nordakian is required to read from the Almuth each day. Although many of the religious doctrines were modified by the dissident priesthood, much of the document remained intact."

"Since being informed I would be working with you on Dakistee," Carmoody said, "I've been studying the Dakis language at every opportunity. I've also been studying the books you and your sisters wrote, as well as the files available through Space Command."

"That's wonderful, Gracie," Christa said. Pointing to a symbol on one of the illuminated displays, she asked, "Do you know what this readout is for?"

"I think the label says 'air quality.'"

"Very good. This display seems to be giving information about the environmental conditions on the lower level. We didn't locate the engineering area down there, so there has to be more to this facility than we've found so far. I tried to make Hubera understand that, but his mind was closed to anything I said. Perhaps it was because he was still angry about being inconvenienced when the sentries refused to allow him entrance to the tunnel. But if he really wanted to see it, he could have come down after I amended the orders. Instead, he ordered the *Murray* to depart the planet. I don't understand the reason for his visit. If all he wanted was an update, he could have ordered me to send him a report."

Carmoody had listened in silence and just nodded when Christa was finished.

"Anyway, we have a lot to do and not much time to do it if I have to leave soon."

Carmoody looked on as Christa investigated the console information and progressed through all the different displays available.

"There has to be a *lot* more to this facility than we've so far discovered. There are far too many readouts here for just this floor and the lower one, but the information is too general to pinpoint anything. We have to locate the engineering area. It's too bad Admiral Hubera wouldn't loan us some people for even a few hours."

"If there are more floors, there has to be a way of controlling the elevator to stop at them."

"Yes, that's true. There are no visual controls in the elevator, so they must be audible. One thing I haven't tried yet is to contact the main computer orally." Speaking loudly in Ancient Dakis, she said, "Computer, can you respond?"

They waited for a full minute, listening for any response but heard nothing.

"What does that mean?" Carmoody asked. "That it can't respond audibly, or that it didn't hear or recognize the command?"

"I don't know. Perhaps there are no auditory sensors on this floor, but that wouldn't make sense since this appears to be a vital security area."

"Can you input requests for information through the console?"

"I didn't see anything that permitted that. Let's look through them again."

After twenty minutes of searching, the two women conceded that no provision for posting queries to the computer existed via the console.

"What now?" Carmoody asked.

"This is just one console of three on this side of the entrance, and there may be three on the other side. Let's check them all to see if they contain different functions. Do you feel comfortable going it alone?"

"I think so. If I have any questions or problems, you'll be nearby, right?"

"Right."

"Okay, let's do it."

◆

At one point, while they worked, Christa snapped her fingers lightly to get Carmoody's attention. When Grace looked over, Christa pointed to the rotunda. A small army of bots were emerging from hidden closets around the huge circular room. They began to work with amazing speed, scrubbing and polishing floors, walls, and ceiling. One bot, tasked to clean the windows on the security rooms, paused and stared for a couple of seconds at the two female officers, then continued its work. When the rotunda was finished, all bots scurried back to their hidden locations and disappeared from view.

"Amazing," Carmoody said. "Do they have the same bots at Fort Carver?"

"I don't know. I never saw any. If we hadn't just seen them emerge from their storage locations, I wouldn't have suspected they were here in such quantity."

"I guess the rotunda was once a busy place," Carmoody said, "so they were probably designed to get the job done as quickly as possible while the area was unoccupied. Did you notice the way that one bot stared at us?"

"Perhaps it was the first time in almost two hundred centuries it had seen a live person and was confused by our presence. Or perhaps it was simply alerting central control that people were in this security room. They cleaned the other security room but never entered this one."

"That's probably it."

◆

Hours later, the two women completed their work with the security consoles.

"Anything?" Christa asked when Carmoody had wrapped up her efforts.

"I found no way to access any part of the system, other than the personnel database."

"Same here," Christa said. "I've never been so stonewalled by a computer system. I think the personnel database is the only data system connected to these consoles, except for an environmental data feed. They must have intended security personnel to perform basic monitoring services 24/7 so engin-eering personnel would only have to be summoned when conditions varied outside established parameters."

"That doesn't help *us*, though."

"No, it doesn't."

"What next?"

"We now know how to operate these consoles, and we can establish security controls. Let's set up a password and lock each of the consoles so they're safe from tampering by the archeologists, just in case the dig site people get in. Then we'll grab some lunch and tackle the issue with the elevator."

◆ ◆ ◆

"We'll reach the planet in two days time. It will be early morning, local time, Excellency," Gxidescu reported. "Our spies there report no Nordakian Space Force or Space Command ships are currently in orbit. We should have a clear field for our operation."

"Excellent. Our attack will no doubt come as quite a surprise to Azula Carver. I wish I could see her face when she learns how we respond to infidels who dare involve themselves in our sacred matters. It would be most fitting if we could find proof that she created the false Almuth delivered to our homeland. But we may never know how she managed to convince the King and certain church elders that it was genuine. I regret that we won't be able to put *her* on trial and exact retribution. A traditional stoning, with a large audience, would be glorious. But Region Two is far beyond our reach."

"Yes, Excellency."

"Are the sacred Warriors of Jubada ready?"

"They have been practicing each and every day of our journey. They are ready and most anxious to take possession of the land promised in the scriptures of Jubada."

"When we arrive at the planet, we must be ready to launch as soon as we place the jamming satellites. It may be weeks before anyone arrives to investigate, but we can't guarantee that, so we must be entrenched and ready to repel all attempts to displace us. Our maps tell us that the planet is sparsely populated, with most people located in one of three major locations. As each outlying area is conquered, we'll move to the next. The three large population centers will be reserved for last. By then we may have been able to recruit, or conscript, additional soldiers for our holy struggle. I wish we had been able to acquire more reconditioned fighters on Nordakia, but we won't rest until the entire planet is ours. The followers of the One True Word will again have a homeland. And as we plant our crops, the ground will be enriched by the blood of infidels. Those idiot puppets of the royal family on Nordakia actually believed we would go to a hot, miserable little planet like Slabeca while a planet rich in agrarian potential was allowed to lie fallow. The fools."

◆ ◆ ◆

"Be careful what you touch in here," Christa said when they entered the elevator, "and don't say anything in Dakis. What we want to do first is examine every inch of the walls to see if there might be camouflaged controls. I realize it seems unlikely, but you've seen what they did with the consoles. When we touch something, we want to be as certain as possible that it won't have adverse consequences."

After forty minutes of examining the walls, Carmoody threw up her hands. "I can't see anything that indicates the walls are anything more than just walls."

"Nor can I," Christa said. "Okay, on to Plan B."

"What's Plan B?"

"We ask the elevator for information, like we did in the security rooms."

"The security rooms didn't answer us," Carmoody said.

"No, but maybe the elevator is feeling more talkative." Switching to Ancient Dakis , Christa said, "Computer, can you hear me?"

A disembodied voice said, "State floor and destination, or close the door and you will be delivered to the housing floor."

Christa and Carmoody looked at one another and smiled.

CHAPTER ELEVEN
~ October 23rd, 2285 ~

"Computer, list the available stops," Christa said.

"There are five levels available— Administrative Offices\Operations, Housing, Medical\Research\Library, Recreation, and the Vault level."

"What's this level?"

"You are currently at the Rotunda entrance."

"Are there any other entrances?"

"Negative."

"What's the Vault level?"

"It is a level where the Vault is located," the computer interface said simply.

"What's in the Vault?"

"State floor and destination, or close the door and you will be delivered to the Housing level."

Christa looked over at Carmoody, who nodded and responded with, "Helpful."

"Computer, take us to the Vault level," Christa said.

"Level accepted."

The elevator just sat there until Christa remembered to say, "Hudaksei."

As had happened on the previous trip down, the floor seemed to fall out from under them, but this time they were prepared and barely nervous that the stop might be considerably more sudden than anticipated.

The doors opened to complete darkness, as had been the case with the last trip. Christa gave the command for illumination and the hallway before them was brilliantly lit in a second.

"Left or right?" Christa asked as they stepped into the corridor.

"We went right last time. Let's try left this time."

Where the corridor had disappeared into darkness on their first trip, they could actually see the end before additional lights came on this time. Christa walked right up to the door and said, "Open," in Dakis.

Rather than opening immediately, a disembodied voice said, "ID?"

Christa thought for a second and remembered the name of an official she had seen while in the rotunda security room trying to access the computer files. She rattled it off.

"Password," the voice said.

"I don't remember."

"Then you must go to security, identify yourself, and request a new password."

It was no use arguing with a computer. They never relented. She would have gotten just as far if she started an argument with the marble tile on the floor.

"I'm going back up to the security station, Gracie. I'll be right back."

"Why don't we just check out the rest of the floor today, and we can do the security thing tomorrow."

"Well, we could— but I'm anxious to see what it is they felt they had to password-protect down here."

"Okay, Christa. Do you want me to accompany you?"

"No, I'll be right back. With the speed of that elevator, the trip should only take about five minutes."

◆

Carmoody was still standing by the door when Christa returned. "I set up IDs for each of us. Your ID is 'Grace Carmoody,' and the password is 'Fort Carver.'"

"That's easy enough to remember."

"There was no sense making it difficult since we're the only ones likely to be using it. Okay, let's take a look at what's inside."

Christa provided her new ID and password when queried by the computer, and the two entrance doors slid open noiselessly. After giving the verbal command for illumination, she and Carmoody stepped into a cavernous area that disappeared into darkness at the far recesses without giving the slightest indication of how far it might extend. Christa could see at least fifty meters into the distance before darkness masked the rest. The roof of the chamber had to be at least twenty meters high, and the width of the area easily matched that. It took a couple of seconds for the impact of the room's immense size to be fully realized, and then a couple more before the room's contents registered. Christa's jaw dropped as everything coalesced. "Oh— my— God!"

"Are those what I think they are?" Carmoody asked, just as shocked by the find as Christa.

"I can't imagine what else they might be."

"There must be thousands."

"Tens of thousands, I'd say," Christa replied.

"Why are they here?"

"That's the million dollar question." Christa took a deep breath and added, "I never expected anything like this. I must report this immediately."

"We'd better change the password to something a little more complex. I have a feeling we're not going to be working alone here for much longer, and we don't want the wrong people getting into this area, if you know what I mean."

"Yes, I know what you mean. No one without top-level security access can be permitted in here. And don't mention the ability to select the level in the elevator. In fact, don't mention anything about today to anybody until we get orders on how to proceed."

"Understood."

As the two women reached the surface, Christa reminded Carmoody to mask her emotions.

"You look like you just lost your best friend, Gracie."

"I'm sorry. I was thinking about what we just found. I'll clear my mind."

A few seconds later, Grace managed a completely impassive expression. Christa nodded and they stepped out into the late afternoon sunlight. Ten minutes later, they were in Christa's shuttle sending a message to Jenetta, with a copy to Admiral Holt.

As Christa ended the message and sat back in the pilot's seat, the computer announced that a message had just arrived from Higgins.

"That certainly can't be a reply to the new message," Christa said as she called up the 'view messages' screen and selected the latest message to play. It was encrypted, so she positioned herself where the computer could verify her identify via retinal scan and held it until the computer was satisfied.

"Hello, Christa," the affable face of Admiral Holt said as the scan process completed. "Although Admiral Carver may have other thoughts on the subject, I'll tell you now that Admiral Hubera doesn't have the authority to boot you out of my deca-sector, and I'm quite upset that he attempted it. As a member of the Admiralty Board, Admiral Hubera votes on many vital issues that affect all of Galactic Alliance space, but his vote is just one of ten, and as an individual he has no power to command, although he deserves the respect owed his rank. Since he was never a line officer, he was never eligible to be a base commander and has never had the authority to direct the work efforts of Space Command personnel, except those of his aides and office staff, as well as the corps of cadets when he taught at the Academy. My instructions to you are to remain where you are until you hear from Admiral Carver. It's her decision and her decision alone to recall you to Region Two or have you remain on Dakistee until you decide your mission has been completed.

"Brian Holt, Rear Admiral, Upper, Commanding Officer of Higgins SCB, message complete."

"Some good news at last," Carmoody said. "I would have felt completely lost without you here, especially after this latest development. What do we do now?"

"We've reported the situation as required by Space Command regulations, so I suppose we're free to continue our investigation until someone orders us to stop."

"Let's go."

◆

When they were again in the Vault, they walked along the main corridor, staring up at storage racks that stretched towards the ceiling.

"Of all the things I expected we might find down here," Christa said, "this would have to rank as perhaps the last."

"From everything I've read, they seemed like such an enlightened people. I don't understand it either."

As they moved deeper into the cavernous area, Christa ordered the lights on. It was surprising that after nineteen thousand, four hundred years, everything worked as well as it did.

Eventually the two women arrived at a raised platform that seemed like a control station. They climbed the stairs and discovered a computer console arrangement similar to that in the security rooms. There was not a speck of dust on any of the four chairs there.

"I guess there must be a virtual army of bots down here," Carmoody said. "Everything is so pristine."

"Yes, it would appear so. I wonder if we'd have any better luck accessing the main computer system from down here. Let's give it a try."

The women took seats as Christa touched the console table to illuminate it. The readouts jumped to life and began displaying an incredible amount of information. As a viewing monitor powered on, it displayed the picture of a woman.

"Who's that," Carmoody asked.

"It must be one of the facility's officials. Her title says Chief Administrative Director."

"She's a Dakistian? She looks kinda like us."

"The people of Dakistee didn't look all that different from humans."

"But Nordakians look so different. Aren't they direct descendents?"

"The dissidents who left in search of religious freedom didn't have FTL, so generations lived and died in space. There's speculation that the species mutated during their trip to Nordakia because of inadequate radiation shielding."

"Wow. I never read that."

"It's just speculation, but there's no arguing that the original inhabitants of this planet weren't as tall and didn't share the Nordakian ability to change skin color. Their skin color seemed to vary between a rich Moroccan brown and a Northern European light pink. In the news broadcasts of the period, I saw none of the extremes represented by deep blacks or albino colorations, and no Mongolian yellow coloration."

"The dissidents were lucky they left when they did. Their bodies may have mutated, but at least they didn't fall victim to the plague that sterilized the population of this planet and eventually led to its extinction."

"Uh, yes. They were lucky."

"Can we determine anything more about this individual?" Carmoody asked, pointing to the image on the viewer.

"There's a button here marked, 'Kudlaknee.' That means 'Presentation' in Dakis. Perhaps it's like a vid biography."

As Christa pressed the button, the viewer changed to show a series of numbers. Readouts jumped to life and the viewer changed to show a graph with steadily increasing wave forms.

"What's it doing?" Carmoody asked.

"I have no idea," Christa replied. "But I don't like it."

"Tap the button again. Perhaps it will revert to the image."

Christa tapped the button once, but there was no change. She then tapped it twice, and still nothing changed. The console continued to display fluctuating information values and the waveform on the viewer continued to show increasing activity.

"Look," Carmoody said suddenly, pointing to a robotic arm that was descending from the ceiling far above. The slight whirring noise from its servos had attracted her attention.

The articulating arm moved with precision and latched onto a long box in a storage rack. After securing itself, it waited as the box was released by the rack's holding mechanism.

"It's lowering a coffin to the floor in front of us," Carmoody said. "Ewww! I hate dead bodies. Especially mummified bodies. Put it back. Quick."

"I don't know how. Besides, I'd like to see the skeleton, if it hasn't turned to dust in twenty thousand years."

"You *want* to see a skeleton?"

"I want to see the original bone structure of Dakistians. I've seen images of the current skeleton. They have four more ribs than humans, but otherwise it's pretty similar. I understand the internal organs are pretty similar as well, allowing humans and Nordakians to breed."

"Nordakians and humans have procreated?"

"I'm not aware of any offspring yet, but there have been marriages."

While they talked, the box had neared the floor and an automated dolly arrived to accept it. Christa climbed down from the platform as the articulating arm carefully positioned the box on the cart. With her first good look at what she had thought was a coffin, she said, "I think our original assessment was incorrect, Gracie. This isn't an immense mausoleum; it's a stasis repository."

"Stasis? That can't be. Stasis isn't viable for more than forty-two years."

"I didn't say I thought they intended to sleep longer than that, just that this box is no coffin. Perhaps the people who functioned as caretakers were unable to awaken the sleepers, or perhaps a decision was made to let them sleep their lives away because there was no hope left for a cure to the plague."

"You think someone would just walk away and leave tens of thousands of people to die in their sleep?"

"I don't know, Gracie. I'm just speculating on possible reasons for so many people having died in their sleep, if indeed all these chambers are occupied."

On the platform, the console suddenly started producing a bleating sound. Christa and Carmoody hurried to determine the cause.

"I don't see a problem," Carmoody said. "No flashing lights or anything."

"Maybe it's a gentle reminder instead of an emergency alarm. Perhaps it has something to do with the stasis chamber that was just lowered. Look at the display— the waveforms have adopted a regular pattern."

"But what do they mean?"

"I don't know," Christa said as she stared at the viewer. "You don't suppose…"

"Suppose? Suppose what?"

"That the person in that stasis bed is being revived."

"After nineteen thousand, four hundred years? Imposs-ible."

"So was a material that's impervious to all forms of energy weapons until we discovered the properties of Dakinium. Perhaps the Dakistians discovered a method of suspended animation where all bodily functions totally cease."

"Scientists have dreamed about that for centuries, but it's been conceded that such a process is impossible. A slowing of all bodily functions is the best they can accomplish."

"Alyysian physiology allows them to be completely frozen, then thawed and revived centuries later. It doesn't work with humans because our bodies are mostly water, and water expands by fifteen percent when frozen. That expansion destroys fragile cell structures. We've all seen what happens when you freeze a tomato and then thaw it out."

Carmoody nodded. "Yes, we did that experiment when I was in pre-school. What a soft, soggy mess that tomato became. You couldn't even pick it up because the outer skin had broken open."

"We know we're more advanced in many areas than the Dakistians were, but we also know they were ahead of us in others. This might be one of those areas."

The automated cart had begun to move away from the loading spot. Carmoody saw it and asked, "Where's that going? Or more importantly, should we follow it?"

"Yes, let's see where the computer is sending it. If it realized the body is deceased, it might be headed for a crematorium. We should try to stop it if that's the case."

The two Space Command officers hurried down from the platform and raced after the cart. The entrance door opened for the cart and remained open for the two women. They followed the cart to the elevator and then joined it inside. They felt the elevator begin to rise, then stop after several seconds and open. The cart exited and turned to the right, but the lights didn't come on until Christa gave the command.

The automated cart wound its way through a maze of corridors until it entered a large ward. When it stopped near the center of the room, another articulating arm lifted the enclosure from the cart. As the box came free, the cart left the room. Christa and Carmoody watched as a table rose from up the floor near the wall and the articulating arm placed the box on top of it. The arm then attached connection wires and tubes from the table to the box. The top cover of what they had thought was a coffin, at first, had been completely opaque until then, but, as they watched, the dark color faded until the cover was as transparent as glass.

"Amazing!" Christa said as they looked down at a female form that appeared to be middle-aged. She had magenta-colored hair with red highlights and, unlike the skin-tight stasis suit typically worn by stasis bed occupants, she was clothed in what looked to be a simple white terrycloth gown. Overall, she looked like someone who had climbed into the box just moments ago and closed her eyes. Christa remembered the debilitated condition of Jenetta's body after ten years in stasis. The two officers didn't observe any indications of respiration, but the condition of the body suggested that it might be receptive to resuscitation. "Gracie, go to the surface and call the Marine Central Command. Tell them we need a full medical team here immediately— preferably one with a doctor who has expertise in stasis recovery cases."

"On my way," Carmoody said as she turned and ran from the room.

Christa reached into a pocket and brought out a tiny case that held four rings. Each about the size of a personal log ring, these were decidedly different because there was no hole in the center. Instead, each had a small optical lens. She touched the edge of one to her tongue, then placed it on a nearby piece of equipment with the lens pointed in the general direction of the stasis container. Taking a small view-pad from another pocket, she centered the image on the box, adjusted the focus, and began recording. The ring would now record everything that happened around the stasis box until either the recording was stopped or it ran out of storage space in about two week's time.

Christa then placed another ring in front of a viewer located on a central desk. It appeared to be identical to the viewer they'd seen in the Vault. She synced the two recording devices so they would share a common time-frame for later analysis.

◆ ◆

As Carmoody emerged from the tunnel, she immediately placed a call to Marine Central Command using her CT. The proximity of Fort Carver allowed the use of CTs anywhere in the Loudescott area. When the first facility had been discovered, a portable communications unit had been set up, but a more powerful unit of the sort typically found on a base had long ago replaced that. The computer generated a carrier and made the connections via satellite to the Marine Base halfway around the planet.

As soon as she had made her needs known and had told the communications operator that the request came from Lt. Commander Christa Carver, she was put through to the base hospital. A dispatcher there said that shuttles would be in the air in minutes with a full medical team. Carmoody had the dispatcher transfer her to Supply, where she requested that a base communications system be delivered to the new facility ASAP. Carmoody signed off and hurried back down to the Medical and Research level where she found Christa staring down at the body through the transparent cover.

"A medical team is on the way," Carmoody said. "They should be here within thirty minutes. I also requested a more powerful com system for inside the facility. Perhaps we can stay in contact with the surface if we have stronger signals."

Christa nodded, then said, "She looks so much at peace, doesn't she?"

"Yes. Any sign of life?"

"None yet. It may be too much to hope for. Just because her body has been perfectly preserved doesn't mean she can ever be revived."

"It would be such a shame," Carmoody said.

"What would?"

"To sleep for twenty thousand years, only to die without truly waking up."

CHAPTER TWELVE
~ October 23rd, 2285 ~

"I'm not familiar with this equipment, Commander," the chief medical doctor said to Christa as they stood looking at the viewer mounted on the central desk. "I don't know how to interpret these symbols. I can't tell if they're reporting the health of the patient or evaluating the hot chili in the mess hall."

"The symbols are Dakistian, Doctor, but that's as much as I can tell you. Can you at least tell me if she can be revived?"

"If, as you say, she's been entombed for nineteen thousand, four hundred years, the chances are astronomical. I agree she looks perfectly preserved, but that doesn't mean anything. She might have died almost twenty centuries ago, but something that was pumped into the body and stasis chamber might have destroyed all microbial life so there was nothing in the chamber to destroy the body."

"But the instruments seem to indicate they're measuring life signs."

"We can't know that. Perhaps that's the way their instruments appeared when life ended. Our monitors show a flat line, but that doesn't mean the ancient Dakistians designed theirs the same way."

A nurse, just one of a dozen medical personnel ringing the stasis chamber suddenly shouted, "Doctor Johannes, the patient's eyes are open."

"I— could have been incorrect, Commander, with my earlier statement. Nurse, are her eyes blinking?"

"No, Doctor. They're just wide open. Wait, they just blinked."

"It appears I was wrong, Commander. It seems that we have a nineteen thousand, four hundred year old patient on our hands."

"It's a lot more serious than that, Doctor. We have an entire cavern full of these stasis chambers. I don't know how many are occupied, but we could suddenly find ourselves awash in nineteen thousand, four hundred year olds."

"If that's true, I'm going to need a *lot* more help. Four doctors and eight nurses can't handle a cavern full of patients."

"I can't say it's going to happen right away. The awakening process with this individual was an accident. I was trying to determine how the control console worked. But it's possible I could have started a chain reaction of awakenings."

"If that happens, we're going to need transportation to take some of them to the hospital facilities at North Pendleton." Looking around, he added, "This entire medical facility can't handle more than a hundred patients at a time."

"We have a full floor of dormitories above this level. There are no medical facilities on that floor, but it's capable of housing about twelve thousand."

"Twelve thousand? Then they must have planned for a mass awakening."

"Or it was to provide housing for people waiting to undergo the process."

"What about food?" the doctor asked. "How much do you have down here?"

"None, as far as I know."

"Then you'd better lay in what supplies you can, just in case those others begin to awaken."

Turning to Carmoody, Christa said, "Gracie, you'd better see to that. We want to be prepared— just in case."

"Right away, Ma'am."

"Doctor!" the nurse shouted.

The shout brought the Doctor's attention back to the stasis chamber. The top had split down the middle and the two halves were sliding down into the base.

"Masks," Johannes shouted. "Everyone!"

A nurse, having already donned a full-face mask, hurried over with masks for Christa and the doctor.

"The patient also," Johannes shouted.

A nurse reached into the chamber and pulled a mask onto the woman as Doctor Johannes and Christa hurried over. Another nurse began sweeping the area around and over the chamber with some kind of electronic device.

The Dakistian was improving by the second. Her eyes seemed able to focus as she stared up at the people surrounding her. "Who are you?" she mumbled in ancient Dakis. The masks picked up the voice of the wearer and broadcast it clearly through tiny speakers on either side, but Christa was the only one who understood the words.

"You're among friends," Christa replied. You've just awakened from a very long sleep."

"Am I the first to awaken?"

"Yes."

"Good. That is as it was intended. Who are you?"

The nurse with the electronic device said, "I'm not picking up the presence of any dangerous, airborne pathogens. The sensor in the patient's mask gives the same clean readings."

"Everyone can remove their masks," the doctor said. "What's the patient saying, Commander?

"She wanted to know who we are," Christa said after removing her mask, "and if she was the first to awaken. I said she was among friends and that she was the first."

"Ask her if she feels any pain."

"Do you feel any pain?" Christa asked the woman.

"What language were you just speaking?"

"It's called Amer. It's the defacto standard in this part of the Galaxy now."

"But you also speak Dakis?"

"Yes. Although my words may sound a little strange to you. The language has changed somewhat during the many annuals you've slept. I've studied the differences, but before now I haven't had an opportunity to practice with someone from your time."

"My time? How long have I slept?"

"A very long time."

"*How* long?"

Christa remembered the shock Jenetta felt when she was told she had been asleep for ten years, but this woman would have to be told at some point.

"You've been asleep for about nineteen thousand, four hundred annuals."

"Nineteen thousand annuals? It has taken this long to find a cure for the sterility?"

"A cure was never found for the sterility problem."

"And you just let us sleep for a hundred ninety-four centuries?"

"Uh, no, not— *us*."

"Commander," the Doctor said, "I understand her desperate desire for information, but shouldn't we tend to her basic medical condition first? Please."

"Yes, Doctor." Turning back to the woman, she said, "I'll be happy to answer all your questions a little later. Right now the medical people are very concerned for your well being. First, how do you feel?"

"Can I remove this mask?" the woman asked.

Christa relayed the request to Johannes.

"Not just yet. Although we believe she can't infect us, she's at risk from germs we're carrying. We need to make sure her immune system is functioning and that she has been properly inoculated first."

With Christa translating, the basic medical examination was completed quickly. The woman felt fine and seemed to be in excellent shape. When the initial questions were answered, she was helped out of the sleep chamber so a physical exam could be completed. Unlike a stasis bed occupant, the patient was not debilitated in any way and was able to stand erect without assistance.

"She's in excellent condition," the doctor said when he was finished. "In fact, she appears healthier than most of the civilians I've examined on this planet. She can remove the mask now. I've administered the vaccinations she needs."

Christa made a motion to the woman that she could remove the mask. The patient understood immediately and pulled the mask off.

"Thank you, Doctor," Christa said." If you have no object-ions, I'd like to take her to get some clothes and perhaps something to eat. I know I'd be a little hungry after twenty thousand years without a meal."

"Commander, this woman has just awakened from a sleep that lasted almost two hundred centuries. I can't allow her to leave yet. She must be watched constantly until we know her condition is stable."

"You said she's in perfect health, so it shouldn't be a problem if we don't leave the facility. Perhaps one of the nurses can tag along? A female nurse would be best."

"Very well." Turning towards the group of medical personnel that was hanging on every word, the doctor said, "Nurse Racceht, would you accompany the Commander and the patient, please?"

"Of course, Doctor Johannes."

To Christa, the doctor said, "After you've completed your tasks, please bring her back here. We'll establish a twenty-four-hour watch over her."

"Of course, Doctor. Now, if you'll excuse us?"

As the doctor stepped out of the way, Christa escorted the woman from the Medical Center, with Nurse Racceht close behind.

"My name is Christa Carver," she said to the Dakistian. "What's your name?"

"I am Madu Ptellewqku. I am the Director of this institute. You said the sterility was never cured? How were you created? Are you a descendent of the people who left the planet?

"It's a very long story. Why don't we go up to one of the dormitories? I'll send for some clothing, and then we can sit and talk."

"I have clothes in my office."

"They've probably turned to dust by now."

"We anticipated a long sleep, although certainly not two hundred centuries. Our clothing has all been stored in vacuum containers after being thoroughly irradiated to destroy any organisms. It should be fine, although a bit out of style. Are you wearing a military uniform?"

"Yes, I am."

"That's a relief. If that was the current style among civilians, I would be most unhappy."

Christa smiled. "A fashion expert once said, 'If you're unhappy with today's fashion, just wait a week.' That's how often fashion changes these solars. As a result, there is no *real* fashion trend anymore. If you visit any space station, you'll see people wearing every fashion from the last hundred annuals."

"Space station? You mean like off-planet stations?"

"Yes. Most inhabited planets have at least one station in orbit to facilitate freight and passenger traffic."

"Inhabited planets? People travel between planets?"

The trio had reached the elevator and, as they stepped inside, Director Ptellewqku said, "Administrative level." The trip took just four seconds. As they stepped out, the Director activated the lighting and turned to the left. Christa let her lead the way.

"The galaxy has changed tremendously during the past two hundred centuries. Some of the changes are going to be quite a shock. People no longer think in planet-centric terms. At its widest point, the Galactic Alliance stretches more than three thousand light-annuals across."

Director Ptellewqku stopped walking and stared wide-eyed at Christa. "Three thousand *light-annuals*?"

"Yes."

"How is that possible? It must take tens of thousands of annuals to traverse that distance."

"Not anymore. It can be done in months now."

"We have faster-than-light speed? But our scientists have always said nothing can travel faster than light."

"Yes, that was the prevalent thinking. Then, a few hundred annuals ago scientists reported that they had discovered neutrinos traveling faster than light. It began a whole new investigation into the accepted theories of the time."

"Neutrinos?"

"Subatomic particles. Anyway, the old thinking about nothing traveling faster than light was eventually discarded and scientists began looking at FTL in a whole new way. FTL travel has been common for a very long time."

"And now you can travel thousands of light-annuals in mere months?"

"Yes."

"I think it will take time for me to become accustomed to this new world."

"New universe."

"Yes, new universe. Ah, here's my office."

Director Ptellewqku led the way through a large outer office and into her inner office. As she pressed her hand against a plate on the wall, a panel slid out of the way to reveal a large, walk-in closet. She disappeared inside while Christa and the nurse took seats to wait.

Several minutes later, the director appeared again still wearing the simple terrycloth gown. "The water in my bathroom doesn't flow."

"That was to be expected," Christa said. "After so many centuries, the pipes will probably have to be flushed."

"I see. Well, I'll make do," the director said as she disappeared into the closet again.

When she again emerged from the walk-in closet, the director was dressed in a stylish skirt suit that resembled a Terran fashion of a decade ago. There was only so much that could be done with clothes and it had all been done a thousand times already.

"Very attractive outfit, Madame Director," Christa said.

"Thank you, but please call me Madu."

"I will, Madu, if you will call me Christa."

"It's a deal." Looking at the officer dressed in hospital whites, Madu said, "And your name is?"

The nurse just looked at her questioningly.

Christa interrupted with, "I doubt if the nurse speaks either Dakis or Ancient Dakis."

"Ancient Dakis?"

"The language has changed slightly over the centuries so we make a distinction between the two dialects. The version you speak is referred to as Ancient Dakis, while the version spoken by the people of Nordakia is called Dakis."

"Nordakia?"

"The dissidents who left here so long ago named their colony Nordakia."

"I see. And that is where you're from?"

"Uh, no. Actually I was born here on Dakistee, but my lineage is Terran."

"Terran?"

"Yes. We're called either Terrans or Humans. We originally come from a planet called Earth, which is located about one hundred light-annuals from here. Our physiology is very close to yours, but there are some slight differences. There has been a lot of speculation about our two races having a common origin but nothing conclusive as yet."

"I see," Madu said slowly. "I did notice that your complexion was lighter than my race, and your hair color is definitely different."

"That's not all," Christa said, pulling back the hair that covered her ears.

Madu was clearly shocked. "I saw those on the males in the medical center. Do all your people have those appendages?"

"Yes. We call them ears."

"And you say you were born here on Dakistee. What's the percentage of Dakistians to Terrans?"

"As far as anyone knew, your race died out nineteen thousand four hundred annuals ago, give or take a few decades."

"Died out?"

"This facility was buried under the rubble of a decaying city. Archeologists discovered it less than an annual ago. I was summoned to see if I could gain access because of my knowledge of Dakis and Ancient Dakis. My sisters and I have studied the Ancient Dakis dialect and written books about your people, so we're considered the foremost experts on your race. The archeologists who uncovered this facility were unable to gain entrance, so they asked my sister to come here. She was unavailable, so she sent me."

"You said you were born here. Do *your* people now inhabit this planet, or have our descendents returned?"

"Uh, that's a complex issue. It will take some time to fully explain everything."

Over the next couple of hours, Christa related the history of the past twenty years as best she could, as well as a brief history of the Galactic Alliance. She was summing up when she was interrupted by a call from Carmoody. She held up her hand and looked away as a signal to Madu that she was pausing their conversation.

"Commander, are you receiving me," Christa heard.

She responded with, "Yes, Gracie. You got the new communications unit set up, I see."

"Yes, ma'am. We're still having trouble communicating with the surface, but internal communications seem to be working fine. The Marines are going to set up a couple of repeaters— one in the tunnel about halfway to the surface, and one at the entrance of the tunnel that will relay from Fort Carver where they have the satellite uplink."

"Very good."

"Where are you, Commander? I've looked around here on the dormitory level but haven't located you."

"I'm on the Administrative level. If you want to come down, I'll have the nurse meet you at the elevator."

"I'll be there in a few minutes."

Nurse Racceht was already on her feet when Christa nodded for her to go.

"You were speaking with someone?" Madu asked when Christa lowered her hand.

"Yes, my subordinate."

"But you have no radio."

Christa explained about the miniscule CT implanted under the skin beneath her left ear.

"Interesting," Madu said. "Do you have any other implants?"

"No, but there are other implants available for people with birth defects or special requirements."

"I wish we had had your scientific knowledge twenty centuries ago."

"It might not be too late."

"What do you mean?"

"It's possible that our scientists can find something your scientists overlooked. It might be possible to reestablish your people here. How many stasis beds are occupied in the Vault?"

"All of them. All thirty thousand."

"I suspected that might be the case. Are they all set to wake up at some predetermined time after you?"

"No. I can wake as many or as few as I wish. The controls were set to awaken me first when the console was accessed."

"A population of thirty thousand would be a good start towards repopulating the planet."

"A hundred eighty thousand would be better."

"You mean there are other facilities like this one?"

"Yes, there are six, as represented by the six cylinders required to open the main doors."

"And how many cloning labs are there?"

"Just one. That experiment was a failure."

"Not completely."

"Oh, it worked as far as creating identical clones, but the intent was to create clones that weren't sterile."

"Why didn't you create babies instead of duplicates?"

"We tried that, but the babies were also sterile and, strangely, during that process mutations crept in after a couple of generations. With normal copulation, we discovered that the ovum were perfectly healthy and the spermatozoon were eager to join, but conception never occurred. We also tried in vitro fertilization, but that failed as well. It was decided that the scientists should continue to work on the problem while a good cross section of the society went into stasis. When the problem was solved, they would begin to awaken us and we could repopulate the planet. I never expected to sleep so long. I hope we can eventually discover what happened."

Nurse Racceht returned with Carmoody and the two officers sat down while Christa continued her conversation with Madu.

"I'd tell you if I knew, Madu. Do you know where the other stasis facilities are located?"

"Generally. If I could find a map of the cities, I could pinpoint them exactly, but if the cities have crumbled to the ground, it may be impossible to establish their locations precisely."

"That won't be a problem. We have maps of the cities and can pinpoint any location using topographic mapping techniques. Without them, we would never have been able to find the cylinders that unlocked the outer door."

"Did you find a journal or something that told you how the unlocking process worked?"

"No, I was able to piece it together using the markings on the door."

Madu was quiet for a few seconds. "Our scientists told us no one would ever be able to solve the puzzle without first receiving instructions."

"It is pretty complex, so I guess I got lucky. It's getting late, so you should be getting back to the Medical level to get some rest. We can talk again tomorrow."

"Are you the only one down here who speaks Dakis?"

"Yes, but after I get clearance for the archeologists to enter the facility I can introduce you to some of the Nordakians who're working at the dig site."

"You referring to the descendents of the dissidents who left the planet twenty thousand annuals ago?"

"Yes."

"I don't wish to talk with them— ever."

"Why not?"

"I can't talk about it."

"Is it because of the role the dissidents played in spreading the plague?"

"You know about that?"

"I found a file in the cloning facility that contained documents about the investigation, but it's restricted information.

When the current leaders learned of it, they were aghast and ashamed of their ancestors. I'm one of the few Nordakians outside of the royal family, top political leaders, and top church leaders who knows of the treachery."

"You said before you were a Terran."

"I come from Terran lineage and I'm a citizen of Earth, but I'm also a citizen of Nordakia. And since I was born on Dakistee, I'm one of only seventy-nine citizens of this planet."

"Only seventy-nine people have been born on Dakistee in twenty centuries?"

"Well, there are only seventy-nine citizens. Fifteen annuals ago, the Galactic Alliance declared that until a formal government is established, anyone newly born on the planet is only a citizen of their parent's planet or planets. It's another involved explanation that should wait until tomorrow."

"Will we be able to begin the awakenings tomorrow?"

"I think Doctor Johannes will probably want to wait a few solars to see if any complications arise from your awakening before he approves of others. You seem perfectly healthy, but we have no experience with anyone being in stasis more than ten annuals. We must make sure the inoculations are effective. We don't want to contaminate your race with germs for which we've built up an immunity but to which you're still vulnerable. If something does happen, it would be better if they could concentrate all their efforts on healing just one person. Please try to be patient while we develop a safe procedure for awakening the others. I'm sure it won't be long before we can begin the process."

CHAPTER THIRTEEN
~ October 23rd, 2285 ~

After escorting Madu back to the Medical level, Christa remained there until Doctor Johannes had completed another brief examination and declared her condition to be unchanged from earlier. Christa told Carmoody to get some rest because the next day was going to be a busy one, then went in search of Lt. Uronson. She found him topside, talking with Staff Sergeant Burton just out of hearing range of the two sentries at the entrance to the tunnel. They stopped talking and turned to face her as she approached.

"Lieutenant, we have a situation."

"Yes, ma'am, I've heard."

"How much have you heard."

"I heard that you found a woman who's been in stasis for twenty thousand years. I also heard that the medical people were able to revive her and that she is apparently healthy."

"Is that it?"

"Yes, ma'am. Is there more?"

"Quite a bit, but I can't discuss it out here in case our conversation is being recorded by someone in the archeologist's camp."

"We've laid a scram-line in the trench that surrounds the camp. It creates an unbroken, vertical wall of RF interference that extends ten meters up. They can see us, but not eavesdrop on our conversations. All they'll hear is static."

"Just in case they've got someone incredibly adept at lip-reading, or they've found some other way around that, I'll hold the news until we're in a more secure location, such as below ground."

"Yes, ma'am."

"The significance of this find justifies some changes. I believe this location will shortly be designated as the new command center, and I want to have all our people handy, so I want you to clear everything out of Fort Carver and set up your operation here. Select one of the dormitories near the elevator for the use of yourself and your people. When the old facility is clear, close and password lock the main door. Are you familiar with the process and do you know the password?"

"Yes, ma'am."

"Good."

"When should we begin the move?"

"Whenever you feel ready, but I want it to be completed by 1800 hours tomorrow. Central Command Supply will be delivering foodstuff that will also have to be transported into this facility and stored. They should arrive tomorrow."

"Yes, ma'am."

"Any other questions?"

"Are you expecting trouble, ma'am?"

"Yes. When word gets out about this momentous discovery, every scientist on this planet is going to be trying to get in. Our job will be to keep them out until Space Command Headquarters approves their admittance."

"I don't think a bunch of weak sister, geeb scientists are going to offer us much of a challenge."

"Would you consider me to be an inconsequential opponent?"

"You? No ma'am. Only a fool would underestimate one of the Carver women."

"Yet I'm a scientist— and a woman. The Raiders made the mistake of underestimating me on that basis. Let's not do the same with the civilians here. Some of them may be a much more formidable opponent than you suspect— especially the women."

"Yes, ma'am."

"Carry on."

Christa then walked tiredly across the small base to her shuttle, composing a message in her head as she went. She knew this news was going to be a bombshell, the repercuss-ions of which would last a normal lifetime, so she wanted to make sure her message was absolutely clear, and pithy.

She sat in the pilot chair as she prepared herself to deliver the news, then sat up straight and reached out to activate the recording equipment.

"Message to Admiral Moore and the Members of the Admiralty Board, Space Command Supreme Headquarters, Earth, with copies to Admiral Jenetta Carver and Admiral Brian Holt.

"Ladies and Gentlemen,

"Please forgive this breach of protocol, but I felt my news too important for you to remain uninformed while this mess-age travels to Admiral Carver in Region Two and then back again, and I believe she will approve of my act.

"I don't know if you've yet received word of yesterday's discovery through Admiral Holt. I thought we had discovered an ancient mausoleum at the lowest level of the new facility, but, upon further investigation, I've discovered that it's actually a stasis chamber. During today's investigation of an operator's console there, a process was initiated that delivered one of the believed coffins to the Medical level and began the automated process to resuscitate the occupant.

"Ladies, and Gentlemen, the occupant of that stasis chamber, has since been identified as Madu Ptellewqku, the Director of this institute. Doctor Johannes from the Marine Central Command HQ Medical Center has declared her to be, so far, perfectly healthy after her sleep of almost twenty thousand years. She is awake and alert, and was able to walk on her own within minutes of being awakened. I'm sure I don't have to tell you what this stasis process will mean to the Galactic Alliance if it works as well for humans and other species as it does for the Dakistian people.

"Aside from that, Ms. Ptellewqku has informed me that the Vault at this location contains thirty thousand members from a cross-section of her race. Further, she claims that each of the cities where the cylinders were found also contains such a facility. The population put into stasis totaled one hundred eighty thousand. It would appear that Dakistee is not the deserted planet it was thought to be.

"Tomorrow, I shall renew my investigation of the other levels found at this location, but I felt you should be informed immediately of today's momentous discoveries.

"Christa Marie Carver, Lt. Commander, Mission Commander, Loudescott Base Two, Dakistee, message complete."

After exhaling a sigh, Christa made a quick meal and then climbed into bed. She was asleep in seconds.

◆ ◆

Christa dropped her spoon into what remained of her cereal and was out of the shuttle in a flash the following morning as tugs from Central Command Supply began dropping shipping containers off at the new camp.

Carmoody was already there talking with Staff Sergeant Burton when Christa reached the tunnel entrance. Christa walked up and said, "Gracie, what is this?"

"The food and clothing I ordered yesterday, ma'am."

"All of this?"

"Yes, ma'am."

"How much did you requisition?"

"I had no idea how many might awaken as a result of our actions, so I told Supply we needed enough for a thousand people for thirty days. I also ordered a portable tailoring machine and enough fabric to make three changes of clothing for a thousand people, plus footwear."

"And all this is for just a thousand people? I don't want to think how much we'll need for thirty thousand."

"Did I order too much?"

"No, Gracie. I just wasn't considering how large the shipments would be. Sergeant Burton, you'd better get your 'oh-gee' sleds and cargo bots cranked up."

"Yes, ma'am. We're ready, and we'll begin operations just as soon as these crazy tug jockeys stop dropping containers all over the place."

"Carry on, Sergeant. Gracie, when you're finished up here, join me on the Medical level."

"Yes, ma'am."

◆　◆

"Good morning, Madu," Christa said as she reached the chair in the ward where the woman was reclining.

"Good morning, Christa. Are they going to let me go this solar? They're driving me crazy with their hourly examinations."

Christa smiled. "I know how exasperating it can seem, but it's only because we're concerned for your health. As I told you, we're not only worried about the effects of the stasis process, but also about possible contamination from modern pathogens for which your body has no immunity. You've been vaccinated, but it takes time for an immune system to property develop the antibodies."

"This is a stall, isn't it?"

"A stall?"

"Christa, I wasn't appointed as director of this stasis institute because of scientific expertise in this field. I'm an administrator, which is about the closest thing there is to being a politician without being elected. I know a stall when I see one. You're waiting on instructions from above aren't you, so you're keeping me here until they give you your marching orders. They haven't decided yet if they're going to let you awaken my people, have they?"

Christa smiled. "Madu, I assure you that we will attempt to awaken every one of your people."

"Attempt?"

"I naturally can't guarantee that everyone can be resuscitated. We hope that's the case, but it has been twenty-thousand annuals. But I promise you that you can participate in every effort and verify for yourself that we are doing our best."

"But not until your superiors decide to start the awakenings."

"Come with me, Madu." To a nearby nurse, Christa said, "I'm taking Madu to the surface to see her planet. If there's any problem, I'll summon help, but I don't think we need anyone along."

The nurse looked over at Dr. Johannes, who grimaced and then nodded reluctantly.

As the elevator opened at the rotunda, Madu gasped slightly. The enormous room was filling quickly with delivered supplies that hadn't been taken to the dormitory level yet.

"This is food and clothing for you and your people. When we checked the mess halls, we found no sign of foodstuffs nor clothing in any of the dormitories."

"Every person in stasis has a vacuum canister stored on the Recreation level."

"I wasn't aware of that because we haven't toured that level yet. Well, I'll tell them to forego clothing in future supply deliveries."

As they approached the facility entrance, a PFC there said into a radio, "Outgoing traffic. Hold new sleds."

They waited several minutes until a loaded sled hovered into the rotunda, and then entered the tunnel when the PFC waved them on. Madu was fascinated by the oh-gee capability.

"It's opposed gravity technology. We call it 'oh-gee.'"

As they emerged on the surface, Madu immediately appeared depressed and spiritually crestfallen. "Christa, I'm sorry. I owe you an apology."

"For what, Madu?"

"I didn't really believe you. It just didn't seem like twenty thousand annuals could have passed." Madu turned and let her eyes sweep the horizon in a three-hundred-sixty-degree arc. "But now that I see for myself, I can believe it. My beautiful city has utterly disappeared."

"Twenty thousand annuals of rain, wind, and sun take an extraordinary toll on buildings. As I understand it, the first explorers to this planet were able to speculate it had once been populated only because of the unusual topographic features, which resulted from collapsed buildings in major cities. Perhaps now you can also appreciate why we must awaken your people slowly, rather than all at once. Aside from the health concerns, there're also the issues of habitat and sustenance. We would be hard pressed to feed an additional one hundred eighty thousand people, or even thirty thousand more people, until we could arrange for food shipments and the construction of shelters to house them."

Madu just shook her head gently. "My beautiful city. My beautiful, beautiful city. I wish you could have seen it, Christa. Dakistee had many beautiful cities and places, but nothing like the capitol here."

"I have seen it, Madu. It lives on through images stored in the computers we've found. The planet is still a beautiful world, and, when your people are reestablished, you can begin to rebuild your cities. The GA will help."

"I'd love to see what images you have."

"Of course. But another solar, okay. This solar I'd like you to give me a tour of your institute."

"I'd be happy to show you around."

"Wonderful. We'll pick up Lt. Carmoody when we go back down."

"Uh, Christa?"

"Yes?"

"Does Lt. Carmoody speak Dakis? It seemed like she was following our conversation while the nurse showed no comprehension."

"Grace doesn't speak Dakis or Ancient Dakis. She has reason to be a lot more interested because of her position on my staff, but she doesn't understand more than an occasional word."

"I see. I didn't want her to think I was slighting her by speaking only to you."

"I'm sure she didn't feel slighted, and I assure you that she couldn't have responded. Shall we go?"

As the two women descended into the tunnel behind a sled filled with supplies, Christa contacted Carmoody and arranged to meet her on the Rotunda level.

◆ ◆

Carmoody was in the Rotunda when Christa and Madu arrived. Christa commandeered the elevator for a quick trip without supplies and they stepped inside.

Madu said, "Administrative level," in Dakis, and the elevator replied with, "Yes, Director Ptellewqku."

When the instruction to close the doors was given, Christa and Carmoody braced themselves for the drop, but it never occurred. Instead, the doors at the back of the elevator opened.

Christa grinned as they stepped out. "When we visited your office last time, I didn't realize it was on the same level as the Rotunda. We came here from the Medical level and then returned there afterwards."

"It made sense to do it this way. Newly arriving people were automatically taken to the Housing level where they were met by someone who would escort them to their dormitories to await their sleep appointment."

"How did you select who would be put into stasis?"

"The selection process was a bit unfair, but we did what was best for our society. We established two age thresholds. Using the first, we invited the greatest minds below that point to join the sleepers. Many declined because they wanted to live out their remaining years with their families."

"That's understandable."

"Yes. After that, we used the second threshold, a much lower one, to select a cross section of society because once sterility was overcome, we would need people who could repopulate our world. It's depressing that our scientists were apparently never able to accomplish their task."

"I'm sure that once news of your survival surfaces, the scientists on dozens of world will begin working on a solution."

"I hope so, and that they have more success than my own people."

As they reached the area outside Madu's office, she said, "I just want to check something. I'll be right out." With that, she disappeared through the doorway.

As the door slid closed behind Madu, Christa turned towards Carmoody and said in a lowered voice, "Gracie, I told Madu you don't speak any Dakis or Ancient Dakis. You told me you've been studying it, but I don't know how much you've picked up. I'd prefer that Madu think you don't know any."

"Of course, Christa. May I ask why?"

"Madu compared herself to a politician yesterday. Someone once said that politicians never say what they mean and never mean what they say. If Madu believes you don't understand her words, she may speak more openly in front of you when others are awakened."

"You don't trust her?"

"I don't really know her, so she hasn't won my trust yet. She observed that you were paying attention like you understood yesterday, so don't change that. It's okay to continue listening closely as if you're trying to understand, but if she asks you anything directly, play dumb— even if you understand all or even part of it."

"Okay, Christa."

Madu emerged from the office carrying a viewpad a few minutes later. "I accessed the computer to look up some information. I'd like to wake my assistant up later when we're in the Vault."

"We still haven't verified that it's safe to begin waking others."

"I feel wonderful and there've been no indications the awakening process is detrimental to anyone's health. Besides, it would be good to have a second individual for the medical people to monitor now that I've experienced no complications."

Christa hesitated for a moment, then said, "Okay, but I want the medical people to check you over one last time before we awaken anyone else to ensure that everything is still okay."

"That's fine," Madu said with a smile. "Follow me and I'll give you a tour of this level before we go down to the next."

◆　◆

The tour of the Administrative level took four hours because Christa insisted that she see every room in order to verify personally that no technology with restricted access could fall into the wrong hands. But all they found was ordinary and outdated computer hardware and office assets. Tracking software proved that her CT had visited every part of the level by creating a detailed floor plan as they went.

Before continuing their exploration, they visited the mess hall set up on the Housing level by the Marines. The layout was the same as the mess hall in Fort Carver, so the cooks hadn't had any trouble adapting, but they'd had to bring water from the other facility because there was no water available here as yet.

After lunch, the tour continued on the Recreation level. Owing to the numerous large open areas reserved for sports activities, the tour was completed in half the time of that required for the Administrative level. Four enormous swimming pools were available there, but, like everywhere else in the facility, there was no water. One section of the level contained the tens of thousands of vacuum canisters that Madu said contained the clothes of the sleepers.

Madu again received a clean bill of health from Doctor Johannes, who quipped, "You're the healthiest twenty thousand year old female I've ever examined."

Christa's translation brought a smile to Madu's face.

"Thank you, Doctor," Madu said. Then it's alright to begin awakening some of my people?"

When Christa translated, Doctor Johannes looked at Christa sharply. "I wouldn't go that far. Are you authorizing the awakenings, Commander?"

"I've told Madu that we'll awaken her assistant, subject to your approval. Having a familiar face nearby will make her feel more comfortable as we try to establish a schedule for further awakenings. I believe she harbors some concern that we don't intend to awaken the others. I've explained that we're moving slowly due to health concerns for the awakened and because of logistics regarding food and shelter for so many."

"Provided we can continue to closely monitor both awakened individuals, I have no objections."

"How long do you anticipate you'll have to monitor the Dakistians?"

"I don't know. We're in uncharted territory here. I suppose that if no complications arise, thirty days should be adequate."

"Thank you, Doctor."

CHAPTER FOURTEEN

~ October 24th, 2285 ~

Chairman Arthur Strauss reached down and tapped the com button on his desk and the face of Councilman Ahil Fazid filled the wall monitor in his office.

"Yes, Ahil," Strauss said. "What is it?"

"Arthur, I've just received a message from Dakistee. Commander Carver's assistant exited the tunnel in an agitated manner and contacted someone. I've also received word that a Marine Emergency Medical team lifted off minutes later."

"And?"

"Don't you see? Carver must have opened the facility. I don't know what happened, but something must have occurred down there. This presents us with a great opportunity to take the facility while they're distracted. I'm recommending that we launch the attack as soon as possible."

"You believe the two reports are linked?"

"I do."

"Very well. Send a message to our people there and have them commence the operation immediately."

"Yes, Arthur."

◆ ◆ ◆

"I call this emergency session to order," Admiral Moore said in the Admiralty Board meeting hall. The other admirals were all in attendance, but only aides and senior clerks had been allowed to join them in the large chamber on this occasion.

"We've received a message from Lt. Commander Christa Carver that requires our immediate attention."

"Carver?" Admiral Hubera said loudly.

"Yes, Donald. Now please hold your comments until we view the message." Admiral Moore nodded to the clerk staffing the equipment console. A head and shoulders image of Christa appeared on the full wall monitor, and she began to speak.

When the message was over, the first to speak was Hubera.

"As soon as I heard her name, I knew she was about to hand us a major headache."

"Donald, you can hardly blame Commander Carver for a situation on Dakistee that began twenty thousand years ago," Admiral Platt said. "Be reasonable."

All Hubera did was mutter and grind his teeth.

"One hundred eighty thousand," Admiral Ahmed, the Space Command Quartermaster said. "I think we'd better prepare some food and clothing shipments immediately."

"Yes, Raihana," Admiral Moore said, "but right now I'm more concerned with the diplomatic situation. The Galactic Alliance, after an exhaustive investigation to guarantee that no sentient life existed on Dakistee, made numerous concessions to the archeological community. Now we find that we have given away land we had no right to give."

"It's not our fault they buried themselves several hundred meters below the surface of a planet we thought uninhabited," Admiral Hubera.

"No, not our fault, perhaps, but we'll have to deal with it nonetheless. I've requested an emergency session of the GA Council to apprise them of the situation, but while I wait for them to gather, I wanted to inform all of you of the message. As Raihana says, we'll have to send food and other supplies as quickly as possible."

"These people haven't been awakened yet," Admiral Bradlee said, "so there's no imminent need."

"Even though the speed of our new transports would allow me to send supplies in just a few days," Admiral Ahmed said, "it will still takes weeks to make arrangements and prepare the supplies for shipment. I must be ahead of the curve on this."

"Quite right, Raihana," Admiral Moore said. "By all means make your preparations so we'll be ready when the Council gives us the order to deliver the supplies, as I feel sure they will."

◆　◆　◆

Madu stood at the operations console entering basic information until an image of her assistant appeared on the monitor. As the image stabilized, she pressed the contact point marked, 'Kudlaknee.' As when Madu was awakened, the viewer immediately changed to show a series of numbers as console gauges came to life, then a steadily increasing wave-form filled the viewer. There was only silence for several minutes until a noise from above drew their attention. A stasis box was being carried along by a suspended robotic arm. Another arm accepted the delivered chamber and gently lowered it to the floor where an automated cart was waiting. As with Madu's awaking, the cart accepted the box and left for the Medical level with its precious cargo as soon as the box was securely positioned. The three women followed along.

◆　◆

In the medical center, Dr. Johannes and a handful of nurses watched as the box was delivered. The automated process performed as before, and there was nothing to do until the cover rolled down so the staff would have access to a man who appeared to be about twenty in human terms. Dr. Johannes immediately administered an inoculation.

Christa had expected a female, or perhaps a slightly built man, but the male before them was young, extremely handsome, and very muscular. It would seem that Madu had selected some eye candy for her office. However, perhaps Christa was jumping to an erroneous conclusion. The man might be a very competent secretary.

"That's her assistant?" Carmoody said to Christa in a voice just above a whisper.

Christa shrugged and said, "That's what she told us."

"I want one like that too."

Christa smiled and said, "Perhaps for your twenty-thousandth birthday, I'll get you one."

Carmoody barely managed to suppress a chortle.

Christa and Carmoody stayed in the Medical center until the young man was on his feet and introductions had been made. The two Space Command officers then headed up to the Marine mess hall to have dinner. Madu would spend another night in the Medical center where the staff could watch over her. Meals for her and her assistant would be provided from the small kitchen on that level.

◆ ◆

"Do you think that's really her assistant?" Carmoody asked Christa as they ate dinner in the mess hall.

"I don't know. I suppose it doesn't really matter. I'm sure she felt alone and isolated, despite our best attempts to put her at ease. Whether he was her assistant or a lover, she now has someone she can talk to— and in whom she can confide."

"May I join you, ladies?" Lt. Uronson asked.

Neither of the women had been aware of his approach but both looked up at him now.

"Of course, Lieutenant," Christa said. "Please sit down."

"I heard you awakened another ancient sleeper," Uronson said matter-of-factly to Christa.

"Yes. Director Ptellewqku requested that I permit her assistant to join her."

Uronson just nodded.

"Have you completed the move, Lieutenant?" Christa asked.

"Yes, ma'am. Everything in Fort Carver that wasn't nailed or bolted down is now in this facility. We placed a large boulder atop the emergency exit into the sewer line and sealed the entrance door with the password."

"A boulder?"

"Yes. The exit tunnel door was already locked, but this makes it doubly protected. Of course, there's nothing left in there to steal, but this ensures that we won't have to worry about squatters breaking in."

"Very good."

"Ma'am, I've received orders to send two fire teams and one sergeant to HQ for deployment to another site."

"What?"

"It seems there's a bit of trouble in one or more of the other dig sites and Central Command is rushing people in to safeguard the scientists and the artifacts they've recovered."

"But we only have one squad to begin with."

"Yes, ma'am. But I have my orders."

"How soon are they supposed to leave?"

"As we speak. Sergeant Flegetti is handling the deployment."

Christa jumped up from the table, and said, "Excuse me, I have to look into this. I'll see you both in the morning. Good night."

"Hell of a way to run an operation," Carmoody said to Uronson. "You'd think Central Command would at least have notified the outpost commander before ordering half her security force to another outpost."

Uronson just grimaced and began eating his dinner.

◆ ◆

"Colonel, I need those people here," Christa said to the image of Lt. Colonel Diminjik, the current commanding officer of Dakistee's Marine Central Command, as it appeared on her shuttle's main viewscreen. "We only just managed to open this facility two days ago. I really need at least a platoon here, if not a full company."

"I'm sorry, Commander. There's serious trouble brewing at several warehouse sites and they're all screaming for more protection. We're also having problems in the larger towns with fights and thefts. By contrast, things are pretty quiet at your outpost so you can get by for a few days. I promise to send them back just as soon as I can."

"Very well, Colonel," Christa said with a grimace. She didn't have the authority to order him to send her people back.

After the connection was ended, Christa prepared for bed. She was looking forward to getting some much needed rest after a tiring day, but sleep wouldn't come. She had a bad feeling about the coming days. She knew Madu would continue to press for more awakenings and, with each awakened ancient, the situation would get more complicated.

She continued to toss and turn for several hours, until she finally drifted off with the thought that maybe she should request a return to Region Two. After all, she had completed the task she was sent here to accomplish. Perhaps it was time for the diplomats and bean-counting administrators to take over.

◆　◆　◆

Christa awoke alert, if not totally refreshed, at her usual time and prepared for the new day. Before leaving to grab some breakfast in the Marine mess hall, she decided to send a message to Admiral Holt. She entered the shuttle cockpit as she composed a message in her head.

"Message to Admiral Brian Holt, Commanding Officer of Higgins SCB with a copy to Admiral Jenetta Carver, Commander of Space Command's Second Fleet and Military Governor of Region Two.

"Admiral, last evening half of my small security force was recalled to Central Command for redeployment to another location. I'm left with just half a squad as a protection detail. Perhaps that would have been adequate for the previous facility but not this one. When transmitting messages not directed to you, I've always included you on the copy list so you remain fully aware of the situation here. I've done my best to keep a lid on information about our discovery, but something this big can't be contained for long. To date, I've fully toured three floors and a small portion of the Medical, Research & Library level. The Vault level is almost virgin ground. I've not found any technology that must be secured, but that could change quickly in the Research & Library areas, and even in the Vault. The stasis process is a technological breakthrough that must be explored, but it doesn't violate any GA laws with which I'm familiar. However, I fully expect at any time to be inundated with scientists from around the planet, all of whom will be anxious to meet the ancients and explore the facility.

"Admiral, I must have a larger security force. I understand that personnel are in short supply on this planet, but my need for at least a full squad must take priority.

"Thank you, sir.

"Christa Marie Carver , Lieutenant Commander, Loudescott Outpost 2 Commander, Dakistee, message complete."

Christa reviewed the message before transmitting it. She wanted it to sound like an urgent appeal, but not a cry of desperation. Satisfied that it was appropriate, she tapped the transmit key, then sighed silently and left for the underground facility.

◆ ◆ ◆

"Good morning Gracie," Christa said to Carmoody as she placed her tray on the table and sat down across from her assistant. The mess hall, capable of seating about a hundred fifty, was deserted except for the one cook normally on permanent assignment to the Fort Carver outpost.

"Good morning." Carmoody waited until Christa was settled, then asked, "What's on the schedule for today?"

"I'm expecting an easy day. I need one. I want to survey the Research and Library areas first. If we have enough time, we'll examine the Vault in more detail."

"Great. Now that I know the Vault contains sleepers and not dead bodies, I'm sort of anxious to look around myself. I'm excited about the technology that will let someone sleep for twenty thousand years and then be awakened in prime physical condition. I never thought such a thing was possible. If their medical science was so advanced and sophisticated that they could accomplish that, is there any chance we can succeed with the sterility problem where they failed?"

"I don't know. I certainly hope so."

Christa was only halfway through her breakfast when she received a message from Lt. Uronson."

"Commander," Uronson said, "I'm topside at the tunnel entrance. There's a large contingent walking across the base from the direction of the current dig location."

"I'll be right up," Christa said. "Carver out." To Gracie, she said rhetorically, "What now?" and then grimaced as she pushed her tray away, stood up, and stepped away from the table.

Carmoody did likewise and the two officers hurried out of the mess hall.

Upon reaching the surface, they saw an enormous group of Terrans and Nordakians, perhaps as many as a hundred, standing about ten meters from the tunnel entrance where the sentries had halted them. The four Marines were aiming their weapons towards the crowd, but so far their fingers were only on the trigger guards because the crowd had stopped when ordered to do so.

Christa walked forward until she was less than two meters from the group. As she scanned the faces of the crowd, she realized she recognized all but one. She naturally knew all the members of the original scientific group and their clones. Also in the group were the dig site labor supervisor, his chief assistant, several lesser assistant labor foremen, and the site's emergency medical technician. The one person Christa didn't recognize was a woman who would stand out in any crowd. She appeared to be about twenty-two or twenty-three and stood out not only because of her attractive looks, but because while the others were all dressed in work clothes she was wearing a very expensive business suit. Christa thought she might be from Expedition Headquarters here on the planet, or even a representative from Anthius. Looking at Dr. Peterson, who, as usual, was front center, she said, "What is this, Doctor?"

"We want to enter the facility *we* found."

"That's not possible yet. You know that."

"Just what have you found, Commander, that we're not allowed to see? We're hearing all sorts of rumors, and we'd have to be deaf and blind not to notice all the cargo containers being delivered and removed. We know you've been successful in gaining entrance, so it's about time you came clean."

"As you speculated, I have been able to enter the facility. I'm sure you realized the situation had changed when the Marine presence here was upgraded. But I can't yet allow any civilians to enter because we haven't finished our investigations. Until I do, I can't deem it safe for you to enter. Plus I don't yet know if the facility contains contraband material that must be protected from falling into the wrong hands."

"You're saying we're the wrong hands?"

"Anyone who's not legally authorized to posses such material is the wrong hands, Doctor. Since you don't have permission from the Galactic Council to possess contraband material, yours would be the wrong hands."

"But I do have permission."

"What? What do you mean?"

"I have special permission from the Galactic Alliance Chairman to be granted immediate access to the facility and the right to examine any and all artifacts found inside."

"I'd like to see proof of that. Do you have any with you?"

"I do." Holding out a holo-magazine cylinder, he said," Here it is, Commander."

Christa accepted the cylinder and a document sprung up along the cylinder's length as she activated it. It was a bit difficult to see in the bright light from the rising sun, but she was able to make out the message.

"This is just a general letter stating you have permission to view any artifacts on the planet. It doesn't address the subject of contraband."

"It states that I have permission to view *any* artifacts. It doesn't exclude artifacts that may be considered contraband."

"Neither does it include them," Christa said. "I see this letter was signed by a *third* deputy assistant to the Chairman of the GA Council. Even if it was signed by the GA Chairman personally, it wouldn't override GA laws governing possession and access to contraband property."

"So you're going to ignore our rights?"

"No, I'm going to continue to protect them, as is my duty. That duty requires me to see that unauthorized persons don't acquire or possess contraband materials, and that's what I'm going to do to the best of my ability. No letter from a senior clerk in the GAC Chairman's office abrogates the law."

"We don't want to possess contraband material, we just want to examine it— in your presence of course."

"The last time you examined something you should have left alone, the consequences were almost disastrous. I personally appreciate that they resulted in my birth, but the outcome could have been far different. Technically, you have already violated GA law regarding the possession of contraband because you didn't notify Space Command as soon as you discovered the facility. Instead, you spent weeks trying to open it. You could still be charged because you knew the facility itself was sheathed in Dakinium, which is a crime to possess. However, since you were unable to break in, no charges are currently being considered."

"We didn't possess that facility; we simply uncovered it."

"It's located on the Loudescott dig site. You were aware of its presence and didn't notify Space Command immediately. That technically makes it a crime. But as I said, I'm not pursuing criminal charges at this time— although I still could." Christa hoped the implication was loud and clear. Her only desire was for an end to the verbal sparring, but Dr. Peterson didn't seem disposed to give up that easily.

"Commander, we both know Space Command isn't going to act on such a charg…"

Peterson stopped in mid-sentence as a fighter aircraft suddenly roared over the dig site. The mean-looking little ship had approached at treetop level without warning and the startled spectators were frozen in their positions as it overflew the site from the direction of the current dig. It had hardly passed when a second appeared from the same direction. Although the first had only disturbed the morning quiet, the second began to spit death as soon as it came into range. The first rounds struck the dig area where laborers were toiling to remove millennia of soil deposits, but as it passed over the Marine base location, hundreds of lattice rounds pounded the ground just behind the civilians massed to demand access to the facility.

The military personnel, trained to react quickly, didn't waste time gawking at the fighter. They opened fire with their laser rifles as Christa screamed for the civilians to get undercover in the tunnel. When they simply stared at her dumbly, she began to physically drag a couple towards the entrance. The others finally got the idea and galloped towards the safety of the underground facility as a third fighter appeared above the site and fired its lattice weapons with abandon.

Some of the civilians tripped and fell, but the ones behind them never stopped running. Those who made it to safety left behind a bloody trail of trampled injured. As the third fighter disappeared from view, Christa and the Marines began helping the hurt civilians get to their feet and start again towards the tunnel. A few seemed to be seriously injured, but Christa and the Marines didn't have the luxury of leaving them where they'd fallen while medical help was summoned, so they picked them up and carried them into the relative safety of the tunnel as another fighter began to strafe the site.

From a position just inside the tunnel entrance, Christa watched as the dig site laborers who had continued to perform their usual tasks during her confrontation with the civilians now jumped out of their excavation holes and ran for the safety of the tunnel while others continued to cower in the dig site cavities.

"Doctor Johannes," Christa said as she activated a carrier for her CT. When he responded, she said, "We have an emergency topside. Fighter aircraft are strafing the camp. We have numerous injured. We need every doctor and nurse in the camp up here. Now!"

"We're on our way, Commander. Johannes out."

"Carver out."

Christa stepped from the cover of the tunnel to wave the labors on towards safety, although little encouragement was needed. At least they were spread out enough that they weren't tripping over and trampling their fellows.

There were still too many civilians in the open when the next fighter approached, and many racing for safety fell as lattice rounds rained down on the base. With so many dig site people exposed and running for cover, the fighter began to deploy the small rockets and bombs that had remained nestled beneath its wings until then. As it passed overhead, explosions rippled across the dig site. Tongues of flame reached skyward and black smoke billowed wherever the bombs or rockets landed, while dirt, rocks, and shrapnel briefly filled the air.

As the fighter passed overhead, Christa and the Marines again hurried out towards the fallen civilians, trying to staunch the flow of blood from gaping wounds while carrying the victims to the relative safety of the tunnel.

CHAPTER FIFTEEN

~ October 24th, 2285 ~

Christa was near the camp perimeter when the next fighter appeared. She had no choice but to temporarily abandon the wounded and dive into the perimeter trench as a pattern of lattice rounds began to stitch the ground towards her, kicking dirt and small rocks into the air. But as soon the fighter passed overhead, she was out of the trench and racing towards a fallen victim.

It seemed like a never-ending activity as more and more of the laborers who had been cowering in their dig holes finally realized the open pits offered only a modicum of safety from the death raining down upon them. Each time a fighter completed a flyover, laborers would leap up and race towards the tunnel entrance. When a new fighter appeared, they dove headlong into the nearest excavation until it was safe to run again. It was unfortunate that there were no foxholes in the base compound and that the trench was a hundred meters from the tunnel entrance, but neither Christa nor Uronson had ever contemplated an aerial attack such as this one.

As the number of injured outside the tunnel had grown, several of the Marines had put down their weapons and concentrated on getting the wounded under cover, but as the flow began to ebb, they picked up their weapons and added their strength to those who had continued the return fire. One fighter was damaged enough to break off its attack and another crashed into the forest a few kilometers beyond the area cleared for the dig site.

The fighters continued to make pass after pass, but everyone left alive was finally inside the tunnel. A number of wounded whom Christa didn't expect would survive had been carried into the tunnel so the medical people could try to save them.

From her vantage point inside the tunnel entrance, Christa could see at least two dozen bodies within the camp perimeter. Every one of them had been checked for a pulse before being left on the field. It was impossible to check the entire dig-site because the cover was so limited and the attacks were so frequent.

"Who's attacking us, Commander?" Christa heard from behind. Recognizing the voice as belonging to Carmoody, Christa said, "I don't know, Gracie. All I really know for sure is that the fighters are a Nordakian design."

"Nordakian? But they're part of the Galactic Alliance."

"The attackers aren't Nordakian military. That ship design was retired decades ago and the Nordakians never mounted lattice cannons on any of their ships. Someone apparently got their hands on some old fighters, probably part of a scrap salvage deal that had been stripped of their original weapons. They repaired the ships and then rearmed them with illegal weapons. The lattice cannons probably came from some rogue arms merchants. At least I hope they were rogue. The Tsgardi are well known for illegal arms sales. I'd hate to think the Tsgardi still haven't learned their lesson."

"They must be Raiders then," Carmoody said.

"At first glance that seems like a logical deduction, but..."

"But?"

"I don't know, Gracie. What reason would Raiders have to attack us?"

"Maybe they believe we found more cloning equipment."

"Perhaps. But their intel is usually highly reliable. It doesn't make sense that they would attack us only on speculation that we *might* have discovered something."

"Maybe it's because you've been so tightlipped about the discovery. They might figure it's something so big that you're afraid to let it be known until Space Command can get here in force."

Christa breathed in deeply and then released it slowly as another fighter made a pass over the site. "Perhaps. But killing innocent civilians like this is completely out of character, even for them."

◆

The next fighter to pass over the site would never return to its base. As every Marine on the ground with a laser rifle poured fire into its hull, someone must have struck a fuel cylinder. The fighter exploded in a huge fireball that sent an expanding orb of flame and smoke skyward while a shower of detritus rained down on the camp.

Finally, the fighters seemed to realize there were no more living targets and that their numbers were being whittled down for no gain. They broke off their attack and disappeared over the tree line.

The dig site was in ruins. Smoke billowed from dozens of fires as anything flammable burned uncontrollably. The dig site shelters and mess hall were ablaze, as were the small vehicles used around the site. A small warehouse used to store collected items was a roaring inferno and black, acrid smoke rose skyward from its location. Every few seconds a small popping sound could be heard as small fuel cylinders and sealed containers succumbed to the heat.

"I need a medic," Christa said loudly, "to perform a final check on the bodies outside. The fighters have left."

"I'll do it, Commander," a nurse offered.

"Thank you. Signal us if you find anyone alive."

Christa looked at two Marines standing near her and caught their eye, then nodded her head in the direction of the nurse. They understood and hurried after her with their weapons ready in case the fighters returned.

◆

Christa waited until the nurse and Marines returned, then nodded as she listened to the report.

"All deceased, Commander. They never had a chance. The wounds were all located in places that either killed them instantly or caused them to bleed out in minutes."

"Thank you, Nurse…"

"Gibson, Commander."

Christa nodded. "Thank you, Gibson. Carry on."

"What now, Commander?" Carmoody asked after Gibson turned her attention to the wounded in the tunnel.

"It's doubtful anybody would attack with fighters and then simply leave. It's more likely they were just softening us up a bit so we'd be too disorganized to resist a ground assault."

"A ground assault? Are you serious?"

"I'm afraid so."

"What can we do? We only have half a squad of Marines."

"We retreat, as we did when the Tsgardi Raiders attacked us at Fort Carver. We pull back and seal the facility. Whoever is responsible for the attack is going to get quite a shock when they come down the tunnel, which is another reason I doubt the attackers are Raiders. The Raiders knew the futility of attacking us like this. They would have done something to catch us unaware before we could bottle ourselves inside. And whoever was commanding those fighters wasn't trained for the job."

"How can you possibly know that?"

"There was too much of a gap between strafing runs. Their goal seemed to be to kill as many people as possible, but the time gap allowed most of the dig site people to reach the tunnel in safety. It indicates that their commander didn't have either the experience or training for such an attack."

"It seemed pretty effective to me."

"It was deadly, but not as deadly as it could have been. Come on. Let's get everybody down below."

Christa began walking among the wounded and informing the medical people that everyone had to get inside the facility.

"A few of these people can't be moved until we get them stabilized," Doctor Johannes said.

"I expect the attackers to return any minute, Doctor. Try to get them ready as quickly as possible or we'll have to leave them."

"Leave them? Are you serious?"

"It's either leave a few behind and save the hundreds who are uninjured or ambulatory, or possibly lose everyone."

"Very well. Give me as much time as you can and then we'll move them rather than simply leaving them behind to be killed."

"Okay, Doc. That's what I hoped you'd say."

Christa and Carmoody helped the medical people move the less critically wounded, with the dig site laborers pitching in to carry those not able to walk on their own. Within fifteen minutes, the tunnel was cleared of all civilian personnel except the few too seriously injured to be moved safely. The two Space Command officers returned to the tunnel entrance.

Addressing one of the Marines, Christa said, "Where's Lt. Uronson, Lance Corporal?"

"The Lieutenant was injured, Ma'am. I think he's in the rotunda."

"Injured? Is it serious?"

"Serious enough, ma'am. He was carrying a wounded civilian towards the tunnel when he caught a lattice round. As I understand, it kinda skittered along his rib cage, cutting away the flesh pretty bad. The doc said he'll recover, but he's gonna be plenty sore for a few weeks."

"I'm glad it wasn't fatal. Too bad you didn't have time to get into your armor."

"Yes, Ma'am. They sure did catch us flat-footed."

"Keep a sharp eye on the tree line, Lance Corporal. If you see any movement, it might indicate an assault wave is headed this way. Tell Doctor Johannes immediately and then pull back into the facility as you cover his retreat. Understand?"

"Yes, ma'am."

"I'll be in the rotunda. Carry on."

◆

Christa was shocked when she entered the Rotunda. It was filled from wall to wall with frightened and injured civilians, and at least one injured Marine. Lt. Uronson was propped against a wall with the other injured and Christa had to push her way through to reach him.

"Lieutenant, how are you doing?" Christa asked quietly as she bent over his form.

"The doc says I'll live," he replied through gritted teeth, "but right now it doesn't feel that way."

"Haven't they administered any painkillers?"

"The supply they brought up is very low. I told 'em to use 'em for the more seriously injured. Once we get down to Medical, they'll give me something."

"Why aren't you down there already?"

"I didn't think you'd want everyone to know the secret of the different levels inside the facility and how to access them, so I told our people not to use the elevator."

"I appreciate your point and your effort, but I doubt we can keep the secrets to ourselves anymore. We have to get the injured to Medical."

Christa stood up straight and announced loudly, "I want everyone with an injury to come to the doors at the back of the rotunda. Those who can't move on their own should be helped. Leave the most seriously wounded where they are until we can send stretchers for them."

Amid moans and groans from the injured as they began to move, Christa pushed her way to the rear doors and spoke the Dakis command for open. Dr. Peterson appeared behind her and tried to push his way in. Christa stopped him and the other scientists who were anxiously following him like small children looking for a candy treat. In their lust to learn the secrets the facility held, they had become seemingly oblivious to the grief and suffering all around them.

"Doctor, where are you injured?" Christa asked sharply. To her eyes, he looked perfectly healthy.

"Oh, I, uh, uh, I sprained my back while was I was hurrying down the tunnel."

"If you're not bleeding, you'll have to wait. Please step aside and let the injured through."

"Commander, please, I'm in pain."

"We have to help the seriously wounded first, Doctor. Would you deny aid to those clinging precariously to life because your back hurts a little?"

"Uh, uh, no. Of course not."

"Then please step aside so the medical people can *carry* in those with serious injuries."

Peterson seemed more than a little embarrassed at being challenged and a contrite look came over his face. He stepped back away from the elevator and stumbled onto the foot of Doctor Ramilo, who screamed in pain as the full weight of Dr. Peterson came down on his toes.

"I'm sorry, Dr. Ramilo," Christa said as she moved aside to let three patients through whose clothes were saturated with blood, "but your injury will have to wait as well. Perhaps if you massage your toes, they'll stop aching."

Like Peterson, Ramilo looked embarrassed and did his best to hobble aside as two laborers carried a third into the elevator.

The rest of the space filled quickly, with the last one in being Nurse Gibson. When Christa asked the nurse if she knew the words necessary to move the elevator, Gibson replied that she had heard Dr. Johannes use them. Christa had her repeat them several times, correcting her pronunciation until it was almost perfect.

As Christa stepped out of the elevator, Gibson gave the command for 'Medical level' and 'Close.' Once the doors closed, there was no more sound from that direction.

Still standing near the doors, Dr. Peterson said to Christa, "Commander, my exuberance got the better of my good judgment. I apologize. I'm ashamed of the way I acted."

"Just see what you and your associates can do to ease the suffering in here and all is forgiven, Doctor."

"Of course."

Christa heard a soft chime in her ear and held up her hand to silence any further apologies from Peterson.

"This is Commander Carver," she said.

"Commander, this is Lance Corporal Engolsen. We spotted movement at the tree line and pulled back, but Dr. Johannes and his people are moving so slowly that the attackers may be upon us before we reach the rotunda."

"Hold position at the point where the ramp first doubles back. Everyone who has passed beyond that point will be safe from fire and the attackers should hesitate to enter the tunnel because it offers no cover from our fire. I'll tell you when the medical people have reached the facility. At that point, you'll break for the rotunda. I'll be ready to slam the door closed as soon as your people are inside."

"Roger, Commander. Out."

"Carver out."

Raising her voice, Christa said, "Your attention, please. The attackers are almost to the tunnel. The Marines will attempt to hold them off when the rest of the wounded are brought in. I need you to make as much space as possible available in the middle of the room and get down on the floor. Stay as low as you can so you're not struck by stray and ricocheting fire."

Woeful sounds of mindless fear and sobs of misery again began to rise in the room. Christa did nothing to stop it— she had too many other things on her mind as she made her way to the rotunda entrance. She would be prepared to close the doors instantly. Her fervent hope was that everyone would be inside when the time came to give the command.

Halfway to the entrance, Christa stopped and changed direction, heading straight to where Lt. Uronson was grimacing in pain.

"Lieutenant, I need your side arm, if you please."

"Sure, Commander, take it," he said as he twisted slightly so she could remove his holster belt after he had undone the quick release clasp. The movement caused such pain that his face contorted grotesquely for a few seconds. "Get one for me, would you?"

"I'll do my best," she said as she took the weapon and fastened it around her own waist before hurrying over to the door. From a side pocket of her tunic, she withdrew one of the cylinders necessary for locking the door. She was glad now that she had decided to keep one on her person. It would only take one to seal the virtually impregnable door against attackers, so the other five were stashed in the safe aboard her shuttle. The ancient Dakistians had used six only because it made the unlocking procedure far more complex.

Christa could hear noises in the tunnel and was greatly relieved when the first of the medical team came into view as they turned the corner where the ramp doubled back for the second time. They were moving slowly, being as careful as possible not to jar the injured more than necessary, so it seemed to take forever before they passed her position.

"Lance Corporal Engolsen," Christa said after initiating a carrier for her CT. Not being an officer, the Lance Corporal didn't have a CT, but he apparently had a portable transceiver tuned to the system. When he responded, she said, "Time to come home, Engolsen. Destroy all lighting in the tunnel as you proceed. We're going to minimum illumination so you won't be backlit. The center of the room is clear so come straight in and hit the deck."

"Roger, Commander. We're moving out."

Christa gave the command to lower the light and the room instantly darkened. At first it seemed like the light had been totally extinguished, and people began to scream. "Quiet," Christa yelled as loud as she could. As eyes adjusted to the lower light level, people quieted down as they realized they weren't in complete darkness.

A second later, she heard boots coming on hard, and then the first of the Marines appeared at the second bend in the tunnel. Engolsen was last and he destroyed each Chembrite panel with a sweeping shot from his laser rifle as he ran. Christa was already speaking the command to close the door as the Lance Corporal passed over the threshold and drove for the floor.

"Hit the deck," Engolsen yelled as lattice rounds ricocheted off the walls in the rotunda. The attackers hadn't wasted any time coming on when they heard the Marines vacate their positions but with little light, they had no hard target and were firing wildly.

No more than a dozen rounds made it into the facility before the door slid tightly closed. Christa ordered the lights to full brightness and practically had her face pressed against the door trying to see and feel the barely discernible marks etched into the Dakinium until she identified the one that matched up with the cylinder she held. She attached it to the door in the correct position and gave it a quick twist. Issuing the command 'lock' in Dakis was all that was required to secure the door. She heard the cams shift and a single bolt slide into place. No one was getting in, or out, once that was accomplished unless they had the cylinder she possessed.

Christa breathed her first sigh of relief since the attack had begun. They had been hit hard and many people had lost their lives, but they were safe from further injury for the moment. As she relaxed against the door, Christa noticed that Dr. Petersen was watching her closely. He had to have seen the locking procedure. She had hoped to keep that information from him and the other civilians, but she'd had no choice. At least he didn't know the final details required to unlock the door, and didn't have the cylinders.

"And I thought this was going to be an easy day," Christa mumbled as she let the tension drain from her body for a few seconds.

But there wasn't time to rest, so Christa stood up almost immediately. She was just about to speak when the elevator door opened. She stopped and waited as the most seriously wounded patients were carried in and the elevator doors closed again. There were still injured in the room, but the critical cases needed to be rushed to the Medical level first.

"May I have your attention, please," Christa said loudly. All talking slowly ceased and everyone turned to face Christa. It was the first time she'd had a chance to survey the faces of the several hundred people who had made it into the facility. She recognized perhaps two hundred, but the others didn't look familiar. Most were Terrans, but there were also a number of Nordakians in the rotunda.

Doctors Dakshiku Vlashsku and Glawth Djetch, plus their many clones, constituted a majority of the Nordakians, but there were a few males Christa had never met before. Owing to their natural height, it was easy to spot the Nordakians. Not one was less than seven feet tall, and all were flashing shades of orange and yellow, an indication that they were feeling intense agitation, fear, or anger.

Christa waited until everyone quieted down before saying, "With the door closed and locked, we're safe from further attack. Unfortunately, we're also cut off from all outside communications. Those of you who were here at Loudescott in 2270 have already been through a situation like this. When Raiders attacked then, we sealed ourselves into a virtually impregnable fortress until help could arrive.

"As I said, we're perfectly safe in here, but I had no warning so I was unable to send a message for help. How long it will take for people outside to learn of our situation and arrive with help is anybody's guess. I don't expect food to be a problem. The Marines had already occupied this facility and we laid in enormous supplies. However, water *is* a problem. It isn't flowing from faucets throughout the facility and the water supplies brought in for the Marine presence isn't adequate for a population this size. Until we can find and correct the problem, water will be strictly rationed.

"I'm going to ask Staff Sgt. Burton and his people to pass among you and collect any liquids you have on you. This will be used to help us survive and I must warn you not to hold back. Yield everything you have because anyone hording water or drink will be dealt with severely."

Christa nodded to Burton and watched as his Marines began to pass through the crowd to collect the liquids.

When the meager supplies had been gathered, Christa said, "Thank you. As soon as the injured have all been brought to the medical center, the Marines will begin escorting you to dormitories. Each dormitory can house a hundred people and I'm sure you would prefer to lodge with people who share your interests, so it would be helpful if you divided into groups before you're assigned housing.

◆ ◆

It took hours to get everyone settled into the dormitories on the Housing level. Most were delighted with the accommodations, especially those who had been involved in the Raider's takeover attempt sixteen years ago. At that time, the one dormitory was already occupied by the Marines, so new arrivals were forced to sleep on the floor in the mess hall.

The archeologists went quietly and anxiously. Any opportunity to explore the facility excited them, even if it was merely a dormitory, lavatory, or mess hall. Christa established a guard post at the elevator on the Housing and Medical levels so the civilians would not be able to move between levels. The guard on the Medical level was also required to ensure no civilians left the Medical center unless accompanied by Space Command or Marine personnel.

When everyone was settled in, the dig site labor supervisor performed a head count. After adding the people in the medical center, the total number of missing was eighty-six. How many of that number were dead and how many may have found adequate cover or escaped into the woods surrounding the area was unknown.

Christa finally had an opportunity to debrief Lance Corporal Engolsen. She had chosen to interview him in one of the security rooms in the rotunda.

"Tell me exactly what you saw just before you ordered the withdrawal, Lance Corporal."

"On the extreme left flank, well beyond our camp perimeter, I observed a large armed contingent moving towards our position behind armored personnel carriers. They appeared to all be Nordakians."

"Nordakians?" Christa exclaimed. "Are you sure?"

"I realize it's an assumption, but the troops were all between seven and eight feet tall. They were wearing camouflage armor, but they didn't fit the description of any other race I'm familiar with. And the APCs were the tallest I've ever seen. I only had the tree line to use as a reference, but I've been on the planet for two years and I'm familiar with the tree sizes."

"How many troops do you estimate were in the contingent?"

"I have no way of knowing how many were in the APCs, but I observed at least a hundred soldiers arrayed behind them."

"A hundred?"

"Yes, ma'am."

"Continue. Did you see any others?"

"Oh, yes ma'am. On the far right flank, coming from the direction of the current dig location, I saw another hundred or more armed personnel. But the ones on the right flank were Terrans."

"No Nordakians?"

"No ma'am. Not unless they were midget Nordakians— if there is such a thing."

"So there were two different forces?"

"I don't know if they were part of the same force or different forces. All I can say is that they were different species. And when they began to fire at us, the group on the left used lattice weapons, where the group on the right used laser weapons."

"I only saw lattice rounds enter the facility after you made it into the rotunda."

"Yes, ma'am. The group on the right stopped their forward progress at our camp perimeter, while the group on the left continued towards the tunnel entrance. By then the Doc was moving the wounded, so we pulled back and covered the retreat, as ordered. We barely made it to the first point where the ramp doubles back before the Nordakians entered the tunnel. We dropped a whole bunch and that slowed them considerably, but they just kept right on coming."

"Okay, Lance Corporal, I think I have a good picture of what you observed and the actions you took in response. You did a good job, and that's what I'll be saying in my report."

"Thank you, ma'am. Is the LT okay?"

"He was in a lot of pain when they took him down to the Medical level, but I think he'll be fine with some rest, medication, and treatment of his injury. That'll be all, Lance Corporal."

Engolsen stood, braced to attention, then turned and walked towards the elevator while Christa tried to reason what was going on. Two different groups attacking in unison didn't make sense. But if they were working together, why did the group on the right flank halt their attack while the group on the left flank continued in? And why would Nordakians be involved? Christa had never heard of any Nordakian being a member of the Raiders, although there were rogue elements in any society. And if they weren't working together, which was responsible for the deadly aerial assault that had taken so many lives? Or was that possibly a third group?

CHAPTER SIXTEEN
~ October 25th, 2285 ~

Lower Council Chairman Arthur Strauss was working on his weekly report to the Upper Council when his com system buzzed. If the message had been from anyone other than Councilman Fazid, he would have let the computer record a message, but it might be news of the Dakistee operation. So far, the cost for the operation had exceeded his original estimate by six hundred percent and the Upper Council was beginning to question the wisdom of continuing. He needed a resolution as quickly as possible.

"Yes, Ahil," Strauss said, after tapping the connection button. "What is it?"

"We just received a communication from our ground commander on Dakistee. The operation was commenced as planned, but their attack on the facility was interrupted."

"Interrupted? By Space Command?"

"No, by someone else's attack on the facility. While our people were forming their lines in the treed area adjacent to the dig site, fighter aircraft appeared overhead and pounded the dig site population with bombs and lattice cannon fire. The aerial attack drove the archeological people underground. The death toll was reportedly quite high. Our people knew *you* didn't want fatalities, if possible, so they're anxious for you to understand they aren't responsible. Anyway, after the planes disappeared, our people abandoned the assault plan and moved in towards the underground facility to assess the situation and determine if there was any sense in trying to salvage the attack. They had just reached the perimeter of the camp when they saw another group coming from the opposite direction. Until then they had been firing their laser rifles just to keep the military and civilians contained in the tunnel and were exceedingly careful not to hit anyone. They halted when they discovered the presence of the other ground forces. While that group pressed their attack on the tunnel entrance, our people retreated to their disembarkation point. They want to know how we wish them to proceed. Should they attack the group that has the facility under siege? The sides appear to be roughly equal in size."

"Who is this other group and why were they attacking Loudescott?"

"We don't know who they are. As to why, perhaps they've discovered what Carver has found and are hoping to acquire it."

"How could they acquire that information if we couldn't?"

"Perhaps one of the scientists learned something and passed it on to them. In any event, all they succeeded in doing is driving the Loudescott people into the facility, which we assume was then sealed by Carver. Our plan was devised to circumvent that eventuality."

Straus pounded his fist down on his desk. "If I know Carver, they didn't get what they were after and now neither of us may get anything. We need to find out who this other group is and who's controlling them. This is our territory and if someone is trying to set up an operation here, we need to take immediate action to stop them."

"The ground commander only knows they're Nordakian, they have a ship in orbit, and they've deployed S-Band jamming satellites. Our people had to send an encrypted RF communication to the *Hell Fire* located outside the jamming range, which was then retransmitted as an IDS message."

"Nordakian?" Strauss said absently as he searched his memory for any mention of Nordakian crime syndicates. "There aren't any Nordakian crime groups operating outside their planet's sphere of influence. We've been monitoring them closely for years to ensure they stay in their own small backyard."

"Perhaps they're expanding."

"What kind of ship do they have?"

"It's an old freighter, maxed out to ten kilometers."

"We gave you a destroyer for your operation, so you should have no trouble overcoming a freighter."

"Probably not, but don't forget the *Lisbon* incident. The Milori and Tsgardi mounted torpedoes in cargo containers. When the destroyer *Lisbon* came in close, the Tsgardi blew the container covers and loosed their torpedoes. Expecting only a disabled freighter, the *Lisbon* crew was caught completely off guard."

"Forewarned is forearmed. You know what to look for. Order the commander on the ground to take that ship by whatever means necessary, but spare the cargo section if possible. It might have value. If our people decide we should kill every Nordakian on board, then I authorize you to wipe them out. I wanted to limit the deaths on the ground to keep Space Command from coming after us with blood in their eyes, but they won't seriously mourn the loss of a pirate ship and crew."

"Yes, Arthur. I'll pass on your instructions immediately."

◆　◆　◆

"Well, where is she?" Vejrezzol asked when Gxidescu reported to his quarters.

"I'm sorry, Excellency. It appears there's a problem."

"I'm not interested in your problems. I want to see her, or her corpse. You said she was here."

"By all accounts, she is here. All my contacts said she had arrived at Loudescott. But no one told me she had an impregnable underground bunker. During the aerial assault, she must have made it inside, along with those from the dig site who weren't killed. They've sealed the doors and there's no way to get them to come out. We can't even communicate with them. If we could, we might be able to get the others to surrender her. We've tried everything we could think of, without success."

Vejrezzol picked up a holo-tube and threw it against the wall with all his might. "You said we could get one of Azula Carver's clones if we attacked Loudescott first, so we abandoned our plan to destroy the Marine base at North Pendleton and came here instead. Now you tell me you missed Carver in the attack and there's no chance of getting her at all. We've lost the element of surprise and have nothing to show for it. We can't attack North Pendleton now because they'll be on alert for any aggression. We must pretend we're not a part of anything happening on the planet. I'm very displeased with you, Sebaqd."

"I'm most humbly sorry, Excellency."

♦ ♦ ♦

Lt. Colonel Andre Diminjik was working at his desk when he received a call from the Base Communications officer. He stabbed at the button on his com unit and watched as the face of Major Garfield appeared."

"What is it, Pete?" Diminjik said.

"We've encountered something strange, sir. We didn't receive our daily traffic from Higgins so we started investigating. Whenever we try to transmit, our messages bounce back at us. It appears we're being jammed."

"Jammed? Are you sure?"

"Yeah, I'm pretty sure. It looks like someone put a jamming satellite or two in orbit."

"That's crazy. They had to know we'll just knock it down."

"Maybe they just wanted to interrupt our communications for a few hours."

"Well, it's time to end their little game. How about RF?"

"Working fine."

"Great. I'm issuing a base alert. Send the word, Pete."

"Yes, sir."

As Major Garfield cleared the line, Diminjik called Air Defense Control and ordered a sweep of space around the planet. In minutes, four FA-SF4 Marine Fighters were lifting off. They pointed their noses almost straight up and disappeared in the blink of an eye. With inertial compensation, the pilots didn't have to contend with g forces.

Forty minutes later, the fighter pilots reported that the S-band jamming satellites were destroyed and communications were restored. The pilots also reported the presence of a cargo ship in orbit, but since it wasn't engaged in hostile actions they didn't have the authority to challenge it. Only a Space Command officer could require a freighter to 'heave to' for boarding and inspection.

◆ ◆ ◆

"So who put those satellites up there and why?" Lt. Colonel Diminjik put to his assembled senior staff awhile later.

"It has to be the freighter," Marine Captain Luduro said. "They're the only ones up there."

"Someone could have placed the satellites and left orbit," Major Garfield offered.

"I've been putting in requisitions for planetary and space surveillance systems since they posted me here, but they just keep telling me the budget doesn't permit it at this time. We didn't even know that freighter was there because it's in geo-synchronous orbit on the other side of the planet. How can they expect us to do a proper job if they won't give us the equipment and personnel we need?" Diminjik took a quick, deep breath and exhaled it just as quickly to show his exasperation. "Could those destroyed satellites possibly have anything to do with the demonstrations going on at the three warehouses?" Diminjik asked.

No one offered any thoughts and a couple just shrugged.

"Okay," Diminjik said. "I sent a message to Higgins describing the situation and asking for their take on things. I also asked, once again, for some proper equipment. We should hear back tomorrow. Dismissed."

◆ ◆ ◆

It had been a long and exhausting day, and Christa was glad to finally climb into bed to get some much needed rest. The Marines had reserved two of the private rooms associated with their dormitory for Christa and Carmoody, and Lt Uronson had the third. The fourth, with four bunks, would be shared by the noncoms, although Sgt. Flegetti had been temporarily redeployed. All enlisted personnel below the rank of Sergeant were billeted in the main room, but it was far better than most barracks assignments, and almost like having a private room without a door. A half-wall separated every two bunks, and a full wall separated all rows. The bunks all had great mattresses and a white-noise generator at the head of each in case anyone's bunkmate snored or talked in his or her sleep. Bots changed the bed clothes every morning if the bed was unoccupied or returned every hour to check until it was unoccupied.

Christa had just slipped into a sound sleep when she was awakened by a call to her CT.

"Carver," she said, as she touched her Space Command ring to activate the carrier.

"Christa, it's Gracie. I'm sorry to wake you but we have a problem. Dr. Johannes just called to inform me that he's lost two people."

"That was to be expected, Gracie. Some of the injuries were pretty severe. I didn't expect them all to make it."

"No, I mean that two people are missing."

"Missing? Who?"

"Madu and her assistant."

Christa came fully awake with that news. "How long?"

"No one can recall seeing them since the attack."

Christa jumped out of bed and began dressing. "That happened during breakfast. And they're just noticing it now?"

"Well, they've been a little busy. Dr. Johannes said they didn't notice they were gone until all the patients had been tended to and he was making his final rounds before turning in."

"They couldn't have gotten out of the facility without being noticed during the attack and then there was no chance at all after I locked the door."

"Do you think they might have sneaked off to find a quiet place where they could be alone for a while?"

"I don't know. Where are you?"

"I'm in my room— getting dressed."

"As am I. I'll meet you in the corridor. Carver, out."

A few minutes later the two women met in the short hallway outside their rooms.

"Should we check the whole Housing level first," Carmoody asked, "or start with the Administrative level? She has a sofa in her office."

"I don't think they'd run off to make love during a crisis."

"What else could prompt them to leave the Medical level?"

"There's only one thing I can think of."

Carmoody was quiet for a couple of seconds as she thought. "No, she wouldn't do that. You explained why we couldn't awaken the other sleepers at this time."

"Yes, I explained. But that doesn't mean she was listening, or agreeing with me. Let's go check. If I'm wrong, we can cross that off the list of places we have to search."

◆ ◆ ◆

Five minutes later, the two officers entered the Vault. Christa, in the lead, turned and pushed Carmoody back behind a large piece of machinery when they rounded a corner and saw activity further into the cavern. Peering around the machinery, Christa saw that the main floor was filled with stasis beds. Dozens of people in simple white terrycloth gowns were milling around hooking up portable machines to stasis chambers in place of the large automated unit in the medical center, while others helped awakened sleepers climb out of their stasis chambers.

"She's awakening sleepers," Christa said. "I guess she didn't believe everyone would be awakened eventually and decided to take matters into her own hands."

"Or she intends a takeover of the facility," Carmoody said.

"Perhaps both. I've got to slow her down. You stay here. If I get caught, report to Staff Sgt. Burton and tell him what's going on down here."

"Why don't we just go get him and the Marines?"

"I would if there were more than a handful available. We can't take the sentries off their posts on the Housing and Medical levels, and Lt. Uronson is out of action, so that leaves just Burton and six of his people. I really want to avoid anyone getting injured. If I get caught, we'll have no choice, but perhaps I can stop this and not get caught."

"Good luck," Carmoody said ingenuously.

"Thanks."

Christa began working her way further into the cavern using machinery to mask her presence. As she neared the control platform, she saw Madu busily entering data at the console. The overhead articulating arms were selecting stasis chambers and gently lowering them to the cavern floor.

As Christa watched, one of the chambers slipped from the grip of an articulating arm and crashed to the deck. Madu screamed and jumped down from the platform, then rushed to where the chamber had landed. Christa knew this was her chance. She climbed up to the metal platform from behind while everyone's attention was diverted and accessed the console. She knew the consoles well enough by now to immediately cancel all operations that had not yet been initiated. She next overwrote Madu's administrative password with a new one and then locked the console.

Christa made it back to where Carmoody was waiting before Madu returned to the platform and the two women were able to slip out of the Vault without anyone noticing.

"What did you do?" Carmoody asked as they rode the elevator to the Housing level.

"I password locked the console after canceling all uninitiated operations. The console is almost identical to the one in Fort Carver where the clones were being produced. The main difference was the module that tracked and selected people in stasis. There's nothing we can do about the sleepers she's already awakened, but she won't be awakening any more unless perhaps one of the people she woke up is a computer expert. She might even be an expert herself, but I doubt it."

"What now?"

"Now? Now we go back sleep, if we can sleep."

"What about Madu and those awakened sleepers?"

Christa was quiet for a few seconds, then said in Dakis, "Computer?"

The words, "Computer active," seemed to come from everywhere in the elevator at once.

"Computer, how are your operating instructions established?"

"From the console in the office of the Chief of Operations, or by verbal command here in the unit."

"Computer, you will not respond to any requests to descend to the Vault level until I amend this instruction."

"Security ID and password required."

Christa gave the ID and password she had entered into the security console to gain access to the vault. She had assigned herself Tier One rights and changed the permissions of all other Tier One rights holders to Tier Two. That included Madu, so no one could override Christa's commands.

"Instruction set altered," the elevator computer said.

"Okay, Madu and her people are stuck on the Vault level unless access tubes are available, and we've seen no indication of any yet."

"There *must* be engineering accesses to all levels."

"You'd think so, but I've been looking and haven't seen any. If I couldn't spot them, perhaps Madu can't either. I'll tell Staff Sgt. Burton to be ready in case they pop up somewhere, and tomorrow, today actually, we'll begin a systematic effort to learn more about the construction of this prison we find ourselves in."

◆ ◆ ◆

Despite being exhausted, sleep didn't come easily to Christa. The problems she faced with the Ancients, the attackers outside the facility, the medical condition of the injured, and the nightmare of trying to keep hundreds of inquisitive dig site people corralled kept playing over and over in her mind. She finally drifted off into a troubled sleep and awoke still tired.

As soon as she had dressed, Christa contacted Staff Sgt. Burton.

"Sitrep," was all Christa said when Burton answered the radio call.

"All's quiet, Commander. The sentries on the Medical and Housing levels reported that no civilians have attempted to use the lift, and the sentry in the rotunda reports no sounds coming from the entry door."

"Excellent. Carver out."

Christa took a deep breath before she said to herself, "Maybe things aren't be as bad as I feared."

◆ ◆ ◆

Admiral Holt smiled when he saw that his morning mail contained a message from Christa. As he listened, his smile turned into a scowl. He immediately prepared a message to Lt. Colonel Diminjik in which he stated most strongly that if Carver didn't get her Marines back immediately, Diminjik might learn firsthand what happens when the deca-sector's commanding officer is angered.

◆ ◆ ◆

"Are they mad?" Captain Permenans of the destroyer *Hell Fire* said.

"I understand the order comes directly from the Chairman of the Lower Council," Commander Sivins said, "whoever that is."

"If we attack a freighter, Space Command won't stop chasing us until we run out of space. We gave up attacking freighters years ago because the Spaccs almost wiped us out for doing it. We're not going to start that war again, are we?"

"Space Command isn't going to mourn the loss of this ship. According to HQ, it's a pirate ship in disguise populated by a Nordakian crime syndicate. Their people have already attacked the Loudescott dig site on the planet and killed dozens of civilians. We had just begun to mount our operation when they showed up and began killing everyone they could. I saw the action first hand, and I can tell you they won't get any mercy from Space Command or the Galactic Alliance Council. The company doesn't need any competition from a bunch of flashing freaks, so the top brass wants them gone, permanently. Got it?"

"Yeah, I got it. When am I supposed to do this?"

"You pick the time, but the sooner the better. That massacre on the planet hasn't been reported yet, but it won't be long before someone wonders why they haven't heard from Loudescott and why they aren't getting any replies to their messages. When that happens, they'll send someone to investigate. I can't keep the Marines tied up forever at those three warehouses."

"Okay, we'll start getting ready. I only have two dozen fighters aboard, so I hope they don't have hidden laser weapons."

"Since the Spacs reinstituted the ban on mounting exterior weapons five years ago, the only thing you have to worry about is their fighters and whatever they might have hidden in the cargo containers. I've been told to warn you to watch out for torpedoes launched from specially rigged containers."

"Torpedoes? Great!"

"I didn't say they have them, just that you should watch out for them. Remember the way the Tsgardi and Milori used them?"

"Yeah, I read all about it at the time."

"If they don't have torpedoes, it should be a simple takeover. Wipe out the crew, then put your own people aboard and have them take the ship to Raider-Four."

"Yeah, if they don't wipe us out first."

"When that's done, stand by in case we need to hitch a ride. So far, no one from Loudescott has seen our faces, but if that changes this planet could suddenly become a little too hot for any of us."

"Right. Anything else?"

"That's all."

"I'll attack the freighter as soon as I can get there. Out."

"Out," Sivins said and ended the communication. The *Hell Fire* was so far distant from the planet that the conversation had taken twenty-five minutes from start to finish, but Sivins had wanted to ensure that the ship remained well outside DeTect range of the planet and approaching ships. The *Hell Fire* had only been intended as a means of escape for people participating in the ground operation, but it could also serve as a fighting resource in an emergency. Sivins had never really expected to involve it in the operation because the Lower Council originally said they wanted to minimize deaths. Now they were ordering a wholesale slaughter.

CHAPTER SEVENTEEN
~ October 25th, 2285 ~

"What's up first on the agenda," Carmoody asked Christa during breakfast, "and what are you going to do about Madu and her people?"

"If we operate on the assumption that the Dakistians can't leave the Vault level, we can ignore them for a while."

"But they'll need food and water."

"Yes, that's true, but Madu also deserves a lesson for her actions."

"But the people she awoke didn't do anything to deserve such treatment," Carmoody said.

Christa took a deep breath and released it. "You're right. They're innocent and don't deserve to suffer. The trouble is they outnumber us dramatically. If we release them, we won't be able to control them."

"It doesn't seem like we're going to be able to control things for long no matter what we do."

"Yes, and angering Madu and her people could make things worse. I guess we'll have to free them from the vault level and try to get them working with us instead of against us."

◆ ◆

An hour later, Christa and Carmoody, supported by Staff Sgt. Burton and a fire team in their armor, descended to the Vault level. As the door opened, an angry Madu stood facing the two officers. Behind her were a dozen angry-looking Dakistians. Christa was glad the Marines behind her looked every bit as intimidating as the Dakistians.

"It was you," Madu said to Christa, "wasn't it?"

"If I knew what you were talking about, I could answer."

- 189 -

"You somehow locked me out of the system. I couldn't awaken any more of my people, and I couldn't open the lift doors."

"Guilty on both counts," Christa said. "I told you we would awaken all your people when the time was right. This isn't the time."

"Why not?" Madu asked angrily. "You've seen that I awakened without any medical complications. And you said you ordered enough food for a thousand of my people. The Housing level can easily accommodate ten times that number."

"Yes, you appear healthy and we have enough space and food for a thousand of your people, but there's one thing we don't have."

"And what's that?"

"We don't have enough water for a thousand people."

"Water has always been abundant on my planet. Twenty thousand years shouldn't have changed that. The vegetation looked lush when I was outside."

"That's outside. We're inside and the water isn't flowing in the pipes."

"So send some people to fill water containers."

"Um, that's not possible. Do you remember when all the medical people were suddenly called away last solar, giving you an opportunity to come down here?"

"Of course."

"They were called away because the dig site was attacked by aerial fighter craft and then a ground assault. Dozens of people were killed and many were wounded. I had to seal the facility to keep them from getting in and continuing the carnage."

"Who would attack us?"

"I don't know. All I know is that they made a formidable effort to kill everyone outside and apparently intended to continue those acts in here."

"You're lying," Madu said. "This is some sort of trick to have me voluntarily agree to suspend awakening more of my people."

"You don't have to believe me. Come up to the Medical level."

"This is another trick— to separate me from my people."

"Bring as many as can fit into the lift. The doctors will want to check them all anyway."

Madu looked at Christa intently for a few seconds without speaking. "No, I'll bring just ten. The others will wait for me down here." Turning to one of the men behind her, she said, "If I don't return shortly, you know what to do."

◆ ◆ ◆

A few minutes later, they entered the first ward on the Medical level. Madu was able to see with her own eyes that every bed contained a bandaged and ailing patient. Christa stopped at the bed containing Lt. Uronson. He was awake.

"How are you feeling, Lieutenant?" Christa asked.

"Better than yesterday, that's for sure, ma'am. The doc's got me loaded up with nano-bots. I don't know if it's the pain-killers or not, but I swear I can almost feel them patching me back together."

Christa smiled. "Maybe it's a little of both."

"How did we make out yesterday, ma'am? I was a little out of it."

"You were the only military casualty. As you can see, a lot of civilians were injured, and I believe several dozen were killed. There are a lot missing, but we don't know how many escaped into the woods instead of coming to the facility. We probably won't have an accurate count until we can get out of here."

"Yes, ma'am."

"Don't worry about anything except getting well, Lieutenant. The facility is sealed so we're perfectly safe for now."

"Yes, ma'am."

As they walked through the ward, Christa said to Madu, "Satisfied?"

Madu's eyes traveled over the prone bodies for a second before she said, "Yes. You were being truthful. I apologize—again."

"Again?"

"Each time I've doubted your word, I've found I was wrong for doing so."

"I realize it takes time to build trust. In time, I have no doubt you'll trust me implicitly."

"I've never trusted anyone implicitly."

"Then perhaps I'll be the first," Christa said with a smile.

◆ ◆

While the doctors examined the newly awakened ancients, Madu, Christa, Carmoody, and the Marines traveled back down to the Vault level.

"How did you do it?" Madu asked Christa.

"Do what?"

"Block me from accessing the console in the Vault and the lift. Neither will obey any of my instructions."

"I'm not an administrator."

"What does that mean?"

"You're adept at controlling people. I'm adept at controlling computers."

"From what little I've seen, you seem adept at both."

Christa smiled and said, "Spoken like a true administrator."

Madu returned her smile and said, "This time I'm being ingenuous."

Looking to change the subject, Christa said, "Do you have any engineers among the people you've awakened? We desperately need to get the water flowing. We can't last long with the meager supply we have, *especially* now that there are so many more of us."

"None listed that as a profession. We can ask if anyone is knowledgeable. Of course, if I had access to the computer I could perform a search."

"We'll see how things go."

"Christa, I promise I won't awaken anyone else without your approval. I didn't understand the real issue at the time."

"It goes beyond that, Madu. I promised you we would awaken everyone but according to a timetable that will allow for an orderly process. You chose to ignore my words."

"Yes, and I regret my actions. I promise you I won't go against you again."

We shall see, Christa thought as she smiled politely.

◆ ◆ ◆

"Just what the hell is going on," Lt. Col. Diminjik said loudly to his senior staff. "There's no reason for these protest marches. The demonstrators have good jobs. They're well paid and they have great living accommodations. So why are they picketing the warehouses? Not a single one is even carrying a sign. It's as if even they don't know why they're protesting. I need some answers."

"I think you put your finger on it, sir," Marine Captain Verdeen said. "They *don't* know why they're protesting."

"What are you saying, Captain?"

"One of my undercover people overheard two of the protestors talking in a bar last night. They were comparing notes on how much money they're being paid to march. Don't you see, sir? There's no real passion behind this movement. They're being paid to protest."

"Paid? Somebody's paying them to protest? Who?"

Verdeen shrugged. "Maybe some big corporation is looking to cash in on the security angle. If Anthius believes we can't protect the warehouses, they'll have to hire private security firms like Peabody."

"That's fine with me. We shouldn't be guarding private warehouses anyway— even if they are non-profit. The GAC ordered us here because they feared bad publicity from

Raider robberies. If they got off their keesters and finally set up a government on this planet, planetary security would become responsible for babysitting these warehouses and we could get back to our real job."

"Since these protestors are doing it for the cash, it's doubtful any of the marches will turn violent. Shouldn't we send the extra personnel back to their regular duty assignments, sir? You said Carver was pretty upset about losing half her squad."

"She still has half a squad. That's more than enough to guard a single entrance to an underground bunker. She acts like she's expecting a Raider attack like the one she experienced fifteen years ago. That was before we had a Marine presence on this planet. It could never happen now."

◆　◆　◆

"Listen up," Wing Commander Deel 'Death Dealer' Fowler said as the entire air wing of the destroyer *Hell Fire* approached the planet from the blind side. The base at North Pendleton would not be able to detect their presence unless they flew outside the line-of-sight umbra.

"You've all been briefed with every fact we know about the enemy, although the intelligence is sketchy at best. We know that that they have fighter aircraft operating from the old freighter. We don't know if the freighter has laser arrays or torpedoes, but just because you can't see them doesn't mean they ain't there. Our job is to take control of that freighter, leaving it intact enough to be space-worthy, although it's not necessary that it have an atmosphere inside. So don't target the engines. Just fill it full of holes and evacuate the air.

"I realize everyone is a bit out of practice since the company stopped attacking ships in space, but it'll come back real quick to you veterans of the old days. You new guys stay alert and don't be lulled into thinking an old freighter can't put up a fight. Jenetta Carver killed two of our better warships with an old freighter because they were careless and assumed the old bucket didn't really present a threat."

"Okay, there it is," he said as the freighter appeared on his DeTect monitor. "Squadron One, you'll take the larboard side, and Squadron Two will go to starboard. Make them breathe vacuum."

◆ ◆ ◆

Vejrezzol was pulled away from his study of the Almuth by an urgent com message from Gxidescu. As captain of the *Gastropod* since the takeover, he was noticeably excited.

"Your Excellency, a large number of small craft are approaching from the stern."

"What kind of small craft?"

"It can only be fighters, but we don't know where they came from. They just appeared on our DeTect screen."

"Obviously they must have come from a ship in space. They must be Space Command. Sound the alert. Launch all fighters and man our laser arrays. This is our moment. God will protect us as we protect ourselves."

"Yes, Excellency."

Vejrezzol jumped up from the desk in his quarters and hurried towards the bridge.

◆ ◆ ◆

As the Raider fighter wing approached the *Gastropod*, they were able see the sides of containers being opened and laser arrays being extended.

"This is Death Dealer," Fowler said over the com. "They do have arrays. Scramble and show them how this game is played. Keep zigzagging until everyone in the main ship is dead."

"Roger Death Dealer. Squadron One taking the larboard."

"Squadron Two taking the starboard."

If the attacking fighter squadrons had been able to simply make a straight run at the *Gastropod*, the fight would have lasted only minutes. But since the fighters weren't armored, they couldn't afford to take a serious hit from even a low-power laser array. By zigzagging, they never gave the dissident defenders a chance to get a target lock, but it also prevented them from effectively targeting the *Gastropod*.

As fighter after fighter passed the freighter and swung back for another pass, they strafed the main ship again. Air was evacuating from hundreds of small holes by the time both squadrons had completed their first pass. Since they needed the main ship operational, they weren't permitted to use their rockets or the task would have been completed with the first pass.

The Raider force was about to make a second run when the *Gastropod's* fighter squadron showed up. The three fighters that hadn't been shot to pieces at Loudescott and one with a continuing power problem engaged the Raider ships, but they were seriously overmatched. They gave it their best, but they all died in the attempt to knock down at least one Raider attacker.

With the way open, the Raider fighters again began making attack runs on the freighter. They still had to dodge the lasers and keep a wary eye out for other fighters, but they were slowly making the main ship look like it was wrapped in Swiss cheese.

◆ ◆ ◆

Alarms were sounding all over the *Gastropod* as anxious people having difficulty breathing, struggled to squeeze into space suits. The space suits would save their lives, but they restricted movement to a barely acceptable level for the people who required free movement for fixing problems.

"Get the ship moving," Vejrezzol screamed at Gxidescu. "We're a sitting target here and our miserable gunners couldn't hit the planet."

"Yes, Excellency," Gxidescu said, who then gave orders to the bridge crew.

The ten-kilometer-long ship was designed neither for fast maneuvering nor for quick escapes. It only had a tenth the power of a warship, and as it turned towards open space, the engines strained to move the enormous mass.

◆ ◆ ◆

"What now, Commander?" the Squadron One leader asked.

"Slow the attack but keep zigzagging. Their gunners haven't scored a single hit yet. If they start to build an envelope, target their generator to keep them at sub-light speeds. They just made our job ten times easier. By moving the ship away from the planet, we won't have to worry about the Marines at North Pendleton coming up to investigate when we repair the ship later. We'll let them get far enough away and then continue our attack. We have plenty of time. The *Hell Fire* will close in when we need her."

◆ ◆ ◆

"Status report," Vejrezzol said with some urgency. "What was that explosion?"

"They knocked out the temporal field generator with rockets when we tried to build an FTL envelope," Gxidescu said. "We're limited to sub-light speeds."

"Why haven't they attacked the ship with rockets before?"

"They may not be looking to kill us. They probably only want us to yield."

"Never," Vejrezzol screamed. "We will never surrender."

"Yes, Excellency. But the ship is depressurizing and we can't patch the holes while we're under full power."

"Have all non-essential personnel placed in stasis beds for their protection, then seal off the bridge section. All other oxygen reserves will be held for the EVA suits."

"Yes, Excellency."

"Why didn't the enemy simply approach with their ship and order us to yield if that's what they want?" Vejrezzol asked.

"Perhaps they believed we would fight and thought this to be an easier solution."

"But their ships are only fighters. They can't continue to follow us forever. They have limited fuel."

"Their mother ship must be tailing us even though it doesn't show on the DeTect screens."

"But they haven't even identified themselves yet. Are they Space Command or Nordakian Space Force?"

"We don't know, Excellency. If they don't identify themselves, we may not know until they board us."

"They won't board us!" Vejrezzol screamed. "We shall never surrender."

"It may be our only option. The main ship can't achieve FTL now and we don't have any tugs that can tow us FTL because we used the entire budget to procure the six fighters. The enemy can disable our sub-light engines any time they wish. What are we to do?"

Standing, Vejrezzol said, "I shall pray for guidance. I won't believe God has deserted us. I shall be in my quarters."

◆ ◆ ◆

"You're never going to believe this," Lt. Colonel Diminjik said to Major Garfield when he'd tracked him down. "I just received a message from Admiral Holt himself. He says that if I don't return those two fire teams to Commander Carver immediately, I'm going to be numero uno on his shit list."

"Not much ambiguity there. What are you going to do?"

"I'm going to order you to send that damn half squad back to her, not that she needs them."

"I'm on it. I'll have them on a MAT to Loudescott within the hour."

"Make it thirty minutes if you can, Pete. I have enough problems. I don't need the deca-sector area commander on my ass as well."

"Will do."

◆ ◆ ◆

As the Marine Assault Transport arrived at Loudescott, the pilot called Sergeant Flegetti to the cockpit. When Flegetti arrived, he immediately noticed they were hovering three hundred meters AGL instead of setting down. MATs almost never hover because pilots are supposed to treat every LZ as hot.

"Flegetti, sir," he said to the pilot. "You wanted to see me."

"Any idea what's going on here Flegetti?"

"What do you mean sir?"

"Take a look down there." As Flegetti strained to see over the instrument panel, the pilot said, "There's no activity down there— at all. The living shelters have all burnt to the ground and some are still smoldering. There are blast craters scattered over the entire site, and those objects sprawled everywhere sure look like bodies to me."

"Yes, sir," Flegetti said somberly. "To me also."

The pilot increased power and the ship began to climb. "I'm taking us up to a safe altitude," he said. "Get your people into their armor and let me know when they're ready. We're going in fast in case there's a reception committee."

"Yes, sir," Flegetti said as he disappeared through the cockpit door.

◆　◆

Flegetti com'd the cockpit fifteen minutes later. When the pilot responded, he said, "We're suited and ready, sir."

"Roger. Strap in. We're going down."

A few seconds later, the MAT seemed to fall from the sky, but it was a controlled fall. As it neared the ground, the pilot pulled out of the dive and touched the craft down with hardly more than a slight bump. The Marines in the rear compartment were out the door and running towards the tunnel entrance as the dirt kicked up by the landing was still settling to the ground.

◆　◆　◆

Lt. Colonel Diminjik tapped the com to take the call from Major Garfield and heard, "We just got a message from the pilot who took Carver's half-squad back to Loudescott. He says the site has been attacked and there are dead bodies all over the place. They seem to all be civilians, but Carver only had half a squad left after you pulled most of her people off for temporary redeployment, so the military dead would be limited. The pilot said the sergeant with the two returning fire teams reported that the facility is locked down and supposes the rest of the dig site people made it inside when the attack came. The dead were mostly killed by large caliber lattice weapons."

"Lattice? That means Raiders. Dear God. How many bodies, Pete?"

"The pilot estimates he could see about sixty from the air."

Diminjik hung his head sadly for a few seconds, then came alive with anger and said, "Pete, I want every fighter we have in the air as soon as possible. I want them to board that freighter in orbit and determine if it's responsible for this massacre."

"But we don't have the authority to board a ship in space."

"Damn the authority. I'm declaring this a planet-wide emergency and invoking martial law. I want the ass of every-one involved with this slaughter, and I'm not particular how we get it. Understand? I'll worry about authority and proto-cols later. I'm gonna catch hell for this one way or the other, so I might as well go down swinging."

"Yes, sir. I understand. We'll find the people responsible."

CHAPTER EIGHTEEN
~ October 25th, 2285 ~

Christa set Madu up with a temporary ID that gave her privileges to perform searches into the sleeper database and save the results but that wouldn't permit her to awaken any-one.

"Roughly two hundred hits," Madu said, "on the parameters I entered."

"Only two hundred engineers out of thirty thousand sleep-ers?"

"No. I only searched for mechanical engineers who specialized in water systems and even omitted purification specialists. We're just interested in getting the water flowing, right?"

"Initially," Christa said. "But once it's flowing, we'll need people who can test it for potability."

"I made a list of the purification specialists as well."

"Okay, let's wake up a dozen of the engineers and get them working on the problem. I'm glad this stasis system of yours doesn't require extended time for recovery. Our people wouldn't be able to go to work for solars after a stasis sleep of just a few annuals."

"I hope that when our population is awakened we'll be able to show we have much to offer the Galactic Alliance if the GA can solve our sterility problem."

"That's my hope as well," Christa said.

◆ ◆

A few hours later, the awakened sleepers had been examined by the medical people and then eaten a hearty meal before beginning efforts to find out why the water wasn't flowing in the facility. Christa was praying that with the enemy attackers waiting just outside the door the problem was not an external one.

◆   ◆   ◆

"All non-essential personnel are now in stasis beds and the entire ship is depressurized except for the bridge and the officers quarters here at the center of the ship. The enemy fighters are no longer following us, Excellency," Gxidescu said when he reported to Vejrezzol.

"Did they turn around and return to the planet?"

"No, they just halted and remained where they were. We watched until we traveled beyond a point where the DeTect system could see them."

"Halted? Why?" Vejrezzol asked.

"My best guess is that they're waiting for their ship to come pick them up."

"Then change course immediately while they can't see us."

"Yes, Excellency."

◆   ◆   ◆

When the entire planet was placed under martial law, the protestors at the three warehouses melted into the population centers. The Marines had recorded images of everyone at the demonstrations, and, when the alert was over, the intelligence people would track down every last protestor to determine if they had any culpability for the massacre.

◆   ◆

"No joy, Major," Captain Edward 'Shooter' Conlon said when his squadron had completed its search. "I don't know where she disappeared to, but I know she's not in orbit over this patch of dirt anymore."

"Roger, Shooter. Bring 'em home."

"What now, sir?" Lieutenant Hollister asked Major Garfield. "Shooter was the last to report in. The cargo ship must have left orbit."

"That in itself makes it suspicious. They might have done what they intended and then bugged out. Send an announcement notifying all Space Command ships in the deca-sector to keep an eye out for that bucket. And be sure to tell them it might be heavily armed. Shit, I've got to report this to the old man now. He ain't gonna be happy."

◆ ◆ ◆

"Commander, is the rumor true or not?" Dr. Peterson asked.

Christa had come up to the Housing level because the sentry there reported that the scientists were demanding to see her. She dreaded the meeting, but she went. And she could see no way of denying the question she knew would be put to her.

"Yes, Doctor. It seems that this planet is not unpopulated after all."

"You're telling us that someone has slept for twenty thousand years and been awakened successfully? That's extra-ordinary. We *must* be allowed to interview this person immediately."

"Doctor, we're not talking about an ancient artifact. We're talking about a living, breathing person. You don't get to *demand* an audience. The Ancient will make the decision whether to speak to you or not."

"Yes, yes, of course. I'm sorry, Commander. My enthusiasm got the better of me."

"Didn't we decide yesterday that you were going to be more careful with that enthusiasm of yours?"

"Commander, you're a scientist. You have to realize how exhilarating a discovery like this is. No one, and I mean *no* one, has ever spoken to a twenty-thousand-year-old person before."

"That's not exactly true. I've been talking with her for days. And the medical staff has examined her from her toes to her head, several times. They don't speak Dakis, but I was happy to interpret."

"You know what I mean," Peterson said with obvious irritation. "Nobody has spoken to someone that old before this week. And we have a number of people for whom Dakis is a first language."

Peterson was naturally referring to Drs. Vlashsku and Djetch and their clones. Since their native language was derived from Ancient Dakis, it wasn't difficult to master the slightly different phonetics.

"I'll speak to Madu and ask her if she desires to speak with you. If she says yes, I'll arrange an interview. If she says no, I'll respect her wishes."

"Yes, yes, of course. How many others are there if *she's* not willing to speaking with us?"

"There are a few others. No more than a hundred eighty thousand, I would say.

"A hundred eighty thousand? And they're all in this facility?"

"No, thank heavens. We only have thirty thousand here. The others are in other locations around the planet. However, location information will not be shared until the proper time."

"Commander, I remind you that this is an archeological dig site and the entire planet has been placed into the custody of the Archeological Expedition."

"That *was* true, Doctor. But now that we know this planet was not uninhabited, I would be very surprised if all contracts aren't immediately nullified by the GAC. Or, at the very least, modified with the provision that the Ancients must agree to let you stay. I suggest you tread lightly with the legal inhabitants of this world if you wish the Expedition's privileges to continue. In other words, from this point on, be on your best behavior. If your enthusiasm gets the better of you while in the company of the Ancients, the Expedition Headquarters may order that you be shipped off planet in a cargo container on the next transport available."

◆   ◆   ◆

"As expected," Admiral Moore said to the assembled Admiralty Board, "the GAC has decided to immediately suspend all previous agreements with the Archeological Expedition regarding rights on Dakistee pending verification that the sleepers reported by Commander Carver really are the original inhabitants. The agreements provide several standard boilerplate clauses that allow this, and, in fact, mandate it. Anthius must immediately halt all shipment of artifacts off planet. The warehouses will be seized and held until the proper authority is identified. The dig sites may continue to operate for the time being, but the extension of that privilege is only for six months, or until a Dakistian authority is established and ready to assume a leadership position. If an official authority is not available by that time, the GAC may extend the privilege in additional six-month increments.

"We have been ordered to assist the Dakistian sleepers with food, clothing, and temporary shelter until the proper aid agencies can gear up and support the Dakistian effort to become self-dependent."

"Who will we put in command of our effort on Dakistee?" Admiral Burke asked.

"We're fortunate to have one of the three foremost experts on the Dakistee people, who also happens to be a senior Space Command line officer, already on the planet."

"No," Admiral Hubera said. "No, no, no. We can't put Carver in command of that effort."

"Why not?" Admiral Moore asked.

When Hubera didn't respond right away, Admiral Hillaire said, "Yes, Donald, why not? Is it because you don't like Admiral Carver?"

"I never said that."

"You haven't had to, Donald," Admiral Platt said. "We all know it. *Everybody* in Space Command knows it."

Admiral Hubera just mumbled something unintelligible and ground his teeth.

"Does anyone else have a better candidate to recommend or wish to voice some reason why Commander Christa Carver shouldn't have this temporary duty assignment?" Admiral Moore asked.

After a few seconds of silence, Admiral Moore said, "No? Then all in favor, signify by raising your hand." After a quick glance around the table, he said, "Let the record show that the vote is nine yeas and one nay."

"I suppose you also want to give her a medal for finding and awakening the Dakistians," Admiral Hubera said.

"Are you making such a recommendation, Donald?"

"Me? Of course not."

"Then I think we can dispense with any discussion on that topic. Commander Carver will be notified as soon as possible of her new posting as Commander of the Dakistee Outpost. Now, on to other business."

◆ ◆ ◆

Christa, Madu, Carmoody, and Madu's assistant were seated at one end of an enormous table in a large conference room on the Administrative level when two Marines escorted the Loudescott scientists into the room. Madu immediately jumped to her feet. Her assistant stood up quickly as well.

"What are *those*?" the director said in horror as she stared at the Nordakians in the group who'd had to bend low to get through the doorway without banging their heads on the frame. Fortunately, eight-foot ceilings were the minimum height in the facility, while most common rooms, such as this one, had ten-foot ceilings.

"I realize you're unfamiliar with greeting alien species," Christa said calmly as she also stood, "but you should remember to remain cordial at all times. These gentlemen happen to be your kinsmen. They are the descendents of the dissidents who left your planet twenty thousand years ago."

"Surely you're joking," Madu said. "Their skin keeps flashing different colors."

"I'm perfectly serious. The speculation is that the space-ships weren't adequately shielded, and the generations who lived and died aboard ship before it reached Nordakia suffer-ed mutating effects. Fortunately, the differences seem to be limited to abundant height and visual appearance. They have variable skin chromaticity, and while their color is normally a soft aqua, they can adjust the color to almost any shade unless they're excited. At that time they lose control over the color and it reflects their mood."

"And they're all bald?"

"Yes, that's another aberration, but it's a minor one. It's only hair, and it's limited to the male population. The women have full heads of hair."

"I won't speak with them," Madu said adamantly. "They're part of the dissident group who destroyed my planet."

"Madu, the people who caused such grievous harm to the population on Dakistee were small in number and died two hundred centuries ago. I realize that for you it seems like last solar, but the Nordakians are a peaceful race of people who want nothing more than to get to know you and have you know them. You must put aside your past feelings and judge these people not on what some long dead psychopaths did but on their own merits. If you do, I think you'll be surprised to see how much you have in common. To begin with, there's your common heritage and a common religion."

"We don't have a common religion. They want to follow some perverted version of the Almuth that elevates their priesthood to almost god-like status while completely subjugating women. They preach hate and death to anyone who doesn't believe as they do while telling everyone dumb enough to listen that their religious doctrine espouses only love. They will smile and say, 'I love you, my brother,' as they push a meter-long Skree through your body. My Almuth decries *all* violence, not just violence against people who share your parochial religious beliefs."

"No, they follow the same Almuth as you. They embrace the One True Word."

Madu looked at Christa with suspicion, then relaxed when she saw Christa was apparently being completely open.

"You're sure?"

"I give you my oath as a Space Command officer and a Lady of the Royal House of Nordakia."

"A Lady of the Royal House? You never mentioned that before."

"There's been little time for us to exchange histories."

"What service did you perform to achieve such an honor?"

"As you know, the reason for the award is often confidential. I'm sorry, but I can't tell you."

"Something military, I suppose?"

Christa neither acknowledged nor denied the prying remark. If Madu expected to learn through elimination of possible choices, she was going to be disappointed.

Madu finally stopped waiting for a response and turned to the visitors. "Do any of you speak Ancient Dakis?"

"Our Dakis is audibly close," Doctor Dakshiku Vlashsku said.

"Audibly?" Madu said.

"The dissidents who took our very gullible ancestors from this planet changed the written language so none of their followers would be able to read the original Almuth, but speech cannot be changed as easily. However, it has evolved over the centuries you've slept as technology mandated the need for new terms and old pronunciations blurred. But, because we read from the Almuth every solar, it has not strayed too far."

"And which doctrine do *you* follow?"

"Azula Carver, Lady Christa Carver, and Lady Eliza Carver discovered the original text on this world. They brought it home to Nordakia, where it was immediately embraced as the True Word of God by the Royal Family, the nobility, and most of the priesthood and population."

Madu turned to look at Christa and said, "*Azula* Carver?"

"Azula Jenetta Carver is the original from whom Eliza and I were copied," Christa said. "Jenetta also holds the rank of Admiral in both Space Command and the Nordakian Space Force, and you will often hear her referred to by that title."

"I see," Madu said, turning to face Doctor Vlashsku again. "You said, '*most* of the priesthood and population.' Not everyone on Nordakia accepts the Dakistee version of the Almuth as the One True Word?"

"There's a very small faction who have refused to accept it as genuine. They've been growing increasingly distant from the rest of the population and we've heard rumors they might leave the planet and attempt to form their own colony somewhere else."

"As your ancestors did?"

"Apparently. The priesthood had so effectively masked the truth that no one on Nordakia even suspected our species didn't originate on Nordakia. It was only when Azula Carver and her sisters discovered the Almuth here that we finally learned our species originated on this planet."

"The Carver *sisters*?" Madu said, glancing over at Christa.

"Yes." Sweeping his arm towards the many clones in the room, Doctor Vlashsku said, "Following their example, we all now identify our clones as our brothers and sisters."

"I see," Madu said. "Christa never mentioned that so many clones had been made."

"It was an accident. My associates and I managed to open the cloning facility and the equipment was activated inadvertently. By the time Admiral Carver and her sisters were able to understand the process well enough to cancel it without harming any embryos, seventy-nine clones had been created."

"Christa mentioned there were only seventy-nine citizens on the planet but never said that all were clones."

"There can be no more," Vlashsku said. "Space Command disassembled the equipment and removed it long ago because it's a serious violation of Galactic Alliance law to produce clones intentionally."

"Before we continue this discussion," Christa said to the group, "won't everyone have a seat?"

The original scientists took seats at the enormous conference table and their clones took seats around the periphery.

"As much as this conference is an opportunity for all of you to meet Madu, it's also an opportunity for her to meet you," Christa said. "Please restrain your enthusiasm and give everyone a chance to talk and ask questions. It appears we shall be down here for some time, so there will be many more opportunities to convene if both parties wish it." Looking at Madu, Christa said, "I'll let you act as your own moderator. The floor is yours, Madam Director."

"Thank you, Christa."

"Commander?" Doctor Peterson said anxiously, just as Madu was about to speak.

Christa held up her hand to Madu. When Madu stopped, Christa said, "Yes, Doctor?"

"Could you please tell us what's going on?"

Christa smiled slightly. In Amer, she said, "I apologize to everyone in the room who doesn't speak Dakis or Ancient Dakis. Doctor Vlashsku just gave Madu a very brief synopsis on the evolution of the language, the creation of the clones, and the situation regarding the acceptance of the Almuth found on this planet." Christa turned to Madu and repeated her remarks in Ancient Dakis.

Turning back to the others in the room, Christa continued with, "It's unfortunate this conference room isn't equipped with translation equipment. The Dakistian culture had evolved to a point where only one language was spoken over their entire world, so there was no need for translation devices. And since most everyone on this planet spoke Amer prior to finding the Dakistians, people haven't typically carried a translation device with them. When Madu was awakened, we ordered a quantity of translation devices from Central Supply. Unfortunately, they hadn't yet arrived when events spiraled out of control. Until we can resolve this problem, I suggest that everyone who speaks both Dakis and Amer pose their questions in both languages. Perhaps Doctor Vlashsku will interpret for the Amer-only speakers, and I will translate for Madu. Is that acceptable to everyone?"

As everyone in the room nodded, Christa turned to Madu and explained what she had just said. Madu nodded in response.

◆ ◆

The next several hours were filled with statements of eye-opening importance for both sides. No one had any desire to break for lunch, and they might have refused to break for dinner if the Administrative level hadn't suddenly begun to vibrate from the sound of alarms whooping in every corridor.

Christa rushed from the room to find the two Marine sentries posed with their rifles at the ready but unsure where to direct them.

"Remain here at your posts," Christa said to the Marines as Carmoody and Madu emerged from the conference room. Taking Madu's arm, she said, "Madu, Gracie, come with me." Looking back at the sentries, she said, "Keep everyone else inside."

Others from the room were already trying to get out when the Marines turned and immediately blocked the doorway with their rifles, forcing the people back inside.

"Madu, do you know what that alarm means?"

"The pattern, three whoops, a pause, and then three again, means there's a serious problem on the Vault level."

"What kind of problem?"

"The pattern doesn't identify it, but it's most likely environmental."

"Let's get down there."

◆

As the lift doors opened at the Vault level, a Dakistian Christa hadn't seen before began talking excitedly at Madu. "Engineering room Six is flooding." He said. "Follow me."

The man turned and raced into the Vault without another word. It took several minutes of running to reach the rear wall of the cavern where the man paused just long enough to open a door that led to a long corridor. Madu followed him in with Christa just behind and Carmoody bringing up the rear. They hadn't gotten to this end of the cavern previously, so the two Space Command officers had been unaware that the area even existed.

◆

The excited man opened another door halfway down the corridor and stood back so Madu, Christa, and Carmoody could enter. Inside were gargantuan tanks that rose ten meters towards the cavern's roof. Christa wanted to ask how they had gotten the equipment down here, but there were more important issues at the moment. Stairs that descended to a lower level were slowly disappearing into a rising tide of dark water as a dozen men and women standing on a raised steel platform that extended out along the giant tanks just stared down into the water.

As Christa likewise looked down at the flooding area, a hominid form suddenly broke the dark surface in an eruption of foam and bubbles.

The man, gasping for breath, shouted, "It's useless. I can't stop it. The valve is stuck."

Madu looked at Christa in shock.

"How high will the water rise if we can't stop it?" Christa asked the man standing next to her.

"If we read the charts correctly, the aquifer and water table in this area is quite high. I estimate the water could rise to about three meters above the floor of the rotunda."

"That's the highest floor in the facility," Madu said. "The water will be over our heads. It will even be over the heads of the Nordakians."

Christa grimaced, shrugged, and said, "Well, it appears we won't have to worry about a lack of drinking water anymore."

CHAPTER NINETEEN

~ October 25th, 2285 ~

"Attention, all crew," Captain Permenans of the destroyer *Hell Fire* announced over the ship-wide com system. "We've recovered our fighters and we're about to move in on the freighter. Our distance from the planet is such that we don't have to worry about Marine fighters becoming involved, and we've already destroyed the freighter's FTL capability so they can't escape us. My hope is that we can move in quickly and take the ship without further damaging the cargo section. We will not target the sub-light engines unless there's no other way to stop the ship. If they refuse to surrender, we'll pour everything we've got into the bridge area until we kill every last mother's son aboard that ship.

"Now lock down anything movable because we're going in. Then report to your battle stations. Captain, out."

"Helm, take us to the freighter."

"Aye, sir," the helmsman said as he keyed the estimated position of the cargo ship into the computer. It was another two minutes before the temporal envelope was built and the ship began to move, but it arrived at the new location within five minutes. "Uh, we're here, Captain," the helmsman said, "but there's no freighter."

"What?"

"I said…"

"I heard you, dammit. Where is it?"

"This is where they should be if they had maintained their course at sub-light, sir."

"Com, find Wing Commander Fowler."

A few minutes later, the com chief said, "I have Fowler for you, Captain."

Permenans picked up the earpiece and stuck it in his ear. "Fowler, where the blazes is that freighter?"

"Uh, I don't know, sir. Isn't it where it's supposed to be?"

"If it was where it's supposed to be, I wouldn't be asking *you*."

"Uh, yes, sir. It was on the heading I radioed in when we received the order to hold position and wait to be picked up. I watched them on my DeTect and they continued on that course until we lost the signal."

"Are you sure you destroyed their temporal field generator?"

"Yes, sir. We blasted it to bits. I guarantee that."

"Damn. Captain out."

Permenans yanked the earpiece out and glared at the Tac officer. "Tactical, find that blasted freighter."

"Aye, sir. It's not on the DeTect so we'll have to hunt for it. I'll establish a search pattern using the last known position as the center of the grid."

"Don't tell me," Permenans said with annoyance, "tell the helm."

"Yes, sir," the tac person said as he dedicated himself to the task.

◆　◆　◆

Commander Conte, XO of the GSC destroyer *Portland*, entered the bridge just after having breakfast. The third officer was sitting in the command chair, so Conte walked to the Captain's ready room and waited until the doors opened to admit him.

"Morning, Jerry," Captain Gregory said. "Have a seat. You're way too early for our daily briefing. What's up?"

"Did you see the com traffic advisories this morning, sir?"

"Yes, I did."

"And, uh, did you happen to notice the one about being on the lookout for a freighter?"

"You mean the one from the commanding officer of North Pendleton on Dakistee?"

"Yes, sir."

"I didn't see anything special about it. The tac officer will watch for all ships listed on the advisory, as always."

"Read the description again, sir— if you would."

Gregory looked at Conte suspiciously, then called the advisory up on his com unit. "I'll be damned," he said after reading the notice. "You think this is the same freighter we tailed from Nordakia, don't you?"

"If it's not, it came from the same shipyard. And if it is, they either had no intention of going to Slabeca, or they have the worst navigator in the universe."

"The Nordakians thought they might make a run to Obotymot, but no one ever considered Dakistee."

"It makes sense though that they might hope to re-colonize their original home world instead of that hell of a planet they announced as their destination."

"How far are we from Dakistee, Jerry?"

"I estimate we could make planet-fall in seventy hours."

"Have the helm change course for Dakistee and have the tac officer keep an extra sharp eye out for that freighter."

"Aye, Captain," Conte said, getting up and walking towards the door.

"And Jerry?" the Captain said.

Conte stopped and turned. "Sir?"

"Good pickup. Thanks."

"Aye, sir."

◆　◆　◆

"Tell me you have good news, Pete," Lt. Colonel Diminjik said to Major Garfield as soon as he arrived at Loudescott.

"I wish I could, sir, but the reports about the bodies were accurate. The Graves Registration people are directing the effort to get them into body bags for transport back to North Pendleton. So far, the count is seventy-one. I have as many people as possible searching the forest around the site looking for anyone who made it into the cover afforded by the trees, including any who might have expired from their wounds. Those lattice weapons are nasty. Most victims seemed to have died from blood loss within minutes of being wounded."

"Any sign of Carver?"

"Negative. She must have made it into the facility here. We haven't found any sign of dead or wounded Marines, either. I've had two people banging on the door with rifle butts and hammers since we arrived, but so far there's been no response from inside and we already know communications are out when the door's closed."

"If anything happened to her after I refused to immediately send back her half squad, the Admiral will have my ass— roasted."

"A half squad wouldn't have made a difference, sir. A full *regiment* wouldn't have made a difference here, unless they had fighters or SAMS. These people were all killed by air attack. The ground is littered with spent lattice rounds. Since the appropriations people have been refusing to give us a proper satellite network, there's no way we could have taken steps to prevent this slaughter."

"Yeah, thanks, but that doesn't make me feel any better. Keep trying to let those people in the facility know it's safe to come out. I've put every shuttle I could commandeer into orbit around the planet. If we can't have a satellite network, we'll use a people network to watch for approaching ships. I told the owners of the shuttles to send their bill to the GAC."

"Jeez, Colonel, you're digging yourself in deep."

"Pete, this happened on my watch. There's no way I'm coming out of this without having my butt roasted good and proper. This will probably be my last command, so maybe I can help the next poor bastard who commands North Pendleton by employing a few theatrics."

"Yes, sir."

◆ ◆ ◆

"That's your response to this disaster?" Madu said wildly. "That we no longer have to worry about a lack of drinking water?"

"Calm down, Madu. It's a serious problem, but not as bad as you seem to think."

"You say that now, but you'll be gurgling a different song when the water reaches your nose."

"The water isn't going to reach my nose or yours. I doubt it will even reach the next level."

"How can you say that? You see the way the water is rushing in."

"We know the facility is tightly sealed or we would have communication with the outside. So, in order for the water to rise, it has to compress the air inside the facility. Right now, the pressure pushing down on the water outside the facility is sufficient to compress the air in here. But once the pressures equalize, the water will stop rising."

Madu looked skeptical, but said, "Are you sure?"

"It's elementary physics. You can try an experiment on your own and see for yourself. Take a glass and invert it, then press it down into a bowl of water. The water will only rise inside very slightly as you push the glass lower."

"But the Vault level is in danger of being filled, right?"

"That has to be our biggest concern right now."

"There are thirty thousand people down there."

"But they're all encased in self-contained stasis chambers."

"But each chamber is plugged into the electrical system. They rely on receiving a small amount of power from the facility to keep their systems operating. If the water fills the cavern, the power to each stasis unit might be lost."

"How long will the chambers continue to operate with no power being fed to them?"

"It depends on the level of energy in the small backup storage cells each chamber contains. After twenty thousand years, the cells might have decayed to a point that they no longer hold a normal charge. Fortunately, once the processing cycle is complete, very little energy is required to keep it that way. But in cases where the storage cells are completely drained, the occupant might survive for only several solars because the process will reverse when the energy runs out. The sleepers could awaken under water with only enough air to survive for a couple of hours, if the chamber doesn't automatically open."

"Okay, *that's* a very serious concern then. Is there a way to determine the strength of the storage cells without awakening the sleepers?'

"I can run a program and create a list of the sleepers according to the energy level of their sleep chamber power cells."

"Good! You work on that while I try to find some way to stop the rising water."

"How?"

"I have no idea— yet. Now go."

As Madu disappeared through the door, Christa turned to look at the men and women standing on the platform. They were all looking at her with curiosity. As Director of this facility, Madu was the ultimate authority. Yet they had just witnessed this slightly odd-looking stranger with the wild hair color order her about as if she was subordinate— and, after accepting the order without question, Madu had hurried to complete the task.

"Ladies and Gentlemen. I'm Commander Christa Carver. This facility is currently under martial law and I'm the senior ranking officer. I need you to follow my instructions as if they were coming from Madu. Do you understand my words?"

Christa waited until each had nodded.

"Do any of you have a problem with that directive?"

Each of the assembled people shook their head to indicate a negative.

"Good. First, I need suggestions for ways to stop the rising water. Who wants to go first?"

The assembled group, all mechanical engineers who had never worked together before, looked at one another but offered nothing.

"Someone must have a suggestion," Christa said. "Who is the senior person here?"

The man who had met Madu, Christa, and Carmoody at the elevator raised his hand partially. "I guess I am."

"And your name is…?"

"I'm Aestolul Derkardlek."

"Well, Aestolul, how would you solve this problem?"

"We've already tried everything we could think of."

"Surely you didn't try everything possible. The water is still rising. We must stop it to ensure that your fellow sleepers don't drown."

"Uh, we could wake them and bring them to a higher level."

"No, that's not possible. We'd run out of food in a solar. We have to stop the water from rising."

"But you heard Semuthl. The valve is stuck open."

"How can we close it?"

"It's underwater."

"I realize that. How could we close it if it wasn't underwater?

"We'd use a hydraulic power unit, and, if that didn't do it, we'd shut off the water line outside the facility and swap out the valve."

"I already know we can't shut off the water line. I suppose you're going to tell me we don't have a hydraulic unit either."

"Well, we don't."

Christa nodded. "Yeah. Okay, let's rack those brains, everyone. What else can we try?"

Her words were met with blank looks from everyone.

"Somebody must have an idea."

When no one offered anything, Christa looked around the area searching for a kernel of an idea.

As she looked upwards, she said, "What would we lose if this entire section flooded?"

"These tanks contain a reverse osmosis filtration system," Aestolul said.

"If this area was flooded and the process ceased, we would be dealing with unfiltered water?"

"The filtration process would only cease if the hydrostatic pressure was less than the osmotic pressure."

"So if this area was completely submerged, it wouldn't affect the filtration?"

"We'd probably lose the electronic sensors and be unable to monitor the flow."

"But the water would continue to flow in and be filtered."

"Of course. We can't stop it, remember?"

"If this door to the corridor was closed, is there any other way for the water to get out?"

The engineers conferred for a few seconds and then Aestolul said, "Water will flow around the pipes where they pass through prepared access holes in the walls."

"Is that all?"

"The total volume could be significant."

"Okay, we have two tasks ahead of us. First, I need someone to find the environmental system controls and increase the air pressure. The more we increase the pressure in here, the more we slow the flow of incoming water."

"I can do that," Aestolul said.

"Good. Second, can anyone here weld?"

One of the engineers raised his hand. "I've done hobby welding."

"Good, you're now our welding master. Get everybody outside and weld the entrance door closed. Then track down all the places where water could leak out, stuff them with whatever packing material you can find, such as clothing, rags, or even wood, and weld something in place to prevent the water pressure from pushing the packing out."

"But I don't have welding equipment."

"This is the utility section of the facility. I'm sure there's welding equipment somewhere down here. You're in charge of this operation and everyone here is part of your team. Task half your people to look for welding equipment and packing material and the rest to hunt for possible leak holes outside the filtration room. Now, go find what you need and get to work."

"Yes, ma'am," he said and started giving instructions to those around him."

◆ ◆ ◆

"There she is, Captain," the tac officer aboard the *Hell Fire* said as the ship dropped its envelope ten million kilometers from the *Gastropod*.

"At last."

"What are your orders, sir?"

"Sound General Quarters."

◆ ◆ ◆

"Sorry to disturb your meditation, Excellency, but the DeTect system indicates that a ship is approaching on a direct course— it's coming on very quickly," Gxidescu reported to Vejrezzol.

Vejrezzol jumped up and ran to the bridge. "Why haven't you engaged the alarm?" he demanded of Gxidescu.

"You didn't tell me to do that, Excellency."

"Fool. You're the captain. I shouldn't have to tell you."

Gxidescu looked over at the security station and nodded to the tac officer. Alarms began to sound throughout the ship.

In two more minutes, the com officer said, "All gunners are at their posts, Captain."

As Vejrezzol climbed into the first officer's chair, he said, "Do you think this is the ship that launched the fighters?"

"That would be my guess. They must be here to complete what they began."

"Are the— cargo containers ready?"

"Yes, Excellency. All is prepared."

"Good. They're about to get the surprise of their lives."

◆ ◆ ◆

"What have you learned?" Christa asked as she climbed up to join Madu on the platform where the computer console was located. Madu was just standing there staring at the monitor.

"The news is bad," Madu replied. "The diagnostic module incorporated into each chamber is so slow that it could take solars to run the procedure on all thirty thousand units."

"Solars? We don't have solars."

"I know. That's why I said the news was bad."

"Oh. I thought you meant the information you'd collected was bad."

"That too. Of the twelve chambers checked so far, four have almost no power reserves at all. If they lose power for more than ten minutes, the process will begin to reverse and the sleeper will be awakened."

"Four out of twelve? That is bad. We can't feed ten thousand additional people for very long."

"How did you make out with the water problem?"

"I've ordered the air pressure to be increased and the filtration room closed and sealed. I have the engineers searching for every place where water might escape so they can attempt to block its flow. If we get lucky, we can reduce the flow to a trickle outside the room. If we can do that, we might be able to find a way to pump the water out of the drains."

"The drains? But we're hundreds of meters below the outside water table."

"Yes, but the drains in every sink, shower, and head must feed into a central area where the water is then automatically pumped to the top level and fed into the local sewer system."

"Head?"

"Sorry. It's the term the military uses for the lavatory, the 'convenience,' or the commode."

Madu nodded her head. "That makes sense. I mean the theory, not the fact that you call the commode a head. Why is it called a head?"

"Tradition— and pithiness, I guess. Head is a single syllable, where lavatory and convenience are four. Even commode is two. That's the pithiness part. The tradition is a little harder to explain. Before sea-going ships had power, they used sails to gather wind for propulsion. The wind, by necessity, had to come over the stern to be of use on large vessels, so the commode would be located at the bow, or head, of the ship so the smells wouldn't pass over the entire ship."

"I see. That makes sense as well. Not the name, the location."

"Madu, let me take a look at the procedure you're running. Perhaps I can get a little more speed out of it."

Madu stepped aside to allow Christa full access to the console. Christa looked at the information on the monitor, then began typing in commands at a furious pace.

"How is it that you know this system?" Madu asked. She was clearly in awe of Christa's apparent familiarity.

"I gained a lot of knowledge working with the system at the cloning facility. The programs are different, but the operating system is identical and that's the most important part. And I got a good refresher course when I worked with the security stations in the rotunda. Computers have always been a hobby of mine and essentially they all work the same way. You just have to understand the 'language' they speak."

After a few more minutes, Christa said, "The procedure you were running was apparently intended to operate as a background task. It constantly checks the chambers. When all chambers have been checked, it starts over again, so it's been running continuously for twenty thousand years. The information is stored in the data files, so we only have to create a report rather than checking all the chambers again. I've asked it to tell me how many chambers would not survive thirty solars without power."

"Why thirty solars?"

"Because the Higgins Space Command base is only about thirty light-annuals away. This planet is far too populated for the attack to go unnoticed for long. Someone will find it strange that they haven't heard from the Marine outpost or the archeological camp, or that their messages are going unanswered. I don't know the size of the attacking force, or forces, but I'm sure they can't stand against the might of a Space Command warship. Even if no warship is closer to us than Higgins, one will arrive here in within thirty solars."

A few seconds later, the report popped up on the monitor.

"Great Nallick save us," Madu muttered. "It's even worse than we thought."

CHAPTER TWENTY

~ October 25th, 2285 ~

Traveling at Sub-Light-100 after dropping out of FTL, the Raider destroyer *Hell Fire* closed quickly on the *Gastropod*, which was still traveling at Sub-Light-50.

"All gunners," Captain Permenans said over the ship-wide com, "prepare to open fire, but not until I give the command." To the com chief, he said, "Send the message."

"Attention freighter," the com chief said into his headset microphone. "Heave to and prepare to be boarded or you'll be destroyed."

After a minute during which no transmission was received, the com officer sent the message again.

"No response, Captain," the com chief said a minute later.

"Okay, they've had their chance. Put me on ship-wide, chief."

"You're on, Captain."

"Attention, gunners, we're going in. You have permission to open fire when you have a lock. Try to avoid hitting the engines. That's all."

◆　◆　◆

"Laser gunners, fire at will," Vejrezzol announced. "Tactical, hold your fire until I give the order."

All gunners acknowledged the order, then hunched over their consoles, watching the large target dot on the screen in front of them. As the ship came into range, the laser gunners let loose with their fire, but the low-power lasers were virtually ineffective against the armor of a warship.

When the *Hell Fire* reached a point one thousand kilometers abreast of the *Gastropod*, Vejrezzol said, "Now!"

As the words reached the tactical officer, he depressed the two lighted switches on his consoles. The sidewalls of two cargo containers flew off and two fourteen-meter-long torpedoes burst from the steel containers.

◆ ◆ ◆

An alarm began shrieking aboard the *Hell Fire's* bridge as the two deadly missiles streaked towards the warship.

"All gunners target those torpedoes!" Captain Permenans screamed. "Tac, eject counter measures. Helm, evade, evade, evade."

Arms of coherent light reached out for the streaking tubes of death as the gunners tried to destroy them. The tac officer ejected counter measures designed to confuse the targeting systems and cause the torpedoes to exhaust their precious fuel while the helmsman twisted the joystick and sent the *Hell Fire* on a wild and twisting erratic path away from the freighter. With each maneuver, the missiles had to change direction to follow, but they slowly closed the gap. There wasn't enough time to build the FTL envelope, so the warship had to rely on its sub-light speed, the maneuvers of the helmsman, the counter measures, and the skill of the gunners.

As the first of the torpedoes closed to within a kilometer, one gunner scored a hit that caused the torpedo to explode. All gunners then shifted their attention to the remaining torpedo.

The second torpedo almost reached the ship before another gunner scored a hit that destroyed the targeting system. The torpedo skewered off in a twisting, turning action, ultimately exploding a good distance from the ship.

"Alright," Captain Permenans said, "they've had their shot. I doubt they've got any more of those things. Now it's our turn."

As the *Hell Fire* neared the *Gastropod* again, the gunners opened up on the cargo ship with everything they had, anxious for a little payback after what they had just been through.

◆ ◆ ◆

"We can't possibly escape," Gxidescu said. "The hull is open to space in hundreds of locations."

"Then we shall have to give them our final surprise. Helm, cut power and cease course correction. Allow the ship to go where it will."

"Yes, Excellency."

◆　◆　◆

When the sub-light engines shut down, Captain Permenans smiled. "Got 'em," was all he said as the *Hell Fire's* helmsman cut power to the engines and allowed the ship to drift towards the *Gastropod* as he matched its speed.

◆　◆　◆

"They've taken the bait," Vejrezzol said.

"But why didn't we wait until they pulled alongside before we fired the torpedoes?" Gxidescu asked. "We might have gotten them."

"No— they would have come no closer. I didn't expect they'd even come *that* close. And they needed to see a last ditch effort before they'd prepare to board us. Now they believe they've seen it."

Vejrezzol waited until the *Hell Fire* was less than a hundred meters from the *Gastropod* and had sent out shuttles to board the freighter.

"Okay, Gxidescu, it's time to give them the real surprise we've reserved for them."

"Yes, Excellency," Gxidescu said somberly.

◆　◆　◆

"Even if we began waking sleepers immediately we couldn't possibly awaken all the sleepers who are at risk," Madu said.

"Calm down," Christa said. "Your people may be able to slow the flow of water enough so it doesn't present a danger. If they can't, we'll start waking the sleepers at the lowest level and work our way higher as the water rises."

"But if the power shorts out as the water rises, the chambers at the top will be inaccessible."

"We'll find a way, even if we have to use some of the emptied chambers as boats. But there still may not be a need to awaken anyone."

"These aren't your people. That's why you're not concerned."

"When I took command of this outpost, everyone in it became one of *my* people. I take my responsibility seriously, Madu."

Madu took a deep breath and then let it out slowly. "I'm sorry, Christa. I take my responsibility seriously, and I believe you do the same. I'm just frightened we won't be able to save them all."

"We'll save every single one. I promise."

"Can I awaken some of the more brilliant minds now? Just in case?"

"We still have the issue of food, Madu."

"You said you stocked enough for a thousand people for thirty solars and that help will be here before that time is up. How many mouths do we have currently?"

"About five hundred, I think. I haven't had time to collect information."

"Then we should be able to awaken five hundred sleepers."

Christa sighed. She knew Madu wasn't going to give up. But she also knew the Admiralty Board might be angry about waking the sleepers before she had received permission.

"If I allow you to awaken five hundred, will you cease asking for more unless we know it's an emergency?"

"I promise."

"Okay," Christa said as she keyed in her password after using her body to block sight of the keyboard. "You can awaken five hundred, so pick the ones you feel will be of most value in this emergency."

Madu smiled. "Thanks, Christa. Your actions continue to reinforce the trust that's been developing in me."

"Madu, I want to see everyone in this vault awakened, but only when we can guarantee that all can be properly housed and fed unless we must do it sooner to protect their lives. If we had the resources, I'd tell you awaken all of them now."

"I believe *you*, Christa. My concern is that your superiors may not agree with your philosophies or actions."

"Knowing what I do about the actions of the religious dissidents responsible for the attempted death of your entire population on this planet, I can understand your reticence to trust those you feel are outsiders, but you must remember that you're part of the Galactic Alliance now unless you wish to withdraw. Until that unlikely event, Space Command will do everything we can to protect you from harm."

"We can withdraw from the Galactic Alliance?"

"Of course. The Alliance is composed of planets that have banded together for the good of all member worlds. If you don't wish to be a member, the planetary government can pull out."

"With no repercussions?"

"There are always repercussions from any action. You'll have to decide if the advantages outweigh the disadvantages."

"Which are?"

"Uh, I think that discussion should be set aside for another time, Madu. We have much more important matters to think about now. I believe you wanted to awaken five hundred people."

"Yes. Of course," Madu said as she turned her attention to the console and began looking through lists of names.

◆ ◆ ◆

Admiral Holt's chief aide took a deep breath and pressed the talk button on his com unit. "Admiral, Captain Dommler and Colonel Reilly would like a few minutes of your time to discuss an urgent matter." When the message, 'Send them in,' appeared on his monitor, the aide nodded his head towards the Admiral's inner office.

Captain Richard Dommler, the officer in charge of fleet communications in the deca-sector, walked down the hallway just slightly ahead of Colonel Michael Reilly, the Commander of Marine forces in the deca-sector. They paused for just a second to straighten their tunics, then stepped into the area where the door sensor would detect their presence and alert the Admiral. As the door slid open, they stepped smartly into the room.

"Gentlemen, come in," Admiral Holt said affably. "What's this urgent matter you need to discuss? Does the squash court in the officer's gym need repainting?" When the admiral's jest failed to bring the expected grins, Holt knew the matter was serious indeed.

"Admiral," Dommler said, "We have a major problem on Dakistee."

"I'm listening, Robert. Have a seat and continue."

At the invitation to sit, the two officers parked themselves in the overstuffed chairs that floated in front of the Admiral's desk.

"Sir," Colonel Reilly said, "I've received a message from the North Pendleton base commander that the dig site at Loudescott was attacked by an unknown force. Dozens of people were killed by lattice weapons mounted on aerial craft. There was an unidentified freighter in orbit over the site at the time, but it has since disappeared."

Holt's affable expression had turned cold and hard as Reilly talked.

"Lt. Colonel Diminjik has scoured space around the planet and found no sign of danger. The new facility at Loudescott is closed, and we're assuming the survivors have sealed themselves inside. We have no report of their condition or the number of survivors."

"Of the dead, how many were civilians and how many were military?"

"All were civilians. It appears they were gunned down as they tried to reach the safety of the facility."

"Sir," Dommler said, "every ship in the deca-sector has been alerted to keep an eye out for that freighter. We believe it might be the one carrying religious dissidents from Nordakia to Slabeca. The Nordakian Space Force asked us to watch them for a while because their intelligence arm suspected the ship might make for Obotymot instead."

"I'm familiar with that issue. So you think those psychopaths attacked Dakistee with the intention of taking the planet for themselves?"

"They may have tried it, and then discovered that their plan was unworkable."

"Damn," Holt said, "as if things weren't difficult enough in this deca-sector with most of our forces still not returned from our war posture along the old Frontier border. Now we have a shipload of maniacs running around slaughtering innocent civilians in the name of religion. I don't mind if crazy zealots want to die for their God, but why do these nut jobs always need to take others with them— as if such tactics ever solved anything in centuries of religious hatred on Earth. Won't they ever learn that they really accomplish nothing with violence except to bring more of it down on their own heads?"

Dommler and Reilly maintained their silence and a staid appearance during the Admiral's little rant.

"Okay," Holt said, "where are we with the search?"

"No one has sighted the freighter yet. The destroyer *Portland* was the ship assigned to babysit the freighter until it seemed reasonably certain they were headed towards Slabeca. It's presently only a couple of days from Dakistee and Captain Gregory has announced he'll commence a search as soon as they reach the area."

"Good. Frank's a good officer. He'll know where to look. Anybody else out that way?"

"We have several other ships about a week to ten days out. All are headed for the area at top speed."

"I wish we had a few scout-destroyers available. What about that diplomatic corps yacht?"

"I don't know, sir. I could check to see if it's available. It's only lightly armed, though."

"That's fine. We only want their speed for assistance in the search. Let's pull out all the stops, gentlemen. I want that freighter found, and if they *aren't* the ones responsible for this attack then I want to know who *is*. This kind of atrocity ended when the Raiders were sent packing and I don't ever intend to let anyone gain another foothold like that in my deca-sector."

◆ ◆ ◆

"Gxidescu," Vejrezzol said, "What's going on? I gave the order to fire."

"There seems to be a problem, Excellency," Gxidescu said from the tactical console. "The explosives have failed to detonate."

"Try again."

"I have, Excellency. I've sent the code three times."

"Find the problem!" Vejrezzol screamed.

"There might be a break in the wiring. A conduit may have been pierced when the warship was firing on us."

"Gxidescu, those infidels will be boarding us at any minute!"

"The ship is depressurized, Excellency. We can't leave the bridge without EVA suits."

"That's unacceptable."

"Yes, Excellency. But nevertheless, it's fact."

"Distribute weapons. We'll fight them when they attempt to enter the bridge."

"We have no weapons on the bridge. We never anticipated a need for them since taking control of the ship from the real crew."

- 233 -

"We *are* the real crew."

"Yes, Excellency. Of course, you are correct. We are the real crew."

◆ ◆ ◆

"Captain, we're about to enter the freighter," XO Pasquale said from the bridge of a shuttle. "Any final orders?"

"Just play it by ear, XO. If any of them still live and want to continue living, accept their surrender. If they insist on dying, help them move along the path to whatever God it is they worship."

"Aye, Captain. Message received and understood."

◆ ◆

Thirty minutes later, the boarding parties were outside the bridge. A deck by deck search had shown that only the bridge was still pressurized, and they had found no one in EVA suits. Pasquale had sent for the portable airlock they'd brought in the shuttle, and once in place, the XO and three of his people entered and forced open the doors to the bridge.

As they stepped onto the bridge, the Raider boarding party was wide-eyed to find themselves facing eight Nordakians, all of whom were flashing in colors of orange and red. There were no weapons in evidence, but the Raiders continued to train theirs on the bridge crew nevertheless.

"I'm Commander Pasquale of the *Hell Fire*," the XO said as he removed his helmet. "Do you surrender this vessel?"

"What is the *Hell Fire*?" Vejrezzol asked.

"It's a Raider destroyer. Now, do you surrender this vessel?"

"And why have you chosen to attack this ship?"

"We don't allow competing companies to operate in our territories. Do you surrender?"

"Competing companies? We're not in competition with you or any other company. We are on a religious pilgrimage."

"Religious pilgrimage? You killed a hundred people on Dakistee."

Four more Raiders entered the bridge as the airlock completed its cycle.

"They were all infidels," Vejrezzol said. "It was done in the name of God, so it was required. For our acts, we shall ascend to paradise and sit at the feet of Nallick, as shall all true sons of the Most Holy."

"You believe that murdering innocent people is required and reserves a place in paradise for you? You're even sicker than some of our people who kill simply because they enjoy it."

"Blasphemer!" Vejrezzol screamed. "Infidel! You shall die for your words."

Vejrezzol pushed aside his cloak. As his hand came up, Pasquale saw that it contained a lattice pistol. He threw himself to the side as Vejrezzol fired a three-round burst. Only one struck Pasquale, while the other two rounds struck the man standing behind him. The men on either side of Pasquale were on Vejrezzol in an instant. Their heavy EVA suits helped drive him to the deck while the other Raiders covered the bridge crewmen. Once disarmed and restrained, all Vejrezzol could do was scream oaths and obscenities as he urged his followers to disregard the weapons pointed at them and rush the Raiders. None were so foolhardy as he.

As Pasquale climbed to his feet, he looked down at the breast-plate on his EVA suit. The metal re-breather unit had stopped the lattice round cold. A laser would have burned through in an instant, but lattice rounds couldn't penetrate anything solid. The man behind Pasquale had taken one hit to his re-breather and one to his helmet. He was also fine.

"Captain," Pasquale said to his com link, "we have eight Nordakian prisoners. We'll need eight extra-large stasis beds in order to transport them to the ship."

"Nordakians?"

"Yes, sir. They claim to be on a holy pilgrimage."

"Holy..."

"Yes, sir. They see killing everyone who doesn't believe exactly as they do, a holy crusade."

"To each their own," the Captain said. "The beds are as good as on their way. Did the Nordakians give you any trouble?"

"Nothing we couldn't handle, sir."

◆ ◆

When the new slaves were safely loaded aboard the *Hell Fire*, Pasquale called for instructions.

"I've assigned a team of six engineers to replace the FTL generator," Captain Permenans said, "and the rest of our engineering staff has been sent to begin sealing the hull so it can be pressurized. With any luck, we'll be out of here and headed for Raider Four within a couple of days. You'll remain aboard as Captain until you reach our base."

"Aye, sir. Pasquale out."

◆ ◆

Captain Permenans was awakened in the middle of the night when his bed began shaking violently. A second later, alarms began sounding in his quarters and the corridors. He made it to the bridge in eighteen seconds. Still in his pajamas, he shouted, "What is it?" at his second officer.

"It's the freighter, sir. It just exploded!"

CHAPTER TWENTY-ONE
~ October 26th, 2285 ~

"You're exhausted, Madu," Christa said. "You should go get some rest. You've identified the people who must be awakened. The computer can do the rest."

"I know. I just want to be here in case something goes wrong."

"I know the feeling, but you need rest. It was a very long solar, and the new solar actually began some time ago. If we were on the surface, we could have watched the sunrise and eaten breakfast already."

"You should talk," Madu said with a weak smile. "You look like you've been up for several solars without any rest."

"But I'm used to it. The activity never stops aboard ship. When an officer isn't on watch, there're meetings and conferences, training sessions, and self-studies. We have to stay on top of everything going on in Space Command and be prepared to meet any situation or emergency. Meal times in the officers' mess are sometimes the only chance we get to socialize. And when I *can* find some free time, I like to spend it in the gym."

"That sounds terrible. It sounds like all you do is work, sleep, and eat. Why do you do it?"

"I guess because I love it. As on any job, there are times when you experience frustration, but most of the time I feel like I make a difference in the Galactic Alliance. For example, my efforts in solving the mystery of opening this facility has led to finding one hundred eighty thousand people entombed for twenty thousand years— people who will shortly join the citizens of the GA and again be able to enjoy life. You can't put a price tag on something like that."

"Christa, if I'd had any lingering doubts that you intended to awaken all my people, they would have been expelled just now. The way your face lights up when you talk about your job speaks volumes. I can usually recognize when someone is lying or hiding something, and I also recognize sincerity when I see it."

"Then look at my face when I say, 'You need rest.' Come on, I'll walk with you to the dorms. Did I hear your assistant say he had set up a room for you?"

"Yes. How about you?"

"The Marines reserved a room for me in their dorm section."

The two women joined the awakened sleepers who were walking to the elevator with escorts. Christa had arranged for dorm spaces to be opened up to accommodate the newly awakened Dakistians. She had also assigned Carmoody to see that the Dakistians were not disturbed by the Loudescott people, so the archeological people were in a separate wing and would not be allowed access to the Dakistian wing. The dozen Dakistians working on the problem with the rising water could move back and forth between the Vault level and the Housing level, but the others could not go back down once they went up.

◆ ◆ ◆

Despite her weariness, sleep didn't come easily to Christa. The problems with the rising water, which had been slowed but not stopped, the unknown situation outside the facility, and the known situation inside all kept her tossing and turning. Thus far, the archeologists had remained somewhat subdued despite their eagerness to interview, and probe, every Dakistian. Christa had made it known that protocol breeches would be dealt with severely, but she didn't know how long that would keep them at bay.

◆ ◆ ◆

"The situation on Dakistee has stabilized somewhat," Councilman Ahil Fazid said as he stood at the table and read his report on the operation. "At last word, the *Hell Fire* had engaged the freighter from which the fighters had come and destroyed its FTL temporal generator. The Captain announced his intention to pursue once he had recovered all his fighters. Without FTL, the freighter can't possibly escape, and even if they employ tugs, their maximum speed will be only Light-75.

"Most of our people on the ground have returned to their previous positions around the planet. A core fighting force remains in a hidden location a thousand kilometers from Loudescott ready to return should they be needed, and a few key personnel are still at the site."

As Fazid sat down, Chairman Strauss said, "Ahil, how do you feel about this operation?"

"Feel, Arthur?"

"Yes. We never expected this other force to intervene during our assault. Were they aware of our plan and intervened only to disrupt us, or was it coincidental?"

"I don't think we can know that until Captain Permenans has a chance to interview the freighter crew."

"Despite this setback," Councilwoman Erika Overgaard said, "do you still expect to achieve the intended goals?"

"Certainly not all of them. The intervening attack drew far too much attention to Loudescott. By this time, I imagine almost every Marine on the planet is bivouacked at the dig site, and Space Command probably has two dozen ships on their way to the planet. But part of our plan might still succeed. Simply learning what Carver discovered inside and being in position to confiscate it, or part of it, after the forces are drawn down could make the operation a huge success."

◆　◆　◆

"We have an urgent message from Admiral Holt," Admiral Moore said to the assembled Admiralty Board. He nodded to his aide and the full wall monitor lit up with the head-and-shoulders image of Admiral Holt.

After the message had played, Admiral Moore said, "As you can see, the situation is serious. Although we believe it was the religious dissidents, we must remain open to the idea that it might have been Raiders again. If they're feeling bold enough to attack a planet this close to the center of Region One then we have good cause to worry."

"Admiral Holt made no mention of Commander Carver in his message," Admiral Platt said. "Do we know if she's safe, or has she perhaps fallen into the hands of the Raiders?"

"I have no other information in that regard," Admiral Moore said.

"Leave it to Carver to get us involved in another serious mess," Admiral Hubera said.

"Commander Carver can hardly be held accountable for an attack on our outpost at Loudescott," Admiral Bradley said.

"Wherever one of the Carvers is located, you can be sure trouble will follow. We ought to assign them all to Border Patrol duty along our border with the Aguspod," Hubera grumbled.

"The Carvers are frequently at the center of trouble because dangerous and sensitive assignments require the talents of the best and brightest," Admiral Hillaire said. "Assigning even one of them to patrol duty along a border would be akin to locking a fine piece of artwork in a dark closet where no one ever saw it."

"When I met with Carver on Dakistee, I knew we'd have trouble there. She should be on her way back to Region Two."

"You were on Dakistee recently?" Admiral Moore asked. "Is that where you went on the short vacation you took?"

"Uh, it was a small side trip. I went to Belagresue for a couple of days and visited Dakistee on an inspection visit because the *Murray* was available to provide transportation for the four-day round trip."

"Inspection visit?" Admiral Burke said. "Since when are you authorized to perform inspections at any of my bases without prior approval from this board?"

"I wasn't inspecting a base. I was merely checking up on Carver."

"And since when have you been authorized to *check up* on an officer in another chain of command?" Admiral Platt asked.

"I was only trying to ascertain if the situation on Dakistee warranted more investigation or not. That's the responsibility of this Board, after all. I was only doing my job."

"In the future, Donald, you should refrain from making inspection visits unless directly authorized by this Board," Admiral Moore said.

Admiral Hubera grumbled something and nodded, his eyes on the table in front of him.

◆ ◆ ◆

Captain Permenans entered the small interview room next to the brig and stared at the captive there.

Vejrezzol, wearing Raider restraints, was seated at the only table, his hands locked against his waist and his ankles locked to each other. A guard wearing a stun baton stood at either shoulder, but they were hardly necessary. The pain that could be instantly administered through the collar was enough to convince any prisoner not to resist his captors. Vejrezzol had already felt the pain a dozen times as his guards, in response to strings of vile curses, administered attitude-correction measures.

"Are you ready to talk now?" Permenans asked, "or should I return later after you've received more— training."

"When I reach paradise, Nallick will have an honored place set aside for me because I've resisted your tortures."

"The collars don't permanently harm your body, so they won't speed you on your way to your Nallick, but no one can withstand the pain indefinitely. You will answer my questions. If you answer now, you save yourself the pain. But if you insist on being stubborn, I can wait."

"Then wait in Hell."

Permenans nodded at the guard and held up two fingers. The guard immediately issued a level two shock. Vejrezzol screamed as the pain shot through his body, and he soiled himself— again.

"I'll return a little later to see if you've changed your mind. If you're hoping for pity, you can forget it. You'll receive none here. We'll treat you just as you treated those civilians on Dakistee."

Vejrezzol tried to answer, but his mouth and tongue refused to follow his wishes.

Permenans smiled and said, "We'll talk again later," then left the room.

◆ ◆ ◆

Christa spent part of the day examining the work of the engineers responsible for stopping the leaking water. It seemed that every time they stopped one, another appeared somewhere else. Aboard ship, there were numerous materials for stopping leaks of air, such as self-sealing membranes and injection gels that solidified within seconds, but there were no such materials available in the facility. They used cloth rags, clothing, towels, or anything else they could jam, wedge, or pack into openings and then braced the openings with wood or metal foraged from everywhere. So far, the effort was adequate and pumps were keeping the Vault deck clear by moving the water into sink drains.

Christa still hadn't completed her investigation of the facility, so when her other duties were handled, she and Carmoody resumed their explorations.

◆ ◆ ◆

Over the course of the next week, Christa and Grace visited every room in the complex that hadn't been visited before. They discovered some interesting technology, but nothing illegal or completely unique. Christa decided the archeologists could tour the facility, as long as they didn't annoy the Dakistians or attempt to take samples of the equipment or furnishings.

◆ ◆ ◆

"Before we begin today," Admiral Moore said, "I want you to view a message from Admiral Carver." Admiral Moore nodded to his aide, who then started the playback.

A head-and-shoulders image of Admiral Carver filled the full wall monitor as her words played in the CT of every officer or the earpiece of anyone who didn't have an ID chip.

"Greeting from Region Two. Everything is well here, or at least as good as we have a right to expect as we struggle to establish control over this territory and that of Region Three.

"My message today concerns the events on Dakistee. Admiral Holt was gracious enough to extend the hospitality of his command while Commander Carver carried out her special assignment in his deca-sectors. For this reason, Commander Christa Carver has been forwarding copies of all reports to him at Higgins, and he has had the authority to modify her orders as needed. However, Commander Carver recently reported that another officer attempted to alter the orders I issued. I regret that it's taken so long for you to learn of this, but the distance between Earth and Quesann makes more timely messages impossible.

"On October 22nd of this year, Admiral Hubera visited Dakistee for the purpose of grilling Commander Carver. At the conclusion of the session, he ordered her to immediately terminate her investigation and return to Region Two on the next available transport.

"Ladies and Gentlemen, I'm sure you understand the seriousness of Admiral Hubera's actions. He had no authority to issue orders which directly countermanded my orders. I therefore accuse him of tampering with my command. The formal charges, prepared by the Judge Advocate General's office on Quesann, provide the complete details and are appended to this message, as is the message I received from Commander Carver immediately after the incident. Admiral Holt advised her to ignore the order from Admiral Hubera as he had clearly exceeded his authority, and she has remained on Dakistee to conclude her investigation."

Admiral Hubera, whose mouth had been working with increasing rapidity, although nothing had come out as the message played, suddenly jumped up from his seat and began screaming at the monitor as if Jenetta could hear his tirade. "I'm a member of the Admiralty Board and I'm fully within my rights to interrogate any officer or non-com in Space Command you, you…" Hubera grabbed at his chest and fell back into his chair where he fumbled in his pocket for medicine. He slipped a tiny pill into his mouth and sat back, his face a pasty color.

"Are you alright, Donald?" Admiral Moore asked. "Do you need medical assistance?"

"No, I'll be okay in a minute," he mumbled.

Admiral Moore waited until Admiral Hubera's complexion returned to its normal ruddy color, and he had sat up in his chair before giving the order to continue with the vid message. The next part was a copy of the message submitted to Admiral Carver by Lt. Commander Carver. Nine of the admirals present watched and listened closely.

When the message was over, Admiral Moore said, "Admiral Hubera, we previously became aware of the fact that you made a surprise inspection visit to Dakistee without authorization from this board, but you neglected to mention that you issued countermanding orders to an officer in another chain of command."

"All I did was question Carver about her efforts on Dakistee."

"You deny that you ordered her to terminate her investigation before it was complete and return by the next available transport to Quesann?"

Hubera was silent for a minute, and then said, "I did nothing wrong and I shall present my defense at the proper time."

"Very well. Due to the serious nature of the charges and the evidence presented against you, I'm obligated to suspend you from further participation on this board until the charges have been resolved. I recommend that you either avail yourself of the services of the JAG office or retain private council for representation. Do you have anything to say at this time?"

"I have plenty to say. These charges are ludicrous. I have never exceeded my authority as a member of this board. I take my duties seriously and know the extent of my rights and powers. This will be amply demonstrated at the proper time."

Admiral Hubera then stood up and proudly walked towards the door that led to the office section of the building.

♦ ♦ ♦

"It's definitely a freighter," the tactical officer aboard the *Portland* said as he stared at the DeTect screen, "because it appears to be maxed out with ten kilometers of cargo. But it's not under power. And there appears to be a much smaller ship alongside. It could be a single-hull cargo ship, or something else."

"Something else?" Captain Gregory said.

"Perhaps a Space Command ship performing an inspection."

"No. I'd know if there was another SC ship in this immediate area. Helm, let's go take a look."

"Aye, Captain," the helmsman said as he keyed in the course information sent to him by the tac officer.

♦ ♦ ♦

"Captain, a ship is headed directly towards us," the tac officer aboard the *Hell Fire* said."

"Freighter?"

"No, sir. Based on the size, my guess would be Space Command destroyer."

"Damn. Cancel all operations. Emergency recall. Tell them to get back here or stay and face Space Command on their own."

Aboard the freighter, the Raider crewmen dropped everything they were doing and ran for the shuttle bays in the maintenance section as fast as their legs would carry them. Once the hatches were sealed, the shuttle pilot hit the remote to open the bay doors without even depressurizing the bay. Objects that hadn't been locked down hit the sides of the shuttle as the depressurization pulled them out along with the atmosphere. When the bay door was wide open he released the magnetic skids and applied all the thruster power he had available. The shuttle blasted out of the bay like a champagne cork from a bottle and into the bay on the *Hell Fire* like a meteor caught in a gravity well. Before the bay door was even closed, the *Hell Fire* was moving and building its temporal envelope.

◆   ◆   ◆

"The second ship is moving away, Captain," the tac officer aboard the *Portland* said.

"Fast?"

"Yes, sir. She just went FTL."

"Should I pursue, sir?" the helmsman asked.

"Negative. I'd love to, but there might be injured aboard the freighter who need emergency assistance. Just keep closing on the cargo vessel."

"Aye, sir."

◆

As the *Portland* neared the freighter a minute later, the sensors were able to provide a reasonably clear image of the ship.

"What do you make of that, Tac?" Captain Gregory asked.

"It looks like just the cargo section of a freighter. The front end where it would attach to the freighter is badly mangled. My best guess is that the freighter blew up."

"Damn pirates. It probably refused to stop so they blew it to hell. Com, notify the shuttle bays that we're going to launch as soon as we're close enough. Without a ship at the front of that hulk, we won't have to worry about attack."

"Aye, Captain."

It took time for the shuttles to launch and enter the maintenance bay at the center of the cargo ship, and then more time to get the bay hatch closed and the area pressurized. Engineers, with a Marine escort, slowly began to move out in both directions. Everyone was in full EVA gear and would remain that way until it was determined it was safe to remove the suits. The link section doors had closed automatically when they had sensed a pressure drop from the end where the freighter had been, and the engineers had to open each as they progressed after determining that the atmosphere conditions on the other side were stable.

"Captain," Commander Conte said as he reported in, "There's something strange here."

"What is it, XO?"

"There are stasis beds lined up in the link tunnel for as far as we can see, sir. These are all extra-long beds, the kind used by Nordakians."

"Empty or occupied?"

"All that we've passed so far have been empty with the covers open, but I can see beds ahead where the covers are still closed."

"When you reach that point, let me know if the beds are occupied."

◆

A few minutes later, Conte reported in again. "The beds here are occupied, sir. The people inside are all Nordakians."

"Okay, I'm sending over a couple of medical teams."

"Yes, sir."

◆ ◆

An hour later, Commander Conte reported in again. "Sir, the docs say the people in the beds appear healthy. Some have been asleep for months and some for only days."

"Tell the medical teams I want two from each group sent over here and awakened, but keep them all separated so they can't coordinate any fictitious stories."

"Aye, sir."

♦   ♦

Captain Franklin Gregory entered the interrogation room where one of the awakened sleepers was being held. His stasis bed indicated he had only been asleep for a few days. He had already been identified from the database information supplied to the *Portland* by the Nordakian authorities when the *Portland* was tasked with babysitting the freighter. According to the files, he spoke Amer, but so far he had claimed ignorance of the language and so he was wearing a translator.

"Sir," Gregory said, "The Nordakian authorities have identified you and told us you speak Amer fluently, but we shall continue with this little charade if you prefer. I want you to tell me of your role in this fiasco. I warn you that I already know most of the story, so if you lie or misrepresent the facts, I will know."

Gregory stared hard at the Nordakian, who seemed totally unfazed by the glare. He refused to offer any information.

"You have nothing to say?"

When he didn't speak up, Gregory said, "Very well. You will be charged with sedition and turned over to the courts for trial and sentencing. If you are found guilty, and I'm quite sure you will be, the sentence will most likely be stiff. Sedition and piracy are about the only laws on the books that still mandate the death penalty for extreme violators."

"Nallick will save me," he said, "unless he wishes me to join him in the hereafter."

"Is that all you have to say?"

When the Nordakian said nothing else, Gregory stood up and left the interrogation room.

CHAPTER TWENTY-TWO
~ November 5th, 2285 ~

Admiral Holt was working at his desk when the message from Captain Gregory arrived. He selected it from his queue for immediate playback and sat back to watch and listen.

"Sir, we have found the freighter we sought. A second maintenance bay near the stern of the cargo section contains a parts inventory for Nordakian fighters and lattice cannons, although there are no fighters in the bay. Still, I feel reasonably comfortable saying we've found the parties responsible for the attack on Loudescott.

"The main ship itself has been destroyed. At first we believed a Raider vessel was responsible, but my engineers have discovered that the entire cargo section was set with charges. It's our speculation that the leader of this group intended to destroy himself and all his followers, but the circuitry failed to detonate the cargo section so only the freighter was destroyed. The fate of those aboard the main ship is unknown. They might have died in the explosion or set a delayed charge and escaped in a smaller craft. There are no tugs in the ship, which is extremely unusual for a freighter.

"The cargo containers, in addition to being laden with food, clothing, medicine, and all the essentials needed for a new colony, are filled with stasis beds. We've found one hundred thirty-two recently used beds in the cargo spine tunnel. I'm guessing that a ship we spotted next to the cargo section just before we arrived was waking sleepers and taking them aboard. The ship went FTL just as we reached the site. I chose not to pursue in case there were people aboard the cargo section who needed our assistance.

"Unless you issue orders to the contrary, I'll have my tugs tow the cargo section to Higgins. At Light-75, it will take approximately sixty-three days for the journey.

"Franklin Gregory, Captain of the *Portland*, message complete."

Admiral Holt sat back in his chair and thought about the message as he tried to fit all the pieces together. Did the Raider ship, if it was a Raider ship, play a role in the attack on Loudescott? And if they did, what were they after? And exactly why did a religious dissident group supposedly bound for Slabeca launch an attack on Loudescott in the first place? Mostly, he wished he knew the fate of Christa and the other military people assigned to the dig site, but that wouldn't be known until the person in charge decided to open the door of the facility.

◆　◆　◆

"I have an update from the *Hell Fire's* captain," Councilman Fazid said when it was his turn to address the Lower Council. "Apparently, the people who attacked the Loudescott site are religious dissidents who have a grudge against Jenetta Carver. The attack was intended to be the opening engagement in an effort to take control of the planet. It seems they believed the planet would just fall into their hands. Maps found on the bridge of the freighter were more than a decade old, so they weren't aware the planet had become so heavily populated. It's obvious the people in command have had no military training or experience, and the rest are simple farmers and tradesmen. In any event, we don't have to worry about a rival crime organization operating in GA space.

"We subdued the ringleaders, but lost a number of good people when the freighter exploded. One of the dissidents said our people must have triggered a self-destruct charge they had set to denote, but which failed to explode. The person in charge still refuses to talk, but Captain Permenans has vowed that he will before he's turned over for slave indoctrination.

"Following the takeover of the freighter, the Captain began an assessment of the cargo and found that it was mainly colony supplies, but he also discovered a great many Nordakians in stasis. He began awakening them and conveying them to the *Hell Fire,* but the sudden appearance of a Space Command warship necessitated their immediate departure from the scene after just a hundred thirty-two had been transported aboard. But— we do have a hundred thirty-two new slaves, plus the eight-man freighter crew for our mines in the Aguspod territory."

"Is the operation over then, Ahil?" Councilwoman Overgaard asked.

"No, but most of the people involved have completed their tasks and returned to their former roles. The expend-itures from this point forward will be minimal, but we're still hoping for significant gains. The profit from the slaves alone will cover most of the expenses for the operation. It's doubtful the Spaccs will bemoan the loss of these religious zealots."

"It almost seems like we've done Space Command's job for them," Chairman Strauss said.

"Inadvertently, I suppose we have. But it's proved profit-able."

◆　◆　◆

On November 14th, three weeks after sealing the facility, Christa made a decision to open the door. They'd heard no explosions to indicate that anyone was attempting to break in, and it was safe to assume that Space Command was either already there or about to descend en masse on whomever might be waiting to oppose them. She'd earlier told the Dakistian engineers to return the air pressure in the facility to normal levels. There was a slight increase of water on the floor of the Vault level, but nothing to get unduly concerned over.

With her meager Marine forces at the ready, she and Carmoody prepared to unlock the door. Even Lt. Uronson was on hand. He had made considerable progress with the help of the nano-bots, and, while not ready for full duty, he was determined to be there to assist. Forced to take up residence in the facility during an emergency meant that all but the Marines bivouacked there had no extra clothing, so everyone had been wearing the light grey jumpsuits included with the provisions sent from North Pendleton when Christa expected to feed and clothe awakening sleepers. For this occasion, both Christa and Carmoody were back in proper uniform.

Christa carefully placed the cylinder against the correct circle on the door and turned it as required. When she gave the command to unlock, she was gratified to hear the faint sound of a locking bar retracting into the door. Christa and Carmoody stepped away and joined the Marines with their weapons at the ready before giving the command to open. If there was an enemy camped on the doorstep, she was ready to close it just as quickly.

As the door slid back into its pocket without warning, a blur of bodies outside jumped to face the opening. The Marines inside the facility tensed for action, then relaxed as they recognized the half dozen Marines who had been lounging in the tunnel. The Marines outside the facility likewise recognized their fellows inside and relaxed their stance.

Sergeant Flegetti stood upright, breathed, smiled, and stepped forward into the facility to report to Lt. Uronson. "Sir, it's great to see you again. We didn't know if any of the squad had made it." Noticing the cane Uronson was using to stand, he said, "Uh, were you injured, sir?"

"A lattice round took a joy ride around my rib cage while I was helping an injured civilian. But the doc says I'll be a hundred percent in a few weeks."

"That's good news, sir. Did all our guys make it?"

"Yes. I was the only casualty, which is amazing. It was a surprise attack, so we didn't have a chance to get into our armor."

"Damn, I wish we had been here to help out, sir. We arrived back a few hours after the attack. We didn't know nothing about it until the MAT pilot was about to land and spotted all the bodies around the LZ. He pulled up so we could get into our armor before coming in hot to drop us off. The Colonel is topside. Do you need help getting there, sir?"

"I can make it, Sergeant," he said, waving off the offer of assistance.

"Yes sir," Flegetti said as he stepped back out of the way.

Christa walked topside behind the Marines with Madu and Carmoody. The Marines in the tunnel had radioed ahead, so Lt. Colonel Diminjik was hurrying towards the tunnel when they emerged. Lt. Uronson braced to attention and saluted Diminjik, who returned the salute and hurried past the Lieutenant to get to Christa.

"Commander Carver, I am delighted to see you alive and well, ma'am. We've had some anxious times since learning of the attack here."

"It was pretty gruesome, Colonel."

"Yes. Perhaps it will provide some comfort to know that the people responsible have been apprehended."

"Wonderful. Who were they and what was the reason for the attack?"

"A band of religious dissidents from Nordakia apparently had designs on taking over Dakistee for their new colony. I guess they realized they had bitten off far more than they could chew and bugged out after attacking this site."

"But why pick this site?"

"I don't know, ma'am. I imagine you'll learn quite a bit more when you're briefed for your new post."

"My new post?"

"As commanding officer."

"Commanding officer of what?"

"You've been named as the commanding officer for the Dakistee outpost."

"You mean the Loudescott outpost."

"No, ma'am. You're the new commanding officer for the Dakistee Outpost, which includes responsibility for the entire planet. I report directly to you now."

Christa just stared at Diminjik for a few seconds, then said, "When did this come about?"

"As I understand it, the Admiralty Board made the appointment several weeks ago. May I say I'm delighted to serve in your command. I hope this appointment means we'll be getting a few of the things I've been requesting for the improvement of planetary security."

"Thank you, Colonel. I'm at a bit of a loss for words right now. Perhaps after I find out exactly what's expected of me, I can brief you."

"Yes, ma'am. As soon as I received word you had opened the facility, I notified the ships in orbit. The captains will be down shortly to confer with you."

"What ships?"

"There are two SC destroyers and a diplomatic yacht over us."

Christa couldn't resist glancing skyward, although she knew she wouldn't be able to see ships in geosynchronous orbit without special optical equipment. Even at four hundred meters in length, an SC destroyer is a small target when it's thirty-five thousand kilometers up.

As Lt. Col. Diminjik turned to confer with Lt. Uronson, Madu said to Christa, "What's going on?"

"The Colonel has just informed me that I've been put in command of the planet."

"My planet?"

"Well, mine also." Pointing towards Fort Carver, Christa said, "I was born about a kilometer in that direction."

"Don't we get a say about who is in charge?"

"You will. In situations like this, the military usually assumes command until a planetary government is established. The Galactic Alliance is a civilian organization made up of elected representatives from all the member worlds. Space Command and the Space Marine Corps are the enforcement arm, but we take our orders from the Galactic Alliance Council. They assign us to act in a protectorate capacity until you set up a government and are ready to assume control of your own affairs."

"And who decides when that is achieved?"

"You do, once the established government represents a majority of the citizens. At that point you tell us you're ready to take over and we leave."

"Just like that."

"Yes, just like that. Of course there will be all kinds of official diplomatic signings with newsies hanging on every word and thousands of images being recorded for posterity." Christa smiled and added, "You can't turn over a planet without dozens of people getting their name in the news."

"And until then, you're in charge?"

"It looks that way." Christa sighed lightly. "I'd rather be back aboard my ship, but the Colonel said the order comes from the Admiralty Board so there's no getting around it."

"What is it you wish to avoid? It can't be the responsibility."

"I don't fear the responsibility. It's the political part I dislike. With a situation like we have here, the schemers and connivers are going to be lining up to take advantage of me any way they can. They'll use their political connections to try to bend me to their will and will scream to the heavens when they fail to sway me. I'm not a politician and have never had any aspirations in that direction. But in this job I'll be forced to deal with them on a daily basis. It will be a miserable, thankless job."

"Yet you'll do it, and do it better than anyone who *wants* the job."

"I'll do it because I've been ordered to do it. As far as doing it better— I don't know."

"I know. I fear people who want the power but try to evade responsibility. You take responsibility unhesitatingly and don't desire the power. Christa, I'm behind you one hundred percent. At first I was a little worried about having one person named as acting governor, but I'm not worried about it being you."

"I'm not the governor, Madu, just the military commander of the outpost."

"With the planet under martial law, isn't that the same thing?"

"Uh, I suppose it might be viewed that way."

The arrival of a shuttle drew their attention towards the landing pads. There were two more shuttles in the distance lining up for final approach to the shuttle port. Christa and Madu began walking towards the pads with Lt. Col Diminjik and Lt. Uronson following.

◆

"Commander Carver," the Space Command officer said by way of introduction after the formal protocols had been satisfied, "I'm Captain Turcotte of the GSC Destroyer *Brisbane* and this is Captain Allisone of the GSC Destroyer *Bremen*." As a third officer joined the group, Turcotte said, "And this is Commander Survossa, Captain of the Diplomatic Yacht *Wellington*."

Good day, sirs and ma'am," Christa said. "Allow me to introduce you to Madu Ptellewqku. She is the director of the institute below our feet where a portion of the Dakistee population has been sleeping for the past two hundred centuries."

All three of the captains, plus Lt. Col. Diminjik, stood looking at Madu with mouths agape. Christa translated what she had said to the officers so Madu would understand why they were staring at her the way they were. She smiled when she realized none had known she was twenty thousand years old.

"And this is Lt. Col. Diminjik," Christa said. "The Colonel is the commander of North Pendleton Marine Base." Gesturing towards Grace, she said, "This is Lieutenant

Carmoody of my staff, and the injured officer next to her is Marine Lieutenant Uronson who commands the Marine presence here at Loudescott."

"Were you injured in the fight here, Lieutenant?" Captain Turcotte asked.

"Yes, sir. I took a lattice shot to my rib cage. I was lucky it bounced off the bones and only tore up a chunk of flesh."

"I hope it heals quickly, son."

"Thank you, sir."

"Commander," Captain Turcotte said to Christa, "is there somewhere we can talk privately?"

"Fort Carver is available," Lt. Col. Diminjik said.

"Fort Carver?" Captain Turcotte said questioningly.

"The outpost facility here at Loudescott was long ago nicknamed after Admiral Jenetta Carver. Everyone seems to use that as its designation rather than the official designation of Loudescott Outpost."

"I see. Then by all means let's convene our meeting in Fort Carver."

"What did you mean by privately, sir?" Christa asked.

"Senior Space Command and Marine personnel only."

"I see." Turning to Madu, she said, "The captain wants to brief me and probably debrief me as well. Lt. Carmoody will get you a translation device so you'll be able to communicate with everyone now that order has been restored. I'll see you back in the facility after we're through." To Grace, she said, "You can begin the evacuation of the civilians now that the area has been secured. I'm sure most are anxious to get out and contact their families, and they'll want to hold services for the people they lost. The Dakistians will most likely remain in the facility until accommodations above ground can be arranged. And please get Madu a translation unit so she can communicate without an interpreter."

Grace said, "Yes, ma'am," while Madu nodded first to Christa, then to each of the officers. The two women headed back to the facility together although they couldn't yet communicate with each other effectively.

It took a few minutes to arrange for transportation to Fort Carver. Two oh-gee general purpose vehicles showed up after Lt. Col. Diminjik made a call to his headquarters shuttle.

◆

The dormitory rooms were inappropriate for a meeting so they had their choice between the mess hall and the one-time cloning lab, since turned into a rec room of sorts. Captain Turcotte, the senior-most officer, decided on the mess hall. The few enlisted people who were grabbing a quick meal were instructed to take their food to the rec room and the mess cooks were told to turn off all equipment and take a break until called back in.

Before sitting down at a table, the five officers prepared a beverage. Christa naturally selected a huge mug of Colombian.

◆

"First," Captain Turcotte said to open the meeting, "Admiral Holt sends his regards, Commander. He was concerned for your safety, as well as that of the military and civilians with you. He was confident you had been the one to seal the facility and ordered our three ships to remain here until you opened it up again in case you needed our support for whatever it was you found in the facility. He believed this would happen not long after our arrival."

Captain Turcotte took an object about the size of a wedding band and stuck it to the table after touching part of the outer ring area with the tip of his moistened fingertip. Everyone immediately recognized it as a vid camera. He then took a small device like a viewpad from his pocket and adjusted it until an image of Christa was sharp and clear.

"This is a debriefing of Lt. Commander Christa Carver on Dakistee following her emergence from the sealed facility at Loudescott. In attendance is myself, Captain Jerome Turcotte of the GSC Destroyer *Brisbane*, Captain Corrine Allisone of the GSC Destroyer *Bremen*, Commander Pieter Survossa,

Captain of the Diplomatic Yacht *Wellington*, and Lt. Colonel Andre Diminjik, the commanding officer of North Pendleton Marine Base."

Over the next hour and a quarter, Captain Turcotte questioned Christa about the attack and her actions during the past several weeks.

"Thank you, Commander. I think that should satisfy most of the questions Intelligence has. They believe they know who was responsible for the attack perpetrated here. The *Portland* discovered a cargo section not far away. The freighter had been destroyed and evidence now suggests it was self-detonated. The fate of the crew is still a mystery, but the cargo section contained thousands of Nordakians in stasis beds. They're believed to be religious dissidents who were reportedly on their way to Slabeca to build a new colony.

"Admiral Holt has instructed me to officially inform you that the Admiralty Board has named you as Commander of the Dakistee Outpost. Upon learning of the sleeping Dakistians, all previously established contracts with the Archeological Expedition Corporation on Anthius have been suspended pending confirmation of the reported facts. The contents of the antiquity warehouses have all been impounded and no more relics may be sent off-world without the consent of the GAC.

"It may sound to some like you've been given a winning hand, Commander, but, in my opinion, you've just been dealt a handful of jokers. I'm glad I didn't draw one like this."

Christa took a deep breath and then released it slowly before saying, "I have to agree with you, Captain. Being placed in command of a military outpost that has responsibility for the entire civilian population of a planet seems almost as bad as the deal my sister has with Regions Two and Three, albeit on a much smaller scale. But someone has to do it, and I suppose fluency with all three of the major languages spoken here makes me seem like the ideal candidate."

"Where will you establish your headquarters, ma'am?" Lt. Col. Diminjik asked.

"Here, I suppose. It's close to where we've awakened the first of the Dakistian population and these facilities are practically indestructible. That could be useful if any more dissidents get it into their heads to attack us again.

"Captain Turcotte, I have a favor to ask. We had no water in the other facility when I was forced to seal the main door. In trying to resolve the problem, the Dakistians opened a valve that then couldn't be closed again. I'd like some of your engineers, or possibly some from Captain Allisone's ship to see what they can do. The filtration room had to be sealed off and is presently filled with water, so it'll be necessary to open that area and work underwater to fix the equipment."

"I'm sure either my engineers aboard the *Brisbane* or those aboard the *Bremen* will be able to repair or replace the valve."

"I'll gladly make some engineers available," Captain Allisone said. "With both groups working on the problem, it should be resolved quickly."

"Thank you both," Christa said. "Captain Turcotte, how long will you be sticking around now that things have settled down?"

"When I received word that you had opened the facility and that you were apparently well, I sent a message to Admiral Holt. I should have a reply in the next couple of days and perhaps we'll know the answer to that question then."

"What will happen to the dissidents found asleep in the freighter?"

"I imagine that if they had no knowledge of what their leaders were doing regarding the attack and really believed they were headed to Slabeca, they'll be allowed to continue their journey to the new colony. If they have a change of heart now that their high priest is gone, it'll be up to the Nordakian Royal Family to decide whether or not they're allowed back on Nordakia or Obotymot. Do you think they'd be welcome here?"

"No. The ancients that will be awakened are the people most damaged by the original priests who wanted to follow a new Almuth. I doubt they'll have any pity for this new group of dissidents and probably won't invite them to share this world."

◆　◆　◆

As Christa walked towards the tunnel entrance of the new facility later, a trickle of dig site civilians were trudging back to their shelters on the far side of the dig area. There were no Marines on guard duty because that post had been cancelled when the attack came and there was no real need for them at present.

Bots were scrubbing the empty rotunda as Christa entered and they scampered back to their storage locations as soon as she stepped from the tunnel. Crossing to the elevator, she descended to the Housing level. There was no one anywhere in sight near the dormitories as Christa walked to her room to pack the few personal items she had left there. She planned to move back into her shuttle until it was time to move into a private room at Fort Carver.

Her back was to the door when she heard it open and she turned to see who would enter without knocking. She was surprised to see the young woman who had been among the crowd the day of the aerial attack. The woman was wearing the expensive suit she had worn that first day, but Christa assumed that, like everyone, she had been wearing the grey jumpsuits since the first day. Of more immediate interest was the lattice pistol she was aiming at Christa's midsection.

CHAPTER TWENTY-THREE
~ November 14th, 2285 ~

"Who are you?" Christa asked. "And what do you want?"

The woman took several steps into the room on her thirteen-centimeter stiletto heels before responding. They were hardly appropriate footwear for an archeological dig site, and, since she was taller than average to begin with, she didn't need the height, so she must have been wearing them out of vanity. For that matter, the expensive outfit with its skirt more suited for a business office in a large city was dramatically out of place here as well.

"I'm not surprised you don't recognize me," the woman said. "I've changed quite a bit since the last time we met."

Christa took a few seconds to look the woman over carefully. That she was beautiful was beyond debate. She probably would have won any beauty contest she cared to enter. She had gorgeous legs and a shapely body that was highlighted by the tight skirt and fitted jacket. The extra-high heels and form-flattering outfit made it seem like her legs ran all the way to her armpits. The cut of her jacket and blouse allowed admirers to see her creamy white skin and the gentle curve of large breasts.

"I'd definitely remember if we'd met before," Christa said.

"Let me give you a clue. I've changed considerably since we were on Raider One."

"I was never on Raider One. That was Jenetta."

"Yes, but you *are* Jenetta after all. You may have a separate identity now, but you have all of her memories."

"There were no children among the slaves on Raider One and you're too young to have been anything else at that time."

The woman smiled widely. "And yet I was there at that time."

"What's your name?"

"Not just yet. I've waited for this moment for a long time and I'm having too much fun to end it prematurely."

"Well, Miss Notjustyet, I'm not amused by having that pistol pointed at me. Would you mind lowering it?"

"Not at all," the woman said as she turned her head slightly and said, "Kasim, come in here."

In response to her command, the chief assistant to the dig site labor supervisor appeared in the doorway. He was also carrying a pistol. As he aimed it at Christa, the woman lowered hers.

"Better?" the woman asked.

Christa grimaced slightly and didn't bother to respond to the absurd question.

"I'm sure you know Kasim. He has a secret that concerns you. Would you like to know what it is?"

"More riddles?"

"An old one. Tell her Kasim."

Kasim grinned and said to Christa, "I'm your father."

Christa looked at him like he was crazy, then suddenly understood the remark.

"Yes, you do understand, don't you?" he said as he saw the change come over her.

"The pieces fit. Now tell me why?"

"I needed to experiment— to ensure— and to prove, that I understood the process. Didn't you ever guess it might be me?"

"You were one of the suspects, but there was no way to establish it one way or the other unless someone confessed. It would have been foolish to simply point fingers."

"Yes, that's true. I would have denied it, of course."

"Why tell me now?"

"I thought you'd like to know. And I'll be leaving here today, finally, so there's nothing you can do to me."

"Going to another dig site?"

"Never again, I hope. I have Doctorates in Archeology and Antiquity Preservation and Evaluation. It's been hell playing nursemaid to the simpletons at this site. Miss— has promised me a post befitting my education and abilities now that I've put in my time as a lackey at this flea circus."

"Taking a step backward for a moment, how did you get into the facility sixteen years ago?"

"Through the sewer tunnel that idiot Priestly found. The day after he found it, he was all over the place bragging about a new find. Of course, he wouldn't give any details or tell anyone where it was, but I followed him the next day when he returned to the immediate area to continue his explorations. It was easy to locate it after he was gone."

"And the Zelem?"

"From old man Peterson's tent. Anyone could walk in there, but my position enabled me to do it without anyone giving it a second thought. I had taken some of his Zelem months earlier and stashed it away, so it was available when I needed it."

"Okay," Christa said, looking at the young woman, "one mystery solved. Now how about the other one?"

"Not just yet. I want to savor this meeting."

As she had been talking, Christa had inched carefully closer to the pile of clothes on the bed. At the bottom of the heap, and not visible presently, was the laser pistol she had gotten from Lt. Uronson the day of the attack. She had no desire to harm either of the people holding her at bay, but she would do whatever was necessary to keep them from harming her. That they would aim pistols at her meant they intended something sinister. They couldn't just walk away now and expect to have the incident forgiven and forgotten. At the very least, they would have to stand trial for threatening the safety and well-being of a Space Command officer. So it might be that they intended to harm her and escape in the confusion. If that was the case, she should keep them talking as long as possible. And if an opening occurred, she had to make a grab for her pistol.

"So," Christa said, "assuming you were on Raider One eighteen years ago, how old would you have been at the time?"

"I was as old as my tongue and a bit older than my teeth," the woman replied.

"At least that's an imprecision I can understand. But it doesn't provide any clue to your identity. You say we've met before but name a time when you should have been a small child and specify a place where no small children were present. That would have to mean that you *weren't* a small child at the time."

"Bravo, Christa. I knew that exceptional mind of yours would eventually tumble to the correct solution, although it would seem so unthinkable to anyone else that they wouldn't dare mention it."

"In a book titled *The Sign of Four*, famed fictional detective Sherlock Holmes said, 'When you have eliminated the impossible, whatever remains, *however improbable*, must be the truth.'"

"Too true."

"Since you say we met, I would have to assume it wasn't a time when Jenetta was unconscious. One can hardly meet someone when they are unaware of everything around them."

"True again. You were most definitely aware of my presence." The woman smiled. "This is such fun. Are you having fun?"

"The crewmembers Jenetta stunned when taking the two battleships weren't technically on Raider One. They were merely docked with it, so the meeting couldn't have occurred on one of them."

"I suppose I could argue the point since the ships were docked, but I won't. I wasn't one of the crewmembers."

"Jenetta only met two people outside the detention center. There was the old hospital attendant who took her for her brainwashing sessions and the aged male doctor who performed the work. So you couldn't have been either of them."

"I could also argue that point, but I won't. I wasn't either of them."

"All of the guards in the detention center were male, so you weren't one of them. And you look nothing like any of the female slaves who were rescued. It seems I've run out of possible candidates."

"Pity. You were doing so well— especially with that Sherlock Holmes hypothesis. Why did you give up on that?"

"I know firsthand of the work the Raiders have done with age prolongation. And Mikel Arneu told me of the intensive efforts to find a way to restore youth, but those old people were all men."

"Exactly. So why did you eliminate them?"

"You're saying I shouldn't have?"

"When you have eliminated the impossible, whatever remains, *however improbable*, must be the truth."

"You're a *man*?"

"Come now, Angel, do I look like a man?"

"You..."

"Uh oh, I've let the cat out of the bag, haven't I?"

"Only one person has ever called Jenetta, Eliza, and me *Angel*."

"It seems that our game is nearly over."

"You can't be Mikel Arneu."

"Why not?"

Christa just looked on in silence as she thought. Finally, she said, "Because Mikel Arneu had such low esteem for women that he would never have become one."

The woman laughed. "Yes, I was that way. I guess I've changed in more ways than one. Perhaps it was seeing things from a different perspective that changed my attitude. I admit

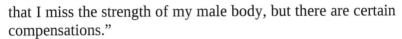

that I miss the strength of my male body, but there are certain compensations."

"Such as?"

"You would know as well as I do. Instead of threatening everyone to get them to do my bidding, I've learned that cajoling is just as effective— sometimes more so with men. Most are exceedingly eager to please me."

"But why change your sex? You never seemed to have difficulty getting people to do what you wanted."

"As you know, I was pressing my scientists to find a way for eternal life and for a way to restore my lost youthful looks. Year after year they worked and year after year they failed to find the secrets. Like you and your *sisters*, I had received the age prolongation treatment so I knew I had possibly thousands of years ahead of me, but I also wanted to be young again. Well, my scientists finally found a way, but there was a qualification. It seems that the youth restoration process they developed would only work on women. It had something to do with the estrogen levels in the body or something. Men don't have sufficient levels of the hormone for the process to work.

"I kept after them to find a different formula, but after a decade of work they said it was no use. They said they could only restore youth to female bodies. What was I to do? If I wanted a young body, I had to take the plunge and go through the DNA manipulation to change me to a woman. You'll no doubt be pleased to hear that the pain you experienced with your DNA manipulation was like a walk in an EVA suit compared to what I went through. Apparently, creating a uterus and ovaries takes massive amounts of energy. I was always hungry and it seemed like I never stopped eating throughout the day. But that wasn't the worst. It was a full year before I reached a point where I didn't groan in pain every time I moved. Reconstructing a pelvis is no simple matter, even when it's done without surgery."

"My, my, how you do carry on," Christa said with a smile.

"I knew you'd be pleased to hear how I suffered."

"You have no idea. Tell me, what name do you use now?"

"You can still call me Mikel. There's no sense giving you my assumed name, Angel, and you'd probably feel compelled to make some remark I wouldn't like."

"You surely don't think you can take me out of here and send me to a whore palace somewhere, do you?"

"That was part of the plan at first, but things sort of got out of hand here with those aerial attacks. That wasn't us by the way."

"I know. We've learned who was responsible."

"Then, when I discovered there was no superior technology down here like the cloning process at the other facility, the trip appeared wasted. Still, I couldn't just leave without paying a visit."

"You don't…"

Christa's words were interrupted by a knock at the door. When Arneu and Kasim turned partway around at the sound, Christa made a move for the laser pistol. She knew they intended to kill her before they left. As long as no one outside the Raider organization knew of his sex change, Arneu could come and go anywhere at any time. Now that he had told her, he couldn't let her live. Christa knew this might be her only chance to survive the day.

As Christa swung back with the pistol, she saw that Kasim was also turning back. He spotted the pistol in her hand and fired his lattice pistol at the same time Christa fired.

All three rounds from Kasim's three-round burst hit Christa. The first lattice round entered her right side just below the rib cage. The second round hit her right shoulder, cutting through muscle and ripping up everything down to the bone. The third round hit her left cheek just ahead of the ear, removing a swath of flesh from there to the rear of her skull. Most of the left ear was gone, along with the skin over the skull behind the ear. The damage to Christa's right arm caused her to drop her weapon but not before her shot had taken out Kasim.

With the laser set to narrow beam, the entire force of the energy struck Kasim in the center of his chest, passing completely through his body at one point as the laser beam swept across his chest for a dozen centimeters. His heart was so severely damaged that it was barely pumping. Although a laser pistol seared flesh closed as quickly as it opened it, the heart damage meant Kasim had mere minutes left to live. The lattice pistol fell from his hand as his life-force began to give up its impermanent hold on his body.

Christa and Kasim fell to the floor at the same instant, landing within a meter of one another. It was difficult to know who had screamed first, but a cacophony had echoed around the room for several seconds.

Through the two-or-three-second interval while the shooting had taken place, Mikel Arneu had stood transfixed by the door, her weapon still dangling in her hand as if she had forgotten it was there. When the door flew open, it caught Arneu in the back and she dropped the pistol, but as Madu burst into the room Arneu suddenly regained her wits and stepped back while extending a foot to trip the director.

Madu fell face forward towards the floor and Arneu ducked out the door. The Director wound up on the floor looking at Christa and Kasim, both of whom still had their eyes open. There was no blood by Kasim, but it was pooling up considerably by Christa. Madu jumped up and ran out the door.

With what must have been his final breath, Kasim managed to say to Christa, "I gave you life— and now I've taken it back. Fitting, don't you think?"

Christa heard the words, but was unable to respond. She was going into shock and her last image was of Kasim's dead body as everything turned black.

◆

Doctor Johannes burst into Christa's room with Nurse Gibson right behind him and Madu behind her. As soon as

Johannes saw the amount of blood, he stopped and turned, putting a hand up to Madu.

"Please wait outside," Johannes said to Madu. "We need room to work." As she stepped back out, he closed the door.

Johannes immediately knelt next to Christa and put his hand on her neck. "Good Lord, no pulse at all. She probably bled out."

"This one is dead as well," Nurse Gibson said.

Standing up, Johannes said, "Okay, let's get this straight. Commander Carver is seriously injured, but she's not dead."

"But you said she has no pulse. That means she's dead."

"She's NOT dead. Do you understand?"

"Uh, yes, Doctor. But why isn't she dead if she has no pulse and isn't breathing?"

"Help me bandage her wounds," he said as he knelt next to Christa and began wrapping gauze around her head. "The reason is not simple. First, I just heard she's been named as Commander of the Dakistee Outpost. She's in charge of the entire planet. We don't want people to think it's this easy to assassinate the top person here. Second, the Carver women have some kind of unique physiology that lets them heal from wounds that would kill anyone else. Perhaps something can still be done for her. But mainly, I don't want to be the one whose signature is on the death certificate, so I'm not ready to pronounce her dead. Admiral Holt should be the one to release any information like that."

"I've heard about their amazing recuperative powers, but surely that doesn't apply here. She's expired, Doctor. She cannot come back to life."

"We don't know that, so I'm going to assume she'll recover. We'll get her into one of the stasis chambers the Dakistians use."

The job was hastily done, and, when Christa was bandaged and an oxygen mask placed over her face, Johannes used a bed sheet to soak up the pooled blood, then jammed the saturated sheet into a plastic disposal bag before going to the door.

Two orderlies with an oh-gee stretcher were waiting outside. He gestured them in and they placed Christa on the stretcher.

"Take her to the Vault level," Johannes said. "We're right behind you."

Gibson hurried after the stretcher-bearers as Johannes said to Madu, "She's very seriously injured and we're not equipped to work on her here. I'd like to place her in one of your stasis chambers and take her to Higgins where she can get proper attention."

"Of course," Madu said. "How long will it take to get to Higgins?"

"Higgins is about thirty light-annuals away. The diplomatic ship in orbit can make the trip in just over a solar."

"The stasis chamber that I was in has more than enough power to sustain the process for that long without being hooked into our power system."

"Great. Let's go."

Carmoody had heard the news, and, in her haste to get to Christa's room, ran into Madu as she and Doctor were headed towards the elevator. Madu explained the situation quickly and the three ran after the first group.

Once in the Vault, Carmoody logged into the computer so Madu could do what was necessary. Christa hadn't yet restored Madu's full access rights, although that would have happened soon now that the crisis was over.

Madu's chamber was gently lowered to the deck and Johannes worked with Gibson to get Christa situated inside.

It was necessary that Madu have the computer place the chamber back in the racks to initiate the process, but that took less than ten minutes. When the chamber was again lowered to the deck, the process was in full effect. Christa would be preserved at her condition when the process was initiated. As the computer lowered the chamber, the two orderlies situated the oh-gee stretcher beneath.

"Take her to the surface," Dr. Johannes said. To Nurse Gibson, he said, "You have ten minutes to get whatever you need or do whatever needs doing. We're accompanying the Commander to Higgins."

"Yes, Doctor."

"I'll see you topside. Remember, talk to no one."

"Yes, sir."

♦ ♦

An hour later, the Diplomatic Yacht *Wellington*, captained by Commander Pieter Survossa, left orbit and headed for Higgins at the fastest speed available in Dakinium-sheathed ships— Light-9793.48.

CHAPTER TWENTY-FOUR
~ December 4th, 2285 ~

Admiral Jenetta Carver opened her message queue as she sat sipping from her first cup of Colombian in what was usually a long line of such refreshments throughout the day. A message marked Priority-One from Admiral Holt naturally grabbed her attention. It should have been delivered to her regardless of the hour and how she was otherwise engaged. She would find out later who on her staff had dropped the ball and make sure it didn't happen again. For now, she punched the play key and watched as the somber face of Admiral Holt appeared on her monitor.

"Jenetta, Christa was injured in a shootout with a dig site person at Loudescott. It's imperative that you drop whatever you're doing and come to Higgins as soon as possible."

"Brian Holt, Rear Admiral Upper, Base Commander, Higgins Space Command Base, message complete."

Jenetta stared at the screen for several seconds while she thought. It wasn't like Brian Holt to send such a brief and cryptic message, and he wasn't prone to melodramatics. There was more here than his words indicated. If Christa had been injured, her physiology should see to the repair of the damage, although doctors had never been able to determine the level of severity from which the Carver system couldn't recover. For instance, would their bodies replace an entire limb over time? Perhaps Christa had lost an arm or a leg and her body wasn't repairing the damage.

Since the message time was eighteen days to Higgins, it would take thirty-six days to get a more accurate picture. In that time she could be more than halfway to Higgins, which was about a fifty-day trip each way. She made her decision.

Jenetta's office was thrown into turmoil as aides tried to reschedule everything that had been planned for the next four months. Much of it resettled onto the shoulders of lower ranked admirals or senior base officers, but some things would just have to wait until Jenetta returned.

The SC Battleship *Ares* was in port, so Jenetta contacted Captain Gavin and told him she needed a ride. He was a bit surprised by the travel orders, but when the Commander of the Second Fleet designated a destination for a ship, that's where it went, and it went when she said. All leaves were immediately cancelled and everyone dirt-side hurried to get back to the ship while on-duty personnel struggled to complete in-progress maintenance operations and stow gear and recently delivered supplies.

Less than three hours after Jenetta had viewed the message from Admiral Holt, the *Ares* left orbit around Quesann, outbound for Higgins Space Command Base.

◆ ◆ ◆

A General Court-Martial for enlisted personnel in Space Command and the Space Marine Corps, as was the case for commissioned officers, was conducted before a judge and a six-to-twelve member jury. But general officers faced a tribunal composed of only five general officers drawn at random. Both court-martial types decided guilt or innocence and determined the sentence to be imposed. A senior JAG officer presided as judge at a General Court-Martial, but the most senior general officer in rank and time in grade of the five selected to hear the case performed as president of the tribunal.

Admiral Bernake, Rear Admiral Upper, sitting in the center of the five admirals, said, "The accused will rise and face the court."

When Admiral Hubera and his civilian attorney had risen and faced the five admirals, Bernake said, "Admiral Hubera, you have heard the list of charges and specifications. How do you plead?"

"Not guilty to all charges," Hubera said loudly and proudly.

"The record will show that the accused has pled not guilty to all charges. The trial will begin tomorrow, December 8th, at 0900 in this courtroom. This Court is adjourned until that time."

◆ ◆ ◆

"Come," Jenetta said when the computer informed her Captain Lawrence Gavin was at her office door on the Admiral's bridge aboard the *Ares*. In response, the computer opened the door to admit the Captain of the ship.

"Good morning, Jen," Captain Gavin said as he strode in. Although she was a four-star admiral, Jenetta preferred an informal rapport whenever protocol didn't dictate that they behave differently.

Newly promoted Lt. Commander Jenetta Carver had been posted to Captain Gavin's battleship *Prometheus* almost two decades earlier and their friendship had grown out of mutual respect for the other's abilities. Gavin had been offered a flag numerous times, but he preferred to remain as a ship's captain for as long as he could. Jenetta would have preferred a battleship captaincy as well, but war and other events had seemingly conspired to keep pushing her up the ladder. She allowed it to happen because she honestly believed she could make a difference. That was true, and, mainly through her efforts and the unremitting efforts of galactic rulers to absorb the Galactic Alliance, the GA had grown five hundred percent of its size at the time she graduated from the Academy.

"Good morning, Larry," Jenetta said almost absent-mindedly as he walked to the beverage dispenser and prepared a mug of coffee.

As Gavin took a seat facing her desk, he said, "You have a troubled look on your face. Anything you can discuss?"

"I've been reviewing all the reports Christa submitted during the months she was on Dakistee. Progress was slow at first until she solved the problem of how to open the door, and then things slowed even more as she waited for special cylinders to be located in the ruins of collapsed buildings around the planet. After she managed to open the door, only one report was transmitted before she was forced to seal the facility to save the dig site people and the secrets of the facility. But she continued to record reports, and the computer sent them as soon as the facility was unsealed and communications were reestablished. The last report was prepared an hour before she unsealed the entrance door to the tunnel. After that, nothing. Her injuries must be horrific or she would have sent something."

"I wouldn't be too concerned," Gavin said. "She inherited that famous Carver physiology. By the time we get there, she'll probably be back on her feet and anxiously looking for her next assignment."

◆ ◆ ◆

"Our involvement on Dakistee has ended," Councilman Ahil Fazid said to Chairman Strauss on the com from his office. "All of our people, save one, have pulled out. We lost the man who was functioning as an assistant labor supervisor. He was good. We'll miss his information and evaluations."

"What happened?"

"According to Mikel Arneu, or perhaps I should say Nicole Ravenau, our man tried to shoot it out with Christa Carver. Apparently, they fired at the same instant and killed each other, dying within minutes of one another where they fell. He was using a lattice pistol from several feet away and she was using a laser pistol."

"Damn," Strauss said. "Damn, damn, damn. Carver is going to be coming after us with a vengeance now. Are we *sure* Arneu had nothing to do with it?"

"He— she— says not. She never fired her weapon."

"What was she doing there and why was that laborer armed?"

"Well, Arneu has carried a grudge against Jenetta for a long time— ever since she destroyed Raider One and made him look foolish. He may have been trying to exact a little revenge on her sister, whom he actually had as a prisoner for a short time until she escaped from the Tsgardis guarding her."

"So that ass wanted to even the score a bit and has succeeded in dropping us into the shit. Well, I'll deal with him later. What about the operation? Were there *any* positives?"

"We wound up with new slaves the GA isn't going to spend much effort looking for, and they're all prime specimens. There's nothing else though. According to Arneu, there was no new technology to grab. It was just a sleep depot for ancients. Carver succeeded in waking up a few hundred."

"Ancients? How ancient?"

"Twenty thousand years was quoted."

"*Twenty thousand* years? And they were successfully revived?"

"According to Arneu's report, they're all healthy. They popped up out of their stasis chambers and were ready to go in an hour."

"An hour? After sleeping for twenty thousand years? And you don't consider that significant? Do you have any idea what that technology would be worth if we could patent it?"

"But Space Command isn't going to let anyone patent it, Arthur. It was found on Dakistee, so any attempt to patent it would point a finger to the member of the organization who tried. The Dakinium we could have used without seeking a patent but not this."

Strauss sighed. "I suppose you're right, Ahil. I'm just groping for something to bring to the Upper Council. They're going to be plenty upset that we spent so much and came out of this with so little."

"Not every venture is going to reap a bonanza, but we have to take a chance every once in a while where the payoff could be great. At least this wasn't the debacle Gagarin orchestrated."

"Yes. Although costly, this was not on the same scale as that disaster. However, there was another cost in this mess.

We've lost the use of a valuable contact at Space Command Supreme Headquarters. Hubera will never be acquitted of the charges brought against him. That old oaf lost his temper and went too far when he ordered Carver to quit the site. He'll be censured and possibly demoted. He might even lose his place on the Admiralty Board. Damn it! People holding senior positions in Space Command are too valuable to lose without having at least turned a decent profit on the loss."

◆ ◆ ◆

"The court-martial of Admiral Hubera begins tomorrow morning," Admiral Moore said to the other eight members of the Admiralty Board. "The trial is closed to spectators and live broadcast, but I've ordered that the images be transmitted here so we can watch the proceedings in real time. Attendance is not mandatory."

"I still can't fathom what he was thinking when he ordered Commander Carver to disobey her orders and desert her post." Admiral Bradlee said. "If, in fact, he did order that."

"It's no secret that Donald is prone to losing his temper where Admiral Carver or her sisters are concerned," Admiral Hillaire said. "We've listened to his tirades here for years. I think he just lost his temper— and his better judgment. If, in fact, he is guilty of doing what he's charged with."

"Is there any chance Admiral Carver might have over-reacted and overstated the issue?" Admiral Platt asked.

"I suppose it's possible," Admiral Moore said, "but from what I've observed over the years, the *Ice Queen* never over-reacts. Every action seems to have been thought out to the nth degree, except during battle. And even there she gives as much thought as possible to examining the issue before deciding on a course of action."

"Yes," Admiral Hillaire said. "I've never heard of an instance where she lost her temper or acted rashly."

"In any event," Admiral Moore said, "it's the duty of the court to determine the facts and I'm sure they'll meticulously examine all the evidence before reaching a conclusion."

"What if it comes down to a matter of Donald's word versus Commander Carver's word? According to Admiral Holt, she's still in a coma. She obviously can't testify until she regains consciousness, and, since she was shot in the head, her memory of the event may be faulty."

"The court can use her official report to Admiral Carver as a deposition. I'm as dismayed as anyone that she hasn't regained consciousness yet. Admiral Holt has informed me she's getting the best care Space Command can offer. If the court requires an in-person appearance, we'll just have to wait and see if she recovers."

"We haven't yet discussed awarding a commendation for the way she managed the situation after the attack and a medal for sustaining an injury in the later shootout," Admiral Plimley said.

"She'll naturally receive a purple heart for being injured," Admiral Moore said, "and she should receive a commendation for her work on Dakistee and for her handling of the situation following the attack. If she doesn't recover, she should receive additional recognition, so perhaps the discussion of rewards should wait until we know the outcome."

◆　◆　◆

Admiral Hubera and his attorney arrived at the windowless courtroom early. The room was empty of people and they sat to discuss the case while the clock at the rear of the room slowly ticked off the seconds.

Normally used for Inquiry Board hearings, the room didn't look like a traditional courtroom. A meter-high raised platform at the front of the room held a long, judicial-style bench that accommodated five officers rather than a single judge. There was no jury box and there would be no gallery for the trial. Two tables, one each for the prosecution and defense, faced the front of the room. There was a witness chair against the left sidewall, several chairs for court officials against the right sidewall, and a dozen chairs behind each of the tables for additional council and aides. The gallery seating had been removed and stored elsewhere so the room imparted a sense of openness— or perhaps emptiness. Witnesses, when there were witnesses to be called, would be located in a separate room and escorted in when their testimony was required. Nine video cameras mounted around the room's ceiling would record every utterance and movement for every second of the court-martial.

◆ ◆

A few minutes before the court-martial was to start, people began arriving. First were the JAG prosecution attorneys and then the court clerks and Marine security detail.

As the clock struck the appointed hour for the start of the court-martial, the five admirals filed into the stark room from a rear door and took their seats. Each either knew, or knew of, Admiral Hubera from earlier times, but each had sworn an oath to be completely impartial and offered no sign of greeting.

As soon as the admirals were seated, Admiral Bernake picked up a small silver rod and tapped three times on the silver tubular chime suspended in a small frame in front of him on the bench.

"This court is now in session on this 8th day of December, 2285," a female chief petty officer announced loudly.

"The chief petty officer will read the charges," Bernake said.

The chief read the charges, already well known to judges and council, then retook her seat.

"Captain Cereus?" Admiral Bernake said.

"Sir?" Cereus said as he rose to his feet quickly.

"You may begin."

"Thank you, sir. I ask the court for permission to replay the report by Commander Christa Carver that has already been entered into evidence.

Admiral Bernake nodded and the clerk replayed the message.

When the vid had finished, Cereus turned to the Defense table and said, "Admiral Hubera. Would you please take the stand, sir."

The chief petty officer, in her role as court clerk, administered the oath and Hubera took the witness chair against the left sidewall.

"Admiral Hubera," Cereus said, "on October 22, 2285, you visited Dakistee for the express purpose of conducting a surprise inspection of the Loudescott Archeological dig site. Is that correct?"

"It is."

"What authorization did you have for conducting such an inspection?"

"I am a member of the Admiralty Board. I need no other authorization. We are charged with overseeing all aspects of Space Command operations."

"Prior to this inspection, how many times had you visited Dakistee to conduct a surprise inspection?"

Hubera was clearly surprised by the question and looked over at his attorney, who simply nodded.

Looking back at Cereus, Hubera said, "None."

"I see. Well then, how many surprise inspection visits have you made since becoming a member of the Admiralty Board?"

Again Hubera looked at his attorney before answering. When his attorney didn't object to the question, Hubera mumbled, "None."

"I'm sorry, sir, I didn't quite catch that. Did you say, 'None?'"

"Yes," Hubera replied tersely.

"I see. Then, since this was your first ever surprise inspection visit anywhere, perhaps you can tell us why you went to Dakistee."

"I object." Hubera's attorney said. "Admiral Hubera has already answered that question."

"Sustained," Admiral Bernake said.

Cereus turned and walked a couple of steps in obvious thought and then returned to where he had been. "You dislike Commander Christa Carver, do you not?"

"I'd never even met her before that day on Dakistee."

"Technically correct, but not completely accurate. Commander Carver is a clone of Admiral Jenetta Carver, whom you've known since your days as an Academy instructor. Is that not correct?"

"Yes, Jenetta Carver was once a student of mine at the academy."

"And you've had an intense dislike of her ever since."

"No, that's not true."

"No? Then when did your intense dislike of her begin?"

"I never said I disliked her."

"Come now, Admiral. Your tirades in the Admiralty Board Hall whenever any subject pertaining to Admiral Carver has come up are legendary."

"I, uh, have reservations about her ability to perform in the role she's been assigned."

"That's been your position ever since she destroyed Raider One, has it not?"

"I haven't changed my position simply because she's had a few small successes."

"A few small successes? I believe that if you ask almost anyone in the service, they will acknowledge that Admiral

Carver has had a greater impact than anyone before her in the history of Space Command."

"That doesn't mean she deserves to be a full Admiral."

"While you're still only a Rear Admiral, you mean?"

"I object," Hubera's attorney said.

"Withdrawn," Cereus said before turning and walking a couple of steps in obvious thought before returning to face Hubera.

"Admiral, is the vid message report sent by Commander Christa Carver an accurate report of what occurred on Dakistee?"

Hubera looked at his attorney, who shook his head almost imperceptibly.

"No, it is not."

"Perhaps you could tell us, in your own words, exactly what happened."

"I met with Commander Carver aboard the *Murray* and asked her to give me a report regarding her progress."

"And?"

"And she gave me a report."

"And?"

"And what?"

"And what was your response when she was done?"

"I thanked her and dismissed her."

"That's all?"

"Yes, that's all."

"You never ordered her to leave Dakistee and return to Region Two immediately."

"I don't recall giving such an order."

Turning to face the president of the court, Cereus said, "If it please the court, I received new evidence just hours ago. It's in the form of a message and I request permission to play it."

"I object," Hubera's attorney said. "I wasn't advised of new evidence so I haven't had an opportunity to review it to see if it has any bearing on the case."

"The message was a recording made by Commander Christa Carver," Cereus said. "It has a direct bearing on the case. If I might be permitted to have it played, I'm sure the court will agree. After the playback, I'll be happy to give the defense time in which to formulate a response, if he feels one is necessary."

"What is the nature of this message?" Admiral Bernake asked.

"Commander Christa Carver was speaking to a subordinate via her CT when Admiral Hubera entered the room aboard the *Murray* where she was waiting to give her report. She immediately braced to attention and never closed the carrier, so her side of the conversation with Admiral Hubera was recorded in full."

"I object. The voice recording of someone without their knowledge and consent is illegal unless a court order has first been obtained."

"Captain Cereus?" Bernake said.

"If it please the court, that law is not applicable in this instance. The recording doesn't contain a single word from Admiral Hubera since his CT wasn't activated. We can only hear Commander Carver's side of the conversation."

"Objection overruled. Play the message," Bernake said.

The judges listened in rapt attention until the message ended. Although only one side could be heard, the evidence was damning.

"I object," Hubera's attorney said. "How can we know when that recording was made or where it came from?"

"It's time and date stamped," Cereus said, "and available from either the computer system aboard the *Murray* or the communication system on the surface of Dakistee since it had to pass through both systems when Commander Carver made the connection to Lieutenant Carmoody. As everyone knows, all CT communications are recorded and saved for a one-year period."

"The recording shall be logged as evidence," Bernake said.

Hubera slumped in the witness chair, then sat erect again when he remembered where he was.

"Admiral," Cereus said to Hubera, "what do you say now? Has the recording refreshed your memory? Do you still deny ordering Commander Carver off the planet?"

"I, uh, might have said something to that effect. Hearing the tape, as you say, has refreshed my memory of the day."

Cereus nodded. "How did you feel when you were refused entrance to the tunnel?"

"How would any senior officer feel? I was upset that Marines had orders to fire on Space Command personnel if they tried to get in."

"But you heard Commander Carver say that as far as she knew, she and her assistant were the only Space Command personnel on the planet."

"She said that later, not at the time I was turned back. You asked how I felt when I was refused."

"Quite right. But you were still upset later?"

"I might have been."

"And that was the reason you ordered her off the planet?"

"Yes. Uh, I mean it might have been part of it if I did order her off the planet."

"There's little doubt about that now. Would you like to hear the recording again?"

"No," Hubera said testily.

"Admiral Hubera, regarding your surprise inspection, would you please tell the court why you chose this occasion to do something you had never done before?"

When his attorney didn't object, Hubera said, "I was taking a brief vacation at the Belagresue Colony when my flag secretary suggested the quick trip. He had learned that the *Murray* would be passing through the system and knew we could be on Dakistee in less than two days."

"Your flag secretary is Captain Robledo. Is he not?"

"He was."

"And he ceased to be your flag secretary when?"

Nervously, Hubera said, "He was arrested two weeks ago."

"You're referring to the charge of treason that SCI filed against him?"

"Yes."

"And do you know the basis for that charge?"

"SCI said they discovered evidence that he was in the employ of the Raiders."

"So the person who had your full trust and confidence and was privy to all the secrets of the Admiralty Board was a Raider spy?"

"He has been charged, but not convicted yet."

"I see." Cereus turned and walked a few steps in thought before returning. "Assuming he *is* convicted, it would mean you've been feeding top secret information to the Raiders for many years."

"Objection," Hubera's attorney said, "it calls for speculation."

"Sustained," Bernake said.

"It sounds, Admiral Hubera," Cereus said, "like you've been putting your trust in the wrong people while spending decades denigrating the people to whom that trust really belonged."

"Objection!" Hubera's attorney said loudly. "Mr. President, I really must protest."

CHAPTER TWENTY-FIVE
~ January 18th, 2286 ~

Madu climbed the steps of the temporary stage erected in a large gymnasium on the Recreation level and walked to the podium at the center. She stared out over the neatly arranged rows of chairs and tried to visualize them filled with attentive citizens. In five hours, every Dakistian who had been awakened would be seated out there. She wished the audience could be larger, but Christa hadn't restored her computer access before the attack and Carmoody refused to let her use hers, fearing that Madu would again attempt another mass awakening. Madu sighed and delivered her prepared speech to the empty room.

Madu had been messaging the commanding officer of North Pendleton for an update on Christa's condition every day but kept receiving the same message that Christa was still in a coma. Madu had begun to doubt Christa would return to Dakistee. She had seen the enormous pool of blood beneath Christa's body in the dormitory room. Christa might be a different species, but the loss of that much blood had to have had a serious impact on her health and condition. Madu knew that a Dakistian definitely wouldn't have survived the loss, and Terrans didn't seem that dissimilar. She had been surprised to see that either the doctor or nurse had cleaned up the telltale pool before the stretcher-bearers were allowed into the room. It seemed a strange thing to do during an emergency where seconds were precious.

Madu rehearsed the speech three times in the gym before being satisfied with her delivery. The speech would be the easy part because she could rehearse it until she had it down cold. The difficult part would be the question-and-answer segment of the program. She already had far too many questions and not enough answers echoing around inside her own head.

◆　◆

When Madu next entered the gym, it was filled to capacity. Knowing how many sleepers had been awakened allowed her staff to only set out enough chairs to accommodate that number. She would therefore know immediately how many had chosen not to attend this vital meeting. To her delight, there wasn't a single empty chair. The meeting was limited to Dakistee citizens only, so she knew no one had skipped the meeting.

As she reached the steps to the stage, she received a standing ovation. She smiled and waved as she walked to the podium and then basked in the applause for a few seconds before raising her arms. The clapping subsided and the audience retook their seats.

"Hello, and welcome to the First Dakistee Constitutional Resurrection Convention," Madu said into the microphone. "I'm quite sure none of us ever expected to sleep for as long as we did. We believed our brilliant scientists would find a solution to our problem and we would be awakened within a few decades, or perhaps half a century at most. When I was awakened and told I had slept for twenty millennia, I didn't believe the people who had restored me to consciousness. I suspected ulterior motives. I was wrong. I learned we were never awakened by our own people because the scientists never found a cure for the plague that doomed our civilization. Unless that now happens within our lifetimes, our people might indeed be doomed.

"Perhaps the best news greeting our reawakening is that the galaxy has passed us by. Ordinarily, that kind of news is tragic, but, for us, it might represent our salvation. It's now possible to travel faster than light and go places never dreamed of when we were born. It means that while we slept, oblivious to events that were happening, and while the galaxy remained ignorant that we were waiting to be awakened, great strides were being made in science and medicine.

"The person to whom we all owe our lives is Lieutenant Commander Christa Carver. She's of Terran lineage but was born here on Dakistee just a short distance from this facility. It was she who solved the riddle of opening the door to this facility, a task that scientists told me would be impossible to anyone who hadn't been briefed in the process. The complex procedure was intended to ensure that thieves didn't break in during the decades we slept without guards at the entrance. We could sleep secure in the knowledge that when we awakened, everything would be just as we left it. And it was, thanks to the Space Command personnel who protected the facility after Commander Carver unsealed the entrance and who still guard the entrance to ensure we aren't disturbed by the archeologists at the nearby dig site.

"I'm sure most of you have been to the surface in recent weeks. Our beautiful city is now just a memory, thankfully preserved in images, as are all the other cities on our world. During the time we slept, our planet's infrastructure has crumbled to dust. We *will* rebuild it. We *must* rebuild it. It will take time, which brings us back to the point I touched on earlier about finding a cure to the plague.

"To date, I've awakened fewer than six hundred sleepers. The first to be awakened were people who could support my effort to awaken more in case Space Command tried to prevent me from doing so. But once I was sure Commander Carver was only trying to ensure an orderly and safe awakening process, the people awakened were those most able to assure our future survival. That means most of you. Our first goal must be to find a cure for the condition that prevents us from natural procreation. If the most brilliant people of our earlier time couldn't solve the dilemma during their lifetime, the new effort must be massive— all consuming in fact. I refuse to believe it will be futile.

"To accomplish our number one goal, we will need funding. I've been told the Galactic Alliance will treat the project as a humanitarian effort, but we all know that humanitarian efforts don't always accomplish their idealistic goals. We also know that nothing moves an effort along better than money, so we must have huge sums of money to fund the research and development work. That's the only way we'll get the attention of the most brilliant of the brilliant in this new universe we've awakened into.

"We must work together with the one main goal always uppermost in our mind. If we can do that, we can look forward to one day seeing our world populated with the new offspring of the young men and women still waiting in stasis to begin their new lives.

"Thank you for listening to my plea. I'll now open the session up to questions."

Madu pointed to a man who appeared senior to most of the people in his seating area.

"Madame Director, I was under the impression that this session was to be dedicated to resurrecting our constitution. Other than your opening sentence, I've heard no mention of it."

"Professor Olivegzelt, I felt I had an obligation to present the problem most important to all of us at this time and then allow the group to take the remainder of the session in whatever direction they wished. Resurrecting the constitution is important, but, in my opinion, pales in comparison to the procreation issue. Do you have a particular question about the constitution?"

"Yes. When will it become the law of the land again?"

"Within this facility, it is the law of the land. Outside is another issue. When the Galactic Alliance performed an in-depth survey of the planet and found no sign of sentient life, it assumed none existed. It never realized we were asleep so far below the surface. At that time, it awarded contracts to a non-profit archeological organization to uncover the remnants of our 'long dead' civilization. There was no malicious intent. They were simply explorers looking for answers. When the GA learned that the planet was still inhabited by a sleeping population, all contracts were rescinded according to included clauses providing for this possibility. The items that have been recovered and not yet shipped off planet were seized and will be turned over to us when our government is formed. In the meantime, the planet is under martial law and will be governed by Space Command."

"A military, not even our own, is going to dictate what we can do and when we can do it?"

"Space Command's mission is to keep the peace and provide a means to settle arguments and conflicts peacefully. I had gotten to know Commander Carver pretty well in the short time we worked together and I can promise you that she is not a dictator. She is not seeking power, glory, or personal wealth. She's assured me that as soon as we're in a position to assume control of our planet, the Galactic Alliance will return full control to the elected government."

"Completely? And they'll leave— completely?"

"If we wish to remain a part of the Galactic Alliance, there will of course be a presence here— a small presence, as is appropriate for embassies. If we decide to separate ourselves from the Galactic Alliance completely, they will leave completely."

"I'll believe it when I see it."

"Anyone else?" Madu asked, looking out at the audience again.

"How are we supposed to raise the money we'll need to support our research?" one of the engineers who had worked on the water problem asked. "The planet is in ruins. There's *nothing* left up there. Except for where the archeologists have pulled back the surface cover, it looks like a prehistoric world."

"I have a few ideas on that, but I'm going to need lots of help on this project. We know that when we went to sleep there had to be vast wealth in precious stones and minerals stored in large, secure warehouses located around the planet. We must begin an intensive effort to find them before some archeological group does."

"And what if they've uncovered them already?"

"They haven't, according to the item lists I've seen of the things they've sent to the planet Anthius where the central repository is located. They're following traditional archeological search procedures, peeling back the layers of time slowly and methodically, being extra careful not to destroy anything. They believed they had all the time in the world to discover what lay hidden, so there's been no massive effort to search for deep vaults that might contain vast wealth. If we act swiftly, we can locate the government caches before they stumble onto them."

"But where do we even begin? We have no organization or structure and no assets."

"We have this facility to begin with. And there are five others just like it. Most importantly, we have a hundred and eighty thousand Dakistians. They included some of the finest minds in our population when it was time to sleep. We can do this and will do this."

"But we have no government. Where do we start?"

"We start small and build, as is always done with any organization."

"But who will lead us?"

"I nominate Madu Ptellewqku for interim leader of our government," someone shouted from over on the right side of the seating.

"I second that nomination," another said as a chorus of voices took up a chant of "Madu, Madu, Madu."

The young engineer looked around, shrugged his shoulders, and sat back down as the chant increased in pitch.

Madu finally held up her hands for quiet. "I'm honored to be nominated to run the interim government. If that's what you want, I promise to do the best job I can. But I have to ask if there are any other nominations."

When no one spoke up, Madu said, "Very well. Can we have a show of hands to see if I have your full support?"

A number of hands shot up quickly, followed by a slow but steady rising as people thought about the vote and decided to go along. A few people appeared undecided and abstained, but the overwhelming majority raised their hand in support.

"Thank you for this show of support tonight. I will do the very best job I can while I function as your President."

◆　◆

"Did I do okay, Madam President?" Madu's assistant asked later when the program was over and the citizens had left the gym.

"You couldn't have timed it better, Toydan. And Marcillos did his role perfectly as well. I thought that idiot Professor Kequilisk was going to bollix everything, but he finally had the good sense to stop asking foolish questions and sit down. I needed someone to provide a little dissidence and awoke him because he always opposed everything. My plan came together perfectly."

"What now, Madam President?" Toydan asked.

"We have a lot to do. We have a planet to conquer and a disease to whip. We're going to be quite busy before we can move into a new executive mansion."

◆　◆　◆

"We just received a dispatch from Anthius," Dr. Manson's assistant said to her as she returned to her office following lunch. "They say the cylinder you brought to Commander Carver will not be coming back to you. It seems the cylinder is constructed from some special metal listed as a controlled distribution substance."

"Is it dangerous? Was it radioactive or something?"

"I don't think so. There's just some law that says we can't possess it."

"That's ridiculous. It has to be Carver again. That bitch is trying to make sure I don't get my ornament back. I knew I shouldn't have brought it to her."

Manson strode angrily into her office.

"You had no choice," her assistant said, following her in. "Anthius ordered you to."

"I bet she put pressure on the curators at Anthius to fabricate this ridiculous story. I wish I could have found something to lay on her, but she's as squeaky clean as a nanotech robot. Her sister might be called the Ice Queen, but she should be nicknamed Snow White."

Her assistant giggled. "That's funny."

Manson looked at her assistant somberly. "What's funny about it?"

"I've heard Carver is still in a coma. If you remember the story, Snow White was in a coma after she bit into the poisoned apple given to her by a witch." Manson was staring at her like she had just scored zero on an IQ test. "Don't you get it? Commander Carver was attacked by a witch and now she's in a coma."

"Don't you have some filing to do, Paula?"

Her assistant stopped smiling and said, "Yes, ma'am."

When she was alone again, Manson looked at the empty display stand on her desk where the cylinder used to rest and said, "Coma or not, I'll get even Carver. Just you wait."

◆ ◆ ◆

"What's the matter, Lieutenant?" Lt. Uronson asked a morose Carmoody in the mess hall as he took a seat across from her. "You look like you lost your best friend."

"I might have. There's still been no improvement in Commander Carver's condition. I'm beginning to worry she may never return to work."

"Oh. Well, it *has* been a long time for someone to be in a coma, but a lot of people have been comatose for much, much longer and still recovered."

"I wish we could have found that woman Madu saw in the Commander's room on the day of the attack. I don't know how she got out of here without anyone else seeing her."

"It was pretty crazy just then with all the dig site people packing up and returning to their camp. It's too bad this facility doesn't have cameras set up at important locations. It's SOP in the Marine Corps. We'd never have an entrance to an important facility without vid coverage. When the Corps took over Fort Carver, we had to add security cameras at the entrance because there weren't any. I guess the Dakistian people were more trusting than we are."

"Or more impractical," Carmoody said in a lowered voice.

"Yeah, that too. Where will you go now?"

"I don't know. I thought I'd be able to stay here for a while and work with the Commander, but now I don't know."

"You like her, don't you?"

"She's great. She's brilliant and funny and was more like a friend than a commanding officer. I really enjoyed our time together. I've never worked with anyone who was so dedicated, and yet so— so— easy to get along with."

"Well, don't count her out yet. She might surprise you and come walking through the door when you least expect it."

"I wish."

◆　◆　◆

"Come in, Pete," Lt. Col. Diminjik said to Major Garfield when he heard the office door open. His chair was tipped back as far as it would go and he was staring out the window with his fingers interlaced and resting on his stomach.

"You look the perfect picture of relaxation, sir," Garfield said with a smile.

"I'm just enjoying the calm before the storm."

"Storm? The weather is calling for average temps and clear skies for several days."

"Not that kind of storm. I'm talking about the political kind."

"But everything seems calm enough. The protests are over, the brass hats didn't hold you responsible for any of the trouble here, and we've been promised more personnel. Things seem to be rosy."

"We've been promised more people because we're going to need them. As soon as they start awakening those hundred eighty thousand sleepers, this planet is going to go from a quiet little outpost to a Mecca for entrepreneurs looking to cash in on the new opportunities here."

"But that will be the worry of the Outpost Commander, not you."

"Right now I'm worried they might stick me with the job."

"What about Carver?"

"Yeah, what about Carver? No one seems to know. I saw a news piece yesterday that said the newsies on Higgins are complaining because they're not allowed to interview her. Hell, they say they can't even find out where she's being cared for. She's not in the base hospital nor any of the usual care centers. Holt won't even discuss it with them other than to say she's not available for interviews. The scuttlebutt is that she's still in a coma and not expected to recover."

"But she's a Carver. Don't they have some special healing power or something?"

"Perhaps her injuries were too extensive even for that. Anyway, if she doesn't make it back here, I'm afraid they might stick me in the CO spot until someone else can be appointed."

"Aren't you there already, pretty much?"

"All I really have to worry about right now is this base. And that's fine with me. There's no way I want that Dakistee Outpost CO job. You know me— I'm not good at dealing with civilians, politicians, or newsies."

"Few military people are."

"Carver is. She's the ideal candidate, if she recovers."

"Wouldn't it bother you to be subordinate to someone with lower rank?"

"She's an O-4. That's just one pay grade behind me. And she's the clone of a full admiral with all the same capabilities and knowledge of Admiral Carver. No, it doesn't bother me to report to her. I'm happy to have her to run interference for us, and perhaps she can get us some of the appropriations money

I've been asking for. I just hope she recovers and gets back here soon. This planet is going to implode in the near future and I don't want to be the one stuck holding the reins when it does."

CHAPTER TWENTY-SIX
~ January 29th, 2286 ~

"This is Neal Neally, reporting outside the Space Command Judicial Headquarters in Arlington, Virginia where the court-martial of Rear Admiral Donald M. Hubera has just concluded," the reporter said to the oh-gee camera focused on his face from a meter away. The judicial building could be seen in the background. "Reporters were barred from the courtroom, so my information comes from a Space Command document with key highlights prepared for the press.

"The trial was not a lengthy one, but it was paused for six weeks until the court-martial of Captain Robledo was concluded, owing to complaints of prejudice and innuendo filed by Admiral Hubera's civilian attorney. As has already been reported, Captain Robledo was found guilty of all charges and remanded to the prison colony on Saquer Major for the remainder of his life. He will be housed in the same, no-visitor detention block as the former Flag Secretary of Admiral Elersey, Captain Dumona, who was found guilty of similar charges back in 2268. Two other senior officers, whom it was proved also accepted bribes or payments from the Raiders, were likewise incarcerated at that time. Admiral Elersey was censured and dismissed from the service for incompetence. In this new case, no other Space Command officers were found to be complicit with Captain Robledo.

"Admiral Hubera has been found guilty of the charges against him, but, owing to his lifetime of excellent service to Space Command, the court decided he will only be reduced in rank to Captain and permitted to retire from Space Command. We do not yet have a copy of the proceedings log, but I understand it shows that Captain Robledo was at least partially responsible for provoking Admiral Hubera into taking the actions he did.

"This is Neal Neally, reporting live from the Space Command Judicial Headquarters in Arlington, Virginia. We'll bring you additional coverage as new information comes our way. Good day."

◆ ◆ ◆

"It's a shame Donald allowed his opposition to Admiral Carver be so inflamed by his Flag Secretary that he lost control of his better judgment," Admiral Moore said to the other admirals as they ate lunch in their private dining room. "And we'll never know just how long it's been happening. Robledo might have been inciting aggression towards Jenetta and her sisters for years."

"I think I'll almost miss his haranguing," Admiral Platt said. "It was quite tedious at times, but he often enlivened an otherwise dull afternoon."

"I'll miss him," Admiral Hillaire said. "I often enjoyed his repartee on various issues."

"Now that surprises me," Admiral Bradlee said. "You two always seemed to be ready to duke it out."

"That was part of the fun. He'd get my blood boiling and I'd do the same to him. As Evelyn says, he usually enlivened things, although he could be tedious at times."

"I suppose we'll have to prepare a slate of potential candidates to fill his seat," Admiral Ahmed said.

"Perhaps not," Admiral Moore said. "I've been informed that things are finally moving ahead on Nordakia. As you know, the Academy there has reached full enrollment and all officers in the Space Force now speak Amer fluently. They are required to use Amer exclusively when aboard ship. Space Force officers who failed to commit the Space Command Handbook to memory have received a separation date. They'll be moved to the space merchant services. Once that happens, we'll be able to begin the merger of the Space Force with Space Command. Admiral Yuthkotl will join us here as a member of the Board."

"It's been a long time coming," Admiral Plimley said.

"Yes. It was a shame we couldn't have Admiral Carver take over the transition as we once planned," Admiral Ressler said. "I have no doubt it would have sped the process immensely."

"It's a shame neither of her sisters had sufficient rank to take on the job," Admiral Woo said.

"Speaking of Admiral Carver," Admiral Bradlee said, "perhaps we should consider bringing her here to fill Donald's seat, even though Admiral Yuthkotl might be joining us. None of us are getting any younger and we need to begin infusing some new blood into the Board."

"The problem," Admiral Platt said, "is that she's still very much needed in Region Two. And since we've never assigned anyone to Region Three, she's handling that workload as well. I doubt we could free her up out there. Who else could hold that part of space together as well as she has?"

"If we assigned someone to Region Three," Admiral Woo said, "we'd have to find them a fleet somewhere and we just don't have the resources for a third fleet right now. It's far better to have Jenetta in control of both territories for the time being. That way she can send her ships where they're needed. I see it as the most effective use of our ships, even if it does place an incredible strain on the Second Fleet and on Admiral Carver."

"I received a note from her yesterday," Admiral Moore said. "She's on the way to Higgins to see her sister."

"Is there any update on Commander Carver's condition?"

"No. The last word from Admiral Holt was that she's still comatose."

"Being comatose for two months is not a good sign," Admiral Hillaire said.

"Her head wound was extremely serious," Admiral Plimley said. "The shoulder wound wasn't too bad, but the lattice wound to the abdomen had to be. Since it was under her ribcage, it had to have passed completely through her body. The blood loss from the torso and shoulder wounds, combined with the damage from the head wound, would kill most people."

"Is Admiral Carver intending to come here?" Admiral Bradlee asked.

"She didn't mention it," Admiral Moore said, "but I'm sure she will if we request it."

"I think it would be good to get a personal update on Regions Two and Three. We haven't spoken in person since the start of the THUG war. I'd like to hear her personal assessment of the situation there now. There must be things we should know that she can't put into official reports."

"Very well," Admiral Moore said. "I'll send her a note requesting she stop here before going back. She'll probably want an opportunity to see her family on Earth anyway after having traveled so far to see her sister."

◆ ◆ ◆

Without requesting it, the *Ares* received a straight-in flight path by Higgins SCB Approach Control. It was just one of the perks always afforded to visiting admirals. Jenetta was on the Admiral's bridge with her aide, Lt. Commander Ashraf, in addition to a communications chief, a tactical officer, and navigator, but the ship was naturally being piloted from the Captain's bridge.

As the ship drew near the docking ring, Jenetta had the tactical officer 'erase' the walls, overhead, and deck. It was like approaching the station in a glass bubble. Only the seating, consoles, and grid lines on the deck gave some perspective of where the floor actually was. It would be far too easy to get disoriented without the thin red lines on the deck, so even the tactical officer had no control over them.

"I love this sensation," Ashraf said to Jenetta.

"It makes you feel sort of god-like, doesn't it? I mean, it seems like you're whisking through the ice-cold vacuum of space without even an EVA suit."

"Yes, it reminds me of when I was small and we kids would sit on the front fender of my grandpa's oh-gee truck on his farm back on Earth. No noise, nothing obscuring your vision, just the wind rushing gently across your face and through your hair."

"I can get you a fan if you want," Jenetta quipped.

Lori smiled and said, "That's alright, ma'am. I can do without. Besides, there's no wind in a vacuum."

"True," Jenetta said, smiling.

◆　◆　◆

"Welcome to Higgins, Admiral," The affable face on the large monitor said, as the ship docked.

"Thank you, Brian," Jenetta said from the command chair on the Admiral's bridge. "I hope you haven't arranged a pretentious greeting ceremony."

"No more than what is minimally required for a visiting admiral who recently brought peace to the entire GA."

Jenetta smiled slightly and accepted that some small ceremony was required. She would bear up and attempt to curtail it as quickly as possible.

◆

When Jenetta stepped from the docking platform into the docking ring proper, a small band began to play and spectators began to scream her name. She smiled and waved, although the worry about her sister kept her from getting into the mood. Still, she performed her role adequately and delivered a small speech, then thanked everyone for their enthusiastic welcome. Her security detail kept her admirers at arm's length because she had feared bringing her Taurentlus-Thur Jumakas, Tanya and Cayla into the throng. The hundred-sixty-pound cats were always nervous in crowds and their fierce protective nature could be problematic if someone not in a Space Command uniform got too close.

When at last they could get away, she climbed into the open-topped limo and waved to the crowd as it sped away.

"That was what you called minimal?" Jenetta said to Admiral Holt.

"That was about as minimal as the PR office would accept. They cited me chapter and verse about the length of the speeches and the band size required in the regulations until I told them to go hang the regulations and cut everything in half."

"Thank you. Now tell me about Christa. Your notes haven't given me any details. The news reports say she remains in a coma."

"Wait until we're in my office, please."

"Brian, what's going on?"

"My office, please, Jenetta."

"Very well."

◆

When they arrived at Admiral Holt's office, all he did was nod to his aide and walk down the corridor. Jenetta followed along behind and held her tongue until the doors had closed behind them.

"Now, why all surreptitious behavior?" Jenetta asked.

Holt took a deep breath and released it slowly. "Jenetta, it's my sad, sad duty to inform you that Christa died in that shootout on Dakistee. According to the doctor, she bled out in minutes. The man who shot her died just a meter away, allegedly by her hand. Her laser weapon caused massive internal injury to him and he probably expired before she did."

"Christa's dead?" Jenetta said as the shock reached down and took ahold of her. "But she's supposed to be in a coma here at Higgins."

"I didn't want anyone to know until you heard the news first, in person. Even the Admiralty Board doesn't know she died. They still believe she's in critical condition, lying in a coma."

Jenetta walked to one the overstuffed chairs that faced Holt's desk and sank down. "You know, when you've been in as many fights as I have and you always come out unharmed, or at least minimally harmed, you almost begin to believe you'll live forever. Thousands of people have died around me over the years— millions if you count the enemies of the GA, so it's a shock to realize you're still mortal. Christa was born in a unique manner, but I loved her as if we had shared space in my mother's womb and grown up together. I remember the hug we shared just before she left on this mission. I feel like a part of me has just died, which I guess it has since she was my clone. And now— I have to tell my family she's gone." Jenetta hung her head as grief took hold.

Holt sat down in his chair behind the desk and tapped a button on his com unit. "Send her in," was all he said.

A few seconds later, the door to the corridor opened and a Lt. Commander entered. Jenetta looked up, then jumped to her feet in surprise.

"Eliza, what are you doing here? How did you get here?" Jenetta said.

"Eliza? Sis, I'm Christa," the officer said.

"But you're…"

"I know, I know, I've been in a coma. But I woke up this morning and I feel great. The doctor told me I've been out of it for months, so I guess my brain kinda shut down to concentrate on healing my body. I can't argue with the results. My face and ear are as good as new, and you'd never know I was shot in the shoulder or the stomach. Boy, did that ever hurt. Ya know, I really thought I was dead when that Raider archeologist shot me. But my injuries are all healed, I'm as good as new, and I'm ready to go back to work. And you're not going to *believe* the things I'm going to tell you about Mikel Arneu and the events that have taken place on Dakistee."

"Uh, Christa," Admiral Holt said rising to his feet, "Would you wait in the outer office until your sister and I have concluded some other business?"

"Of course, sir. I'll be waiting outside for you, sis."

Jenetta turned back to Admiral Holt as Christa left the office. "She doesn't know, does she?"

"No, she doesn't."

Jenetta sank back down into the chair as Admiral Holt did the same.

"Did you intend to tell her?" Jenetta asked.

"I figured I'd leave that choice up to you."

"Tell me how."

"How to tell her?"

"You know what I mean."

Holt grinned. "It was thanks to a lot of people, none of whom know anything about this."

"I'm listening."

"Admiral Moore authorized a black project fifteen years ago after you brought us the cloning equipment. He wanted us to learn everything we could about the process and also explore other possibilities."

"Other possibilities?" Jenetta said, nodding. "Totally black?"

"Blacker than black. I doubt that even half of the Admiralty Board members know about it. After the Admiral Elersey court-martial, things that were hush-hush went almost dead silent. Richard didn't want to take a chance on leaks because the project represented such a potential bombshell. Evelyn Platt and Roger Bradley know, and Shana Ressler probably knows because she's the budget person, but no one else had a need to know and probably weren't included in discussions."

"Just four members of the Admiralty Board?" Jenetta said.

Holt nodded. "The project was named Springboard. I have no idea how many people were on the inside track on this one, but I'm sure it wasn't more than a handful, other than the scientists who actually worked the project."

"And this black project is still underway?"

"No, it was wrapped up about four years ago after the funding ended but not before they accomplished their goal.

They documented exactly how the clones are produced by the Dakistee equipment and how the clones acquire all the knowledge and memories of the host. And, they found one more thing. They discovered that if they can get to a host within one hour of death, they can replace him and provide all the memories he had at the time of his death."

"But Dakistee is at least four days from here. That's well beyond the time which you say was required to recover Christa and all of her memories."

"Yes, but the first physician on the scene had the good sense to put Christa into one of the stasis beds used by the Dakistians. Those beds are far superior to anything we have, or ever envisioned, because they preserve the subject in virtually the same condition they were in when they entered the chamber."

"The attending physician on Dakistee knew of Project Springboard?"

"No, but he'd heard the stories about your incredible physiology and wanted to get Christa to us in the same condition in which he found her in case it was possible for us to heal her."

"So, bottom line, how many people are in the know on this use of the equipment?"

"Only half a dozen know the whole story. A dozen more know that something important required them to perform certain tasks in complete secrecy but not what was involved."

"For example?"

"The two pilots who took Christa's body in a sealed container and ejected it so it would burn up in the star we orbit. They had no idea what was in the container. They were told it presented a possible environmental threat to the station and had to be disposed of in a permanent fashion."

"So Christa's original body is gone and we have a clone who doesn't know she's a clone."

"Well, she was a clone before, so she knows she's a clone. Her memories are complete up to the minute she blacked out from loss of blood."

"You've put me in a tough spot, Brian."

"I know. But if our places were reversed I would have wanted you to do it for me— and for the GA. The people of the GA and Space Command need their heroes, Jen, and Christa *is* a hero. She saved most of those Loudescott people and discovered the thousands of sleepers who were entombed in the bowels of the planet."

"Yes, but you know how I feel about cloning. It's a slippery slope when you start justifying 'just one' and then 'just one more.'"

"We'll have to see that doesn't happen— except in extreme cases like this one. Look at it this way— Christa was already a clone, so we didn't create another clone. We just replaced the body she previously occupied because it was damaged."

Jenetta breathed in deeply and released it before saying, "I wonder what I would have said if you had asked me before you authorized it."

"Maybe that's why I didn't ask. You can be a bit stubborn at times where moral issues are concerned."

"Is this a moral issue or simply a psychological one?" Jenetta asked.

"It shouldn't be an issue at all. We send people into the hospital to fix them, right? We use prosthetic devices to return their mobility and functionality. In this case, we're just using the resources we have on hand to repair a damaged body."

"But where does it stop? Instead of replacing a damaged and useless limb, why not just create a clone with 100% functionality and dispose of the old body?"

"Because we would have to kill the person with the damaged limb so there was only one unique individual. There was no decision like that with Christa because her body was already dead. We just restored her life force to a replacement body— what the Milori call a 'husk.'"

"You knew that no matter how I felt about this, there'd be nothing I could do now. I can't order her to be killed to restore balance to the equation."

"Ordering her death wouldn't restore anything, Jen. It would just rob us of an incredible human being."

Jenetta nodded and stood up, facing Holt's desk. Holt rose to his feet as well and came out from behind his desk to stand facing Jenetta.

"You knew all along I would object," she said, "but that I would give in."

"I *hoped* it would work out that way."

Jenetta suddenly turned and wrapped her arms tightly around his neck. Stretching just slightly, she planted a kiss on his cheek and continued to hold him for a few more seconds. As she pulled back, he saw that both her checks were wet from tears.

"Thank you, Brian," she said. "Thank you for everything. Thank you for giving Christa back to me, and thank you for sparing me the agony of making that decision."

"That's what friends are for," he said with a kindly smile.

~ finis ~

♦♦♦ *The adventures of the Carver sisters will continue* ♦♦♦
in:

Retreat and Adapt

Watch for new books on Amazon and other fine
booksellers,
check my website - www.deprima.com
or
sign up for my free newsletter to receive email
announcements about future book releases.

APPENDIX

This chart is offered to assist readers who may be unfamiliar with military rank and the reporting structure. Newly commissioned officers begin at either ensign or second lieutenant rank.

Space Command	Space Marine Corps
Admiral of the Fleet	
Admiral	General
Vice-Admiral	Lieutenant General
Rear Admiral - Upper	Major General
Rear Admiral - Lower	Brigadier General
Captain	Colonel
Commander	Lieutenant Colonel
Lieutenant Commander	Major
Lieutenant	Captain
Lieutenant(jg) "Junior Grade"	First Lieutenant
Ensign	Second Lieutenant

The commanding officer on a ship is always referred to as Captain, regardless of his or her official military rank. Even an Ensign could be a Captain of the Ship, although that would only occur as the result of an unusual situation or emergency where no senior officers survived.

On Space Command ships and bases, time is measured according to a twenty-four-hour clock, normally referred to as military time. For example, 8:42 PM would be referred to as 2042 hours. Chronometers are always set to agree with the date and time at Space Command Supreme Headquarters on Earth. This is known as GST, or Galactic System Time.

A

Admiralty Board:

Moore, Richard E.	Admiral of the Fleet
Platt, Evelyn S.	Admiral - Director of Fleet Operations
Bradlee, Roger T.	Admiral - Director of Intelligence (SCI)
Ressler, Shana E.	Admiral - Director of Budget & Accounting
Hillaire, Arnold H.	Admiral - Director of Academies
Burke, Raymond A.	Vice-Admiral - Director of GSC Base Management
Ahmed, Raihana L.	Vice-Admiral - Dir. of Quartermaster Supply
Woo, Lon C.	Vice-Admiral - Dir. of Scientific & Expeditionary Forces
Plimley, Loretta J.	Rear-Admiral, (U) - Dir. of Weapons R&D
Hubera, Donald M.	Rear-Admiral, (U) - Dir. of Academy Curricula

Ship Speed Terminology	*Speed*
Plus-1	1 kps
Sub-Light-1	1,000 kps
Light-1 (*c*) *(speed of light in a vacuum)*	299,792.458 kps
Light-150 or **150 c**	150 times the speed of light

Hyper-Space Factors	
IDS Communications Band	.0513 light years each minute (8.09 billion kps)
DeTect Range	4 billion kilometers

B

Strat Com Desig	Mission Description for Strategic Command Bases
1	Base - Location establishes it as a critical component of Space Command Operations - Serves as home-port to multiple warships that also serve in base's defense. All sections of Space Command maintain an active office at the base. Base Commander establishes all patrol routes and is authorized to override SHQ orders to ships within the sector(s) designated part of the base's operating territory. Recommended rank of Commanding Officer: **Rear Admiral (U)**
2	Base - Location establishes it as a crucial component of Space Command Operations - Serves as home-port to multiple warships that also serve in base's defense. All sections of Space Command maintain an active office at the base. Patrol routes established by SHQ. Recommended rank of Commanding Officer: **Rear Admiral (L)**
3	Base - Location establishes it as an important component of Space Command Operations - Serves as homeport to multiple warships that also serve in base's defense. Patrol routes established by SHQ. Recommended rank of Commanding Officer: **Captain**
4	Station - Location establishes it as an important terminal for Space Command personnel engaged in travel to/from postings, and for re-supply of vessels and outposts. Recommended rank of Commanding Officer: **Commander**
5	Outpost - Location makes it important for observation purposes and collection of information. Recommended rank of Commanding Officer: **Lt. Commander**

C

Sample Distances

Earth to Mars (Mean)	78 million kilometers
Nearest star to our Sun	4 light-years (Proxima Centauri)
Milky Way Galaxy diameter	100,000 light-years
Thickness of M'Way at Sun	2,000 light-years
Stars in Milky Way	200 billion (est.)
Nearest galaxy (Andromeda)	2 million light-years from M'Way
A light-year (in a vacuum)	9,460,730,472,580.8 kilometers
A light-second (in vacuum)	299,792.458 km
Grid Unit	1,000 light-years² (1,000,000 Sq. LY)
Deca-Sector	100 light-years² (10,000 Sq. LY)
Sector	10 light-years² (100 Sq. LY)
Section	94,607,304,725 km²
Sub-section	946,073,047 km²

The two-dimensional representations that follow are offered to provide the reader with a feel for the spatial relationships between bases, systems, and celestial events referenced in the novels of this series.

The millions of stars, planets, moons, and celestial phenomena in this small part of the galaxy would only confuse, and therefore have been omitted from the images.

Should the maps be unreadable, or should you desire additional imagery, .jpg and .pdf versions of all maps are available for free downloading at:

www.deprima.com/ancillary/maps.html

E

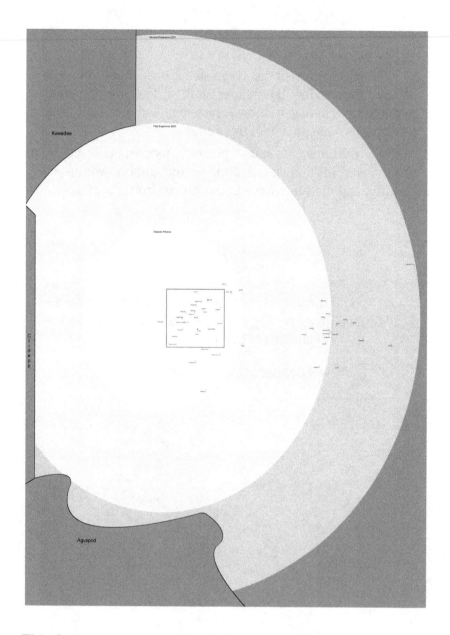

This first map shows Galactic Alliance space after the
second expansion. The white space at the center is the
space originally included when the GA charter was signed.
The first circle shows the space claimed at the first expansion in 2203. The second circle shows the Frontier Zone
established with the second expansion in 2273.

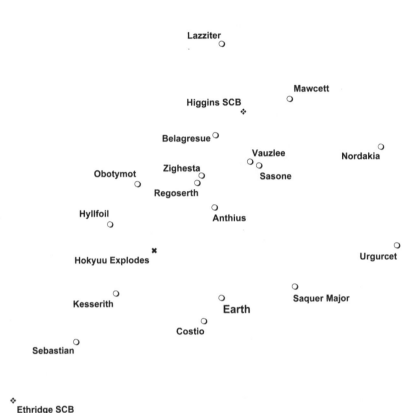

Lazziter

Mawcett

Higgins SCB

Belagresue

Vauzlee
Nordakia
Sasone

Obotymot
Zighesta
Regoserth

Hyllfoil
Anthius

Hokyuu Explodes
Urgurcet

Kesserith
Saquer Major
Earth

Costio

Sebastian

Ethridge SCB

This second map is an enlargement of the 'inset area' shown in the previous image. The mean distance from Earth to Higgins Space Command Base has been calculated as 90.1538 light-years.